"This gripping novel pro...................................herhood and
family secrets, and prov......................................r out of our
reach. A captivatingly h...........................soon forget."
—LISA TUCKER, bestselling author of *Once Upon a Day*

"Amy Hatvany's powerful language, delicious imagery,
and tender treatment of motherhood is a love letter to
women everywhere, who try and sometimes fail, but
who always get back up again. She is a gifted writer."
—RACHAEL BROWNELL, author of
Mommy Doesn't Drink Here Anymore

"Haunting, hopeful, and beautifully written, *Best Kept Secret*
takes a brave and honest look at the slippery slope of
addiction and the strength it takes to recover. I couldn't put
this book down, and I can't stop thinking about it."
—ALLIE LARKIN, bestselling author of *Stay*

"This novel is a testament to the power of a mother's love.
I suspect this story will resonate with more women, more
mothers, than this author might ever know."
—T. GREENWOOD, author of *The Hungry Season*
and *This Glittering World*

"One of the most compelling books I've read in years. This
could be any woman's secret—be it your sister, your best
friend, or the mother you see on the playground. This heartfelt,
heartbreaking, and ultimately uplifting novel will start an
important dialogue about the secrets we keep . . .

Cadence didn't sit down one night and decide that downing two bottles of wine was a brilliant idea.

HER DRINKING SNUCK UP ON HER—AS A WAY TO sleep, to help her relax after a long day, to relieve some of the stress of the painful divorce that's left her struggling to make ends meet with her five-year-old son, Charlie.

It wasn't always like this. Just a few years ago, Cadence seemed to have it all—a successful husband, an adorable son, and a promising career as a freelance journalist. But with the demise of her marriage, her carefully constructed life begins to spiral out of control. Suddenly she is all alone, trying to juggle the demands of work and motherhood.

Logically, Cadence knows that she is drinking too much, and every day begins with renewed promises to herself that she will stop. But within a few hours, driven by something she doesn't understand, she is reaching for the bottle—even when it means not playing with her son because she is too tired, or dropping him off at preschool late, again. And even when one calamitous night it means leaving him alone to pick up more wine at the grocery store. It's only when her ex-husband shows up at her door to take Charlie away that Cadence realizes her best kept secret has been discovered . . . .

Heartbreaking, haunting, and ultimately life-affirming, *Best Kept Secret* is more than just the story of Cadence—it's a story of how the secrets we hold closest are the ones that can tear us apart.

Also by Amy (Yurk) Hatvany

The Language of Sisters

The Kind of Love That Saves You

best
kept
secret

A Novel

Amy Hatvany

WASHINGTON SQUARE PRESS

New York   London   Toronto   Sydney

WASHINGTON SQUARE PRESS
A Division of Simon & Schuster, Inc.
1230 Avenue of the Americas
New York, NY 10020

First Washington Square Press trade paperback edition June 2011

WASHINGTON SQUARE PRESS and colophon are registered trademarks of Simon & Schuster, Inc.

For information about special discounts for bulk purchases, please contact Simon & Schuster Special Sales at 1-866-506-1949 or business@simonandschuster.com.

The Simon & Schuster Speakers Bureau can bring authors to your live event. For more information or to book an event contact the Simon & Schuster Speakers Bureau at 1-866-248-3049 or visit our website at www.simonspeakers.com.

Designed by Meredith Ray

Manufactured in the United States of America

10 9 8 7 6 5

Library of Congress Cataloging-in-Publication Data
Hatvany, Amy.
   Best kept secret : a novel / Amy Hatvany.—1st Washington Square Press trade pbk. ed.
      p. cm.
1. Women alcoholics—Fiction. 2. Single mothers—Fiction. I. Title.
   PS3616.E358B47 2011
   813'.6—dc22   2010038165
ISBN 978-1-4391-9331-0
ISBN 978-1-4391-9333-4 (ebook)

For Scarlett and Miles

Ring the bells that still can ring
Forget your perfect offering
There is a crack in everything
That's how the light gets in. . . .

—"Anthem," Leonard Cohen

One

Being drunk in front of your child is right up there on the Big Bad No-no List of Motherhood. I knew what I was doing was wrong. I knew it with every glass, every swallow, every empty bottle thrown into the recycle bin. I hated drinking. I hated it . . . and I couldn't stop. The anesthetic effect of alcohol ran thick in my blood; the Great Barrier Reef built between me and my feelings. I watched myself do it in an out-of-body experience: *Oh, isn't this interesting? Look at me, the sloppy drunk.* It snuck up on me, every time. It took me by surprise.

I tried to stop. Of course I tried. I went a day, maybe two, before the urge burned strong enough, it rose in my throat like a gnarled hand reaching for a drink. My body ached. My brain sloshed against the inside of my skull. The more I loathed drinking, the more I needed it to find that sweet spot between awareness and agony. Even now, even though it has been sixty-four days since I have taken a drink, the shame clings to me. It sickens my senses worse than any hangover I've ever suffered.

It's early April, and I drive down a street lined with tall, sturdy maples. Gauzelike clouds stretch across the icy blue sky. A few earnest men stand in front of their houses appraising the state of their lawns. My own yard went to hell while I was away and I have not found time nor inclination to be its savior.

Any other day I would have found this morning beautiful. Any other day I might have stopped to stare at the sky, to enjoy the fragile warmth of the sun on my skin. Today is not any other day. Today marks two months and four days since I have seen my son. Each corner I turn takes me closer and closer to picking him up from his grandmother's house. For now, it was decided this arrangement was better than my coming face-to-face with Martin, his father.

"What do they think will happen?" I'd asked my treatment counselor, Andi, when the rules of visitation came down. My voice was barely above a whisper. "What do they think I'd do?"

"Think of how many times you were drunk around Charlie," she said. "There's reason for concern."

I sat a moment, contemplating this dangerous little bomb, vacillating between an attempt to absorb the truth behind her words and the desire to find a way to hide from it. I kept my eyes on the floor, too afraid of what I'd see if I looked into hers. Two weeks in the psych ward rendered me incapable of pulling off my usually dazzling impersonation of a happy, successful, single mother. Andi knew I was drunk in front of Charlie every day for over a year. She'd heard me describe the misery etched across my child's face each time I pulled the cork on yet another bottle of wine. She knew the damage I'd done.

"Cadence?" she prodded.

Finally, I managed to look up at her round, pretty face. For the most part, I like Andi, except when she suggests I might be wrong about something. In the two months I have known her, this has happened more often than I'd like.

She met my gaze and smiled softly. I didn't respond, so she spoke again. "Try to think about it as what's best for Charlie."

"Isn't it best for Charlie to see his parents get along?" I asked. I've read enough advice books on how divorced parents should act in front of their children to feel pretty confident I was right about this one. I longed to stand before Martin and put on the face that said everything was okay. I wanted to prove to him that whatever darkness had reared its ugly head inside me had subsided; I had it back under control.

"Yes, seeing you getting along would be best," Andi conceded. "But it's not realistic. Martin just filed to take custody away from you. Your emotions are running insanely high. Even with the best intentions it would be hard not to confront him."

"I don't want to confront Martin," I said. "I just want to talk to him. Explain that I'm better. That I'm getting help with this . . . problem."

"Pleading your case is just going to stir up a bunch of negativity. Charlie is five years old. Even if you manage to restrain yourself from fighting, he's smart enough to pick up on facial expressions and the tone of your voices. You don't want to upset him."

"I could fake it," I said. I knew it wouldn't take much. When we were married, Martin and I fought and then went to bed with an invisible force field between us. In the morning, I gave him a smile, a kiss, and then made a pot of coffee and his lunch. Shape-shifting into what made Martin happy was something I already knew how to do.

Andi looked at me with her gentle, tigerlike topaz eyes. "Have you considered that maybe 'faking it' is what got you here?"

I was eight months pregnant when Martin and I decided I would leave my reporting job at the Seattle *Herald*. I'm not sure where I got the idea that working from home while taking care of an infant would be easy; I guess I thought freelance writing would grant me flexibility and plenty of free time to be with my son. Of course, after spending three years juggling the incessant demands of both self-employment and motherhood, I realized there was nothing easy about it. There was one person in charge of my day, and his name was Charlie.

"Mama!" he said, jumping on my bed one morning in May, a few months before he turned four. "Time to wake up!"

I groaned, rolled over beneath the covers, and peeked at the clock. Six o'clock on a Sunday. *Oh, sweet Jesus.* "Charlie, honey, can you go back to bed? It's too early."

"No, it's not!" He bounced on the mattress, jarring my throbbing head. Finishing off that bottle of merlot had been a bad idea. Since Martin moved out the previous November, my usual limit was one glass, maybe two a night, and then it was only to help me sleep. But then the night before, with Charlie already down for the count, I figured it wouldn't hurt to enjoy another glass while I worked. When the contents of my cup grew low, I splashed in a little more to top it off. Before I knew it, there was none left to pour.

Now, I propped myself up on my elbows and looked at my son through scratchy, dry eyes. He was starting to lose his baby-ish looks—his dark, wispy curls were mussed, his cheeks were pink, and his ears stuck out from his head like a chimpanzee's. My little monkey.

"Do you want to cuddle with me for a while?" I asked, hoping he'd take the bait.

"No!" Charlie said. "I want pancakes. And yogurt."

I flopped back down and threw my forearm over my eyes, causing the pain to ricochet like a bullet beneath my skull. If I didn't do something for this headache soon, it would take over and I'd never get anything written today. I had barely started my article on the Northwest's Top Ten Bed-and-Breakfasts for *Seattle* magazine, and while it was originally due the week before, I managed to sweet-talk the editor into extending my deadline through tomorrow. I couldn't afford to screw up and not get paid.

Charlie pushed me playfully and giggled. He was not going to give up.

I sighed and forced myself to rotate up and out of bed. The room spun around me, so I kept my eyes closed and took deep breaths until it passed. *Ugh*. I felt awful. I hoped I wouldn't be sick.

"Pancakes!" Charlie hollered, and I cringed, clutching my forehead with one hand.

"*Shh*, honey. Mama has a headache."

He leapt off the bed and sped down the hall in his Spider-Man pajamas. The noisy clamor of cartoons quickly echoed throughout the house.

I trodded after him, my bare feet slapping against the hardwood floors. I wondered when I had changed out of my jeans and into my pajamas the night before; I didn't remember doing it. *I must have been really tired,* I thought hazily. *I'm really not getting enough sleep.*

In my tiny, black-and-white, fifties-style kitchen, I immediately went for the super-size bottle of Advil on the counter and shook four out into my hand. I popped them into my mouth and used my cupped palm beneath the faucet to splash them down with a water chaser.

I fought with the coffee filters for a minute, but soon managed to get a pot brewing, throwing in an extra scoop of aromatic grounds for a super-charged medicinal kick of caffeine. Charlie raced in from the living room and threw his arms around my legs, squeezing them tightly.

"I love you, Mama," he said.

"I love you, too, Charlie bear." I hoped my voice didn't sound as weary as I felt. I reached around and cupped my hand against the curve of his head.

He let go of me, padded over to the refrigerator, and grabbed a strawberry yogurt from the bottom shelf. I kept most of his snacks within reach so he could get them himself. I'd read somewhere that giving him tasks like this to accomplish on his own would encourage his self-esteem. It also reduced the number of things I needed to do for him each day from one hundred to ninety-nine.

"Did you turn off the TV?" I asked absentmindedly, then realized the sound of cartoons had ceased.

"Yep!" He sat at the chrome-legged, black Formica kitchen table that put in double duty as my desk. The house was too small for an office, so my laptop and printer took up one end of the table, and at meal time Charlie and I took up the other. It was all the space I needed, really, since most of my work was done online and over the phone.

"Let me get you a spoon," I said, reaching into the silverware drawer and setting the utensil on the table. "Eating yogurt with your fingers isn't such a hot idea."

With an impish grin, he wiggled his fingers threateningly over the open cup.

"Don't you dare," I said. Too late. He dropped his fingers in the creamy pink yogurt and scooped a bite into his mouth.

"Charlie," I said, exasperated. "No." I snatched a dish towel from the counter, took him by the wrist, and wiped his hand clean. I gave the bottom of his chin a gentle pinch. "Don't do that again, okay? You're a big boy. You know better than that."

"Okay," he said. He dutifully picked up his spoon and began to eat. My head screamed at me to go back to bed, but I knew it would be impossible.

While I inhaled my coffee from a black, soup bowl-size mug, I zapped a few frozen pancakes in the microwave. When they were done, I cut them up into bite-size squares and served them to my son. I nibbled on one without butter or syrup, hoping the carbs would take the edge off my nausea.

"All done!" Charlie said, pushing away from the table and jumping down from his chair. "Want to come play with me?"

I smiled at him. "I need to work for a little while. Can you watch TV quietly?"

"But I want you to *play*," he whined, yanking on my hand.

I took a deep breath, then exhaled. That was that. As always, work would have to wait for his nap time. I knew spending time with my son was more important, but the money I'd received in the divorce settlement wasn't going to last forever. If I watched my pennies and pulled in at least a little bit from freelancing, it would be enough to live on for a couple of years. Martin paid child support to cover basic things like Charlie's clothes and food, but in order to survive on my own long term, I needed to step up my professional game. Something that was difficult to do, considering I wasn't all that crazy about freelance journalism in the first place. After I left the

Herald, my career had morphed into a matter of convenience rather than a passionate pursuit, but it was all I knew how to do. So for the time being, I didn't have a choice but to make it work.

"Mama!" Charlie said, jerking on my hand again. I allowed him to lead me into the living room, a small space made to look even smaller by the arrangement of an overstuffed khaki love seat and two matching, comfy lounge chairs with ottomans. There was a flat-screen television hanging above the river-stone fireplace—an indulgence Martin encouraged before he moved out, a purchase I reluctantly grew to enjoy. The built-in cherry shelves on each side of the fireplace were stuffed with my books, a few candles and pictures, but mostly Charlie's toys.

He let go of my hand and ran over to the enormous pile of brightly hued Duplo blocks that already lay in the middle of the tan, skeleton leaf-imprinted area rug. He sat down and gave me a toothy grin.

"Here," Charlie said, holding out a single red block. "This is yours. Mine are the rest."

"Okay," I said, walking over to join him on the floor. The combination of Advil and caffeine had finally kicked in—the elephants tromping through my head began to slow down. I took the block from him. "Where do you want me to put it?"

"I'll do it," he said, snatching the toy back immediately.

"Okay," I said, smiling. "Gotcha, boss." I watched him play for a few minutes, amazed by the intensity of my feelings. No one told me that the love I'd feel for my child would be so pervasive and consuming. Charlie came howling from my body and in an instant, my own soul was woven into his so completely it became impossible to extricate one from the other.

"Here," my son said again, handing me another red block. He pointed to the top of the tower he had built. "Put it there."

"Yes, sir," I said, setting the block where he wanted it. "Like that?"

"Good job, Mama," he said, patting me on my knee with his plump hand. He suddenly jumped up and launched himself full-force into my lap, pushing me over onto the floor with his arms around my neck.

"Oomph!" I said, laughing and hugging him to me so he wouldn't crash his head into the nearby bookcase.

"I love you to the stars and back!" he announced.

"All the way to Timbuktu," I answered.

"All the way to Kalamazoo," he finished. The words were our nightly routine when I tucked him into bed, what I whispered in his ear before he drifted off to sleep.

Charlie pulled back and landed a wet, slightly open-mouthed kiss on my cheek. His breath smelled faintly of the peanut butter and syrup he had had on his pancakes. I almost wished I could take a bite out of him, I loved him so much.

We played for a couple of hours, coloring and building with more blocks. I took a hot shower, trying to scrub the cobwebs from my brain, while Charlie sat on the bathroom floor, chattering away about Spider-Man and what kind of superhero outfit he wanted me to sew for him.

"Mama doesn't sew, baby," I said from behind the shower curtain. Where he had gotten the idea that I could, I had no clue. I opted to throw away his socks rather than darn them; he'd even seen me do it.

"That's okay," he said simply. "You can learn."

We both got dressed, then went outside to the backyard so Charlie could climb on the wooden jungle gym Martin had tried to put together for Charlie's second birthday party. At the last minute, I ended up having to call the toy store to send an employee to finish the job.

"I can do it, Cadee," my husband had said.

"Uh-huh. And is it supposed to lean against the fence?" I only meant to tease him, but he dropped his tools to the lawn and stormed off toward the garage.

"It's a safety thing, honey!" I called out. "We don't want the other kids' parents to sue!" He didn't answer, and every time after that when a project needed to be done around the house and I asked him to help me with it, he'd shake his head and say, "I don't know, Cadee. You don't want me to screw it up. Maybe you'd better call a professional."

Now, the May sun was warm on my face, and my eyes wandered over the overgrown clumps of vibrant bluebells and delicate forget-me-nots along the fence. Yard work—another thing I didn't have time to do. The outside chores had always been Martin's. At least, when he came home from work long enough to do them.

"Watch me, Mama!" Charlie said over and over again as he went down the slide or made his way up the ladder. "Watch this!"

"I'm watching," I reassured him, my arms crossed over my chest. My thoughts danced with the descriptions I needed to be writing. I wished I could just sit Charlie in front of a movie and get started. I knew some writers could get words on the page no matter what was going on around them—with music playing or children chattering in the background—but I wasn't one of them. I needed silence to work.

I pushed Charlie on the swing and chased him around the moss-covered pear tree until it was time for lunch. "What do you want to eat?" I asked as we walked up the back steps into the house.

"Orange," Charlie said.

"Oranges?" I said. "I don't think we have any."

"No. Not oranges. *Orange*."

"Ohhhh," I said, realizing what he meant. It was his favorite color. I fed him macaroni and cheese and sliced peaches.

After he ate, I snuggled with Charlie on the couch and watched an episode of *The Berenstain Bears*. As I held him, his eyelids drooped and his breathing deepened. When the show ended, I glanced at the clock. It was almost 1:00.

"Time for your nap, baby," I said, kissing the top of his head. When he didn't respond, I knew he was asleep.

I carried him into his room, marveling at the heft of his dead-weight, careful to keep jostling his body to a minimum. I lay him down, slipped off his shoes, and tucked his favorite blue blanket up around his neck, making sure the silky edge was against his face, the way he liked it. Quietly, I shut the door behind me, listening for any movement. He didn't make a sound. *Success.*

Back in the kitchen, I grabbed a poppy seed muffin I'd baked the day before, thinking it might be better for me than finishing off the entire pot of cheesy pasta. I started to type the description of a popular San Juan Islands, Fidalgo Bay, 1890s Victorian. I was cheating a little, using online reviews for references and interviewing the establishments' owners over the phone instead of in person, but the logistics of lugging Charlie along for a road trip to visit them all were too complicated to consider.

I'd barely gotten a page completed when I heard Charlie's door open. His bare feet pattered down the hall.

"You need more sleep, baby," I said, turning to look at him when he came through the kitchen's arched doorway.

"Nope!" he said cheerfully, though his cheeks were rosy and his eyes half-lidded. "I'm hungry."

"You just ate lunch. And you only rested half an hour. You need to get back in bed. Mama needs to get some work done."

He clambered up into a chair and looked at me expectantly. "I'll help you."

I sighed, tapping my fingers on the top of my thigh. "No, honey. You can't. This is grown-up work."

He pounded on the table with his fists. "I'll *help* you!"

"Charlie," I said as gently as possible. "You can play quietly in your room, but Mama needs to be by herself for a little while. We'll play later." If he didn't get a nap, I wouldn't get anything accomplished and both of us would hate the rest of this day.

"No!" Charlie said, setting his jaw in a determined line. It was his father's expression, one I had seen on my ex-husband's face too many times to count.

Something in me snapped. I shoved my chair back from the table, then tucked my hands in my son's armpits and lifted him out of his chair. He gave a few rowdy kicks and managed to knock my laptop onto the floor with his foot. It landed on the checkered linoleum with a frightening clatter. All my work was on that computer—I wasn't a master of backing up my copy. If he just killed the machine, I was screwed.

"Dammit, Charlie!" I yelled. My heartbeat galloped in my throat. "Knock it off."

"Don't say 'dammit'!" he screamed, continuing to struggle as I carried him back down the hall to his room.

"You're fine," I told him through gritted teeth. "Mama's here. You're *fine*."

"Daddy!" he wailed, wriggling and writhing to get away from me. "I want my *daddy*!"

It made me crazy how often my son asked for Martin. Charlie and I spent most of our time alone even when his father lived with us. Yet something did shift when my husband no longer came home at night. I was *it*. Responsible for absolutely *everything*. Sometimes I wasn't sure I was up for the job.

I lay Charlie in his bed. "I love you, sweetie, but you need to take a rest." I kept my voice calm, though aggravation skittered along its edges. I smoothed his hair and he kicked at the wall, still crying. I hoped he'd tire himself out and go back to sleep as he'd done a hundred times before. I closed the door behind me again and this time, I stood in the hall, waiting.

Over the next five minutes his screaming intensified. There was the loud *thunk* of something being thrown against his door. A toy, probably. It wouldn't be the first time. The tips of my nerves burned beneath my skin.

"You're a bad mama!" he yelled.

His words felt like a slap. *He's only three. He doesn't mean it. Tantrums are normal for lots of kids.* Still, tears rose in my eyes and I pressed a curled fist against my mouth at hearing my child accuse me of my deepest fear.

Swallowing the lump in my throat, I returned to the kitchen and picked up my laptop, happy to see it wasn't destroyed. I would never get anything done with him screaming in the background; I needed someone to watch him. I thought about calling my younger sister, Jessica, but she was seven months pregnant with twins so I didn't want to bother her. My mother was more the type to visit her grandchild than to babysit him, so with this late notice, that left me with only one option.

I grabbed my cell phone and punched in Martin's number, taking a few deep breaths as I always needed to before talking with him.

"I'm really sorry to bug you," I began, hoping he'd give me a different answer than the one I expected. "But can you take Charlie for a few hours this afternoon? I'm on deadline."

"Why's he screaming?" Martin asked.

I gave him the short version of why his child was pitching a fit. "I know it's my weekend, but if you can help me out, I'd really owe you one."

"Sorry, I would, but I've already got plans," he said.

You always have plans, I wanted to say, but managed to bite my tongue. The role of bitter divorcée was one I worked hard to avoid.

"I can take him an extra night this week, though," he went on to offer.

"The article's due tomorrow," I said, trying to keep the desperation out of my voice. The editor had already cut me some slack; it was unlikely he would do it again.

Martin sighed. "I don't know what to tell you, Cadee. I can't do it. But I'll pick him up Wednesday at five."

After he hung up, I slammed down the phone on the table, adrenaline pumping through my veins. *Goddamn him.* So much for the concept of coparenting. I shouldn't have bothered to call. Charlie's cries escalated into punctuated, high-pitched shrieking. I didn't know what to do. I started to weep, the internal barricade I usually kept high and strong crumpling beneath the weight of my frustration.

After a few minutes of feeling sorry for myself and wondering how my child didn't sprain his vocal cords screeching like he was, I plunked back down at the table, wiping my eyes with my sleeve and thinking I might just polish off that pot of pasta after all. As my gaze traveled toward the stove, the sunlight streaming in through the window glinted off a bottle of merlot on the counter and caught my eye.

I checked the clock. It was almost 2:00. People who worked outside the home had drinks with a late lunch, didn't they? I could have half a glass now, just to take the edge off, and maybe another before bed. Not even two full glasses for the day. Some people drank more than that with their dinner alone. And it wasn't like I did it all the time. I needed to relax. *Just this once,* I thought as my son sobbed himself to sleep in his room. *Just today.*

I swore to myself I'd never do it again.

Pulling up in front of Alice's house to pick up Charlie, the shame is strong enough in me that I must fight the urge to drive away. I'd go anywhere to not feel this. Canada is only a couple of hours north. I could run off and not have to deal with any of it. I could start again, build a new life with our maple syrup-friendly neighbors. I could learn to say "eh?" at the end of every sentence. I could blend right in. I wouldn't have to go to treatment. I wouldn't have to write all those silly assignments or attend AA meetings. I wouldn't need to find some ridiculous notion of a higher power. I could leave. I could . . .

There he is. All thoughts of escape disappear. Charlie comes bounding out of my ex-mother-in-law's front door, his dark brown curls bouncing around his perfect, elfin face. He needs a haircut, I note. Something for us to do today, something to fill the hours we are alone. He is wearing blue jeans and a polo shirt I didn't buy for him, one I would have left on the rack at the store. His smile is wide. His hands flutter in excitement as he races down the stairs toward me.

"Mommy!" he exclaims, and my heart melts into liquid. I throw the gearshift into park, turn off the engine, and jump out to meet him. He leaps into my open arms and clings to me like a spider monkey, his skinny arms and legs wrap around my neck and waist in a viselike grip. I bury my nose in his neck and breathe him in—his nutty, warm, slightly funky little-boy scent. This is the first time in two months that we'll be alone overnight. Two months and four days since Martin came to my house and took him away.

"Where were you?" he demands. "I *missed* you!"

"I've missed you, too, butternut," I say, choking on my tears. I nibble on the thin skin of his neck, growling playfully. It is our game.

"Ahhhh! Stop it!" he squeals.

I nibble again. My lips cover my teeth so I don't accidentally hurt him. He squeals again and wriggles like an eel in my arms. "Let me go!"

"No, I won't let you go! No way!" I say, holding his precious body to mine.

"Mama! Ahhh!! It tickles!!" His sturdy legs wrap themselves even tighter around me and he continues to squirm.

God, oh God, how could I ever have done anything to lose him? How could I have been drunk around this gorgeous little boy? I am sick—undeniably ill.

"Hello, Cadence." My ex-mother-in-law's words land like a gauntlet at my feet. They cause me to peek up from the warmth of my son's neck. Alice stands atop her front steps, arms folded tightly across her chest. Her eyes are stone. Her silver-streaked black hair is pulled back from her face in a tight bun at the base of her neck, not a loose strand in sight. She has applied just enough makeup to avoid being mistaken for dead. She wears her standard khaki slacks and practical, scoop-neck, long-sleeved navy knit top. No frills for this woman. No fussy, floral prints. She is all business, the bare necessities.

"Kill her with kindness," Andi said when I expressed my anxiety about having to see Alice in this first official exchange. "That'll piss her off."

"Really?" I asked, skeptical. "I want to piss her off?"

"No, you want to be kind." She gave me a beatific smile. "The pissing her off part is just a bonus."

Purely out of respect for Andi's advice, I manage to smile at Alice when she greets me. It is a tenuous, struggling movement—my cheeks literally tremble with the effort. "Hi, Alice. How are you?"

"Fine." She gives me a tight-lipped look, one I recognize as her version of a smile under duress. From the moment I met her, it was clear that Alice had envisioned a much more suitable partner for her only child. A lithe, Nordic blond perhaps, petite and demure. Instead, she got me—all wild brown curls and fleshy curves. Big breasts, big opinions.

"You're late," she says.

I twist my wrist up from my son's body, which is still clamped around me, and look at my watch. Ten minutes after 9:00 a.m. Panic seizes me. She'll report me to Mr. Hines, the court guardian. I'll lose my son. I worry that everything I do goes under automatic scrutiny. *How does it look for me to do this?* I wonder, as I order a soda at dinner. *Are they wondering why I don't ask for a real drink? A glass of wine? A vodka tonic with a twist?* I feel like I have to explain every little movement, or lack of movement.

It's similar to how I used to feel when I'd buy wine at a different grocery store or corner market every day. "I'm having a party tonight," I'd explain to an uninterested checker. "Eight people, so I'll need four bottles of wine." Like the checker gave a good goddamn.

"Only a few minutes late," I say to Alice now, not just a little defensively. "Sorry."

"It's fine," Alice says, looking at me with cool disdain.

Charlie chooses this moment to wriggle out of my grasp. He jumps up and down in front of me. "Look, Mama! I can do a cartwheel!" Falling forward, he places both palms flat on the wet grass and does a donkey kick not more than eight inches or so off the ground. He lands on his knees with a *thump*.

I clap for him. "Excellent!" He grins, causing the deep, cherry-pit dimple on his left cheek to appear.

"Charles!" Alice scolds. "Look what you did to your jeans!"

The grin vanishes. He stands, looks down at his now brightly stained green knees. "Sorry."

I reach down, ruffle his curls. "That's okay, buddy. That's why God invented Spray 'n Wash, right?"

"Yeah!" he says. He looks up at me, smiling again, and then to the sky. He waves. "Thanks, God!"

Oh, my Charlie. My eyes well up. *Would you look at that. Look at that sweet soul. I haven't completely screwed him up.*

"God isn't doing your laundry," Alice says lightly as she steps down the stairs.

I look at her, anger tight and warm in my chest. It's that mama bear feeling rearing its head.

She sees my eyes flash. Her expression melts into one of supreme smugness. That's right, it says. Here it comes. Yell at me. Give me something to tell the court.

Kill her with kindness. The chant I played over and over in my head on the way to this moment. I take a deep breath before speaking.

"Thanks for taking such good care of his clothes. I'll wash his jeans today, and bring them back." And then, because I cannot help it, I continue. "Why doesn't Martin do his laundry?"

She lifts her jaw. "Martin is busy working. Martin is busy making sure his son is fed and clothed and brought to school on time. He is very busy being a parent."

Which is more than I can say about you, I hear the unspoken finish to her statement. She doesn't need to speak. Her eyes paint the words: black, ugly brushstrokes in the air between us.

"How nice for him," I spit out. I can't stop myself. "Most single parents don't have someone to pick up their slack." *Dammit. And I was doing so well.*

"Most single parents don't drink themselves into oblivion, either," she launches back. She speaks quietly, over Charlie's listening ears. "*I* didn't."

Her words pummel me. They stop my breath. Sudden, violent guilt invades each cell in my body. She is sacred and pure. I am the evil, rotten mother who couldn't control her drinking. I deserve her hatred. I deserve the pain that goes with it. She is right and I am wrong. I earned every minute of all I have to endure.

Charlie grabs my arm with both hands and pulls in the direction of my car. "Mama, let's go," he whimpers. "I want to go."

"Okay, monkey," I say. And then, to Alice, "I'll have him back tomorrow at twelve o'clock."

"Twelve o'clock sharp," she says.

"Right," I say. "C'mon, Mr. Man." Any fight I had is knocked clear out of me. Round one: Alice. I let Charlie lead me to the car and help him climb into his booster seat, ever conscious of Alice's sharp blue eyes on me. For good measure, I say loudly, "All right, you're all buckled in," just so she can't tell the court I let Charlie bounce around like a red rubber ball inside my car. Anything is a threat now. Anything could be used against me. I step slowly around to the driver's side, open my door, and then force myself again to smile at Alice and wave good-bye. "Say 'bye to your omi, Charlie bear." This is what he calls her, Omi—the German equivalent of Nana.

"'Bye, Omi!" he chimes in. This is out of good breeding alone, I convince myself. Good breeding that I, as his mother, am personally responsible for.

I buckle my own seat belt, start the car, and look at my son in the rearview mirror. "Ready, Spaghetti Freddie?" I ask.

"Ready!" he squeals. He kicks his feet against the seat in front of him in emphasis.

I pull away from the curb, wondering if the real question is, how ready am I?

TWO

I wasn't looking for a husband the night I met Martin, I was looking for a story. Two years after a summer internship morphed into a lifestyle section beat at the Seattle *Herald,* I was twenty-six and anxious to prove to my editor-in-chief that I was capable of writing more than fluff pieces on the newest trends in weight-loss programs or the yearly sand castle-building contest at Alki Beach. One of my sources—a woman I'd gotten to know during an article I did on a state workers' successful holiday food drive—gave me the heads-up regarding a conflict between the pay increase percentage the governor had promised teachers and what the state could actually afford, so on a Friday night I showed up at a benefit dinner intended to raise money for creative arts in public schools. I figured I could chat up the teachers in attendance and see what kind of feature might evolve.

As it turned out, after two unsuccessful hours of trying to track down an educator who was incensed enough with the governor to speak to me without the presence of their union rep, I stood alone by the appetizer buffet table with a glass of wine in hand, nibbling on a cracker spread with goat cheese and caramelized onion. Discouraged, I wondered not for the first time if I actually had the determined nature it took to be a successful journalist. I was weighing the option of making an early exit when a handsome man with bright blue eyes and short, spiked black hair suddenly appeared by my side.

"Do you like sausages?" he inquired.

I laughed out loud, hand over my mouth, trying not to spit out my last bite.

He smiled at me, tilting his head in a disarmingly adorable manner. "A server sent me over to ask if you prefer sausage or chicken for dinner since he didn't have your preference on the list. Why is that funny?"

I touched the back of my hand to the side of my mouth, making sure I wasn't covered in chewed-up appetizer before responding. I was suddenly conscious of my hair, happy I'd chosen to wear the flattering black dress that showed off the best thing about being an hourglass girl in a push-up bra.

"It's a rather presumptuous question, don't you think?" I said.

"Presumptuous, how? I didn't ask if you like *my* sausage in particular." His eyes flashed a wicked sparkle.

I couldn't help myself; I took a sip of my wine and looked up at him over the edge of the glass. "Sorry, I make it a strict policy not to reveal my meat-eating preferences to a man until at *least* the second date."

"Oh, really?" He raised his eyebrows in a way that convinced me he was definitely interested in learning more about my particular appetites. "And when do we go on our first?"

"As soon as you call me." I set my glass on the table, took out my business card from my purse, and handed it to him. My response to Martin was completely out of character—most of my relationships with men grew out of casual friendship, gradually evolving into something more intimate. My reaction to him was physical from the get-go, his pheromones unabashedly speaking to mine. We were seated at separate tables for dinner, but at the end of the night he offered to walk me to my car. The article was forgotten and I went to bed that night with a wide, stupid grin plastered across my face.

We went out for dinner the following week at a cozy Italian cafe. After racing through the usual niceties about the weather and how our day was at work, we dove right into our family histories.

"It was horrible," Martin told me about his mother's pregnancy with him. "I made her very, very sick. But she instructed me that I would be a strong, healthy boy."

"She 'instructed' you?" I said, twirling my hair in what I hoped was an appealing, playful manner. Being near him made my stomach feel as though it was full of a thousand fluttering butterflies.

He nodded with mock gravity. "I learned in utero it was best to do what my mother expected. I mean, look at me!" He swept his hand from his chin down toward his waist. "Aren't I a strong, healthy German boy?"

I laughed and nodded. He wasn't especially tall—five foot eight, maybe? Only a few inches taller than me. But he had the kind of arms I knew were strong enough to beat the begeezus out of any type of assailant. I was a sucker for a man with excellent arms.

"You are absolutely strong and healthy," I agreed. "But what about your father? Didn't he have any say about how you turned out?"

A brief shadow fell over his face. "He died when I was two. A construction site accident."

"Oh, I'm so sorry," I said. "Do you remember much about him?"

He shook his head. "Not really. Nothing more than the *feeling* of him." His mouth shifted into a wistful bend. "Does that make sense?"

"Of course it does." I gave him a tender smile and reached across the table to squeeze his thick fingers. They felt warm and sturdy. We fit. "Did your mother remarry?"

He squeezed my hand in return and made no move to pull away. "No. It's always been just the two of us." He paused. "What about you?"

"My family?"

He nodded. "Brothers? Sisters? Pets? Crazy old aunts locked in the attic?"

I laughed. "One younger sister, Jessica. And my mother. No pets. Or crazy aunts—that I know of." My mind flashed briefly on the possibility of telling him about my grandmother, but I decided against it. Not good fodder for a first date.

"And your father?"

"I think I'd call him more of a sperm donor than a father."

Martin cringed. "Ouch."

I shrugged, pulling my hand back from his. "I was too young when he left for it to affect me very much." I recited this line out of habit; my mother had said it to me often when I bemoaned the fact that I didn't have a father like most of my friends.

"How old were you?"

"Not quite six months. My mom was about eight weeks pregnant with my sister."

"Nice guy."

"I don't know. According to my mom, he just wasn't cut out for the whole family gig, you know? He was an artist. Sort of the free-spirit, one-with-the-earth type. She was a registered voter and dental hygienist. An upstanding citizen." *Total opposites,* I thought. *Not like you and me. We already have more in common than the two of them ever did.*

"Still," Martin said. "I just couldn't imagine taking off like that. As a father. Or a husband."

I smiled. "They never actually got married. But that's good to know about you." Having witnessed the demise of her own parents' disastrous union, my mother insisted she would never venture down the aisle. I was not quite so averse to the idea.

"Is she still a hygienist? Your mom?"

"A dentist, actually. After Jess was born, she worked about sixty hours a week at a couple of different offices to keep us afloat, then went back to school to get her degree. She's had her own practice for over ten years now."

"Do you get along?"

I picked up my fork, toying with the cold remains of my fettuccine. "For the most part. But Jess and I spent a lot of time with babysitters when we were growing up. And she's so busy with her practice now I barely see her. I'm not sure how well I really *know* her." It surprised me to feel the muscles in my throat tighten as I spoke that last sentence. I feigned a cough.

Martin didn't seem to notice the change in my voice. "Babysitters, huh? She didn't have family around to help her out?"

I shook my head. "Her parents divorced when she was twelve and her mom died not too long after that. She was pretty much on her own. It's what she knows how to do."

He nodded. "Sounds like my mom, too. Both my parents' families are back in Germany. I've never even met them."

"How did she support you after your dad passed away?" I paused, then added, "If you don't mind me asking."

"It's fine. She actually bought the bakery where she'd been working. My dad was a planner like that. He knew his job was risky, so he made sure to have good accidental death coverage."

"You had babysitters, too, then, I take it? With her owning a business?"

"Sort of. I just went to the shop with her. A gaggle of German bakerwomen took care of me. Fed me bits of cake to keep me from crying."

"Hmm . . . a whole gaggle, huh?"

He lifted one shoulder up and forward a bit. "What can I say? My mother ran the place. It was in their job description."

"Of course it was. Does she still work?"

"Nope. Sold it a few months ago. She's retired now, and focused on finding me a wife."

I attempted to appear nonplussed as the butterflies in my stomach went nuts. "Uh-huh. So, do you bake? That might work in your favor."

"No, no baking." One corner of his mouth bent upward. "But I could calculate a couple logarithmic functions that would make your toes curl."

"Ew. Math. Do you have any other annoying habits I should know about?" I winked at him and smiled.

He sat forward, crossed his forearms, and leaned on the table. "Hmm . . . let's see. I keep track of pretty much everything in my life on a spreadsheet. Does organization qualify as a bad habit?"

"Only if you expect the same kind of freakish compulsion from me."

To my relief, he threw his head back and laughed.

For a first date, I thought, *this is going extremely well.*

I called my sister the minute I got home. "I really, really like him," I said. "He's smart, he's funny, and I'm pretty sure he thinks I'm smart and funny, too. He took my smart-ass commentary like a pro."

"Did he kiss you?"

"Oh yeah."

"And . . . ?"

"And everything south of the border pretty much melted."

It didn't take long for Martin and me to begin spending almost every evening together. His linear brain served our lovemaking well. He possessed a scientist's determination to understand what pleasured me most.

"Hmm," he'd murmur, running his fingertips up and down the curve of my waist to the generous swell of my hips. "What happens when I do *this*?"

My eyes would close and I'd shudder as goose bumps popped up across my skin.

He'd smile, then move his fingers a little lower. "What about *this*?"

Afterward, he didn't want to sleep. He wanted to talk. Our conversations went on for hours. He thought my burgeoning career as a journalist was fascinating; I admired how he spent his days teaching young minds how to navigate complex mathematical theory. Though he struggled with how little money he was making as a teacher, he said that seeing students suddenly grasp a concept that had previously eluded them more than made up for the lack of financial reward.

A few weeks into dating, things felt solid enough between us that Martin invited me to meet his mother. We had lunch at Alice's favorite German eatery down in Pioneer Square. At her insistence, I agreed to let her order for all of us: feather-light potato dumplings served with a creamy bacon sauce.

"Holy butter, Batman," I remarked after I'd practically licked my plate clean. "That was amazing. Is there a way I can become an honorary German?"

Martin leaned over and whispered in my ear, "German by injection, perhaps? I have just the tool . . ."

I punched him playfully and he pulled away, grinning.

"Tell me, Cadence," Alice said, ignoring our antics. "Do you want children?" She didn't speak with much of an accent, but the edges of her words were noticeably clipped, as though she were forcibly restraining herself from giving you a piece of her mind.

"Mama . . ." Martin began, but I set my hand on his forearm and squeezed.

"No, it's okay," I said. Our conversation had been fairly tame up to this point; part of me welcomed a more challenging subject. "I'm only twenty-six, Mrs. Sutter. I've been pretty focused on my work at the paper. I haven't given babies much thought, to tell you the truth."

"But you want them," she said. "You aren't one of those girls who think they're not cut out to be a mother, are you? A *career* girl." She said "career" the same way she might have said "hooker."

I tilted my head and gave her a closed-lipped, tight smile before responding. I had to be careful here. I wanted to make a good impression. "Well. My career is definitely important to me. And actually, I think it's a *good* thing that women can decide for themselves whether or not they want kids. There's no law that says it's some kind of requirement of womanhood."

"Perhaps there should be," Alice said.

"Mama, please," Martin said. "Leave poor Cadence alone."

"Martin," Alice said. The word was sewn through with warning.

Martin sat back in his chair and pressed his lips into a thin line. His acquiescence was surprising, but I assumed he did it to avoid a knock-down, drag-out with his mother in front of me. I imagined him chewing her out later, after he dropped me off at home. I imagined him standing up for the woman he loved.

"Don't you consider owning your bakery a career?" I said, unable to keep myself from making this point.

Her eyes narrowed the slightest bit, though the rest of her face remained impassive. "Yes. I do. But I would have given it up immediately if having my bakery meant I wouldn't have had Martin. He was the most important thing. Always. No question. He still is."

Martin nudged the edge of his foot against mine beneath the table. I nudged his back and took a deep breath before speaking again.

"Like I said, I haven't thought about it a lot, but if I found the right man, then yes. I'd want to have a baby with him." I looked at Martin. "Someday."

Two months after that luncheon, Martin asked me to move into his Capitol Hill apartment. My mother approved of this living arrangement; his mother did not. The fact that Martin didn't let Alice's opinion sway him reassured me. For a while, we enjoyed that honeymoon stage of nesting, when I still found it adorable that he needed all the canned food labels facing in the same direction and he didn't complain that the contents of my closet were strewn across the bedroom floor.

That blissful period of time came to an end on a crisp December evening. I was curled up on the couch with a book when he stepped in from our bedroom, holding a white sheet of paper.

"A note from my mom," he said, waving it at me.

"Let me guess," I joked. "Thanking me for all my help at Thanksgiving?" I had not been allowed in the kitchen to help with the food preparation during my first holiday spent at Martin's childhood home. "Oh, no," Alice said. "Don't bother. Really. I'll take care of it. You just sit. Relax." So I lounged in the living room with Martin while she whirled around like a madwoman between the dining room and kitchen. The conversation over the dinner table began with her dramatic lamentation: "I can't believe I did this whole meal all by myself! I swear I'll have to hire help next year." I had enough social graces to keep my mouth shut, though Martin and I laughed about it in the car on the way home.

Standing there in our apartment a couple of weeks later, Martin looked uncomfortable, clutching the e-mail. "No, no thank-you note," he said. "Actually, she made a list of what you ate. With calorie count." He swallowed, his Adam's apple bobbing visibly up and down beneath the thin skin of his neck.

My mouth dropped open. "Are you kidding me?"

He took a step toward me. "Now, don't get upset . . ."

"Unbelievable." I threw my book to the floor with a loud *thump*. Martin stopped in his tracks. "You're going to *defend* her?"

"She read an article, honey," he began. "With a list of the calories people typically consume . . ."

"Stop." I held up my hand, just in case he was tempted to believe I wasn't serious. "Just stop it right there." Pursing my lips together, I pushed a couple of breaths out through my nose. "Why are you telling me this? Maybe *you're* concerned about my weight?" I was not a gym bunny. I had a belly. When not safely ensconced in the proper combination of wire and spandex, my breasts bordered on cartoonish.

"No," he sighed. "You know I love your body. She just asked me to tell you about it. I really think she meant well. She says she's concerned about your health."

I snorted at this. "Please. My health is just fine. You're the one with the high blood pressure. Did she make a list for the food *you* ate?"

"No, but–" he attempted, but I cut him off.

"You know what? She can go fuck herself. You both can."

It was our first official fight. The next day, I found the e-mail in the recycle bin and experienced great pleasure in pushing it through the paper shredder at work. Martin brought home flowers that night and apologized profusely for his misstep.

"It's just the way she is," he said. "Maybe you could talk with her. Tell her how you feel."

"I'd feel a little strange doing that," I said. "Couldn't you do it?"

"And say what?"

"That her e-mail was totally offensive. That she hurt my feelings."

He sighed. "She won't get it. She's a very factual person."

"What would you do if it was you? If she hurt your feelings like this?"

"I don't let her hurt my feelings. And even if she did, whining about it is not who she raised me to be. I told you she's old-fashioned. She's also a very strong woman. It's not worth the energy trying to get her to change. She won't."

I forgave him, of course. *Nobody is perfect,* I reasoned. *He just made an error in judgment. Mother-child relationships are complicated.* Since my relationship with my own mother was fairly distant, I attempted to find it sweet that Martin shared a close relationship with his. I understood it, to an extent. Martin was an only child. After his father's death, Martin and Alice became partners in life just as much as they were mother and son. I rationalized her blunt insertion in our relationship as a result of her heritage. Germanic women just said what they thought—no sugar-coating necessary. That was just who she was. Over time, though, this logic wore thin. Martin didn't see it, calling me paranoid. I called him a mama's boy and an idiot. Yes indeed, it does take two people to end a marriage. I'm not so delusional as to think I played no part in our downfall. However, I am still child enough to proclaim that my husband is the one who started it.

We lived together about a year before I found out I was pregnant. Not a minute after I stepped out of our bathroom with the positive test in hand, he smiled and said, "Marry me." I said yes immediately—he was smart, funny, and sweet; all the good things I thought a husband should be. I loved him. I also didn't want to be like my mother, resigned to survive my life alone. I was certain having a husband would make motherhood that much easier to navigate. And besides, Martin was delighted to become a father. I could still be a journalist. I could still live the life I'd planned. I'd just have Martin and a baby living it right along with me.

Alice, of course, was thrilled to learn she would be a grandmother. We told her about the baby a few weeks after the impromptu wedding. At her urging, with the sudden knowledge he was about to become a father, Martin surprised me by leaving the public school system, parlaying his technical savvy into a cushy, well-paying programming position with Microsoft.

"But you love teaching," I said when Martin informed me he was switching careers. Martin's intense fondness for his students was one of the things that made me believe he would be the kind of father neither of us had ever known. "What about becoming a principal someday? Isn't that what you've wanted?" We were driving during this conversation, on our way out to dinner. My hand rested on the curve of my stomach, a first attempt at cradling our child.

Martin shrugged. "The benefits at Microsoft are amazing, Cadee. They'll pay for everything . . . your pregnancy, the birth, insurance for all of us. Plus, there's the opportunity to move up in the company." He threw a brief glance out the window. "I'd never get that with teaching. Not really."

"But—" I began, and he cut me off.

"I want this, honey. I do. I want to be the kind of father my dad would have been proud of. I want our child to have everything we didn't."

I hadn't argued with him further. I tried to be supportive the way I assumed a good wife would. Not that I had any firsthand knowledge of what a good wife actually looked like. But since life presented me with the opportunity to have everything my mother never did—husband, kids, *and* a career—I wasn't going to screw it up. I was going to have it all.

For a while, it felt like I did. Toward the end of my pregnancy, with the security of Martin's new job, I left the *Herald* and started freelancing. My first few articles sold quickly, so I assumed I'd have no problem picking it back up a few months after Charlie's arrival. Aided by a perfectly timed spinal block, giving birth was easier than I expected it to be, though learning to take care of an infant was much harder. Charlie was colicky, and no matter how many times we tried, he refused to take a pacifier or a bottle. The first six months of his life, if he wasn't sleeping, he was nursing. Sleep became a rare luxury, and even with breastfeeding, my body didn't bounce back the way all the books I'd read promised that it would. Instead, it clung to fifteen of the thirty-five pounds I'd gained while pregnant. I was puffy and exhausted. I also discovered that I really didn't want sex anymore; that overwhelming physical desire simply ceased rising up beneath my skin. This startled me and had a profound, immediate effect on my marriage. The one place Martin and I always connected was in bed.

At first, Martin was patient. He said he understood. We'd climb under our covers at night and he'd just hold me. After a couple of months passed, though, that wasn't enough. He'd hold me, but then start to kiss my neck. His hands moved over my hips, urging me to him. I knew what he wanted. I felt guilty, so I forced my body to mimic the correct motions, despite my mind silently screaming to be left alone. This was a new sensation for me. I was used to wanting him, too. At that point, the only craving I felt for physical connection was cradling my child in my arms.

"Mmm, you feel so good," Martin whispered in my ear. My body felt stiff and unresponsive, but I murmured a loving sentiment in return. I crossed my fingers that because it had been so long since we'd last made love, it would be over quickly. If it wasn't, I barely managed to hide my relief when Charlie interrupted us, crying out from his crib in the other room. I extricated my body from my husband's and slipped into my bathrobe.

Each time this would happen, Martin rolled over onto his back, arm thrown over his forehead. "He's *fine!*" he insisted.

"He is not fine," I said. "He's crying."

"You need to let him cry it out," he said, propping himself up on his elbows. "He needs to learn to comfort himself back to sleep."

The fleshy kickstand of his erection stuck out at an odd angle from his body. It was a sight that used to arouse. Since having Charlie, it simply made me tired; yet another task I needed to check off my to-do list.

"According to who?" I asked, heading toward the door. "Your mother?"

Even in the dark, I felt the leaden weight of his eyes on my back as I walked out of the room. When I returned to bed after nursing our son and settling him back to sleep in his crib, Martin was most always already asleep. Or at least, he was good at pretending.

During the day, when Martin was at work and Charlie still slept better than he did at night, I tried to get back in the habit of writing. It took longer than I thought it would, but when Charlie was eight months old, I sold an article to a local consumer parenting magazine. I recounted what it was like trying to figure out what my baby's cries meant, and how frustrating it was that my breasts were the only pacifier he'd use. It was more of an essay than the fact-driven, journalistic style I was used to at the paper, but I enjoyed writing it, and felt enormous satisfaction signing the back of the nominal check the magazine sent upon publication. I set a goal to finish at least five articles a month, which often meant working feverishly a few hours late at night after Charlie was asleep.

"We don't need the money," Martin said. "I don't know why you think you have to work so hard."

"It's not about needing the money," I told him. "It's about retaining my sense of self."

Luckily, my experience at the *Herald* translated easily into my attempts at freelancing. I knew my queries to editors needed to be specific and attention-grabbing; several years spent penning headlines came in handy for that. It wasn't "The Best Way to Potty Training Your Child," but "Potty Train Your Child in Two Days!" Not "An Interview with the Chef at the Space Needle," but "Local Chef Spills All!" I kept a notebook of topics that interested me, ranging from child rearing to profile pieces on local celebrities. I didn't want to put myself in a niche, the way I had at the paper, where I only covered lifestyle subjects, so I kept my eye on the news for controversial issues and tried to jot down ideas for story angles that I might be able to sell. I ended up in a niche anyway, focusing for the most part on parenting and relationships, with a few interviews and how-to career articles thrown in. I wasn't making enough money to support myself the way I had at the paper, but I sold enough work to avoid feeling that I had been completely swallowed by motherhood.

Then came the sweltering August evening when Charlie was about a year old. It was nearly eight o'clock and Martin was just making it home. I was so busy that day taking care of Charlie and furiously writing during his naps, I hadn't managed to shower. Martin strode through the front door, brushed his lips against my cheek, and handed me a brochure for a gun-metal gray, two-seater BMW.

"Is this where you've been?" I asked, looking at the picture of the sleek vehicle. We sat at the table in our kitchen. Charlie was next to us in his high chair, up to his elbows in a before-bedtime snack of cottage cheese and diced peaches. I attempted to convince my child to use a spoon, but he much preferred the hand-to-mouth shovel method. I'd be picking bits of cottage cheese out of his ears for days.

"Yes," he said, lifting his chin almost imperceptibly.

"You told me you were working late."

"I did work late. And then I stopped by the dealership."

"Um-hmm." I pressed my lips into a thin line to keep from saying more.

"So, what do you think?"

I gave him a slightly confused look. "What do I think about what?"

"The car."

I placed the brochure on the table. "It's not exactly child-friendly," I said. "And not very practical for us. At least, not right now."

"Well, it's kind of too late," Martin said. He picked the brochure up and gave it a little wave in the air. "I bought it."

I looked at Martin, my mouth open in a soft O. "What?"

He sighed and dropped back against his chair. "Don't look at me like that. We have the money, Cadence. And my mom pointed out you have your Explorer for carting Charlie around. I needed a better car for commuting." There it was—my husband's linear brain. A plus B equals C.

"You talked to your *mother* about this?"

"BMWs are German cars. I wanted her opinion."

"But not mine."

"Please don't start," Martin said.

"Whatever, Martin." I didn't know what else to say to him. That he made such a big purchase on his own was unsettling, but I swallowed my concerns. *His money, his decision,* I thought. *Who was I to tell him no? He works so hard—he's entitled.*

The year after Charlie turned one, Martin's working late stopped being the exception and became the rule. He rarely called to let me know when to expect him home, and when I'd try to reach him, he claimed he had turned his cell phone off so he could concentrate on whatever code he was writing.

"I was worried about you," I said one morning after Charlie's second birthday in August. He had come home after I was already asleep. "Do you really need to work late *every* night?"

"I'm doing it for us," he said. "For Charlie. I want to get into management, and the only way that's going to happen is if I show them I'm willing to put in the hours." He paused. "I'm playing golf with a couple guys from the office today, too."

I rolled over in bed to look at him. "You are? Is it a work thing?" Microsoft often held employee engagement events—basketball tournaments or picnics on Lake Sammamish—but Martin usually told me about them beforehand.

"No, I took a vacation day," he said. He sat up and patted me on the hip, the same way he might have petted a dog. "I need some time with the guys."

"Oh," I said. I paused. "What time do you think you'll be back? I could make us ribs." My recipe for smoky, oven-baked ribs was almost always a guaranteed lure to bring him home.

He stood up and walked toward the bathroom. "I think I'll be late, honey. Jeff wants to do drive practice and walk all eighteen holes. We'll probably grab dinner out, too."

"Okay," I said, and on the surface, it was. I wasn't bothered that Martin wanted to play golf with his friends. It was that he made plans without letting me know. I also hoped he would want to spend at least part of his day off with his wife and son. Still, I didn't push the issue.

Instead, I tried to up the romance in our relationship. I put sweet notes in his lunches and made sure to kiss him passionately before he left for work. I cooked the food he adored, and despite my insecurities about my post-pregnancy body, I donned the skimpy lingerie he was so fond of in an effort to reignite our sex life. One night, I arranged for my sister to babysit Charlie and planned an elaborate dinner, being sure to text Martin a reminder that we had the entire evening to ourselves. As the candles burned low, I sat in the kitchen wearing a scant red dress, crying. He strolled through the door at midnight, claiming he'd been busy at work and simply forgot about our date.

"Sorry," he said. "Why are you so upset? It's just dinner."

I stared at him through swollen eyes. "No, Martin. It's not. Charlie is with Jess until tomorrow morning and I went to a lot of trouble to make this a special night for us. You know we don't get enough time alone together and you totally blew me off."

He stepped over to the table, picked up the glass of wine I'd poured for him earlier, and took a sip before speaking. "I think you're overreacting. I'm here, now, aren't I? You look great, by the way. But I think you'd look better out of that dress." He winked at me, and I shook my head in disbelief. Was he kidding?

"Good night," I said, pushing back from the table. I strode down the hall and slammed our bedroom door behind me, making it clear I didn't want him to follow. I lost sleep that night and several more after that, wondering if I had enough strength to pull my marriage out of the rut it was in without the help of my husband.

A month later, he volunteered to head up a project that would require twelve-hour days and working weekends, too.

"Weekends? Really?" I said, struggling to keep the petulance out of my voice. Martin typically took Charlie to the park for at least a few hours on both Saturday and Sunday so I could have uninterrupted time to work.

"Leading this project is huge, Cadee," he said. "Opportunities like this don't come along very often. It gives me a chance to move up."

"How long will the project take?" I asked. I didn't recognize this man standing before me. What had happened to the Martin I fell in love with? In his determination to provide for his family, he appeared to have lost track of something infinitely more important—spending time with us.

"Six, maybe eight months."

I sighed. "God, Martin."

His jaw tensed; the muscles worked like tiny gears beneath his skin. "It's my job. I can't help it."

I nodded tightly, telling myself I'd find a way to make it work. I continued to write, though with days filled with carting Charlie to the park and the play area at the mall to help wear out his raging toddler energy, I rarely met my goal of completing five articles a month. I did some short online pieces, trying to build a more varied customer base with quicker turnover when it came to getting paid, but for the most part, writing evolved into more of a hobby than a career—something I slipped into the cracks around my real job of being Charlie's mom.

That first project came and went, and Martin was promoted to a management position and was asked to start speaking at regional technical conferences. He'd let me know maybe a day or two before he had to travel, though there were a couple of times I had no clue he was leaving until he pulled out his suitcase from our closet.

"I'm sorry I forgot to tell you," he said, blaming his busy schedule for this new habit of forgetfulness. I blamed his new obsession with making more and more money, which demanded he *have* such a busy schedule. He bought a custom golf club set and almost every week brought home a different useless gadget from the Sharper Image. He filled our garage with elaborate tools he rarely used and upgraded the stereo system in his new car. He brought home gifts for Charlie and me, too, like a set of high-end pots and pans I'd drooled over at Macy's and a video gaming system Charlie was too young to use. But having these things didn't make up for having a husband who was rarely home.

I tried to talk with him. I told him I was afraid our marriage was disintegrating. He told me I was imagining things. He said he was only doing what any good father should. He had it set in his mind that how we were living was fine. Nothing I said, no matter how I said it, seemed to get through.

The summer of Charlie's third birthday, an important deadline approached on a profile piece I was writing about a local Native American artist for *Sunset* magazine. It was a pretty huge deal for me to land a contract with *Sunset*, especially at the time, since I hadn't sold anything for a couple of months. I was anxious to make a great impression and hopefully build a solid relationship with the publication's managing editor.

I was able to do a lot of my background research online, but needed to visit the artist's home to conduct the interview. When I called her, I quickly discovered she was a grandmother and she was nice enough to encourage me to bring Charlie along. Finding a time that worked for her was a challenge, and as it turned out, our meeting ended up being scheduled precariously close to the day the finished article was due. The day before I was supposed to make the trip to La Conner, a quaint town about an hour north of Seattle where the artist lived, Charlie spiked a temperature of one hundred and three. I took him to the doctor.

"Is he okay?" I asked. Heavy with worry, the muscles of my face pulled downward. I held Charlie in my lap as the doctor examined him.

"It looks viral," his pediatrician said. She peeked in Charlie's ears and up his nose. My son was too exhausted to protest.

"Are you sure? His fever is so high."

She gave my forearm a reassuring squeeze. "As long as he's fussing and giving you a hard time, I wouldn't worry. If his fever hits one-oh-four or he gets too listless and unresponsive, I want you to take him to the ER."

Panic swelled in my chest. "What's 'too listless'?"

"Not eating, not drinking, not crying, not responding when you say his name." She squeezed my arm again. "It's only a cold, Cadence. We'll keep an eye on it to make sure it doesn't turn into an ear or sinus infection, but it's nothing serious. Just keep him hydrated and as cool and comfortable as possible over the next few days."

As usual, Martin was late that night getting home from the office, and even after I'd called his cell phone twice and left messages asking him to pick up Charlie's cough medicine at the pharmacy, he'd forgotten.

"I have to go do my interview tomorrow," I told him. I stood in the living room, holding my son, swaying back and forth. If I set him down, he cried. If I put him in a lukewarm bath, he screamed. My arms were the only place he was calm. "Can you stay home with Charlie?"

"I can't," Martin said. "I have a huge presentation in front of the executive team. I can't miss it."

"And I can't miss this interview," I said. "I'm on deadline. I haven't asked you to skip one day of work since Charlie was born, Martin. Have I?"

"If it were any other day, I'd say yes," he said, avoiding eye contact and my question. He fiddled with the remote control, trying to figure out how to get the screen off the *Rolie Polie Olie* DVD I'd put in to entertain Charlie.

"So your job is more important than mine?" Charlie's skin was sweltering, his breath hot and slow against my neck. I was fairly certain he'd fallen asleep again.

He set the remote down hard on the coffee table and finally looked at me. "My job pays the bills."

"Oh, that's nice," I said, seething. "Because I make less money, my work isn't as significant as yours?"

He didn't blink. "You can't live off what you earn. So yes, in the grand scheme of things, I'd say it's less significant."

It was everything I could do not to tell him to fuck off, but I didn't want to swear in Charlie's ear and wake him up.

Martin saw the look on my face and held his hands up in front of his chest, palms toward me, in a gesture of mock surrender. "You're the one who wanted to do the freelance thing, Cadee. You know you don't have to work."

"I know I don't have to. I *want* to. Is that so hard to understand?"

"It is, actually," he said. His blue eyes flashed. "From the minute you had Charlie you were adamant about not letting other people raise him. You swore you wouldn't be like your mom."

"I'm *not* like her," I said, incensed that he would hit so far below the belt.

"I wouldn't be so sure. At least she had a good reason to be away from you so much. She had bills to pay. You need someone to take care of Charlie tomorrow just so you can go find *fulfillment.*"

I glared at him, fury rising like a wave inside me. "What I *need* is for his father to help take care of him when he's sick." I adjusted Charlie in my arms and he whined, rubbing his snotty nose against my bare shoulder.

He gave me a glowering look. "I do take care of him. I bust my ass to make enough money so my wife can stay home with him. Like we agreed she would."

"Don't talk about me in the third person," I said through gritted teeth. "I'm not just your wife."

"No, you're a mother, too," he shot back. "Shouldn't your child be more important than some stupid interview?"

"Shouldn't your child be more important than some stupid presentation?"

He fell silent after this, visibly fuming to the point that his body shook. I didn't know how he could discount my work like this. I felt torn enough already, needing to leave Charlie when he was ill. His father was the logical choice to take care of him. I didn't think it was too much to ask.

After a few minutes of silence, Martin spoke with an exasperated sigh. "Can't you reschedule your interview?"

I narrowed my eyes at him. "Can't *you* reschedule your presentation?"

Round and round we went. In the end, I gave in and asked Alice to watch Charlie for me, enduring her reproachful stare while I explained why it was so important I make it to the interview. Charlie and

I both sobbed when I left him, and while I managed to finish the article, I had a hard time forgiving my husband for the things he'd said.

Still, I told myself, this was a normal way to live—that every family was busy, that most couples struggled with spending enough time together and finding balance between work and family life. All mothers had to make sacrifices. When Jess or my mother asked how we were doing, I smiled brightly and said, "We're great. Busy, but really great." I repeated this line enough times in my own mind to believe it was true. But my husband seemed to drift further and further away. *Only a temporary side effect of young parenthood,* I reasoned. He'd come back around and everything would be fine.

Of course, it wasn't fine. We fought frequently over his long hours at the office and how much he was missing out on at home. "Charlie doesn't care about how much money you make," I told him as gently as I could. "He cares about how often you're there to tuck him in at night." Martin loved his son, I knew, but he simply brushed off any input I gave him about how his behavior was affecting us. He, however, felt free to dish out criticism about me. As the months passed, his belittling of my career grew worse.

"It's not like you're a hard-hitting journalist," he said one night after Charlie had gone to bed. We were sitting on opposite ends of the couch, once again discussing my need for more time to work. "You spit out cute little essays about what it's like being a mother or how to get a job. The world's not going to end if you don't write anymore."

Tears filled my eyes and the air stopped short in my lungs at his words. I had to remind myself to breathe before responding. "I can't believe you would say something like that to me," I whispered, my chin trembling.

He sighed and rolled his eyes. "Do you have to take everything so personally? I'm only making an observation."

It struck me in that moment just how much like his mother he'd become. "Martin, if you think that wasn't personal, then you've got bigger issues than we can deal with on our own." I swiped my eyes with the bend of my wrist. "I think we need to see a marriage counselor. We need someone to help us learn how to work through this stuff. We keep going round and round on the same issues."

He gave me a cold stare. "No, *you* keep going round and round on them. You nitpick everything. If anyone needs a therapist, it's you."

Did he really not see we had problems? Could he be that self-absorbed? My eyes went dry and a cold sensation crept into my chest. I suddenly realized that not only was I unsure if I still loved Martin, I was pretty certain that I didn't like him anymore. I met his stare with one of my own. "Are you saying you won't even try to fix this with me?"

"There's nothing for me to fix. I'm being the provider we agreed I would be. You and Charlie want for nothing. If you think we have issues, they've got nothing to do with me."

I did go see a therapist briefly, who agreed that if Martin was unwilling to work on our marriage, it was most likely doomed. I also asked her about Charlie, since I worried about how a divorce might affect him. "Happy kids have happy parents," she said, peering at me over her bifocals with kind gray eyes. "Witnessing the two of you constantly at each other's throats could inflict much worse damage on his development."

Armed with this knowledge, and after a few more months of Martin's continued denial of our problems, I gathered up the courage to contact a lawyer and tell my husband I wanted a divorce. He was shocked and angry, but surprisingly didn't put up much of a fight when I asked him to leave. I decided my son and I would be fine. My mother had been a single parent. So had Alice. I had no doubt I could do it, too. Martin was gone all the time anyway. I'd been on my own all along.

The day Martin moved out for good, he stood in front of me in our living room, bags packed. He searched my eyes with his. The fury in his face was so pronounced it almost looked like he was wearing a mask. He inhaled deeply and released the breath with a hiss, like a punctured tire. My gaze traveled the sharp planes of his cheekbones, the high, smooth forehead, the full curve of his lips. I thought how Mother Nature took the best of both of us and put it all into our son.

He took a step toward me and I immediately stiffened, anticipating his touch. He saw this and stopped just short of me. There was barely an inch between us. I could smell him, the woodsy warmth of his favorite soap, the cinnamon spice of his skin.

"Are you sure?" he whispered.

I nodded, a sharp, quick movement, my lips pressed together in a straight, hard line. A new coldness resided in me after his final refusal to even consider counseling; a chunk of ice moved over my heart and froze any feeling I had left for him. I felt distant, detached. It's not something I chose, just something that was.

"Okay, then," he said, turning around to grab the last of his bags. "I guess that's it." The door closed behind him and a moment later, though he'd only just left, it was almost as if he'd never lived there at all.

Three

Charlie! You need to turn off the television and come talk with me." It was nine o'clock on a cool June morning, and I stood in his bedroom with my hands on my hips, staring at a scribbled mess on the wall. Only a month shy of his fourth birthday and my son considered himself a Van Gogh, regardless of the medium upon which he chose to display his work.

His face popped around the doorway, his eyes darting from me to the wall. "What, Mama?"

I pointed at the wall. "Did you do this?"

"No." He dropped his gaze to the floor.

"Don't lie to me, Charles Sutter." I swore I wouldn't be one of those mothers who used her child's full name as a threat, but there I was.

"I'm *not*." He stomped his little foot.

I went over to him and crouched down, taking one of his hands in mine. "Sweetie. No one else lives here but us, and Mommy knows *she* didn't color on the wall. So I'll ask you one more time. Did you do this?"

His dark head bobbed once, but he still didn't meet my gaze. "Sorry."

"I forgive you, Charlie bear, but please don't do it again." I sighed. "Now, let's get you dressed so we can get to play group." The Mommy and Me group I'd been attending since Charlie was five months old was welcoming a new member, Hannah, a former stockbroker who had just adopted an adorable, chubby two-year-old girl from China. She had invited a few mothers over to her high-ceilinged, open-concept rambler for an introductory lunch and play time for the kids.

"I'll do it *myself*!" he proclaimed. He dashed to his dresser and began yanking out handfuls of clothes I had just folded and put away the night before. He tossed the first batch to the floor, reaching in the drawer for another handful.

"Charlie, don't!" I said, running over to stop him. He pulled on the T-shirt I attempted to take away from him.

"No!" he said. "It's my shirt, Mama!"

Oh, dear Lord. I took a deep breath and stepped back. "Charlie, I am going into the kitchen. I will see you there in two minutes, and whatever you have on, even if you're still in your undies, we are going to play group."

He giggled. "Even if I'm *naked*?"

"Yes." Trying not to smile and thus completely undermine my threat, I gave him a stern look and walked out of the room.

An hour later, we arrived at Hannah's place with me in jeans and a ratty blue sweatshirt and Charlie in too-tight purple swim trunks and a bright yellow sweater. Four women including myself showed up, and now stood around the marble-topped island in Hannah's kitchen. Since it was unseasonably chilly, instead of being outside, our children were playing directly off the kitchen in the toy-laden, toddler-proofed "great room," a space that when I was growing up would have been called the den.

"Cadence, you should come to my party on Friday," said Brittany, whose daughter, Sierra, was born a few months before Charlie and seemed to hit every developmental milestone—rolling over, crawling, eating solid foods—well before my son. Brittany, like me, worked from home, which I originally thought would be a commonality that bonded us. I soon discovered that while I planned to make my freelance work a career, Brittany saw hers as a scrapbook supply specialist as an excuse to kick her husband out of the house and throw a party. I genuinely liked the other women in the play group, but outside of our children being about the same age, we didn't really have that much in common. Our relationships remained pretty much on the surface; our conversations centered around the kids. Most of the time, this was enough.

"Oh!" Renee squealed. "You totally should come, Cadence. The new flower hole punchers she has are super cute." Renee was a former elementary schoolteacher, mother to three-year-old Juan, and prone to using the phrase "super cute" in just about every conversation she had.

"I would," I said, trying not to visibly flinch, "but I'm on deadline. I don't think I'll have time." When I first met Brittany, I had tried to forge a friendship with her, valiantly attending several of her parties over the past three years. I even purchased some of her company's products to put together Charlie's baby book, but only managed to complete the first four pages. And using the word "complete" might have been pushing it.

"What about Sunday's knitting night?" Renee asked, as she dipped a strawberry into the cream cheese and Marshmallow Fluff dip Hannah had set out with a platter of fruit. "We're working on a blanket for Hannah's new edition."

I gave a faltering smile to Hannah, who kept her eye on the children as they played. "I wish I could," I said, "but Martin brings Charlie home on Sunday nights. I need to be there." After watching so many of the other women find satisfaction—joy, even—in activities like these, I sometimes wondered what was wrong with me that I only found more excuses not to join them. I felt like I did back in high school, not wanting to be a cheerleader or head up the homecoming committee—I didn't have a bubbly personality and didn't care about the theme of a prom. And yet, I ached to fit in with the girls who did, like a hippo trying to fit in with a herd of gazelles.

"That's too bad," Brittany clucked. She smoothed her sleek blond pageboy. "It must be so *difficult* to work without Martin there to help out."

"I manage." I shrugged and looked down to the floor. These women knew that Martin and I had divorced, but I kept the details to myself. "I need to use the ladies' room," I said, rearranging my face into a cheery expression. "Will you excuse me?"

"Down the hall and on your left," Hannah directed.

I stepped through the entryway and down the short hallway. In contrast to her modern kitchen, Hannah's guest bathroom was a flashback to the mideighties, painted a pale shade of peach accented with a seashell wallpaper border and bright turquoise hand towels. As I put my hand on the doorknob to rejoin the group, I caught a glimpse of myself in the mirror. The space beneath my eyes was bruised from lack of sleep—my best hours for writing came after Charlie was in bed, and these days that time seemed to be getting later and later. My wild curls were pulled back in a clip, but I'd missed several strands and they spun out from the sides of my head like corkscrews. I let go of the doorknob and tried to smooth them, remembering a time when I checked myself in the mirror *before* I went out, not after I'd arrived at my destination.

I sighed. I wasn't sure I even wanted to be here. I should have stayed home and worked on the article about food allergies I needed to turn in to *Alpha Mom* magazine the following week. Play group was more for Charlie's sake than for mine anyway. Still, I showed up, just like I had for Sign with Your Baby classes and Toddler Yoga. I remained ever-determined to do with my child the kinds of things my mother had never done with me. In September, he would start going to preschool five mornings a week instead of just three, so it was easy to reason we could stop coming to play group then. School would provide him all the play time with other kids he'd need.

Back in the kitchen, I walked past the women toward the great room. "I'm going to check on Charlie," I said, and the women smiled and nodded, continuing their conversation about the newest Pampered Chef knife set.

My son sat alone at the toddler table, scribbling away on a piece of paper with a thick, blue crayon. I dropped into the other tiny chair, a little horrified by how much of my hips hung over the seat.

"What are you drawing?" I asked, tilting my head so I could see the image on the page.

"'Pider-Man," Charlie said. He was intent on his work and didn't bother to look up.

"Of course you are." I wasn't sure where his obsession with the superhero came from; he'd never seen the movies or watched the cartoon. I blamed excessive product placement—did a three-year-old really *need* a toy cell phone emblazoned with Spider-Man's face? Probably not, but I'd bought him one, nonetheless.

"Can I help you color?" I asked my son.

"No, I got it."

"Okay," I said. "You're doing a good job coloring on the *paper*." He gave me a mischievous grin, then went back to his picture—an abstract mess of red, blue, and black. Our refrigerator was covered in a multitude of similar depictions. I watched him for a minute, until he set his crayon down and held up the paper in a triumphant gesture.

"All done!" he announced. "It's for you."

"It is?" I took the paper and gave him a huge smile. "I love it. Thank you."

"Welcome, Mama." He jumped up and walked over to the corner where Leah, Hannah's newly adopted little girl, was playing with a pile of blocks. He happily plopped to the floor and she pushed a few toward him. Again, I watched him, proud to see my child sharing the way I'd taught him.

There was a knock at the front door. Just as Hannah took a step to go answer it, the door swung open and in walked Susanne, one of the few women in our particular Mommy and Me group who still worked full-time. Susanne's husband, Brad, stayed home with their daughter so Susanne could run her highly successful insurance brokerage, but when her schedule allowed, she brought Anya to our meetings herself. Susanne was curvy, like me, with straight black hair, a ghostly white, creamy complexion, and was never seen in public without a slash of bloodred lipstick. Outside of my sister, she was also the person with whom I spent the most time. When Susanne wasn't busy working and Charlie was with Martin, we occasionally got together for conversation and a bottle of wine. I admired her blunt nature and quick wit, not to mention her professional success. She was one of those women who seemed to balance it all, and part of me hoped by spending time with her, that particular skill might rub off on me.

"Sorry I'm late," she said as she joined the women in the kitchen. She wore dark, pin-striped slacks and a royal purple button-down blouse. "I had a hard time getting out of the office."

I stood up and went back to stand with the other women around the island, passing Anya as she shot past me to join the other children at play. I tucked the picture Charlie had drawn for me in my purse. "Hey, Susanne," I said.

Her face brightened when she turned and saw me. "Hey!" She leaned over and gave me a quick, one-armed hug.

"Do you guys want a glass of wine?" Brittany asked.

I looked over and saw that she was already pouring chardonnay into thin-stemmed, silver-rimmed goblets. My mouth watered a bit seeing the cool liquid stream out of the bottle's neck. I'd made myself a promise a month ago—no wine until after Charlie went to bed—and I'd managed to stick to it.

For the most part.

One afternoon the previous week, Charlie had woken from his nap and snuck down the hall. When he entered the kitchen, I spun around in my chair, caught with a glass of syrah in my hand. I had told myself napping counted as his being in bed. *Just a few minutes to take for myself. I don't get pedicures or massages; I deserve some kind of escape.*

"Can I have some of your wine, Mama?" he'd asked.

"No, monkey. Wine is for grown-ups," I'd said. "I'll make you some chocolate milk, though, okay?"

"Okay," he'd said.

A few minutes later, we sat at the table together, each of us sipping our separate drinks. His gaze moved back and forth from my wineglass to my face a few times, his tiny eyebrows furrowed above the bridge of his nose. Unable to stand this scrutiny, I stood up and splashed the contents of my glass down the sink.

Now at Hannah's, I glanced at the clock on the microwave—it was only 2:00 p.m. "It's a little early for me, thanks," I said, swallowing back an aching urge to join them.

"Oh, come on," Renee said, raising her glass in a mock toast. "It's five o'clock somewhere!"

"That's true," I said. With a hesitant smile, my resolve instantly vanished. *It's only one glass. And it's not like I'm sitting at home, drinking alone. I'm being social. It would be rude not to join them.*

"Well, then, that settles it," Brittany said. She poured a full goblet and held it out to me. "I don't know about you, but I'm a *much* happier mommy after a cocktail. Or three." She giggled.

"Me, too," Renee agreed. "They don't call it the 'wine with dinner hour' for nothing. Juan whines while I make dinner. Now, I just join him." She gave her glass a little shake to emphasize her point.

I took the glass from Brittany's hand and breathed the drink in—a light, slightly sweet, fruity bouquet filled my nose. The first swallow puckered my tongue and warmed my belly. Every cell in my body seemed to exhale.

"Well, if *everyone else* is having one," Susanne said with a smile. Brittany poured her a glass, too.

"Thank you so much for the food you brought, Cadence," Hannah said. "I can't believe you made all of that for us. My husband will be thrilled."

I smiled at her over my wineglass as I took another sip. "It was my pleasure." While I wasn't into scrapbooking or knitting, I did love to cook, so every new mother in the group—whether it was their first child or their fourth—received a few days' worth of my freezer-friendly lasagnas or vats of hearty beef stew. Hannah was no exception.

"Wow," Renee had said when I showed up unexpectedly at her house with an ice chest full of foil-wrapped meals. Her body was ripe, about to give birth to her second baby any day. "What made you decide to do this?"

"Empathy, I guess," I said, smiling shyly as I stood on her front porch. "There were so many times during Charlie's first month that the idea of needing to get dinner on the table nearly brought me to tears. I was sleeping maybe three hours total a night. I could barely find time to shower, let alone defrost a roast." I shrugged. "I figured a few ready-made meals might help alleviate that for you a bit."

She laughed. "Let's hope so. Thank you so much. It means a lot."

The other women were appreciative of the gesture, as well. After a couple of months of doing it on my own, another member suggested that the idea become a regular practice. From then on, when one of the group's members became pregnant or adopted, it wasn't uncommon for her to have at least a month's worth of meals in her freezer before the baby was due.

"Cadence's food is amazing," Brittany said. "She always brought the best appetizers to my parties. When I could get her to show up."

I took another swallow of wine, almost emptying the glass, choosing to ignore her cloaked jab. "Oh, I see," I said, feeling pleasantly engaged. "You just want me for my hot artichoke dip."

"Well, yes," Brittany said as she lifted the bottle and tilted it to top off my drink. "And for the money you'll spend to up my commission."

All the women laughed then, including me.

"Where is Leah going to preschool?" Susanne asked Hannah.

Hannah looked surprised. "She's only two. Doesn't preschool start when she's three?"

"Oh, no," Brittany said. "You need to get her registered now. Isn't that right, Cadence?"

I nodded. "The waiting list at the Sunshine House is at least six months long. If you want her to get in, you should get her name on it." I recognized the look of panic on Hannah's face, remembering how intimidated I was when I first joined the group. The other women appeared so confident in their mothering skills; I felt like a freshman in a room full of MBAs. It had taken me almost two months just to decipher which of Charlie's cries meant he was hungry and which meant he needed to sleep. Suddenly, the stakes around my choices took on a whole new weight. Breast milk or formula? Organic or processed? Cloth or disposable diapers? Home school or public? The list of potential mistakes seemed endless. It overwhelmed me.

"Don't worry," I said to Hannah now. "You'll figure it all out." I wasn't sure if I was reassuring her or myself.

A sudden cry erupted from the other room—I knew immediately from the pitch it was my son. I set my glass on the counter with a light clatter and rushed to his side. He was standing with his arms straight at his sides, his fingers balled into fists. "She took my block!" he hollered.

Leah stood only a few steps away, a yellow block clasped to her chest. She whipped around to hide it from view. I crouched down to Charlie's level. "Charlie, you were playing with Leah just fine a minute ago. And there are plenty of blocks for everyone to share. Why don't you ask her to build something else with you?"

"No." Charlie pouted.

Hannah stepped next to her daughter. "Leah, you need to give the block back to Charlie. He's your guest."

"No, no," I said. "Charlie can share." I rubbed my son's arm. "Can't you, Charlie?"

Charlie dropped his chin to his chest and shook his head.

I sighed. "Okay, then, I guess it's time we go home." I stood up and took his hand to lead him. He pulled, trying to fight me. I don't know what the experts were thinking when they classified two-year-olds as "terrible." It wasn't until his third birthday that Charlie had occasionally seemed in need of an exorcism.

"Sorry," I apologized to the group. "He needs a nap."

"I do not!" Charlie protested. "*You* need a nap!"

"He's right about that," I said with a deep breath and a forced smile. What I really needed was to get him home. He could go from pouting and cutely sassy to a full-blown tantrum in ten seconds flat, something I didn't feel comfortable having the other women witness. I couldn't help but feel like his behavior reflected how good a job I was doing as his mother. If he lost it, it was like having to wear a dunce cap in front of the entire class.

"Thanks for having us, Hannah," I said. "It was good to meet both of you. Leah's wonderful."

"Good to meet you, too," Hannah said, hiking Leah up onto her hip.

"Here," Susanne said, handing me my glass. "Looks like you might need it."

I regarded the half-full glass, everything in me screaming to grab it and drink it down, knowing how quickly it would dissolve my growing tension. "I really shouldn't," I said.

"All right, then." Susanne laughed and poured the rest into her own glass. "I'll call you soon."

"Mama, let's go!" Charlie said, pulling me toward the front door.

"Okay, okay," I said. I grabbed my purse and waved to the other women. "'Bye, everyone."

With Charlie strapped into his car seat, I set my hands deliberately at ten and two on the steering wheel and slowly pulled out from the curb. I drove along, quietly humming "Fruit Salad" by the Wiggles. Charlie would listen to their CDs constantly if I'd let him, and as a result, I knew all the songs by heart.

As I turned the corner to my street singing "Dorothy the Dinosaur" under my breath, a car blared its horn long and loud, forcing me to slam on my brakes and bumping my chest against the steering wheel. I'd forgotten to put on my seat belt.

"Shit!" I exclaimed. I wasn't going very fast, but still, my heart leapt into my throat and my eyes went straight to the rearview mirror. Charlie had zonked out within minutes of leaving Hannah's house and miraculously didn't seem disturbed by the jarring stop. His pink, bow-shaped lips smacked open and shut, but his eyes remained closed.

"There's a stop sign there for a reason, lady!" the man yelled as he drove past, angrily flipping me off.

With my chest aching and adrenaline pulsing through my veins, I fastened my seat belt and took a couple of deep breaths before pushing on the gas. *I've turned this corner a thousand times—how the hell could I have missed that sign?*

Of course, I knew why I'd missed it. I knew it from the wine-tinged, fuzzy feeling around my edges, the slightly loose, unhinged feeling in my joints. I drove down the block to my house, gripping the steering wheel until my knuckles were white, keeping the speedometer below ten miles per hour. I wondered how I could have been so stupid, putting Charlie's life in danger like that. A moment later, as I pulled into the safety of my driveway, I counted my blessings, thankful that at least I had learned this lesson without anyone getting hurt.

As the economy declined, my freelance work became so sparse I started toying with the idea of going back to Peter Baskin, my editor at the *Herald*, and begging for my old job back. But the last thing I wanted to do was go back to a standard full-time job and put my son in day care twelve hours a day. In fact, the idea made my stomach turn. I didn't want to be my mother, but I also couldn't get away from the sinking sensation that I didn't want to be who I was.

Charlie turned four in August, and that November, I managed to swing a contract with *Woman's Day* for an article about why women take back a husband after he cheats. The managing editor initially asked me to write the article on spec, which meant I would have written it in full and then they would have decided whether or not they wanted to buy it, but I managed to negotiate my way into a contract instead, including a ten percent kill fee if they decided not to publish.

On the Friday before Thanksgiving, my plan was to hunker down while Charlie was at Martin's for the weekend and get the *Woman's Day* assignment done. I'd finished my research and interviewed a psychology professor at the University of Washington to cite as my relationship expert, but I was still having a hard time getting the actual writing started.

I sipped at a glass of wine while Charlie ate dinner—he was leaving soon, so I figured it would be okay to indulge in front of him. For almost six months, since the day of the stop sign incident, I'd waited until after he was in bed for the night to pour my first glass.

Martin showed up around six o'clock, a full hour after the time he told me he'd pick Charlie up.

"Daddy!" my son said when I opened the front door. He ran and jumped up, throwing his bony arms around his father's neck and squeezing hard. Martin squeezed back, lifting his child into the air, letting Charlie's body hang straight down—a human necktie. His skinny legs floated free as Martin rotated, swinging his son back and forth. Charlie laughed.

"Sorry I'm late," Martin said, looking just over my shoulder instead of making direct eye contact.

"Uh-huh," I said. He knew I'd heard that phrase fall out of his mouth enough times for it to lose all meaning; I don't know why he bothered to speak it. I took in his casual work attire, blue jeans and a black V-neck T-shirt with a Windows icon over his heart. A bitter thought floated through my mind: *I pledge allegiance to Bill Gates . . .*

and to all the money that he pays me. . . . And then I remembered that for the time being, between the proceeds of the divorce settlement and child support, Bill Gates's money was keeping me afloat, too.

"So," Martin said, lifting Charlie up to hug him. "Do you have his stuff?"

"It's right there," I said, pointing to the Spider-Man-embossed backpack by the door. I'd packed four changes of clothes and an additional five pairs of underwear for the two-day stay at his dad's. Charlie was successfully potty trained; however, his attempts to clean himself up afterward occasionally went very, very wrong.

"Great, thanks." He stared at the glass of wine I still held in my hand and I quickly set it on the entryway table.

"He hasn't been eating much other than chicken nuggets and mandarin oranges," I said. "So you might want to stop at the store and pick some up."

"We'll manage. We're going over to my mom's tomorrow."

"Ah. How *is* Alice?" Our conversation was tense—I suddenly flashed on how my husband's naked body used to feel pressed against mine in the middle of the night, how he'd set his wide palm across the flesh of my belly. I gave my head a tiny shake, trying to erase the image.

"She's good." He pulled back his head, craning to look at Charlie. "You ready, buddy?"

"Yep!" Charlie said, kicking his spindly legs in emphasis.

I leaned over and kissed my son's cheek, rubbing his back as I did. "'Bye, Mr. Man. Mommy loves you."

"Love you, too," Charlie said.

After I closed the door behind them, I went straight to my laptop, but the words wouldn't come. I was a fake, a fraud. I don't know why I ever thought I could be a writer. I'd sent ten query letters out in that last two months and only picked up one assignment. Every "thanks, but no thanks" response that came in the mail felt like a nail in my professional coffin.

I sighed, leaned back in my chair, and eyed the liter of unopened merlot on the counter. *It's cheaper in the larger bottles,* I told myself when I stood in the wine aisle at the store, debating which size I should purchase. *I'm buying them to save money.* Maybe I could have just a little more. Once I really wind down, I'll be able to work.

I got up, walked over to the counter, and grabbed the corkscrew that lay next to the sink. I'd stopped bothering to put it away. Digging the sharp point into the cork, I twisted until the metal spiral was deep enough to anchor the lever against the lip of the bottle. The scarlet liquid flowed into the glass, and a moment later, the first swallow rolled over my tongue and around my teeth like silk; its rich, heady scent rose up into my senses and made me weak. Within minutes, I finally relaxed enough to feel like I fit inside my own skin. I set up camp with my bottle and a goblet the size of a small grapefruit, marveling at how half a bottle could fit inside a single glass.

Five rapidly typed pages later, my cell phone rang. Glancing at the caller ID, I saw Susanne's name pop up.

"I'm just leaving the office," she said, "and Brad took Anya to his mom's. Can I stop by for a drink?"

I looked at the document open on my laptop, the blinking cursor seeming to mock me. My social life was practically nonexistent—a couple hours spent talking about something other than Elmo and Spider-Man was incredibly appealing. "Sure," I said. "Martin just took Charlie to his house for the weekend."

She blew in through the front door thirty minutes later, a bottle of Chilean merlot in hand. Her black hair was pulled back from her face with a red velvet headband. I gave her a quick hug and we settled on the couch, both with a goblet of wine.

We chatted about work and the kids, but halfway through our second glass, Susanne paused and looked down into her drink. She bit her bottom lip before speaking, managing to smear lipstick on her front tooth. "Was divorcing Martin the worst thing you've ever done?" she asked. "Did it just devastate you?" The words tumbled from her mouth, falling into each other like a line of dominoes.

I swallowed and looked down, too, running the tip of my index finger over the edge of my glass. "Divorce is hard," I began. "But—"

"There's always a 'but.'"

"It's hard," I continued with a small smile, "but staying with Martin probably would've been a hell of a lot harder."

She blew out a long breath. "Okay, so it's a matter of degree, then? How hard would staying be in comparison to getting a divorce?"

"Pretty much."

"But is the thing that might be easier—"

"I didn't say divorce is easy," I said, cutting her off. "I said it seems to be less difficult than staying would have been." A minute distinction, but one I felt compelled to make.

She took a sip of her drink, looking up at me over the rim. "Okay, then," she said, after she swallowed. "Do you think choosing the *less difficult* thing is necessarily the *right* thing? If your marriage is hard, then isn't it your duty to stay and work things out, maybe even come out stronger for it in the long run? Isn't that the whole idea behind taking vows?"

I was silent, grappling with this idea, not sure if I was dizzy from the thought or the wine. "I'm not sure," I finally said. "I suppose challenges do tend to teach us more, but being alone again is another form of that, right? It's challenging." I tried not to sound defensive, but failed.

Susanne set her glass on the coffee table, then adjusted her headband. "I wasn't asking you to justify anything. Really. I'm sorry if it came across that way. I was more just wondering out loud, you know? Philosophizing."

I took a deep breath, then released it, trying to erase the tension that had invaded each cell of my skin, pulling it tight across my flesh. "Why, exactly?"

"Why what?"

"Why are you philosophizing?"

"I'm thinking about leaving Brad," she said.

"Oh." I finished the last swallow in my glass, then set it next to Susanne's on the table. "I thought I picked up on some tension the last time you talked about him." I chose my words carefully here, knowing full well how dangerous the territory can become around saying anything negative about a friend's spouse. They end up staying together, and you're suddenly the bitch who talked shit about her husband.

Susanne laughed, a harsh, dry sound. "'Some tension'? We're strung tighter than a goddamn violin."

"I'm sorry to hear that," I said. "How's Anya doing?"

"She's lovely. Daddy's little girl. I think she loves him more than she loves me."

"Oh, I doubt that," I said. "I don't think kids make those kinds of distinctions. He just spends more time with her. That's all."

"Ever since I went back to work, she doesn't want me to help give her a bath. She doesn't want me to read with her or cook her breakfast, or any of it. She doesn't want *me.*" Her eyes welled with tears, but she tried to hide it by looking away and reaching for her empty glass.

"I'm sure it's just a phase," I reassured her.

"Yeah," she said. "I hope so." She sighed. "Can I have another drink?"

"Of course," I said. I stood up, but felt woozy and ended up falling backward onto the couch.

"Uh-oh," Susanne said, laughing. "Time for rehab, Lindsay Lohan."

I laughed, too, a short, staccato sound. "Yeah, I could use the vacation," I said, then stumbled to the kitchen and grabbed us another bottle of wine.

Four

Some say there is a prescription written for a person in childhood determining whether or not they'll develop a drinking problem. A family history of others who drink, a violent home environment, an angry father, or sexual abuse. One of these circumstances in your childhood? A good chance you'll look to a substance as a way to numb it all out. Two circumstances or more? Pretty much guaranteed. I mean, really, who could blame you?

Serena, a woman in my treatment group, was raped by two of her cousins when she was nine. Her parents didn't believe her when she told them; in fact, they beat her for lying. Those cousins raped her over and over again until her thirteenth birthday, when she shot one of them with her father's gun. He lived and the police ended up ruling the shooting an accident. She snuck a bottle of rum from her parents' liquor cabinet and got drunk that night. She pretty much stayed that way for thirty years until she landed in treatment on a court-ordered deferral after her fourth DUI. Now here's a woman who has a reason to drink. Here's a woman who people feel sympathy for. She was abused, of course she needed to find a way to cope. I'm disgusted with myself, really, how my story lacks the frightening qualifications that the other women in my group seem to share.

Looking back, I can't find a reason for me to be in this nightmare. It doesn't make any sense. This is not who I am. I made a mistake. I overdid it just like I overdo everything else in my life. I'm not an alcoholic. Alcoholics live under bridges and swig from bottles tucked in brown paper bags. They beg for change on street corners and make offers to wash windshields while you're stopped at a traffic light. That's not me. That's not my life. I graduated from college. I own a home. I shower on a regular basis. I still have all my teeth. I had a problem with drinking for a little while there, but it was just the wrong way to deal with the stress of being on my own with a toddler. I'll do my time in the treatment program, get my attendance slip signed at AA like I'm required to, and get the hell out. I'll tell Andi what she needs to hear to stand up in family court and assure the judge I'm cured. And then, I'll get Charlie back and get on with my life.

So here I am, this sunny Saturday morning, practicing doing just that. After picking Charlie up from Alice, I take him to get his hair cut. I choose one of those generic, "we take walk-ins" kind of joints. There is an uneasiness in me while I do this simple errand with my son, a too-bright feeling. I hate it. It causes me to make silly, idle motherly chatter with this hairdresser. She is a melancholy young woman with a pierced upper lip and a pink frosted, blond crew cut. She has more black tribal tattoos than plain, pale visible skin. I wonder if covering her body like this is her own strange way of trying to disappear. The bass-driven music in the salon is nightmarishly loud, but I don't have the courage to ask her to turn it down. I somehow feel like I don't have the right.

"Charlie just loves getting his hair cut, don't you, Charlie?" I say. I hate the high, false pitch of my voice. I'm anxious to appear like his mother again. "He fell asleep in the chair the first time the stylist used the buzz cutters on him. He loved it. Totally relaxed him. It was like he was getting a massage."

The punk girl nods, visibly unimpressed. "Huh. Weird. You want it a two or a three cut?"

I experience a brief moment of panic, not able to remember what length on the clippers I used to have my hairdresser use on my son. Shit. Mothers are supposed to know this kind of thing, like their son's Social Security number or the exact time and date of his first successful stand-up pee. Unable to come up with it, I fake it.

"A three should work. We can always go shorter if we need to." I say "we" like I'm somehow one and the same as my son. I suppose in some senses I am. I suppose this is why it's excruciating to be forced to stay away from him.

It takes exactly twenty-two minutes to finish getting Charlie's hair cut. It is 9:53 on a Saturday morning. Twenty-six hours to go, alone with my child. It looms frighteningly in front of me. I am alternately thrilled and terrified to have such a long stretch of time alone with him. Will I remember what to do? What I used to do was drink. Merlot, in a moss green coffee mug, the moment I staggered out of bed.

There is a wild, fluttery panic in my chest. I am not ready to take Charlie home. There's no booze there, but there could be. It's as easy as stopping at the corner grocery and picking up a bottle. "Drive a different way home," Andi told all of us the first day of our group. "Grocery shop with a friend or shop online and have it delivered to your house. The only thing you're going to have to change is everything."

Her words alone exhausted me. *Really? I have to what? You've got to be joking.*

I don't want to drink. I abhor the idea. The thought of even a sip of alcohol makes the gorge rise in my throat. But I have been at this point before—physically appalled by the thought of taking a drink, and then, something will happen. Or not happen. And suddenly there I'd be, in the line at the store, bottles of wine in my grasp. *I'm smarter than this,* I'd think, and then, gradually, the thoughts would lessen as the alcohol took effect, until they disappeared altogether. Which was the point, I suppose. I've got too much at stake here. Martin's trying to take my son. I need to get my shit together.

We get into the car, Charlie successfully buckled in again. *Now what?* My pulse races, thumping in my throat. I put my hands on the steering wheel and glance in the rearview mirror.

"Hey, champ. What do you feel like doing?" I used a cheery tone in the hopes of concealing my hesitance.

He shrugs. "I don't know." He picks his nose.

"Digging for gold there?"

"No!" His voice is snuffled—his finger remains in his nose as he speaks. He laughs, a rolling, belly giggle that warms me, slows my pulse a bit. "Boogers."

My turn to laugh. "Lovely. Any luck?"

"Yep." He holds up his finger triumphantly, showing me his find.

"Uh, that's gross." I twist around in my seat, snag a tissue from the box I keep in the console. I cry all of the time, even driving down the road. It hits me at the strangest moments, for no reason. For years, I have cried only alone, only in the dark. Much like I chose to drink. I realize there's likely an interesting connection here, but I'm not sure I want to explore it. Andi would. Andi would have a field day with this particular nugget of insight.

I hold out the tissue to my son. "Here, gimme that, you booger monster."

He giggles again. "I'm not a booger monster." He pushes his finger into the tissue; I wipe it clean and shove the tissue into my purse.

"You're not? Are you sure?"

"Yep." He's silent for a minute, seemingly thoughtful. *He's five, Cadee,* I say to myself. *What does he have to be thoughtful about? The political climate of Sesame Street?*

"Whatcha thinkin'?" I ask, hoping I sound lighthearted.

"Are you going to drink any more wine, again ever, Mama?"

Wham. There it is—the guilt, landing like a cannonball in my gut. I swallow twice before I'm able to respond, my voice hoarse. "No, baby, I'm not. Mama's all done drinking wine."

"Good!" is all he says, then kicks the back of my seat again.

I've asked myself a million times in the past two months if he could remember. I've wondered if he was aware, if he really knows what kind of person his mother is. Does he remember those last three days? Does he understand why his father came to take him away? His question is my answer.

"Did your daddy give you the cards I sent this week?" I'm anxious to say something to stem the tide of shame still pushing to overwhelm me. Since entering treatment, I've been mailing a note to my son at his father's house a couple of times a week. Though Charlie will jabber my ear off in person, he's not much of a telephone conversationalist. He listens silently as I chatter on about nothing and I hang up feeling worse than before I'd called. Self-loathing pounds through my blood after I set down the phone. *What have I done to him?* I worry that he doesn't talk because he's angry with me. He doesn't talk because I've damaged our relationship beyond repair. He doesn't talk because he hates me.

When I shared these thoughts with Andi, she assured me this was not the case and suggested I start sending the notes just to tell him how much I love him and to make sure he doesn't believe his mother has simply disappeared.

"Yep, I got them!" Charlie says. "Daddy reads them to me and then I get to keep them in my room. He gave me a book and I get to use real grown-up tape to stick them in. It's blue. With stars on it." Something softens inside me toward Martin when I hear this. At least he's not trying to erase me completely from my son's life. I wonder if I should send a note directly to Martin, as well. *Please,* it would say. *Please let me have my son back.*

Charlie claps his hands together once, excited. "I know what we can do! Let's go see Aunt Jess! I want to see Marley and Jake!"

I twist back around to face the steering wheel, turn the key in the ignition. I don't look in the rearview mirror; I can't look at him. I refuse to look at myself. The engine roars to life and I pick up my cell phone to call my sister and let her know we are on our way. "That's a great idea, sweet boy. Aunt Jess is exactly what we need."

From the day Jessica was born, our mother told us it was evident we would be close. I was barely a year older than my sister, so when Jess was no longer an infant and it was safe for us to sleep in the same crib, our mother said we curled up to each other like a pair of tiny, pink cooked shrimp. Even after we officially reached "big girl status," and graduated to separate sleeping arrangements, Jess and I continued to sneak into one or the other's bed until puberty rolled around and we learned there were certain activities better performed in private. We are reduced to hysterics still, every time we talk about this particular discovery, the summer night before I turned thirteen when she rolled toward me, twisted her head over her shoulder, and said, "What are you *doing*? Do you have a *bug bite* down there or something?" Obviously, I had thought she was already asleep.

Throughout our adolescence, whether we were in trouble with our mother or didn't get asked to the dance by the boy we liked, one of us crept into the other's bed when the house went dark. We whispered condolences, eventually giggling the disappointment away. Not that Jess missed out on too many dances; when we got to high school, she suddenly became the golden child, the adored popular girl. She was also genuinely nice, which made it impossible for me to really hate her, at least not consistently. Even when we fought, we loved each other fiercely. We still do. For a long time, *we* were all the other had.

I was in sixth grade when our mother decided she could no longer afford to pay someone to stay with Jess and me after school. Busy with work during the day and her dentistry classes three nights a week, there were times we saw our babysitters more than we saw our mother.

"You're mature for your age," she said to me as she sat on the edge of my bed to tuck me in. "You can watch out for your sister." As with most of my mother's statements, this was an edict, not an inquiry.

"But what if there's a robber?" I asked.

"There won't be, but Mrs. Stevens will be next door if you need her and you can always dial nine-one-one, right?" She hugged me. "You'll be fine."

Mrs. Stevens was in her seventies and I doubted she'd be of much assistance when it came to fending off a robber, but my mother was right. Over the next few years of spending most of our afternoons and evenings alone, Jess and I *were* fine. We called and checked in with our mom as soon as we were home safely, but after that, we were accountable to no one. We wasted hours watching reruns of *Three's Company* and *The Love Boat,* though we always made sure we were finished with our homework before our mother walked through the front door. We couldn't invite anyone over when she wasn't there, so my sister and I didn't have a lot of time to develop other friendships. A lot of the time we were bored.

"Maybe we should try to find our dad," I said to Jess the summer before I started high school. I was almost fourteen and a little bitter about not being able to participate in debate club because my mother didn't have time to transport me to and from events. The activity bus was reserved for the jocks, so academic students' parents were expected to drive.

Jess screwed up her face, looking at me as though I were nuts. "Why would we want to do *that*?"

"I don't know. I guess I wonder how he'd feel if he knew she left us alone all of the time."

"*He* left us completely," Jess said. "What makes you think he'd care?"

Some part of me knew she was right, but I couldn't get away from the idea of tracking him down. I just wanted to talk with him.

I wanted to understand why he went away. Was I so horrible a baby that once he found out Jess was on the way, he couldn't fathom another one like me? He was the only one who could answer my questions; my mother didn't like to talk about him.

One afternoon while Jess was napping, I snuck into our mother's room to look for any information I could find about the man who had fathered us. My mother's room was strictly off-limits when she wasn't home, so stepping inside was as thrilling as it was terrifying. I half expected flashing lights and a siren to sound when I passed over the threshold, but there was only the sun slicing through the Venetian blinds, casting thin shards of light onto her plush beige carpet. The walls were painted a dark red—conducive, she said, to good luck and restful sleep. Her dresser was tall and black with six wide drawers I was certain would contain some hint of my father's existence.

I opened the bottom drawer where I knew my mother kept our birth certificates and report cards. Digging through a file marked "private," it didn't take long to find a yellowed scrap of paper with his name and a phone number. Why she had kept it, I wasn't sure. Maybe she planned to wait until we were older to help us find him. I didn't have that kind of patience.

"Jacob Miller," I breathed, rubbing the piece of paper between my fingers. "Dad."

I quickly copied the information into the notebook I'd brought with me and slipped the scrap back where it belonged. A glance at the clock told me I had two hours until my mom was due home— plenty of time to make the call.

I walked over to the side of my mom's bed where the phone was. I sat down, careful not to disturb the perfect edges of her poppy red, silk-brocade comforter. I felt my heartbeat pounding in my head, so I took a few deep breaths to try to calm down before picking up the receiver and dialing. *He might not be home,* I told myself. *He might not even be at this number.*

I punched in the number slowly, holding each button down a tad longer than was necessary. It rang three times before a man picked up. "Hello?" he said. His voice was soft, quieter than I had imagined it would be.

I couldn't speak. I swallowed once, then twice, trying to moisten the insides of my mouth.

"Hello?" he said again.

"Is this Jacob Miller?" I finally managed to creak. I cleared my throat.

"Yes, who's this?"

"I . . . um, it's Cadence. I live in Seattle. With Sharon Mitchell?"

He didn't answer for a minute, and I didn't know what else to say. I opened the single drawer on my mother's nightstand, then slammed it shut. Her lamp wobbled.

"Can I help you with something?" he finally asked. His tone was guarded.

"No, no," I said. "I just thought . . . well, you know. That I might get to know you a little."

He exhaled softly. "Oh, Cadence. I don't think that's a good idea."

"Oh," I said, probably a little too loudly. "Okay."

"I'm just not set up for this kind of thing. You understand."

What kind of "thing" was talking to your daughter? I wanted to ask. But instead, I coughed and said, "Sure. I understand."

"Take care," he said, and I heard the dial tone in my ear before I could say good-bye.

I stared at the receiver before setting it back in its cradle. My father wasn't interested in knowing me. The muscles in my throat thickened, and tears pricked the back of my eyes. I smoothed my mother's comforter and went back to the bedroom I shared with Jessica, tossing my notebook to the floor. She was awake then, and sitting on the edge of her bed. Her usually smooth, straight brown hair was mussed from sleep. "Are you okay?" she asked.

I threw myself onto my bed, facedown in my pillow, and didn't answer. I didn't want to tell her what I'd done. The ache I felt was like a boulder on my chest. Before the call I at least had the fantasy of my father. I could imagine him showing up unexpectedly, unable to stay away from me a moment longer. Now there was no doubt—I knew exactly what kind of man he was.

"Fine then, don't talk to me," Jess said, then went downstairs to watch TV. A while later, the bedroom door opened and my mother flipped on the light.

"What's going on?" my mother asked. "Jess says you're sulking."

"I'm not sulking," I said to the wall. "I'm just tired."

"She said you called your father today."

"What?" I flipped over and looked at her. She was still in the light blue scrubs she wore to work and her long brown hair was as smooth as when she left the house that morning.

My mother nodded. "She said she listened at the door while you called him from my room."

"She's so nosy!" I said, spitting out the words. "She needs to learn to mind her own business."

"Come on, now. Don't be mad at her. I would have seen it on the phone bill anyway."

I started to cry. "He didn't want to talk to me."

She came over and sat next to me on the bed. "And this surprises you? I've told you a hundred times he wasn't cut out to be a father. Outside of giving me you two girls, he was the worst decision I ever made." She pushed the hair back from her face, tucking it behind her ears.

"I just thought . . ." I blubbered. "I thought if he heard my voice . . ." I trailed off, unable to go on through my tears.

"You thought if he heard your voice he'd suddenly want to get to know you? An orchestra would swell in the background and he'd miraculously realize what he's missing?"

I nodded, sobbing and wiping my eyes with the back of my hand.

My mother sighed. "That's not the way life works, Cadence. People are going to let you down. I'm sorry you're hurt, but it's an important lesson to learn. You'll get over it. I did." She patted my leg. "Now, why don't you come downstairs and have dinner with us? I brought home Chinese."

That was the end of the discussion. She didn't want to know what he had said, or how it had made me feel. I heard countless versions of this same lecture from my mother over the years. *Buck up, Cadence. Push forward. Don't let anyone see you upset.*

"If you're unhappy," my mother told me if I bemoaned the circumstances of my life, "it's up to you to do something to change it. The only thing complaining will get you is an invitation to leave the room."

"But *Mom* . . ." I'd begin. All I wanted was a little sympathy. I wanted the kind of mother who at least once in a while would pull me into her soft embrace, feed me homemade chocolate-chip cookies, and assure me everything would be okay. I didn't think that was too much to ask.

What I had was the kind of mother who worked sixty hours a week and held up her hand to cut me off midwhine. "Uh-uh-uh," she said. "No buts about it. If you want to succeed, you need to figure out what needs to change and change it. I'm happy to listen to whatever solutions you come up with."

"Everything's so *easy* for Jess," I told her at the beginning of my sophomore year in high school. It was a Saturday and my mother and I were sitting together in our living room. "It's not fair. She's only a freshman and she's already a cheerleader. Everyone just automatically *likes* her."

"That's because she makes an effort," my mother said, looking up from the magazine in her lap. "She reaches out to people. It's not her fault you have trouble making friends."

"I didn't *say* it was her fault."

She cocked her head, raised her eyebrows, and gave me a pointed stare. "Please watch your tone with me, young lady. And jealousy doesn't become you."

"I'm *not* jealous." I sighed, crossed my arms over my chest, and flopped back against the couch. That wasn't true, and my mother knew it. Just the week before, I'd been grounded for mixing a dollop of Bengay into my sister's moisturizer, wanting her to think she had some strange muscular disease that caused her pretty face to go numb.

"You can't just sit back and wait for things to happen for you, Cadence," my mother said. "You have to make them happen."

I didn't know how to explain that I didn't feel like I fit in with the other kids in my class; how every conversation I tried to start felt stilted and forced. It was as though everyone else had been given a handbook on how to be cool except for me.

"I don't know what else I can do," I said. "I'm not into sports and I'm too fat to be a cheerleader."

"You are not fat. You're voluptuous, like my mother." She looked thoughtful for a moment, then lifted a single finger into the air. "I know. You should join the school paper. You like to write. It would look great on your college applications, too."

I did join the paper, and while at first it was only to get my mother off my back about taking charge of my life, I soon found I was good at writing profile pieces on the new biology teacher or articles exposing the astronomical calorie content in our cafeteria's lunch menu. Becoming the editor of my high school paper didn't help me win any popularity contests, but it did give me a reason to talk with people who used to ignore me. After a while, given an appropriate subject, I learned how to fake conversation despite any insecurity I felt. My mother was right about college, too—along with my 4.0 grade point average, my work on the paper won me a full-ride journalism scholarship to the University of Washington. And once I was there, I did what I always strove to do—I tried to make my mother proud.

*   *   *

Charlie is unbuckled and racing toward my sister's front door before I manage to turn off the engine. He looks back at me and waves before disappearing through the entryway. I love how he pushes the door open, knowing he is welcome, knowing he is safe.

I step out of my car, and Jess pokes her dark head out of the kitchen window on the side of her house. She and her husband, Derek, chose this broken-down Craftsman-style home in the north Seattle Wallingford neighborhood for its early twentieth-century charm, figuring they could fix it up and flip it for a quick and painless profit. Two months into living there during renovations, Jess found out she was pregnant with the twins and fell permanently in love with the slightly sloping original hardwoods, the coved ceilings, and built-in, beveled-glass cabinets. Derek, her partner not only in life but in their successful real-estate brokerage firm, soon gave in to her desire to stay. Not that he had much of a choice in the matter. Saying no to Jess was like saying no to breathing. You really didn't have the option.

"Hey!" she hollers. She may be a tiny thing, but the girl has got a set of lungs on her. They served her well in her cheerleading days.

"Hey," I say, and wave back at her. "The munchkin has already invaded."

"I know. He's hugging my legs as we speak."

I smile. Such an affectionate boy, my Charlie. Possibly having something to do with the amount of hugs and kisses I smothered him with from the moment he was born.

"Get your butt in here," Jess commands. "Natalie is playing with the twins downstairs." She pulls back inside. I smile again, thinking how lucky Jess is to have Natalie, a thirteen-year-old neighbor girl who is thrilled to be paid a mere six dollars an hour for her babysitting services.

Within minutes, Jess and I are sitting at her kitchen table. Two steaming mugs of coffee, creamy with half-and-half, sit before us. My sister is what I would look like if I lost fifty pounds and shrunk three inches: the dream of willowy and petite versus the reality of short and substantial. She is one of those sleek, Gap-ad-type mothers who appear to have a personal makeup artist dwelling in their bathrooms, who arrive at their children's preschool in hip, chunky black boots and immaculate flat-front khakis, looking like they've just been to the spa for a massage. She is the kind of mother who always baffled me. The kind of mother I always wanted to be.

Natalie and all three boys are in the basement-turned-recreation-room, a space built specifically with well-padded surfaces and filled with countless toys. Charlie loves being the big boy, teaching, leading, and telling his younger cousins what to do. He'll be busy for an hour, at least, especially with Natalie there to help sort out any conflict. Part of me wants to not let him leave me. I want to snatch him up, hold him in my lap, squeeze him, smell him, and kiss his soft cheeks. The other part is happy for this momentary reprieve; my encounter with Alice has drained me. Wrapping both my hands around the warmth of my coffee mug, I exhale deeply, lift my chin toward the ceiling, and close my eyes.

"That bad?" my sister inquires.

"Yes." I hold my position. Avoiding eye contact with her is the best way to keep her from seeing what is going on with me.

"How'd it go with Alice?" She will not let it be.

I shrug, lower my chin, and open my eyes, only to see her take an enormous bite of the lemon-cream cheese Danish she set out with the coffee. She says something else, but it comes out muffled—along with a few crumbs of pastry—as she tries to chew.

"Nice manners. Mom would be proud."

Her mouth still full, she widens her blue eyes, purses her lips, then flips me off.

"Ooo, nice manicure, too!"

Jess finishes chewing, takes a sip of her coffee, and admires her nails. "Thanks. I just got them done last night." She holds up the Danish. "You should have one of these."

I eye one—the biggest, of course—thick and gooey with bright yellow and creamy white sweetness. I sigh. "No, I shouldn't. My ass is spreading like butter just looking at them."

She pushes the plate toward me. "You had to give up booze, for Christ's sake. Have a damn Danish."

She has a point. I grab the one I want and take a small bite, letting it melt on my tongue. I fully intend to eat only half of it. Two minutes later, I've devoured the entire thing. "Mmm. God, I hate you," I say.

Jess pulls her chin into her neck, perfectly plucked eyebrows raised. "What did I do?"

"You won the genetic lottery. You never exercise, eat like a horse, and don't gain an ounce. You suck."

"Whatever. You have multiple orgasms."

I snort. My stories of four, five, even eight orgasms one night with Martin—back before we went all to hell—drove her mad with envy. It's the one area I can one-up my sister and though I know I shouldn't, I revel in it.

"Okay," I consent, "I suppose that makes us even. Sort of." I sip my coffee. "Where's Derek?"

"Showing property. He's trying to get some horrible couple to buy a condo downtown. He bet me ten bucks he could have them writing an offer by the end of the day."

"Huh." I don't pretend to understand the real-estate industry, though I do attempt sympathetic and interested noises when my sister begins to talk about her job. Since the boys were born almost three years ago, Derek carries the weight of the upfront selling and Jess works behind the scenes to run the business from home. She picks up clients where she can to help make ends meet, especially since the market took a nosedive. Luckily, their brokerage was strong enough to weather the economic downturn, but even so, most months they've been forced to dip into the savings they'd each built up during the late 1990s housing boom. According to Jess, those funds are quickly depleting, so each sale they make today takes on greater significance for their financial survival.

"How's work going for you?" Jess asks.

I shrug. "Okay, I guess. I'm having a hard time getting back into it." For too many months, pulling the words from my brain to write has felt like trying to squeeze fluid from stone. It made sense when I was actively drinking, I suppose, since my thoughts were muddied by alcohol, but Andi says this is normal even now; for up to two years my brain cells will be in the process of rebuilding. Post-acute withdrawal symptoms, she calls it. Memory loss and the lack of ability to focus are only the tip of the dysfunctional iceberg. I already went through Baby Brain; apparently, Booze Brain is a similar experience.

"I did get a call from Peter the other day," I say. "My old editor at the *Herald*?"

"Oh, right," Jess says, taking another sip of her coffee. "What did he want?"

"I guess he was in Chicago a few weeks ago and ended up meeting an editor from *O.*"

She looks confused.

"Oprah's magazine?" I say.

"Oh, right, right."

"He said he thought our personalities would click. She's expecting me to get in contact and pitch her a few ideas."

"That's *amazing*," Jess says, then crinkles up her forehead and lifts a single, perfectly plucked eyebrow when I don't look as enthused. "Isn't it?"

"It would be if I *had* any ideas. I'm not even sure I should be freelancing right now. I sort of let things slide over the past year." More like I let them disappear. I couldn't remember the last time I'd sold an article. "I'm starting to think I might need to find a new career. One that actually pays my bills."

"Are you okay? Do you need to borrow a little bit to get you through? If Derek makes this sale today—"

"That's very sweet of you," I say, cutting her off, "but I can manage. I still have some of the divorce settlement left. But it won't last much longer." I figure if I really cut corners, I can survive about six more months on what's left in my account. After that, I may have to practice inquiring whether customers would like to supersize their meals.

"You'll figure it out," my sister says. "You could always sell the house, right? Maybe move into something more affordable?"

"I suppose so, but I'd hate to move Charlie." The divorce left me with two main assets: the house and my cashed-out half of Martin's 401(k) account, the latter of which I've been using to pay my bills. With the account already so diminished, I didn't want to lose the house. Not yet.

"Well, at least you know a good agent if you need one," she says with a grin.

"Really? Who?" I tease.

"Funny," she says, rolling her eyes, then pauses for a moment to sip her coffee. "So, do any of the editors you usually work with know about your problem?"

"No." I realize I'm gripping my mug tightly enough to make my fingers ache. I relax them. "I was pretty good at keeping it under wraps."

She shifts her shoulders almost imperceptibly. It's suddenly her turn to not make eye contact.

"What?" I push. "I know that look."

"What look?" She moves her gaze to meet mine.

"That one." I put a finger in her face. "You're trying not to say something. Give it up."

"This coming from Little Miss Not Forthcoming." She bats my finger away and points hers back at me. "You're not quite as sneaky as you think you are."

I sit back in my chair. "What does *that* mean?"

"It means, Cadee," she sighs, "that it's not like people didn't suspect what was going on with you."

There is no condescension in her tone, only a factual edge, and it cuts deep. A panicky feeling grips my belly, the kind where it seems that the jig is up on something you thought you had gotten away with free and clear, and suddenly, there you stand, caught, your emotional pants down around your ankles.

She leans forward and takes one of my hands in hers. "We knew. We might not have said anything, but we did know."

I pull my hand back, tuck my fingers in between my thighs, and squeeze them. Tears threaten to roll and I hate them. She hasn't said this to me before now, not once in the last eight weeks.

Jess sighs, pushes back into her chair. "I'm sorry."

"For what?" I keep my tone neutral. Hysteria claws at the edges, just below the surface of my words. Only I can feel this. I will not show it to her. I will not show it to anyone.

"For bringing it up, I guess."

"It's okay." It's not okay. It is very, very far from okay.

"Yeah, you sound like you mean that." We are silent for a moment. And then she continues. "I should have said something. I should have tried to help."

"I wouldn't have let you." I swallow hard and clear my throat. "I didn't know anything was wrong." This is not entirely true. A person can't drink the way I did and not suspect she might be completely screwed in the head. Crazy, even. Like the grandmother I didn't want to tell Martin about on our first date.

Jess takes a deep breath, registers the expression on my face, then asks, "Should we talk about something else?"

"Yes, please," I say with a faltering smile.

And just like that, we do. We talk about the twins, her latest deal, the lack of intelligence she perceives in the Mommy and Me pool. We talk about our mother, who has a new boyfriend with a funny-looking mustache. The sense of normalcy around our conversation calms me, distracts me from the whirling tornadoes in my mind. I am exhausted of thinking, of examining every tiny scrap of information and emotion that flows through me. I long for a shutoff switch for my brain, a way to halt the never-ending supply of synaptic chatter.

Natalie goes home around noon, and Jess and I make lunch for the boys: toasted cheese sandwiches and tomato soup, and for us, mandarin grilled chicken salad. Jess gets Charlie's jeans washed while the twins take a nap, and Charlie and I walk to a nearby park so we don't disturb their rest. Charlie wears a pair of sweats he left at his aunt's house the last time he slept over; the elastic hems hit just above his ankles now. Watching him play, it strikes me just how quickly he has grown.

After we return from the park and the boys wake up, Jess and I decide to get out of the house for a few hours. We take the boys to Tube Time, a venue filled with well-padded, obstacle course-like tunnels and cushioned slides, both designed to wear out even the most energetic kid. Jess and I take turns crawling in after our children when they refuse to get out of another child's way, or when Jake is too frightened to go down the bigger slide. For a while, chatting with my sister and seeing the kids play, I almost feel like myself again.

The afternoon passes and the light starts to fade as we pull into Jess's driveway. Derek calls and tells Jess he has to go out to dinner with his clients to write up an offer on a house. Jess growls playfully at her loss of their bet, happy, I know, to have another commission coming in. Lured by the promise of Jess's cheesy lasagna and garlic butter-drenched bread, I agree to stay for dinner. My nephews have gone downstairs to play, but Charlie runs around the house, alternately clinging to me, then spinning in circles, arms spread wide in the middle of the living room.

"Hey, champ," I say, "knock it off, would you? You'll break something."

"No I won't!" he exclaims. "Look at me! I'm Spida-Man!" He leaps onto the couch and pretends it's a trampoline. Even after a busy day of playing, his energy levels are insane; not hyperactive, exactly. More kinetic. He's pretty much been in constant motion since he learned how to walk. This has been somewhat disconcerting for me to deal with as a woman who views exercise as punishment for her private, passionate love affair with ice cream.

"Wow," Jess observes. "Too much sugar?"

"Too much Alice, more like it. She completely clamps down on him so he freaks out when he gets away."

"I do *not*!" Charlie screeches, the slender cords in his neck standing out like rope. He jumps across my sister's couch, feet together, cushion to cushion. "Don't call me a freak!"

"I didn't call you a freak, I said you freak *out*. Big difference. Now, get down." I try to keep my tone calm, but there is an itch in my chest, a tightening that feels all too familiar.

"No!" He jumps again, once, for emphasis, then looks at me defiantly.

"It's really okay," Jess says. "The boys do it all the time."

"No, it's not okay." I stand up, step toward him, and grab my child around his skinny bicep, maybe a little harder than I should have. "I told you to get down. Now."

"Owww!" he squeals. "Don't!"

I yank him a bit to get him to land on his butt, which he does.

"Cadee," Jess says, her voice quiet. "It's okay."

I look at her, my eyes flashing. The adrenaline is already pumping. Another withdrawal symptom—extreme irritability. It takes nothing—nothing at all—to set me off. *I want a drink* is the first thought in my head. My blood is heating, bursting into tiny, stress-induced flames beneath my skin. I can no longer douse them with wine. My child is my trigger. "Identify them," Andi encourages us in group. "Avoid them if you can." What the hell is wrong with me? Who reacts like this to their own child? I let go of my son's arm, sit down next to him on the couch.

"Sorry, monkey," I whisper.

He sits still, arms crossed over his chest, bottom lip pushed out but no tears. I try to run my hand down his arm, but he jerks away. "Don't!" he says, more quietly than the time before.

"Okay." I rest my hands, cupped together gently, palms up, in my lap.

"Why don't you go downstairs with the boys?" Jess suggests in a happy voice.

Charlie glances at me, tentative, sidelong. He is not ready to forgive me. I don't blame him. I'm nowhere near being able to forgive myself.

I nod. "Aunt Jess is right. Go play, have fun." He walks slowly, head hanging, down the hall and down the basement stairs. The ache in my heart is a palpable thing. I wish for a way to have it surgically removed.

"He'll be fine," Jess says. Her expression is blank, but her eyes can't mask her concern.

I shake my head. "What if I can't fix this? What if I've scarred him for life?"

She sighs. "All of us are scarred, Cadee. We've all got our wounds. No one escapes their childhood unscathed."

I take in a jagged breath. "I feel like I've totally failed him. No wonder he's freaking out. It's not Alice. It's me. It's my fault. Kids need to know what to expect. They need stability and routine to feel safe and I've obliterated all of that for him. When I think about what I've done—"

"Stop it." Jess cuts me off. Her voice is firm. "You can't do this to yourself. Yes, you screwed up. Yes, Charlie has gone through some shit you wish he didn't have to go through. But wallowing around in your guilt about it is going to get you nowhere. So knock it off."

When I don't respond, she walks over and puts her arms around me. She holds me close, her palm pressed against the back of my head, her mouth next to my ear. "You are a good mother."

"No," I say. "I'm not." This is the tape that plays in my head: *I'm shit. I'm selfish and useless and I got drunk in front of my son. I'm nothing but a piece of shit.* It's the sound track that sets the rhythm of my days.

"Yes, you are. Remember when Charlie wouldn't nurse right away in the hospital? Remember how your milk wasn't coming in?"

I sniff, then nod into her shoulder.

"And what did you do that I'm sure to this *day* the nurses at Swedish still talk about? You started massaging your boobs to get those milk ducts going. You rubbed your boobs so hard they were black and blue. I thought you were a rock star mom. You were absolutely determined Charlie would get what you thought was best for him. Right?"

I nod again.

"And what about the time when he had bronchitis and you didn't sleep for eight days straight? Remember how you held him? How you sat in the bathroom running scalding hot water for hours and hours trying to help your baby boy breathe easy? You had tile marks on your ass for a week."

A small, reluctant smile pushes out the corners of my mouth. She is still holding me.

"You're a good mother, Cadee. Not perfect, but good."

I shake my head, but don't say anything more. She doesn't understand. She has no idea just how deep this sense of disgrace goes. How could she?

She sighs. "Okay, then. I'll set up the guest room."

I pull back from her and start to protest, but she stops me by holding up her hand. "No arguments. You're spending the night. Derek won't be home until late and I need the company."

"I should take him home," I say meekly. "He needs to be in his own bed."

"Cadence." This is all she says. Her tone is enough to tell me the debate has ended. We won't talk about it outright. She won't say she is worried about the flare-up of my anger, my inability to manage it without taking a drink. She doesn't have to speak. My sister knows me well enough to hear my thoughts, to know I need help, even when I can't come close to admitting it to myself.

Five

"Mama!" Charlie yelled from the bathroom. "Come *wipe* me!"

I sighed as I stood in the kitchen on a chilly spring morning, picturing my four-year-old son in front of the toilet, palms flat on the cold, green tile and his tiny, naked bottom stuck up in the air. "Coming, baby," I called out. "Mama just needs to take out the garbage." I heard the truck rumble just down the street and knew I had to be quick. The recycle truck only came twice a month, and if I missed today, the bin would overflow.

I grabbed the blue recycle bin I kept beneath my sink, ready to lug it outside, when the noisy clanking of glass stopped me. I looked down and quickly counted the bottles—*two, four, six, eight . . . what the hell?* I kept counting. *Fifteen?*

I didn't want my neighbors—or the sanitation workers, for that matter—to see how many bottles I'd gone through in two weeks. It seemed to happen the same way I cut away slivers from a pan of brownies, telling myself, *I'm only having a tiny bit—really, it's not that much.*

But now I had to get rid of the evidence. I hurriedly padded each bottle with newspaper, shoved them deep into the regular garbage can, and rolled it out to the curb, happy to have stumbled upon such an easy solution.

"Mama!" Charlie screeched from the front porch, where he now stood naked, cupping his genitals with both hands while hopping up and down.

I raced up the stairs. "Get inside, Mr. Man. No naked boys on the porch." It was hard for me to believe he would be five in just a few months; he was already almost as tall as my waist.

"How come?" He giggled.

I smiled. "It's the law. Now, shoo."

He complied, and shot back down the hallway to the bathroom.

"Didn't you clean yourself up?" I asked, shutting the door behind me.

"Nope!" came his cheerful reply.

I sighed again. *Ah, too much to hope.* I joined him in the bathroom. "You know, you're getting to be such a big boy," I said after I finished helping him. "You can do this."

"Nuh-uh. You do it better." He grinned. "Let's go play."

"Clothes first, mister."

I helped him dress, too, and then spent the next hour lying on the living room floor, rolling the same bright orange Hot Wheel Corvette back and forth for what seemed like the nine hundredth time in a row. I tried not to think that what I really should have been doing was trying to write something that might actually make us some money.

I'd all but given up on freelancing; I had a hard time concentrating on anything for more than a few minutes at a time. Coming up with query letters and article outlines overwhelmed me. *I'm just exhausted,* I told myself. *Once I start sleeping better, I should be able to get back in the swing of things.*

Until then, I managed to spit out short pieces for websites like About.com or CareerBuilder, mining old articles I'd written on how to ask for a raise and reslanting them to how to ask for a raise in a downsized economy. E-zines like this didn't pay much—some not at all—but it was enough to at least help get us by. Each month I reluctantly pulled out just enough money from savings to pay the mortgage, utilities, and my health insurance, sickened by the shrink-ing balance. The months I didn't sell an article, I used credit cards to pick up any slack. When those bills came due, a heavy panic swelled in my chest as I made the minimum payment, which I knew wouldn't even make a dent in what I owed. Just thinking about skyrocketing interest rates as I tried to play with my son brought on the same feeling.

I jumped up from playing with my son. "I'll be right back, okay?"

"Okay, Mommy," Charlie said, intent on smashing two Mack truck grilles against each other in a head-on collision.

I zipped down the hall and into the kitchen, knocked down two swallows of merlot—the last from the bottle I opened the night be-fore. I walked back into the living room.

"Want to go to the store with Mommy?" I asked Charlie.

"What are you going to buy me?" he asked, leaping to his feet.

I laughed. "I'm going to buy you lunch," I told him, ruffling his hair with my fingers. "Whatever you want from the deli, okay? I don't feel like cooking." I slipped on my flip-flops and made a silly face at Charlie, who giggled, crossed his eyes, and stuck out his tongue at me.

I loved this moment. It was the one I was always trying to reach. I was happy, Charlie was happy. After the wine, everything in my body felt loose, like it was saturated with oxygen and massaged into a deep state of calm.

We hopped in the car and drove the few short blocks to the store. "Can I ride in the cart?" Charlie asked as we approached the entrance.

"Sure, baby," I said. I typically made him walk. "Hop in." I tucked my fingers into his armpits and lifted him up, struggling a bit to get his feet through the holes in the cart. "You're getting to be such a big boy. Almost too big for this."

"No, I'm still a baby," he said, and jammed his thumb into his mouth. "Th-ee?"

"Oh, do I have to buy some diapers, too?" I asked playfully.

"No," Charlie said. A chuckle rolled beneath the word. He pulled out his thumb and wiped it on my forearm.

"Ew!" I said, pretending to be horrified. "Charlie slime!"

He giggled again and we headed to the deli.

"I want chicken bones," he said, pointing to the hot food section under the glass.

I scrunched up my eyebrows. "You want what?"

"Chicken bones." He shook his finger in the same direction, and I realized what he meant.

"Oh, you want fried chicken? The legs?"

He nodded.

"You got it." I had the deli counter clerk bag up a twelve-piece meal, including six legs, mashed potatoes, coleslaw, and biscuits. I gave his nose a little tweak. "You want some ice cream, too?"

He looked at me with wide eyes. "Really?"

"Why not?" We hit the frozen foods aisle, where I filled our cart with a few containers of chocolate fudge and strawberry cheesecake ice cream, along with a variety of quick, microwave dinners for the rest of the week. With just the two of us and Charlie's picky appetite, cooking wasn't as fun as it used to be.

"Thank you, Mommy!" he said when I added an economy-size bag of frozen Tater Tots to our other purchases.

"You're welcome, sweetie."

"Can I have chips, too?" he pressed. "Wrinkles?"

I cocked my head to the side, confused. "Wrinkles?"

Charlie sighed, impatient with my obvious ineptitude. "The potato chips with all the bumps, Mom. You know. The kind you like with the yucky onion dip?"

I racked my brain for a moment, until it dawned on me. "Oh! You mean Ruffles?"

"Yeah, Ruffles. That's what I *said.*"

I laughed. "No, you said 'wrinkles,' kiddo. But that's okay. I think that's a better name anyway. I think we'll skip them this time, since we're getting ice cream. Okay?"

"Okay!" He threw his arms around my waist. His small hands pushed flat on my lower back; his face pressed into the swell of my belly. "I love you, Mama," he said, his voice slightly muffled.

"Oh, baby. I love you, too." My heart began to beat a little more quickly; I suddenly felt a little anxious about getting back home. On the way to the cash register, I flipped the cart down the wine aisle. The inside of my mouth was parched, like I'd been chewing on a wad of cotton.

"You have to get more wine?" Charlie asked in a quiet voice.

"Just a little bit," I said. "I'm all out."

"And you need to relax." He looked at me, questioning. "Right?"

"Right." I snatched two bottles of my favorite cabernet and merlot mix, thinking those would last me at least until the next night. Setting them in the cart, I clapped my hands together once and smiled at my son. "Let's go home and play some more," I said.

"You're too tired to play with me after your wine," he said reproachfully.

I swallowed back the ache in my throat. "I won't be. I promise."

When he didn't answer, when he wouldn't even meet my gaze, I told myself I had imagined the disappointment weighting his voice when he asked if I needed more wine. I convinced myself he was still happy, that his smile hadn't vanished because of me.

Six

After complying with Jess's order to stay at her house overnight, I'm hunkered down in her guest room, snuggling with my son. Following the controlled chaos of a tomato-sauce-laden lasagna dinner, Charlie and I changed into borrowed pajamas—he in one of Jess's T-shirts and me in one of Derek's—then crawled into bed. I curl around Charlie in the exact manner I used to wrap myself behind my sister. Big shrimp, little shrimp. His butt is pushed into my belly and his fragile spine rests against my breasts.

"You're all squishy, Mommy," he said when we first climbed beneath the covers. He wiggled against me, adjusting to find his comfortable spot.

"Is that a good thing?" I asked with a warm smile. I'm pretty sure my son is the only male on this earth who could call me "squishy" and not only get away with it, but have it make me happy.

He nodded. "For mommies, it is." He closed his eyes and let out a long breath, a spinning top finally winding down.

"Well, thank you, then," I said. "Hey, baby boy?"

His eyelids lifted a bit, but didn't open all the way. "Mm-hm?"

"I'm really sorry I snapped at you today." I kissed the back of his soft head. He smelled faintly of Johnson & Johnson's baby shampoo and the fudge pop Jess fed the boys for dessert. I'm out of practice at the tasks of motherhood; I forgot to make him brush his teeth.

"'S okay. Everybody gets mad sometimes," he mumbled, and something inside me that had been held captive suddenly lifted and was set free.

How is it that he knows this, at five? I wonder after he falls asleep. *How is it so easy for him to forgive and let go?* He didn't learn this from me—or his father, for that matter. Maybe it's something we're all born with, this ability to accept another person's failings and imperfections without lingering contempt. Maybe harboring resentment is an environmental hazard, habitual pollution absorbed into our blood. I wonder if I could get some kind of emotional transfusion. Out with the bad blood, in with the good.

I sigh and my gaze travels through the darkened air around me. The guest room in my sister's house is small, with space enough only for a double-mattress-size Hide-a-Bed couch and a tiny nightstand with a lamp. The door has to be shut before opening the bed; if it's not, privacy while sleeping becomes a logistical impossibility. Two of the walls are built-in bookshelves; a small, porthole-style window lets the moonlight spill in from the night sky to pool on the hardwood floor.

We are used to this bed, Charlie and me. We spent many nights here when Martin and I first separated. The quiet in my own house was deafening. I needed the ordinary rhythms of a household—the sound of a toilet flushing, the low murmur of Jess and Derek's voices to help lull me to sleep.

At the time, anxiety gripped my every breath. My mind spun on its side—an engine stuck in high gear. I regretted every decision I'd ever made. I told myself I should have kept my job at the paper. I never should have married Martin. Once I married him, I should have been a better wife. I should have tried harder to work it out. I should have quit working completely so I could have focused all my attention on being the kind of mother Charlie deserved. I should have been a nicer person so I'd have more friends and a better support system. I should, I should . . .

Oh, how I remember that first swallow of wine. *Relief,* I thought. *Respite.* I didn't know enough then to realize how false that feeling was, a chemical peace of mind that would turn on me. It silently ran wild in my blood and attacked my best defenses. It was an insidious, habitual process; a sip-by-sip, day-by-day gradual prison built. Once trapped, there was no easily recognizable method of escape. I wandered around, banging against impenetrable walls, no tools to chip away at them, no weapons to fight against this invisible foe.

I have no problem accepting the physical aspect of addiction. I did manage to learn a few things in treatment. I get how the brain becomes addicted to a hit of the pleasure chemical dopamine when certain substances are ingested. Gradually, a tolerance is built to the ingested amount; a person needs more of the substance to get the same pleasurable payoff. I get this. It's science; it makes sense. I see how it happened with me. Some people's brains are more easily addicted—our physical chemistry sets us up this way.

What I have a hard time buying into is all the other recovery rhetoric. The admission of powerlessness, the spiritual God crap the Promises staff shoved down my throat the first weeks I was there. Okay, maybe they didn't shove. Maybe they strongly suggested. They gave me assignments to examine my concept of a power greater than me in the universe and other fluffy, overly emotional garbage. The only way I got through it was to look at these assignments like homework in college—get the work done, do it well, show the instructor I had been paying attention. Use perfect presentation to mask the fact that you find the work you've been asked to do totally asinine.

I lie here thinking about this and though I'm exhausted from this day, again, I cannot sleep. Charlie is out cold, his breathing deep and regular, lost to the wild of a little boy's dreams. I prop my head up with my hand, elbow bent, gazing at my son to try to find my center. His smattering of freckles are perfect pinpoints, minute brown dots above the apples of his cheeks and across the bridge of his button nose. His dark eyelashes are the kind that movie stars pay makeup artists thousands of dollars to create. I reach to stroke the side of his face with the tips of my fingers, the perfect, smooth warmth of his skin. The muscles in his face twitch and I pull my hand back, afraid I will wake him. It is a miracle I had a part in creating him, this gorgeous little being. He is the sole evidence that his father and I once shared something other than acrimony.

He is the reason I can never drink again.

I awake the next morning in my sister's guest room and Charlie is already gone. A brief sense of panic quickens my pulse, wondering where he is, but then I hear his high-pitched giggle and realize he is already playing in the living room.

"Charlie?" I call out, wanting to hold him again, desperate to make up for lost time. I hear the *thwap thwap thwap thwap* of his bare feet running down the hall and he rushes back into the room, jumping on the bed next to me.

"Morning, Mommy!" he says, leaning over to give me a kiss on the cheek. His breath is pungent and earthy after skipping his dental hygiene the night before; my mother would have a coronary if she knew I didn't make him get back out of bed to brush his teeth.

"Morning, monkey," I say. I try to snuggle him to me, but he wriggles away.

"Marley and Jake and me are going to play in the wrecked room."

I smile. *God, I adore him.* "It's the 'rec' room, sweetie. Not 'wrecked.'"

"Oh. That's what I said." He leaps back off the bed and is gone in a flash.

I get dressed and proceed to the kitchen where Jess and I sit at the kitchen table, sipping huge mugs of coffee as we watch her husband cook breakfast. Sunday morning means Derek's fancy-pants pancakes at my sister's house. He and I are kindred spirits when it comes to food preparation. No boxed mix for this man. He makes them from scratch, doctors them up with vanilla, cinnamon, or lemon. Whatever he has on hand.

I started cooking when I figured out it would please my mother that she didn't have to. Over the years, I learned that it was a practice that soothed me. Even today, if only for a moment, following a recipe removes me from the prattle led by the chorus of crazies in my head into a world where careful steps taken, measurements made, lead to expected, predictable results. How I wish my life were like this: proper ingredients exposed to the right environment, blossoming into something tantalizing to the senses and easy to digest. Do the right thing, and the right thing should happen. I made a huge mistake, but I did the right thing—I stopped drinking, I'm in treatment. It follows that I should get my child back. It's driving me out of my mind how little control I have over any of this.

Derek stands in front of the stove now, using a pastry brush to coat the griddle with butter. He rolls up to the balls of his bare feet and bounces to an unheard rhythm, pausing a moment from the task before him in order to conduct an invisible band with his pastry brush. Jess rolls her eyes and laughs.

"Hey, Harry Connick Jr.," she says, winking at me. "Don't burn breakfast this time, okay? Our fire alarms are tired of being prodded with a broomstick on Sunday mornings."

Derek flips around to face her and shakes his pastry brush at her in mock irritation. "Listen, woman," he warns, the lines around his warm brown eyes crinkling up as he tries, and fails, to keep from smiling. "Don't start with me. And stop trying to show off in front of your big sister." His normally well-groomed, salt-and-pepper hair is flipped up in the back: a two-inch alfafa sprout. A small beer belly pushes at his sweatshirt; the weight he gained on par with Jess when she was pregnant with the twins was not as easy to lose as hers. I'm not sure why it is that men can gain twenty pounds and still be considered attractive, but if a woman gains the same, it's time for a food addiction intervention on *Oprah*.

"Oh, no," I say, setting my mug down on the table. "Don't blame me for her bad behavior. I had enough of that growing up."

Jess reaches over and smacks me lightly on the top of my thigh. "Hey! You did not. I didn't *have* bad behavior when we were growing up."

I snort. "Yeah, right. I saved your butt on a regular basis with Mom, and you know it. I can't even count the number of times I took the blame for you. Mom was always mad at me, anyway. It was just easier that way."

"I don't know what you're talking about," Jess says, incredulous. "I was sweet and innocent."

Derek snorts at this one, steps over, puts his meaty hand at the base of her neck, and kisses his wife on the top of her head. "Not even close, honey. I wouldn't have married you if that were true." He moves back over to the stove, picks up a ladle, and starts pouring batter onto the griddle. A toasty, sweet scent infused with vanilla bean and lemon zest wafts through the kitchen almost immediately; my stomach growls in response.

Jess grins impishly. "Why *was* Mom always mad at you?"

I shrug, reach for my coffee again, and take a sip, looking at her over the rim of the mug. "You know why. Because I wasn't more like you."

"And how was I?" Jess asks.

"Like her." I smile at my sister. She knows I'm right about this, though she'll argue the point. From the time she could tie her shoes, Jess was the kind of child who washed the dishes the minute a meal was over and went about her chores without grumbling. She picked up her toys and put them away when she was done playing. She kept her side of the closet organized by season and color, her dresser drawers were full of neatly folded shirts and perfectly rolled socks. I, on the other hand, much preferred escaping into a good book or spending hours writing in my Holly Hobbie diary to performing any kind of manual labor. Most days, I was lucky to find a clean pair of underwear or a shirt without some kind of telling stain. I spent a lot of my time trying to emulate my younger sister. I tried to be the kind of daughter it was obvious my mother appreciated.

"You're so organized, Jessica," my mother was fond of pointing out when we were kids. "What a wonderful quality to have."

I stood next to my sister, my body erect, my mind alert, primed to hear what wonderful quality my mother thought I possessed. When she said nothing, I solicited a response. "What are mine, Mom?"

"Your what?" she asked. Her mind had already moved on to other things.

"My wonderful qualities."

"Oh," she said. "Well, let me see. We can't all be organized, now, can we? You're creative. Creative people tend to be messy."

Our mother also took note of how alike she and my sister were. One of my clearest memories is that of our mother sitting on the couch in our small living room with us both, one on each side of her. I was twelve and Jess was eleven; it was a rare evening Mom was home early from work. I had made spaghetti for dinner.

"Did you like the sauce, Mom?" Jess asked. "Cadee made it, but I added the basil."

I shot Jess a dirty look for trying to take credit for the work I'd done. Nobody cared about a stupid teaspoon of basil.

She smiled at Jess, tousling my sister's hair. "My little carbon copy."

"Am I your carbon copy, too?" I asked, wriggling my way over on the cushions to snuggle more closely with my mom. As the oldest, I came first. I was certain her answer would be yes.

"Oh, sweetie," she said, wrapping her arm around my shoulders and giving me a quick squeeze. Her fingers smelled pleasantly of garlic. "A person can't have more than one carbon copy."

I looked at the floor, then back up at her, forcing a smile. "Whose carbon copy am I, then?"

She paused, assessing me. "My mother's, I think. You're starting to look like her." Her hazel eyes narrowed the slightest bit. "Around the eyes, mostly. She had that wild mop on her head, too." Both my mother and sister's hair, though dark like mine, was straight as a board. After months of begging, Mom finally broke down and took me to have mine chemically relaxed. A week later, after all my curls broke off in uneven chunks, I ended up with what the hairdresser mercifully called a pixie style, but more truthfully resembled a marine's boot-camp buzz cut. This was an undoubtedly sorry look for a chubby adolescent girl.

"Didn't you say your mother was crazy?" I said. Our mother had dropped enough comments about her mother's erratic behavior and subsequent hospital stays for me to be curious to learn more. This seemed a perfect opportunity.

"Mm-hmm," my mother murmured, closing her eyes and leaning over to kiss Jess on top of her head.

"*How* was she crazy?" I asked, a tiny nugget of fear materializing in my belly.

"She just was," my mother responded. There was a sharp, irritated edge to her words.

"But how?" I persisted. "What kinds of things did she do?" I didn't like the look on my mother's face when she said I reminded her of her mom. I wanted to do everything I could to avoid seeing it again.

"She wandered the neighborhood in the middle of the night in her nightgown," my mother said with a sigh. "She'd be barefoot, singing show tunes at the top of her lungs. When my father would bring her home and I asked her if she was okay, she picked up her shoes and threw them at me."

As children, Jess and I had giggled at this image of our grandmother standing in the entryway, chucking a pair of penny loafers at our mother. But a still, small, cold space inside me reserved judgment. I felt sorry for my grandmother. From the bits and pieces of the stories our mother had told us over the years, I gathered that she had been abandoned when she was three years old to be raised by an elderly, distant aunt. She married our grandfather when she was only sixteen and gave birth to our mother less than a year later, losing a lot of blood and her ability to have more children in the process. As our mother told it, throughout her childhood, our grandmother popped in and out of the hospital, the doctors prescribing medication that never seemed to work. While she was gone, our mother became the woman of the house.

"I was cooking my father dinner by the time I was seven," she told us. Her chin lifted as she spoke. "I learned to be self-reliant a long time ago, girls. You would do well to do the same." Her father left when she was twelve. Old enough, he said, to sign her mother into the hospital when she needed to be there. He never came back.

As a child, my grandmother's death—years before I was born—scared me. I was left with no way to confirm whether or not what my mother said about her being crazy was true. I took her at her word. She was my mother; what other choice did I have? I worried that insanity might follow me the way my grandmother's curly hair and dark, round eyes had. Did instability already flow through my veins? I swallowed my fears, pressing them into a hard ball inside my chest.

The sound of a thin, metal spatula scraping across the griddle snaps my thoughts back to the present. "How's treatment going?" Derek inquires.

I suck in a breath, set my coffee down. Derek is a salesman; he goes right for the kill, every time. "It's fine, I guess," I say, trying to keep my voice even. "But I do feel kind of stupid getting an attendance slip signed at AA meetings."

"Why do you have to do that?" he asks.

"To verify I showed up. It's a requirement of the program I'm in. I have to show it to my counselor every week."

"What about the custody case?" Jess asks. She reaches behind her head to pull her ponytail tighter. "What's going on with that?"

"I have my first meeting with the guardian ad litem next month. May fifteenth."

"The guardian ad what-what?" Derek asks, turning around to look at me, his eyebrows scrunched in confusion.

I give him a halfhearted smile. "Guardian ad litem. He's appointed by the court to make a recommendation for who should have custody. He's supposed to represent what's best for the child. Charlie, in this case." Again, it seems unfathomable to me that I'm sitting here discussing how someone else will decide what's best for my own son.

"Oh. How exactly does he figure that out?"

I shrug. "By talking to everyone involved, according to my lawyer. Gathering information, looking at all the facts. He's supposed to be a neutral party." Though I was uncomfortable about meeting Mr. Hines, I was trying to approach it like a job interview. I'd never interviewed for a job I didn't end up being offered. I had my mind set that this situation would be no different.

"Are you nervous?" Derek asks, transferring a stack of pancakes onto a platter, then sliding it into the oven to keep our breakfast warm.

"I don't think 'nervous' is strong enough of a word."

"Why aren't you meeting with him sooner?" Jess asks.

"My lawyer told me most GALs like to give the emotion of the dispute some time to calm down before they talk with all the people involved. He's not meeting with Mom until July. I wish we could just get it all over with." I have no idea what I'm going to do with myself while I wait for these meetings to happen. Hours and days and weeks loom in front of me. Time that used to be filled with my son. What was I going to do now?

Jess sets her coffee down and reaches over to give my arm a reassuring rub. "You'll do great. Just be honest with him. Be yourself, do what you normally do."

"You mean I should down a bottle of wine beforehand?" I intend this as a joke, but it falls flat. Neither Derek nor Jess cracks a smile.

"So, how often is Charlie with you?" Jess asks.

"Every other weekend and Wednesday nights for dinner." Before either Jess or Derek can respond, my cell trills. I reach for my purse to catch the call before it goes to voicemail.

"Hello?" I say, standing up and stepping down the hall toward the living room. I can feel my sister's eyes on my back.

"Cadence? It's Laura." Laura was one of my roommates when I was still an in-patient at Promises Treatment Center, where I ended up after the psych ward. She was a twenty-two-year-old girl with a high IQ and a heroin habit. We shared a mutual passion for chocolate and tacky reality television shows and a similar practice of weeping in the dark.

"Oh, Laura, hey." It's strange to have her call me. She isn't part of this world here, with my sister, my family. It feels oddly intrusive, like an adulterous lover showing up uninvited to a family event. "I missed seeing you at group last week. Are you okay?"

"I guess so," she says. "I relapsed last week. Didn't they tell you?"

"No," I say. "They didn't. Andi said you were sick."

She laughs. "That must've been what my mom told her, so I wouldn't lose my place in treatment. I think I get one get-out-of-jail-free card, though. Hopefully, they won't kick me out." She pauses. "Sorry. Didn't mean to shock you." Another pause, her deep inhale of breath in my ear. "So . . . I'm having a really hard morning."

I am quiet, not sure what to say to someone who has relapsed on heroin. "Just say no" seems entirely inadequate.

"I really feel like using," she says. "I want to shoot up."

"Oh." I swallow, dropping to the couch, and look out the front window at another sunny spring morning. It's only ten o'clock and I haven't even finished my first cup of coffee. It seems a little early to be talking to someone about her desire to stick a needle in her arm. But Andi did say we should call each other if we needed to talk. I just haven't felt the need to pick up the phone. "Did you? Shoot up, I mean?"

"No. But I didn't sleep, either. I kept having dreams. Waking up, reaching for the needle I used to keep on the table next to my bed." She pauses. "Have you had those kinds of dreams?"

"Not of needles. But drinking dreams? Yeah, I have." I say this quietly, my eyes stealing down the hall to make sure Charlie hasn't come looking for me in the kitchen. I hear Derek laugh and the sound of silverware tinkling and plates being set on the table. I don't want Charlie to hear me talk about drinking; I'm afraid he'll think I haven't really stopped. I pull my legs up onto the couch and bend them so my heels are jutted up against my backside. I rest my chin on top of one knee.

"Like, what do you dream?" Laura asks, her voice small.

I sigh, softly. "Well, the one I have most is of being in my front yard, trying to cover a hole filled with empty wine bottles with dirt. And there's not enough dirt. All my neighbors are standing around, watching me, shaking their heads."

"But you're not drinking in that dream. You're just ashamed that people might find out that you *did* drink like that, right?"

I nod, as though she can see me, then realize she's waiting for me to answer her. "Yeah, I guess that's what it means, huh?" I clear my throat. "Are you going to be okay, sweetie?"

"Oh, yeah. Sure. I'll be fine. Just trying to do what's suggested, you know? Call someone when you feel weird?"

"Well, I'm glad you did. And I'm really sorry to cut this short, but I need to eat breakfast with Charlie and get him back to my ex-mother-in-law's house. I'll see you tomorrow at group?"

"Absolutely. Have fun with Charlie."

I hang up, unsettled, though I'm not sure why. I tell myself I'll call her later tonight to make sure she is okay. I'll offer to take her out to dinner sometime. It's better than being stuck home all alone.

I take a deep breath and pull myself off the couch. As I'm about to step back down the hallway, there's a knock at the front door. "I'll get it!" I call out, reaching for the glass knob and swinging the door open.

My mother stands before me, slender and lovely, in a lavender pantsuit. Her crisp white linen blouse is ironed in perfect lines beneath her jacket. She looks like spring. She regards me, surprised, but manages to rearrange her features into an immediate smile. As a dentist, she is her own best advertisement. Her dazzling, bleached white teeth practically send out a beacon of light twenty feet in every direction. Her hair is newly cut in a chin-length, sleek bob, about three inches shorter than my sister's. I wouldn't be surprised if they go to the same stylist.

"Cadence!" she says, stepping in to give me a kiss on the cheek, surely leaving a lipstick mark of perfect pale pink. "I didn't expect to see you." She sniffed the air and then crinkled her nose. "Are you wearing perfume?"

"Hi, Mom. Charlie and I spent the night. And it's a body spray." Our mother never allowed me or my sister to wear perfume when we were growing up; she told us it gave boys the wrong idea, but we convinced ourselves she was just being strict.

"Ah. Did I tell you I made my office a fragrance-free workplace? There are a lot of people with allergies to any kind of scent, you know."

"No, I didn't know that."

"You're both here?" She sets her purse down on the entry table. "Where is that wonderful grandson of mine?"

As if on cue, Charlie comes bounding down the hallway. "Nana!" he exclaims, running over to hug my mother's legs. "What did you bring me?"

"Charlie," I scold gently. "Watch your manners."

"It's all right, Cadence." My mom pats him on the head. "I didn't know you were going to be here, darling. So I didn't bring presents. But here," she says, reaching over to her purse. "I think I have some quarters."

"Mom—" I start, but she cuts me off.

"Now, Cadence. Don't deprive a grandmother the chance to spoil her grandchildren." She rustles in her wallet, then hands Charlie six quarters. He holds them cupped in his hands like treasure, his eyes bright. "Make sure you give two each to Marley and Jake, as well, dear."

"I will!" Charlie says, racing back down the hall.

"Charlie, say 'thank you'!" I call out after him.

"Thanks, Nana!" he says, not looking back. He stops at the top of the basement stairs and hollers, "Marley! Jake! Nana gave us *money*!"

I laugh, shaking my head. "You always made me work for my allowance, Mom."

"It's not my job to teach him responsibility, honey. Children learn by the example of their parents." She smiles, this time hiding her teeth with closed lips. "It smells wonderful in here. Derek must be making breakfast!"

Jess steps into the living room and comes over to give our mother a hug. "Hi, Mom. You're early."

I look at Jess. "You were expecting her?" She hadn't told me this.

"Not until noon," Jess says, not meeting my gaze. "We're going shopping for a new bedroom set for her."

"Oh. Well." I keep my voice light. "That's right when I have to get Charlie back to Alice's house, anyway."

"That's what I figured," Jess says. She must have planned it this way. She didn't want me to be hurt that my mother hadn't thought to ask me or didn't want me to come along. My mother has only called me twice since I got back from my in-patient stay at Promises. One call was to make sure I got the flowers she sent me in the hospital and another was to ask when she could see Charlie. After much collusion by Jess, she did come to the family counseling session offered by the treatment center; however, once there, she sat with her hands perfectly folded in her lap and didn't say more than ten words.

"How was the hospital?" she inquired during her first call, before the family session. She asked this in the same tone a person might ask how I enjoyed a trip to Hawaii.

"It was fine, I guess. As psychiatric units go." I made a noise I intended to be a laugh, but it came out more like a fractured breath. "I guess you were right about me, huh, Mom?"

"How was I right?"

"That I'm like your mother."

She was quiet. "I have to go now, honey," she finally said, ignoring my comment. "I have a patient."

That was the way we left things, the last time we spoke, before seeing her today.

"You never were one for decorating, honey," she says to me now, as though that conversation had never taken place. "Jess has such a lovely eye for what will work in a particular space. Like what she did with my office. My patients all ask for the name of the design firm I used." My mother's office is all glass, chrome, and leather, effectively warmed with lush groupings of tropical plants and thick, luxurious throw rugs. Calm, practically hypnotic melodies are piped in through the sound system; tiny Zen sand gardens rest on every table sitting next to a chair, strategically placed there by my sister to ease the stress of the patients about to have a whirring metal drill pressed against the sensitive nerves of their teeth.

"Yes," I say, "she's very talented."

Derek comes up behind his wife, wrapping his arms around her waist and kissing her on the neck. He looks up at our mother. "Hey, Sharon. Are you staying for breakfast? There's plenty."

"Oh, I might have one," my mother says. "No butter, though."

"Come on, Mom," I say, "live a little. Don't you have any vices?"

"We all have plenty of those, don't you think?" The carefree tone of her voice doesn't match the strange cloud in her eyes. A lump forms in my throat and I try to swallow it with a false smile.

"We better eat before the boys devour it all," Jess says, saving me. I shoot her a grateful look. Charlie comes bounding back down the hallway, runs over to me, and grabs my hand, pulling me back toward the kitchen with him.

"C'mon, Mama. I want you to sit by me and I put the biggest pancake from the stack on your plate for you!"

"With lots of butter, I hope," I say. I can almost feel my mother's body tense at those words.

"Yep!" he says. "But I'll let you pour the syrup."

"Oh, well, thank you. How generous!" Once again, my heart fills with a sense of gratitude that he seems to have completely forgotten my brief loss of temper the day before. I squeeze his hand, smile at the rest of my family, and let him lead the way.

My family spends over an hour making pleasant chitchat over breakfast. With my mother there, no one brings up what is going on in my life: the psych ward, my internment at Promises, the custody dispute. My humiliating trifecta.

Instead, my mother goes into more detail about her new boyfriend: a pediatric nurse who came in to her office for a root canal and left with our mother's phone number.

"Geez, Mom," Jess says. "What do you *do* to these guys when you have them in the chair?"

"Jessica!" my mother exclaims, setting her fork down on her plate with a clatter. "I am a complete professional with my patients!" Her expression is more pleased than angry, her voice filled with false indignation.

Jess winks at me. "Oh, sure. Okay, Mom. Whatever you say."

I couldn't have gotten away with teasing my mother like that. But Jess is the baby. The favorite. The rules are different for her—they always have been. It's silly for me to expect them to change now.

When I pull up in front of Alice's house a few minutes before noon, there is an immediate weight in the pit of my stomach at the site of Martin's car. "Daddy's here!" Charlie cries out from the backseat.

What's he doing here? I wonder. It was he who requested that I pick up and bring Charlie back to Alice's house and not his. Maybe he wants to talk. Maybe he is coming to his senses and wants to work things out with the custody issue. Maybe he's had a change of heart. I feel my heartbeat quicken with this thought, tiny hopeful seedlings popping up within me. I get out of the car, then help Charlie disengage from his seat belt. He scrambles out the door and toward his grandmother's house, leaving me to amble behind him.

Martin steps out of the front door, arms crossed over his chest. The skin is dark under his eyes and he hasn't shaved. He still looks handsome.

I give him what I hope he interprets as a friendly smile. "Hey, there. Where's Alice?"

"She isn't feeling well," he says. The sound of his voice braids my stomach muscles into messy, complicated knots. *Why is that?* I wonder. I'm not in love with him anymore. I don't regret the divorce. I suppose it's the guilt. Or, more likely, the humiliation I feel knowing that *he* knows exactly how far I've fallen.

Charlie launches himself against his father's legs. "*Oof!* Careful, there, champ," Martin says.

Charlie looks up at his father, keeping his skinny arms latched around Martin's thighs. "Is Omi sick?"

Martin pushes Charlie's hair back from his forehead and smiles. "Yeah, buddy, she is."

"What's wrong?" I take a few more steps so I am standing at the bottom of the stairs. My legs are shaking; I tense them to get them to stop.

Martin pauses, searching my face. "Head inside, okay, Charlie? But don't bother Omi, you understand? She's resting in her bedroom."

"Can I watch television?" Charlie asks hopefully.

"Yes, you may. The Disney Channel only, though. And not too loud."

"Okay." Charlie lets go of his father, looks back at me.

I smile at him. "Come give me a hug good-bye, sweetie. I'm going to miss you."

Charlie rushes back down the steps and leaps into my open arms. I hug him tightly, breathing him in. "You are my best boy, you know that? I love you so much. I am so proud to be your mama." I don't know how to go about my life without him, how to let him simply walk away from me like this. It goes against every fiber of my being.

"I know," he says, dropping back down to the stairs. "'Bye, Mama!" The door slams behind him and Martin cringes.

Silence weighs between us. Our eyes are locked on each other. I look away, clearing my throat before speaking again. "Nothing serious, I hope? With Alice, I mean." I raise my eyes to him again.

Martin shakes his head. "It's the anniversary," he finally says.

It takes me a moment, but then it dawns on me what he is talking about. Thirty-three years ago today, Martin's father was crushed to death on one of his building sites. It wasn't his fault. It wasn't anybody's fault. A vital, rusted bolt had snapped and the crane fell. Every year on this day, Alice remains in bed, mourning the loss of her husband. At first, when Martin told me about her ritual, I thought it was a little over the top, but I gradually learned that Alice's grief was authentic. She loved her husband and one day a year she found a way to honor him. It was sweet, actually. It was one of the few things I liked about her.

When we were married, Martin had the day circled on the calendar in our kitchen. He made no other plans than to be with his mother.

"Really?" I said, the first year he told me he spent this day with her. "The whole day?"

"She needs me," he explained. At the time, this show of love for his mother endeared him to me. I loved that he was there for her when she needed him so much. I believed he'd be there for me, too.

"Sorry. It's been a few years," I say now, reaching out an arm to rest my hand on the black metal railing. I grip it for reassurance. "I forgot what day it was."

"Yeah, well, it's hard for her," Martin says.

"I know," I say. "I'm sorry she's having such a hard time. I would have brought Charlie back to your place later, if you had called."

He shrugs. "Not a big deal. I was here with her anyway." He looks at me, his blue eyes dimmed by an emotion I can't read. I used to be able to read every one of his thoughts.

I feel a thousand things. I want to scream. I want to beg him to forgive me. I want to cry. Instead, I take a deep breath and make sure I'm looking him straight in the eye as I softly speak. "It kills me that I've hurt him, Martin."

A muscle beneath his left eye twitches and he blinks, but Martin doesn't respond. His mouth opens, as if to speak, but then he closes it again.

Andi was right. The tension between us holds an unbearable weight. Even with Charlie inside the house, any more discussion of us, my drinking, or the custody dispute is too dangerous a risk.

"You okay?" I manage to say.

"I'm fine," he says, and I know it's not true. I know he carries the bulk of his mother's grief. He helps her manage it so she doesn't have to bear the burden alone. There was a time when I would reach out to him, when I would have found a way to offer him comfort. But today, there is no way. Too much sits between us. It's a distance too vast, far too treacherous for us to cross.

Seven

By the time the summer of Charlie's fifth birthday rolled around, I decided I was done drinking. The fact that I limited myself to two glasses a day—and even managed to go a few days at a time not drinking at all—didn't matter. Two weeks before the party I went cold turkey, suffering through a four-day, intense, and debilitating headache, fighting off my craving to drink with a constant stream of Gatorade. After the fifth day, I actually felt a little like my old self and was proud of my abstinence. *If I had a real problem, I wouldn't be able to stop,* I thought. *I have this thing completely back under control.*

Still, my muscles ached and occasionally trembled, and my energy level was low enough for me to worry I had contracted some kind of silent but terminal disease. *Maybe chronic fatigue syndrome. Or fibromyalgia.* I chose to have the party at a nearby park so I wouldn't have to clean my house or worry about the guests' possible scrutiny of the wine stains on the kitchen counter or the piles of laundry I couldn't quite convince myself to fold.

"Can we have Cheetos at my party?" Charlie asked when I took him shopping with me for supplies the day before it was scheduled to take place.

"Sure," I agreed. "It's your birthday, why not?" I deliberately kept my eyes averted from the wine aisle. I wouldn't even walk down it. *See how strong I am?*

The morning of the party arrived on a hot Saturday in August. I filled an ice chest with pinwheel ham and cheese tortilla sandwiches, grapes, and juice boxes, then carefully packed the chocolate cake I'd made the night before. I almost gave in and bought a sheet cake from the store, but I knew Charlie would be disappointed if I didn't bake his favorite "dirt" cake, complete with cookie crumbles and a mountain of gummy worms.

When we arrived, Jess and Derek were already there, chasing the twins on the toddler jungle gym. Charlie raced over to join his cousins and my sister came over to hug me. "I feel like it has been forever since I've seen you," she said, pulling back to look at me. Worry knit itself across the lines of her forehead. "Are you okay? You look tired."

"I haven't been feeling very well," I said, pushing my hair away from my face, happy I'd taken the time to put on some makeup. I wore a lightweight, sage-color princess-waist sundress and black flip-flops. I forced a bright smile at Jess. "It's just stress, I think. Can you help me set up?"

We spread out the plastic Spider-Man tablecloth and arranged a stack of plates, juice boxes, and the gigantic bag of Cheetos. The rest of the guests trickled in, with the exception of my mother, who had called to let me know she'd be a little late.

Susanne came over to help us set up the table while Brittany and Renee went off to monitor the kids on the play equipment. She gave me a quick hug. "Good to see you, hon."

"You, too," I said. She had come to the party with Anya, but not Brad. After the one night we'd talked about their marriage, she hadn't brought it up again, so I figured it was something she didn't want to discuss. I introduced her to Jess, who looked over my shoulder as I was explaining how Susanne and I knew each other from Mommy and Me.

"Oh, shit," Jess muttered underneath her breath.

"What?" I asked, spinning around to look where she was looking. Martin was holding a woman's hand, and the woman wasn't his mother.

"Did you know he was bringing her?" Jess asked.

I shook my head, and my heartbeat rose up into my throat. It was Martin's new girlfriend, Shelley. It had to be. He began dating her a few months ago, and Charlie told me that she was always at Martin's house when he visited for the weekend. "She's nice," Charlie said. "She buys me candy."

Bribery, I thought. *How lovely.*

I hadn't said anything to Martin at the time, knowing he was well within his rights to date whomever he pleased, but this—bringing her to his son's birthday party without telling me first? My stomach suddenly snarled itself into thorny knots.

"I'm going to talk with him," Susanne said, making like she was about to give Martin a piece of her mind. "What a jerk."

I grabbed her arm and held her back. "No," I said. "I don't want to give him the satisfaction. It's no big deal. I'll be fine."

Susanne looked like she didn't quite believe me.

Jess looked doubtful, too. "Are you sure?"

I swallowed, suddenly very thirsty. "Yes." I pasted on my best and brightest smile as they approached. *It was only a problem if I let it become one. I could do this.* "Hello!" I said in my finest singsong voice. "How are y'all?"

Martin eyed me warily. He knew I expressed false hospitality with a bad southern accent. "We're fine. This is Shelley," he said, gesturing to the very thin, very blond woman standing next to him. "Shelley, this is Cadence."

"Nice to finally meet you," Shelley said. "I've heard so much about you."

I shook Shelley's hand and gave her a tight, closed-lipped smile, taking a moment to try to see what it was about her that attracted Martin. She wasn't exceptionally pretty—more like the surfer girl next door with expensive sandals, a spray-on tan, and slightly bucked teeth. She wore tiny jean shorts and a tight hot pink tank top that would have been better suited for one of Charlie's five-year-old female friends. I had her beat in the breast department, though. She could have worn one of my bra cups as a bonnet.

"Shelley!" Charlie cried out. He ran across the bright green lawn and threw himself against her legs. Seeing him show her such affection, my stomach twisted even further. For a moment, I feared I might vomit.

"It's my birthday!" he told her.

"I know," she said. "I bought you a really great present."

"Can I open them now, Mommy?" Charlie asked, pulling away from Shelley to give his father a hug.

"No, honey. We'll wait until after cake, okay?" My molars were grinding as I spoke, and I could feel my heartbeat in my throat.

"Okay!" he said, and he raced back to play with his cousins and friends.

My mother chose this moment to arrive, and upon seeing Martin holding Shelley's hand as she approached the group, she lifted her nose just the slightest bit and said, "I thought this was a family party."

I loved her in that moment, and gave her a brief, grateful smile. "No, Charlie has a couple of friends from preschool here, too. They're all over on the climbing toys." I raised my hand and waved at Brittany and Renee, who were sitting on a bench watching the kids play.

"Hello, Sharon," Alice said to my mother. "How have you been?"

"I'm well, thank you," my mom answered, deliberately not making eye contact with Martin's mother. Her behavior may have been impolite, but I appreciated it nonetheless. "Do you need any help with anything, Cadence?" she asked me.

I shook my head. "I think we're all set. We can eat whenever the kids are ready." I turned to pull the cake out of the box I'd packed it in and Martin stepped over to help me.

"I meant to call and let you know she was coming," he said quietly. I felt his fingers brush against mine as we both held the cake platter and I pulled away like I'd been burned. The cake wobbled, and he set it on the table.

"Let me know *who* was coming?" I asked brightly.

"Cadence." His face told me he saw right through my feigned indifference. "Come on."

I gave him a huge, toothy smile. "Oh, you must mean Shelley. She seems very nice." My heart shook in my chest. "Can you excuse me for a minute?" I asked. "I need to get something from my car."

His blue eyes narrowed and he frowned. "Are you okay?"

"I'm fine," I said brightly. I walked briskly toward the parking lot, almost breaking into a run as soon as I saw my navy blue Explorer. I jumped into the safety of my vehicle and gripped the steering wheel to keep from shaking. I took a few deep, shuddering breaths, trying not to cry. Images from the last ten minutes rushed over me—seeing Martin holding Shelley's hand; Alice's cold, hard stare; the moment my son wrapped his arms around that woman's legs. My chest ached.

A sharp rap at my window startled me. Susanne came around the car and hopped in the passenger seat. "So much for you'll be fine, huh?" she said. She reached into her purse, pulled out a lovely silver flask, and held it out for me. My pulse sped up at the sight of it.

I stared at it, every thought in my head telling me, *No, don't do it, you've been doing so well,* and still, my hand reached out.

In that moment, I couldn't think of a woman who wouldn't do the same thing if something like this had happened to her.

Over the next couple of months, I once again attempted to keep a two-glass-a-day limit, but occasionally awoke to discover an empty bottle or two by my bed. My gut ached with shame. *Why can't I stop this? What is* wrong *with me?* I had to do *something* to figure it out.

In October, I finally went to my doctor for my yearly checkup, planning to talk with her about my insomnia, but not about how I'd been dealing with it. How much I was drinking was the dirty little secret I carried around, the shame I felt was just punishment for my bad behavior. I figured if I found a way to deal with the core of what made me drink—my anxiety and sleeplessness—the problem would go away.

The morning of the appointment I thought about asking Jess to watch Charlie for me, but she was having a hard enough time adjusting to life with toddler twin boys—I didn't need to add more to her already full plate.

Charlie and I sat together in a plush, overstuffed chair in the doctor's office waiting room. I gazed at my son, taking in the blue river of veins beneath his pale skin. He was so delicate, so fragile. "I love you, Charlie bear," I said. I kissed the top of his head.

He looked up at me and grinned. "Love you, too, Mommy." He pointed to the cover of the book we brought along to read. "That's Alexander. He's having a no-good, terrible bad day."

I smiled. "Yes. We all have those kinds of days."

"Not me," he said. "My days are all good. 'Cept when I don't get chocolate. Then I get cranky."

"Me, too, monkey. Chocolate is good for our souls."

He crinkled up his nose, confused. "What's a soul?"

The receptionist sitting behind the counter chuckled quietly, overhearing our conversation, and I lifted my eyes to the ceiling as if to say, *Oh boy. Let's see if I can explain this one.*

"Well, it's kind of who you really are, honey," I began. "What you think and how you feel. Your body just kind of carries your soul around."

"Can you see it?" He tilted his head, still trying to figure it out.

"Hmm," I said, stalling for a little time to think. "Sort of, maybe. Like in how a person treats someone else? That's how you see what kind of soul they have."

"You have a really good soul, Mommy."

"Not as good as yours," I whispered, leaning down to give his perfect ear a quick kiss. My eyes stung and my throat thickened as I pictured the bottle of wine waiting at home for me. I didn't understand how I could hate doing something so much and still not be able to make myself stop. It didn't make sense.

A few minutes later, the nurse called me back to the exam room and I helped Charlie get settled with a pencil and notepad so he could color. The nurse took my vitals, looking down at me over her bifocals as she recorded my weight. "You've gained nine pounds since your last visit," she said without a shred of compassion.

And you *have beady little rat eyes*, I thought, then immediately felt crappy for it and happy I'd managed not to speak aloud. It must have been written all over my face, though, because the nurse frowned and left the room without saying another word.

"I don't *want* to draw," Charlie announced. He set down his pencil and crossed his arms over his chest.

I sighed. "Please, honey. Just for a few minutes. Mama needs to talk to her doctor."

He widened his eyes. "Do you have to get a shot?" he whispered.

"No." I rummaged through my purse and pulled out a slightly crushed Baggie of Goldfish crackers and a juice box, wondering if the day would ever come that I didn't need to pack snacks for an hour-long outing. His face lit up as he snatched them from me. "Try not to spill, okay, Mr. Man?" I said. He nodded and shoved a handful of crackers into his mouth. Crumbs went everywhere. I sighed again.

Dr. Fields entered after a sharp rap on the door. She wore baggy black linen slacks and her white doctor's coat on her thin frame. Walking toward me, she reached behind her head to tighten her blond, practical ponytail at the base of her neck, somehow managing not to drop the thick manila folder she carried in the crook of her right arm.

"Hi, Cadence. Hi, Charlie," she said.

"I don't want a shot," Charlie said. Gummy orange cracker pulp clung to his teeth and I had to restrain myself from using one of my fingernails to scrape them clean.

"Oh, don't worry. You don't get one." Dr. Fields smiled at me, revealing a set of straight, white teeth my mother would have loved. "Long time no see."

I felt myself flush, remembering that I'd been so hungover the morning of my last scheduled appointment, I'd missed it. I couldn't remember the last time I'd been to see her.

"Not to worry," she said, then consulted the chart she cradled. "Looks like your blood pressure is a little high." She lifted her gaze to me. "Everything all right?"

I nodded, maybe a little too enthusiastically. "Oh, sure. A little stressed, I suppose. I'm not sleeping very well." I went on to tell her how my thoughts twirled like batons the moment I tried to drift off. I kept it general, since Charlie was in the room, telling her only that I had worries about my diminishing career and the d-i-v-o-r-c-e.

And I'm drinking too much. The phrase perched on the tip of my tongue, but I couldn't speak it.

"Stress will do that to you," she said. She scribbled in my chart. "Let's try some Ambien and a few Xanax to help get you through the tougher spots, okay?" I nodded. "If that doesn't work, we'll talk about getting you on something longer-acting, like Lexapro." She stopped scribbling and looked at me again. "You shouldn't drink with the Ambien or Xanax. It's a bad combination."

"That won't be a problem," I said. *I'm telling her the truth*, I thought. *If I get my anxiety in check and I can sleep, then I won't have a reason to drink.*

"Anything else?" she asked expectantly.

"No," I said with forced, glittering cheer. "Other than that, I'm all good."

The holiday season passed in a muddled haze. Some days I kept to my two-glass limit, others a switch would flip inside me after a single glass and two bottles would disappear instead. I stopped being able to predict which it would be.

The phone woke me one cold, January morning while Charlie

was at preschool. Three days before, I'd decided once again that I was done with drinking. That was it. I'd stick to the Ambien and Xanax—the doctor had prescribed them, after all. I would never pick up a bottle of wine again.

By noon on the first day without any wine, I was sweating so profusely I had to change my shirt. My skin reeked of alcohol and itched as though it was covered in a million tiny bugs. My muscles shook and my head felt like it just might explode. Still, I didn't drink. I was smarter than what I was doing. It was time for me to knock it the hell off.

"Hey, lady," Jess's voice chirped in my ear. Her pleasant demeanor felt like tiny daggers of ice slicing into my flesh.

"Hey," I said groggily.

"What are you and Charlie doing later today? Want to come over for dinner?"

I paused, trying to come up with a reason to not see my sister. I was in no shape to socialize. "Um, nothing, I don't think. But I'm not feeling well, really, so I probably shouldn't be around the twins."

"Is it the flu?" she asked.

"I'm not sure," I said, faltering. "Just some kind of bug, I think." I couldn't remember the last time I'd spent time with my sister. I was too scared to be around her very long, afraid she might see what was wrong.

"Okay," she said, drawing the word out with an edge of doubt. "Let me know if you change your mind."

I hung up, and the phone rang almost immediately again. This time it was the bank, an automated voice message. "Your December mortgage payment is more than thirty days past its due date. Please make this payment at your earliest convenience or you will be contacted by the loan processor within the next twenty-four hours."

I slammed my cell shut and shook my head, as though to clear it of thought. I hadn't slept more than two hours at a time in three days. I couldn't deal with this kind of shit. I had the money in savings, I'd just forgotten to transfer the payment. I'd take care of it later. I dozed in and out for another hour, setting my alarm to make sure I didn't miss picking up Charlie, then managed to drag myself out of the house.

"How are you, Cadence?" Brittany inquired, waving at me from the driver's side of her cobalt blue Lincoln Navigator.

"Fine," I said, waving back at her as I secured Charlie into his booster seat.

"We miss you at play group," she said.

"Thanks. I'm just really busy, you know?" I was suddenly conscious of the fact that I was wearing a gray T-shirt stained with sweat and my hair hadn't been washed in several days. I jumped into my car and drove off as fast as I could.

Even though he rarely took them anymore, once we got home, I led Charlie into his room and tried to get him down for a nap.

"Will you at least lie down with Mommy and rest? I don't feel good, honey."

"No, I don't want to. I want to go to the park." My son crossed his arms over his tiny chest and set his face in a stubborn expression similar to the one I'd seen on his father's face a thousand times before.

"Not today, baby. I'm sick."

"You're *always* sick," he said.

His words felt like a kick in the gut. My guilt sparked and caught fire in my chest.

"You will take a rest, young man, whether you like it or not."

"No!" He pushed his body into a rigid line, then screamed at the top of his lungs, "You're mean!" I left his room, slamming the door behind me. He shrieked and pounded on the wall for another half an hour before finally quieting down.

I went to the kitchen and stared at my too-long-untouched laptop. A pulsing, electric discomfort coursed through my body. What was I going to do? I was running out of money, I couldn't write, and my mind spun like an out-of-control carnival ride. I felt trapped, hopeless, unable to see a way to fix any of it. And yet, I'd brought it on myself. I *chose* this life. I was the one who convinced myself I was a strong, capable woman who could be just fine on my own. If I couldn't do it, the only person I had to blame was myself.

"God*dammit*!" I screamed, pushing my computer across the kitchen table and into the wall.

Fuck it, I thought. *I need a drink.* My entire body trembling, I stepped over to the counter and poured myself a rather hefty goblet of ruby-hued cabernet. I drank straight through the dinner Charlie threw on the floor and I had no appetite for, waiting for relief to fill me. To my dismay, I remained stone-cold sober. The wine wasn't working anymore. It had lost its desired effect. I opened another bottle.

"Sorry Mommy yelled earlier," I said an hour later as I lay in Charlie's bed, finally relaxed, tickling the bare skin of his back to help him go to sleep.

"Will you come to my house and tickle my back when I'm married?" he asked instead of replying to my apology.

I smiled, my eyes filling with tears. "I don't think your wife would like that very much, baby boy."

He turned his head to look at me. "Well, will you show her how to do it, then?"

"Yes," I said, and I kissed him on the forehead.

The next thing I realized, Charlie was shaking me awake. "Mama!" he said. "Mama, the bathroom floor's all wet."

I attempted to pull myself upright. The room spun around me and my stomach bent in on itself. That second bottle had sent me for a loop. I patted Charlie on the head. "'S okay, honey," I slurred. "Everything will be okay." I blinked at him heavily and he shook my arm again.

"Water's all over the floor," he said. He yanked on my arm and I groaned.

"Okay, I heard you," I said. I braced myself against his bed and pushed my body into a standing position. The clock read midnight.

I staggered down the hall behind Charlie and stepped into a swamp in the bathroom.

"What the hell?" I exclaimed, jumping back out of the mess of water, toilet paper, and poop.

Charlie scrunched up his face and began to cry. "I had to go potty," he said. "And I flushed the way I'm s'post to and all the paper got stuck and the water and poop went over the top." He looked at me with wide, glassy blue eyes. "I'm sorry, Mommy. I didn't mean to do it."

"Don't cry, baby. I'll clean it up. It's just an accident. Mommy's not mad." I didn't have the energy to be mad.

His bottom lip trembled. "Really?"

I wobbled where I stood, and braced myself with a flat palm against the wall. "Really." My head bobbed and I felt like I might pass out. "You go on back to bed. I'll come tuck you in in a minute."

"'Kay," he said, and padded off down the hall. Bleary-eyed, I snatched a huge stack of towels from the linen closet and threw them onto the mess on the floor. Tiptoeing across them, I managed to adjust the toilet so it stopped running and went back to its normal level. I dropped to my hands and knees, swabbed the floor until the towels were soaked, and then took the entire smelly armful to the washing machine by the back door.

"I don't want to do this anymore," I whispered. The tears swelled in the back of my throat. "Please. I can't do this anymore. Somebody help me."

There was no one to hear my cries. I took several deep breaths, grabbed the bottle of bleach, and stumbled back to the bathroom to splash some over the floor. I would have to clean up this mess on my own.

Eight

As I turn into my driveway after dropping Charlie off with Martin, I eye my cozy, red-brick 1920s bungalow as someone might upon seeing it for the first time. The structure itself was beautiful—rare, detailed, latticed brick found only in older Seattle neighborhoods, leaded glass windows, a convex wall making up the front of the house. A substantial weeping willow was the garden's focal point near the sidewalk. Looking out from my living room window seat, I've always thought that the willow looks like the bottom half of a genteel lady, carefully lifting her hoopskirt.

I'm conflicted over Jess's suggestion that I sell my home. My son spent his first five years here, but it's also where I descended into the bottle and endured my darkest days. If we moved into something more affordable, I'd be leaving good memories behind with the bad. Then again, leaving the bad ones might be exactly what I need.

Once inside, I set my purse down on the entryway table and let my eyes travel to the living room shelves. The sight of Charlie's Spider-Man action figures and Lego creations jars something loose inside me. My pulse races. Even though I've just left him, I feel disjointed and panicky without him here. It's like my body is missing its skeleton.

Dropping to the couch, I blow a heavy breath out through my lips. I think about how I used to long for quiet—a leisurely meandering through my days. The first few years of being a mother, especially, when sleep seemed like the fabulous sex you'd once had with a stranger and would never get to experience again now that you were married. I yearned for mornings without a screeching infant, mornings without a husband accusing me of misplacing his keys.

At one point, I remember wondering if I would be better off if Charlie never existed. This shadow of a thought, this brief turning over of my heart to the darkness that lay inside it, this is what haunts me now. Is all that resulted from my drinking some kind of cosmic retribution for spending one selfish moment wishing I had not become a mother? I didn't mean it. Charlie is my gift, the best thing, hands down, that ever happened to me. I'd never heard other mothers discuss whether or not they were actually cut out to be a mother, nor did I have the courage to ask any women I knew if the question ever crossed their minds. The words were obscene enough inside of my head—saying them out loud felt unfathomable.

My cell phone rings and I see Susanne's name pop up on the tiny screen. We've only talked once since I got out of treatment, and while she understands the basic outline of what has happened with me over the last couple of months, I am too embarrassed to tell her too many of the dirty details. She knows I've stopped drinking and Martin has filed for custody. For now, that's enough.

"Hey there," she says. "Long time no talk. What're you up to?"

"Not much," I respond. I gnaw on a hangnail on the outside edge of my pinky finger. "How are you?"

"Stressed. You want to go out for a drink?"

I pause, feeling awkward. "Um, I'm not drinking anymore. Remember?"

"Not even wine?" She laughs and I picture the bloodred curve of her lips. "C'mon, it's medicinal."

My mind flickers briefly on the feeling of a perfectly cool, spherical crystal goblet in my hand and what a swallow of wine might taste like. I have to cough a little to clear the gag from my throat. "I can't. Sorry."

We're both quiet for a moment, unused to conversation with each other unaided by the lubricant of wine.

"What're you guys up to tonight?" I finally ask.

She sighs. "The usual. Bath with a screaming toddler, followed by an enormous martini with my husband. Slightly drunken sex, if he's lucky."

I don't know how to respond. I'm suddenly hyperaware of everyone else's drinking patterns. Andi assures me that "normies"—otherwise known as people who don't have a problem with alcohol—don't register how much wine another person leaves in a glass, or how many shots of scotch their friends knock back over dinner. She says it's a reflection of an alcoholic's obsession with alcohol, how he or she keeps track of other people's consumption rates. I don't think I have an *obsession* with alcohol—I think I notice it more because my problem with it is so recent.

"Well," I manage to say, "I hope you have a good night."

"You, too."

After we hang up, I think about how much it disturbs me to hear about Susanne's drinking. I can't imagine what it would be like to sit down with her and watch her do it, to smell the wine and have it right there, within my reach.

I'm not sure I have it in me to say no to her when I've barely learned to say it to myself.

One chilly but clear January afternoon, I picked up Charlie from school and took him to Golden Gardens Park in Ballard, not too far from Alice's house. *I'm going to be a good mother,* I'd decided the morning after the toilet overflowed. *I'm going to write and clean my house and play with my son.* How I was living was ridiculous. I wasn't a victim. I was a strong, intelligent, and capable woman. I'd succeeded at everything I'd ever set my mind to. I gave up the pretense of being able to stop altogether; instead, I once again limited myself to two glasses of wine a day. I was certain I could practice some measure of self-control. It was like going on a diet—all I needed was some discipline.

"Why aren't we going home, Mommy?" Charlie asked.

"I thought it would be fun to have an early picnic dinner." I glanced in the rearview mirror at my son. "It's so nice outside. I packed submarine sandwiches and Cheetos." I'd called Jess to see if she wanted to bring the twins along and meet us, but both of them had bad colds she didn't want to share.

"What else?" he asked, reaching over to pat the top of the ice chest sitting next to him in the backseat.

I smiled, knowing he was fishing for dessert. "Oreos and milk. But only after you eat at least half of your sandwich, okay?"

"Okay," he agreed. We found a spot near the play area to lay our blanket, then I chased him around the equipment in a game of monster tag until he was ready to eat.

"You're a good monster, Mommy," he said as he shoved a handful of Cheetos into his mouth.

"Well, thank you," I said. I was always the one to play the monster, chasing my son around with fake, menacing growls. He finished his meal in record time, then raced off to play in the sandbox with a group of other children. I sat on a nearby bench to catch my breath and tried not to think about the wine I would have once I got home.

"Your son is adorable," a woman said after she sat down next to me. Her delicate Asian features were accented by a copious blessing of splotchy tan freckles on her cheeks.

"Thank you," I said. "He looks a lot like his father."

"He looks like you, too," she said. "His smile is yours." She leaned over and offered her hand. "I'm Leila."

"Cadence." I gestured toward my son. "And that's Charlie."

"Is he an only child?"

I nodded. "Yep. How about you?"

"Tyson is on the slide. He's four. And Becca's on the merry-go-round. She just turned three."

"Wow, that's a handful."

"Don't I know it. My husband works like a fiend, too." Leila said. "Does yours help you much?"

"I'm divorced," I said. "What school do your kids go to?"

"I'm homeschooling, actually," she said. "We belong to a pretty big group of families who have decided to go that route, so they still get a lot of social time." She had been put in the position of defending her decision to others. I could hear it in her voice.

"Ah. You are a better mother than me," I said, not wanting her to feel she was being judged. "I don't think I could do it."

"I know, it's a lot being home with them all the time. It could drive a woman to drink." She laughed.

I forced myself to laugh, too, because I knew this was what she expected. I'd seen websites devoted to moms who joke about drinking wine out of sippy cups; pages on Facebook dubbed "Moms Who Need Wine." There, drinking was talked about as a way to channel your former, nonmotherly self, laughingly referred to as "Mommy's Little Helper." I understood all of this was meant to be tongue-in-cheek—purely innocent fun. But as I sat there with my hands shaking, thinking of the bottle of wine waiting for me, I did have to wonder if any of those women thought about the other side, too. If they considered, even for a moment, the possibility they could end up just like me.

That night, I stared wide-eyed at the ceiling in my bedroom, unable to sleep. I debated with myself whether or not I could make it through to morning without a drink. I'd finished my two glasses when Charlie and I got home from the park, and I was out of both my prescriptions from the doctor. My heart pumped in my chest at a frightening, demanding pace. My skin was cold and clammy. Tiny seismic warnings rolled out through my muscles. If I didn't get up soon, the shakiness would only get worse. I didn't want to drink— *don't do it, please don't do it*—but my body's insistence on relief was about to take over.

Cold, creepy-crawly twinges moved along in my muscles. My body was desperate for rest but my mind had a different idea altogether. I tried deep breathing, tensing my muscles and then relaxing each one; first my toes, then my feet, my calves, my thighs, moving up my entire body until I got to my head, where I realized I had no idea how to tense my brain, let alone any clue how to make it relax.

Just a glass, I told myself as I rolled out of bed and stumbled down the hallway. Only enough to take the edge off so I can sleep a few more hours. Charlie would be up at 6:00. I needed to get him to preschool by 9:00. My fatigue was profound. My body felt as though someone had poured sand into my head, my eyes, my limbs. *I can't keep doing this. What the hell is wrong with me? I need to get my shit together.*

I stepped into the kitchen and regarded the bottle teetering on the edge of the countertop next to the sink. I hadn't bothered to cork it and a fly danced around its lip. Brushing it away, I picked up the bottle and stared at it as though it might have had something to say. *Drink me,* maybe? Or perhaps, more likely, *STOP drinking me, you stupid bitch.*

My belly warped in a strange dance of revulsion and impending relief. I chose relief. Holding the neck of the bottle with my right hand, I lifted it to my mouth, halfway gagging as I chugged down the first few swallows. My throat clenched in disgust and I pressed the back of my hand over my mouth, fighting the urge to vomit. The wave passed and I took another pull on the bottle. The heat of the wine burned through my body and slowed my pulse. I knew the nausea would cease. It only came back if I stopped drinking.

"Mommy?"

"Shit!" I exclaimed, jumping at the sound of Charlie's tiny voice. He stood in the entryway to the kitchen, watching me. He wore plaid flannel pajamas and clutched his blanket with both hands. I jerked the bottle behind my back and heard its contents splash around.

His lower lip pouched out, quivering, and his eyes filled with tears. "Sorry."

"Oh, honey, I'm sorry." Guilt immediately flooded my senses. "Mommy shouldn't swear. You just surprised me." I placed the bottle on the table and kneeled down next to him. I felt softer after the wine. More pliant. The way I wished I could always feel. "What are you doing up? Did you have a bad dream?"

He nodded and leaned into my shoulder, nuzzling the base of my neck with his damp face. I kissed the top of his head and rubbed his warm back in a small circle. He pulled away, crinkling up his perfectly snub, five-year-old nose. "Your breath smells yucky."

"Everyone has bad breath in the middle of the night, sweetie," I said. His words stung. My mouth felt like it had been used as a litter box and probably smelled about as good. "Come on. Let's go back to bed."

"Can I watch TV?" he asked.

"No," I said. My voice sounded like I'd been gargling gravel. "It's late."

"Please?" he whined.

I sighed, closing my eyes. So much for collapsing back to bed. "Fine. You go curl up on the couch and Mommy will be there in a minute."

"'Kay." He plodded off to the living room and I stepped over to the table. There was only a swallow or two of wine left, and I knew this wouldn't be enough. Tears welled in my eyes as I finished it, already thinking about where I'd stop to pick more up on my way home from dropping Charlie off at preschool.

If I could wait that long.

I wasn't sure that I could. Lifting the bottle to my lips, I sucked the few remaining droplets of wine and a sudden panic filled me. It was gone, and I was nowhere near feeling like I could close my eyes and go back to sleep. The backup bottle of vodka I kept in the freezer was already empty. I hadn't bought more, thinking if I didn't have it in the house, I wouldn't want it. My heart began to jitter in my chest again, demanding that I drink more to appease it. It terrified me how much more I had to drink to find a place of relief. It was the briefest sensation, barely lasting longer than a breath. Most days, I couldn't reach it at all.

Maybe I could zip to the store, I thought. *It's only a few blocks away.* I staggered into the living room, where Charlie had curled up on the couch with his blanket and quickly fallen back to sleep. I'd only be gone a few minutes, ten at the most. He'd never even know I wasn't there.

I stared at him, every motherly cell in me screaming to not do what my body was demanding, but I simply couldn't stand the thought of lying in my bed the rest of the night with a jackhammer in my chest. I could have a heart attack, and what would Charlie do then? I grabbed my keys and slipped out the front door into the frigid night air, being sure to lock the door behind me. Shivering, I climbed into my car and drove as quickly as I could with one hand over my right eye. The last thing I wanted was to get in an accident.

The store was deserted except for the cashier standing at the register with a bored look on her face and the teenage boy stocking the shelves on the cereal aisle. Elevator music played an easy-listening rendition of "Time of Your Life" by Green Day. I grabbed a handcart and kept my body tense and my head down, trying to appear as sober as possible.

I returned to the front of the store with a liter of merlot, a couple of bottles of cold medicine, and a box of tissues.

"My son has a horrible cold," I said. "Poor thing. My husband is waiting with him in the car."

The cashier eyed the liter of merlot I placed on the turn belt.

Then she looked at me. "I can't sell you the wine. It's the law. No alcohol between two and six a.m."

"Oh," I said, suddenly flustered. I had no idea. "Well, I guess I'll have to pick it up later for my dinner party then. Maybe after work."

The checker nodded, though the look of disgust on her face was obvious enough that even I, in my foggy stupor, didn't miss it. She knew I was a liar. So did I.

I sped home, opened the front door, and saw Charlie hadn't moved from his spot on the couch. Relief washed over me. *See? He didn't even know you were gone.*

I took a couple of hefty swigs of the cold medicine, draining half the bottle. Curling up behind my son, I closed my eyes and felt my remedy gush through my veins. Within minutes, I fell into a deeply medicated, troubled void, barely noticing how easily I'd surrendered my chance to dream.

The blare of my cell phone woke me with a start. I struggled to piece together how I'd ended up on the couch with Charlie, who was lodged against me, out cold. *Wine, store, cold medicine.* I leaned forward and fumbled with the phone, which I had left on the coffee table the night before, having failed to plug it into its charger.

"Hello?" I said. The word came out rough and slow.

"Hi, Cadence. It's Lisa, from the Sunshine House?"

Charlie's preschool. Oh, crap. What time was it? I squinted at the DVD player on the shelf: 9:30. Shit. "Hey, Lisa. God, I'm sorry, I meant to call you. Charlie was up with an upset stomach last night. We must have overslept." The lie slipped out too quickly for me to stop it.

"Oh, I'm sorry to hear that," Lisa said. "Does he have a fever?"

"I'm not sure," I said, reaching my arm out to press my open palm against Charlie's forehead, as though the act would somehow support his feigned illness. He stirred a bit, but didn't wake. "No, he feels okay. Probably just something he ate. I'll have him there in about half an hour, if that's okay."

"Sure. We were just worried about you guys." She paused. "Are *you* all right?"

"Yeah, of course, I'm fine!" I say, maybe a little too brightly. "Why?"

"You sound a little hoarse."

"Just tired, I think," I said, clearing my throat. Which was true. My head throbbed. I needed Advil and I needed it fast. "See you in a few." I hung up with a sigh and shook Charlie awake. "Come on, baby. We need to get you to school."

I managed to get him dressed and out the front door in less than fifteen minutes.

"You forgot to give me breakfast, Mama," Charlie said in the car.

"Shit," I said, reaching over to my purse and rooting around as I drove. My head was heavy and I had to fight to keep my eyes open. I found a slightly squished cereal bar beneath my wallet and handed it back to my son.

"It's all mushy," he said.

"It's all I have," I snapped. I heard the crumpling of the foil wrapper and then immediately felt like crying for yelling at my son.

We pulled up in front of the bright yellow church that was converted ten years earlier into one of the most highly rated north Seattle preschools on record. Charlie raced to the front door and I walked slowly behind him. Lisa's pert, pretty face appeared in the window before she came out to greet us in the hallway.

"Hey, Charlie," she said, mussing his hair with her fingers. "Everyone else is already in circle time. Why don't you go join them?"

I smiled and crouched down, wobbling on the balls of my feet as I did so. "Come give me a hug, baby," I said, and Charlie jumped over to kiss me good-bye. "I'll see you in a few hours."

After Charlie was gone, Lisa looked at me, concerned. "He seems like he's okay," she said, "but I'll call you if he doesn't feel well enough to stay." She paused. "Did he eat?"

"Part of a cereal bar," I said. I clutched my forearm over my stomach, hoping I wouldn't be ill. I needed to leave, anxious to stop at the store and pick up more wine. "He didn't have much of an appetite."

"You don't look like you feel very well, either," Lisa said. Her eyebrows pulled together as she spoke.

I made a half-coughing, half-laughing sound. "I don't, really. I might be coming down with whatever it was he had last night." *Liar*, I thought. *You're just a huge, disgusting liar.*

"Do you want me to call Martin and have him pick up Charlie so you can rest?"

"Oh, no," I protested, waving my hand in front of my face. "I'll be fine. I just need a little sleep."

"Okay," she said, her voice still hesitant. "Call me if you change your mind."

"Thanks." I got in my car, thinking there was no way in hell I wanted Martin to know the shape I was in. I drove to the other side of the freeway to the liquor store, not wanting to return to the market I'd been to the night before, fearful the same checker might still be working her shift. I didn't want to be doing this. A violent war waged between my mind pleading no and my body screaming yes. My body won the battle every time.

Once home, I hurried into the kitchen and uncorked one of the four liters of Spanish merlot I'd bought, explaining to yet another checker about the imaginary dinner party I was hosting that night. I also stashed another gallon of vodka in the freezer, thinking I would leave it there and not touch it unless I ran out of wine. I would never have to leave Charlie alone again.

At the sound of the cork popping out of its tight confines, my mouth moistened. I poured the wine into my coffee mug and took three long, hard swallows, holding my breath until I felt the familiar warmth spread throughout my muscles. Tension unknotted itself in every fiber of my flesh. Thus momentarily relieved, I glided over to the kitchen table and fired up my laptop. I wanted to sleep, but I needed to work.

I opened Google, planning to begin research on the celebrated chef at the Dahlia Lounge. I thought I might be able to sell a quick and dirty profile piece on him to *Seattle Gourmet*. But instead of typing in his name, I found myself typing in the words, "Do I have a problem with alcohol?"

A long list of links popped up, and I clicked on one that indicated it contained a questionnaire. As I sipped tiny, measured amounts from the mug of wine I needed to make last for the next two hours before I went to pick up Charlie from school, I took the quiz.

"Have you ever decided to stop drinking for a week or so, but only lasted for a couple of days?" Yes. More times than I can count.

"Have you ever switched from one kind of drink to another in the hope that this would keep you from getting drunk?" Yes. The previous week I'd decided to only drink beer, reasoning it had a lower alcohol content than wine, and ended up drinking a twelve-pack in a single afternoon.

"Do you tell yourself you can stop drinking any time you want to, even though you keep getting drunk when you don't mean to?" Yes. Over and over again.

When I clicked on the results, it said I had a problem and should consider seeking help. Discomfort snuck its way back into my body with every breath. I took the test again, switching my answers around, trying to make the computer prove there was nothing wrong with me. But no matter the answers I selected, no matter the number of times I tried, the results were clear. I didn't understand how this could be. I wasn't a partier—I didn't drink in high school or college. Why was this happening to me now?

Staring at my hand wrapped around a coffee mug filled with wine, I felt utterly detached. I thought that particular appendage might belong to someone else. This couldn't actually be me, sitting here drinking at 10:30 in the morning. This wasn't me, a woman who left her child alone in the house.

Stop it, I thought. But then my arm lifted and before my mind could protest, the wine was on its way down.

Later that day, after picking Charlie up from school, I leaned against the counter in my tiny kitchen, bottle of merlot in my grasp. My son stood in the arched doorway, his almond-shaped eyes growing wide as he watched the scarlet fluid flow into my favorite moss green coffee mug. I tensed the muscles in my arms to control the tremors. I didn't want Charlie to see me spill.

"That's not coffee, Mama," he said, hugging his worn, blue baby blanket tighter to his chest.

I averted my eyes from my child and gulped down two long swallows. It only took a moment for that familiar feeling to wash over me, like hot honey pushing through my veins. I closed my eyes, trying to hold on to it, knowing it would not stay.

"Want to watch TV?" I asked with a watered-down smile. We did this too often, lying on the couch with the curtains pulled, me drinking, my son entranced by cartoons.

"Okay," he said. He turned around and padded into our living room. Charlie crawled up onto the couch and patted the cushion next to him. "Here, Mama. You sit next to me."

"Where else would I sit, baby?" I asked, taking another pull on my wine. I took lurching, unsteady steps out of the kitchen and over to the front door, making sure the stainless-steel chain that Charlie couldn't reach was secured. That way, in case I passed out, he couldn't wander outside.

Dropping to the couch, I snuggled Charlie against me with one arm and gripped my drink at the end of the other. Already a seasoned pro at getting electronics to do as he commanded, he turned on the TV. The racket of banging and whistling side effects filled the room and my son settled back comfortably into the crook of my arm.

I closed my eyes. *Only for a while,* I thought. *Only until he wakes up all the way. Then we'll go to the store. Or the park.* My breath came in short, cutting bursts, so I took another swallow, knowing the wine would slow my galloping pulse.

I pushed myself forward and filled my cup again. My son was watching an infomercial on some sort of kitchen gadget. "You want cartoons instead, sweetie?" A part of me knew I was slurring, but I told myself Charlie wouldn't notice. He had a bit of a lisp himself.

"Yes, please," he said. His eyelids were heavy. So were mine. I switched to the Cartoon Network and turned the volume down. I snuggled us beneath a blanket, my legs outstretched onto the coffee table. My eyes closed. *Just a few minutes,* I thought. *Just a few minutes to rest.*

"We'll go to the park later," Charlie said, making a statement rather than asking me a question. "You'll take me later."

Violent guilt stormed inside me. The alcohol dilated my usually watertight emotions and opened a floodgate of tears. My child knew full well we would stay in the house with the blinds closed. I'd broken enough promises to him for him to know the truth.

Feeling my sobs, Charlie twisted around to look up at me, worry etched his fine features. He brushed the damp curls away from my face.

"What's wrong, Mama?" he asked, resting one pudgy, moist palm on my cheek. "Did you have a bad dream?"

"I'm just so sad, honey," I said, weeping. "Very, very sad."

He used the silky edge of his blanket to wipe my face. "Don't cry," he said. "It's okay. Don't cry. I will take care of you."

His words only made me cry more. It was not his job to comfort me. A mother should protect, not fall apart. I hated what I'd done; I hated who I was. I wasn't sure I could do it anymore. So I did the only thing I knew would erase how I felt—I opened another bottle of wine.

I didn't take Charlie to school the next morning. I was much too drunk to drive and I knew it. I could barely stay conscious. I lay on the couch, knocking back a swallow of wine every time I came to enough to lift the bottle to my mouth. I told myself to stop, but felt powerless against the compulsion. My hand reached out like it was under someone else's command.

Charlie sat with me, watching TV. But the next time I struggled awake, he was gone.

"Charlie?" I called out, my tongue thick and unmanageable in my mouth. "Where are you, baby?"

"In the kitchen, Mommy," he said. A few seconds later he was standing next to me. I peeled a single eye open and saw he had a yogurt in his hands. What time was it? When was the last time I'd fed him? My vision was too blurry to see the glowing blue digital numbers on the DVD player's clock. I wasn't sure if it was day or night.

Charlie touched my face. "Are you okay, Mommy?" he asked. "Please wake up."

I fell back into oblivion. My cell rang several times, but the sound was muted, as though traveling through water. My body was leaden, weighted to the couch; I couldn't have stood up to answer the phone if I'd tried.

More time passed, and then, suddenly, there was a pounding at the door. "Cadence?" Martin said. He knocked again. I couldn't move. I couldn't think.

"Daddy!" Charlie cried. "Mommy's sick."

"Go to the back door, Charlie," Martin's voice instructed. "Can you unlock it and let Daddy in?"

No, I thought, struggling to convince my body to wake up. It would not cooperate. My eyes refused to open. I floated in and out of awareness, trying to balance on the slippery edges of unconsciousness.

I heard the back door squeak on its hinges. The sound of footsteps. Martin's hand on my shoulder, shaking me. "Cadence, I'm taking Charlie with me," he said. "I'm going to pack a bag and bring him to my house." His words were muffled, but I could still detect his disgust. It soaked through my skin and melded with my own.

I still couldn't open my eyes. The front door slammed shut and I drifted back into the dark, far, far away from the truth.

Several hours later, I awoke with a start, my heartbeat chugging in my chest like a freight train. I groped for the bottle of wine on the table, opening my eyes just long enough to see it was empty. *Kitchen,* I thought. *More in the kitchen.*

I rolled onto the floor and crawled into the kitchen, pulling myself up to the table where there was another liter of merlot. The last liter. If that didn't do it, the vodka in the freezer would.

Charlie. The thought of my son pummeled me, and it all came rushing back. Martin, pounding on the door. Taking Charlie away.

"No," I creaked. "No, no, no." *Oh God, he'd taken my son.* What was I going to do? I had to call Martin. I had to make this right.

It took me three tries to get his number punched into my cell phone correctly. It rang once, then went straight to voicemail. "Martin," I said, trying to make my voice sound as calm as possible. "I took a medication that reacted with a glass of wine. That's why I was on the couch." My words were soupy and loose. I could barely understand them myself. "Please. Bring Charlie home." I hung up, knowing he would not call me back, knowing I was a liar.

Oh dear God, what had I done? I can't do this anymore. I can't live in a world where I've hurt my child. He deserves better than this. He deserves better than me.

With my hand around the neck of the bottle before me, my gaze moved to the counter where the bottle of Advil sat. I wondered how many it would take to end this. To end me.

The shrill of my cell phone made me jump. I grabbed it and answered, thinking that against the odds Martin might be calling.

"Cadence?" It was Jess. "Are you okay? Martin called me and said he had to come get Charlie."

I began to sob, in huge, body-racking movements. "He took him, Jess. He's gone. How did he know? How did Martin find out?"

"The preschool called him when you didn't show up with Charlie." She sighed. "What are you *doing*, Cadence? What the hell is going on?"

"I'm looking at a bottle of pills," I said in a sudden wash of calm. What I needed to do was clear. "And a glass of Spanish merlot."

"Cadence, don't you dare," my sister yelled into the phone. "Don't you fucking dare! I'm on my way over, do you hear me? I'm on my way right now."

I sat numbly, waiting with my hand on the glass, floating in and out of awareness. Before I knew it, my sister was through the back door. "Did you take anything?" she asked, snatching both the bottle and the glass of wine and pouring the contents down the kitchen sink.

"No," I said, weeping.

"Where's the rest?" she demanded, grabbing my chin and making me look at her.

"What?" I asked, blinking heavily.

"The rest of the alcohol, Cadee. Where is it?"

"Vodka. In the freezer."

She let go of my chin and strode over to the refrigerator, slinging open the freezer door. She rooted around for a minute, then pulled out the gallon of icy, clear booze. It went down the sink, just like the wine. "Is that it?" she asked.

"Yes."

She stormed down the hallway, then returned with a bag stuffed with a wad of my clothes. "Here," she said, throwing a pair of flip-flops next to my feet. I slipped them on.

Wrapping my arm over her shoulders, she half dragged, half carried me to her car.

"I'm sorry," I said as I climbed into the passenger seat. "I'm so, so sorry."

Her expression morphed into a strange mix of sadness and fear, but she didn't respond. She slammed my door shut, raced around the front of her car, and hopped behind the wheel.

"Where are you taking me?" I asked.

"The hospital," she said. She didn't talk to me about my drinking. She didn't say she knew why Martin took Charlie away. All she said was, "You're going to be fine." Over and over she repeated this to me as I rocked back and forth in the leather front seat of her Lincoln SUV, my heart racing, sobs shredding every breath.

"This is not me," I whispered through the tears, "this is not who I am."

"Yes," my sister said. "It is."

Nine

The emergency room at the University of Washington Hospital was a surprisingly busy place the late-January night I won the staredown with that bottle of pills. It took almost an hour for a nurse to get to us, and when she finally did, Jess ended up answering most of her questions. It had been several hours since I'd taken a drink, but I was still pretty looped. The nurse gave me a dose of something called Librium, which she told Jess would help calm my anxiety. I told her I was pretty confident I'd need more than a single dose.

"Someone will be here to take her up to the fourth floor soon," the nurse said, ignoring my comment. "You can wait with her here, but you can't go upstairs."

"They're coming to take me away, ha ha," I murmured. "To the funny farm, where life is beautiful all the time . . ."

"Shh," Jess said. She pushed my hair back from my face. Her blue eyes shone. When she blinked, a plump, perfectly formed tear rolled down her cheek. As the intern arrived to wheel me to the psych ward, Jess cupped my face in her hands and kissed my forehead. "Please, Cadence. Please. Get better."

"Okay," I said, closing my eyes. I didn't know how that was possible. My drinking was out of control. Martin took Charlie. Sorrow spiraled into my bones like a thousand tiny metal screws. It was agonizing. Any movement made me want to cry out. *Save me, please. Please, please, make this pain go away.*

Once upstairs, I lay on the gurney in a hallway because the room they said was open was still being cleaned after the last patient had used it. *What happened to that patient?* I wondered. *Did she get well? Do crazy people suddenly become sane? Am I crazy?*

A tall, adolescent-looking doctor came to stand next to me, a clipboard in hand. "Hello, Cadence. I'm Dr. Wright."

"You barely look old enough to drink," I said. Though I had begun to sober up, I was still rummy and slurring my words. "Are you sure you're a doctor?"

"I'm a third-year psychiatric resident. So yes, I'm a doctor. I'm going to ask you a few questions, if that's all right with you."

"Fine." I felt deflated. Empty. My entire body was numb. *Who cares if this man was a child. What difference does it make? It doesn't matter. Nothing matters. Charlie is gone.*

"Okay, great. Can you tell me why you're here?"

"I drank too much."

"What's 'too much'?"

"A couple of bottles of wine a day."

"How long have you been drinking that heavily?"

"Heavily?" I felt vaguely stupid for repeating the word, but my thoughts were clouded. I was having a difficult time getting my brain to function the way I wanted it to. "About a year, I think."

"And before that? How much did you drink?"

I sighed. "I'm not sure. It sort of snuck up on me."

"Snuck up?"

"Well, yes. It's not like I sat down one night and decided that downing two bottles of wine was a brilliant idea."

The corners of his mouth turned up the slightest bit, as though he wasn't sure if it was proper etiquette to find a psychiatric patient's sarcasm amusing. "Why don't you tell me how it started, then?"

I rolled my head to the side and stared at the wall. It wasn't hard to remember the beginning, when sipping a glass of wine seemed an innocent enough thing to do.

"It was about two years ago," I told the doctor, closing my eyes. "Right after my husband moved out. I couldn't sleep. A friend of mine suggested that a glass of red wine before bed would help relax me." I pictured those words escaping Susanne's red lips. "She said it was good for my heart, too."

"I see," Dr. Wright said. "When did it develop into more than a single glass?"

"I don't really know."

"So, let me get this straight," he said. "You've been drinking heavily on a daily basis for *two* years, then, not one?"

"No." I sighed again. I didn't want to talk anymore, but felt compelled to make sure I didn't come off sounding like a bigger lush than I appeared. "I wasn't drinking *every day* until the last year or so. But it all *started* two years ago with a couple of glasses a week. Only when I couldn't sleep."

I tried to pinpoint the moment I crossed over from wanting a drink to needing one, but couldn't come up with it. My descent was more of a gradual, subtle spiral. I didn't even feel myself falling while it happened. At first, one glass was all it took. One drink shaved just enough of the edge off my tension for me to function. When one stopped working, I'd pour just a splash or two more, until one glass turned into two. Then three. By the time I realized how bad it was, I couldn't stop. How could I explain to this doctor what led me to this point when I barely understood it myself?

"Why do you think you drink?" he asked.

That's the million-dollar question, I wanted to say. *If I knew why, I wouldn't be here.*

"I don't know," I said instead. "I can't stop. I wake up every morning and tell myself I won't drink. And then I do. Something is *wrong* with me." *I'm nuts. That's what's wrong. I'm completely out of my mind.*

My grandmother was crazy, and so am I. Tears seeped out of the corners of my eyes and trickled into my ears. I didn't bother to wipe them away.

"Is alcohol all you had tonight? Did you take anything else?"

I shook my head. I heard him scribbling. Jess already told the nurse in the emergency room about the bottle of pills, so I'm sure Dr. Doogie already knew. "I thought about it, though."

"Thought about what?"

"Taking pills."

"What kind?"

"The kind I wouldn't wake up from."

More scribbling. "Is there any chance you might be pregnant?"

"None."

"What about sexually transmitted diseases? Have you engaged in unsafe sex practices?"

God. How humiliating. I already feel like I've been put through a meat grinder. What's next, a pap smear? This child doctor has probably seen fewer vaginas than me.

"I haven't engaged in any kind of sex practices." I couldn't remember the last time Martin and I made love before the divorce. The thought of getting to know another man well enough to let him see me naked was too exhausting to fathom. For the most part, my body seemed to have forgotten what desire felt like.

"We'll run some tests on the blood samples you gave downstairs, just in case."

"Okay." I didn't care. Whatever. Let him think I'm a drunk slut. In his mind, the two probably go hand in hand.

"Do you still want to harm yourself?" he asked.

My throat swelled at the kindness in his voice, but still, he didn't get it. I felt no real desire for death. No part of me said, *Now suicide, there's a good idea.* I longed only for an absence of anguish, an end to self-loathing. Death seemed the only viable method of reaching this goal. At that point, it seemed reasonable. I only wanted the pain to end. *Just stop,* most people would say. *You hate drinking. Just make the decision and stop.* If it were that easy, I would have done it.

"No, I don't want to hurt myself," I told him. "But can you fix me?"

He gave me an accommodating smile. "Let's help you fix yourself." He fed me a pill he said would help me sleep. I swallowed it greedily. Anything for oblivion.

The next day, I woke up more hungover than usual. It took me a minute or two to realize where I was.

Oh, right.

Wine, pills, hospital.

Charlie.

Gone.

Each word was a sledgehammer to my chest. I felt disoriented from the medication they had given me in the middle of the night, which I vaguely remembered the nurse telling me would prevent a heart attack or convulsions due to alcohol withdrawal. I rolled out of bed and stumbled to the bathroom. I didn't recognize the person in the mirror. My hair was a rat's nest. I was swollen and disheveled. My eyes were empty.

"This is not me," I whispered again, as I had in Jess's car. "This is not who I am." *Who was I, then?* If not Martin's wife or Charlie's mother? Was there anything left about me worth saving?

I began to sob, a kind of heart-racking, body-bending hysterics I'd rarely given in to before. I cried for my son, for what I'd put him through. I cried for myself, for being so inept that I couldn't get myself to stop drinking. I was an idiot—a weak, immoral creature. I wept for the humiliation of getting caught. *How can I face this? How can I function in a world where I allowed this to happen? What will people say? How will I survive it? What kind of person am I?*

And then, the two-by-four to my head: *What have I done to my son?*

At this point a nurse came into my room and told me breakfast was being served down the hall. After a few more shuddering breaths, I clamped the sobs down as best I could, wiped my eyes with a tissue, and splashed cold water on my face. I didn't know what else to do. I wasn't hungry but I went anyway. I moved as though someone had poured cement into every cell of my body. I went through the rote motions of putting on a pair of sweatpants and a T-shirt Jess had packed, brushing my teeth, and stepping into the hall. Other patients moved with the same laborious effort I felt. There were about ten of us and we sat at rectangular tables in a small cafeteria, not speaking. I stared at the dry lump of scrambled eggs and limp, greasy bacon in front of me. My stomach was tied in too many knots to eat. I sipped at a cup of pale coffee. It tasted like watered-down dirt. I drank it anyway.

"You new?" a woman sitting across from me finally asked. Her hair was stringy and gray, matted flat on one side of her head.

I nodded.

"You a drunk?"

I flashed her a strange look and gave my head a quick shake.

She smiled, showing me a crooked row of yellowed teeth. "Ha. Takes one to know one."

I shuddered inside, my stomach clenching even tighter in on itself. *I am not her. I am not her.*

After breakfast I moved into another room, where other patients sat staring at an older console television which didn't appear to be on. I sat in a corner by the windows at a table strewn with stacks of paper. Upon further investigation, I realized they were all photocopied pages from artistic coloring books. Not Scooby-Doo or Strawberry Shortcake, but rather intricate prints of animals and other scenes from nature. A mountain backdropped by a thin-striped sunset, a lionfish etched with a wild zigzag pattern. I selected a drawing of a leopard, picked up a colored pencil, and began to fill in the spots. I placed all my focus on the pencil to the page. I didn't look up when another person sat down and tried to talk to me. I couldn't respond. I was busy coloring. I filled in each exquisitely tiny space of the leopard, shading each detail as delicately as possible. When I was done with that picture, I picked up another. And then another when I was done with that. As long as I was coloring, I didn't think about anything else.

I couldn't allow myself to think about Charlie for more than half a breath. The hurt was too great, the guilt too debilitating. My heart, my brain, my body couldn't process it. I tried not to think about what he was feeling. It was too much to endure, imagining him crying for me, wanting to know where I was. I considered calling him, but the simple thought of his sweet voice in my ear brought on another onslaught of uncontrollable tears. I wouldn't be able to hold it together while I talked to him. I didn't want to scare him with my hysteria. I didn't want him to think I wasn't getting well.

Moment by moment, I lost myself in the pressure of the pencil on the paper and the careful selection of which shade would best suit the picture I had in front of me. Then the thought of him would come again—*Charlie, gone*—and my heart instantly shattered. There is a place beyond grief, a place where pain hardens into paralysis. This was where I dwelled.

When I finished with the fifth picture several hours later, I sat back. *This is what I've been reduced to,* I thought. *A nut job on a psych ward, coloring away like a child. Like my life depended on it.*

Maybe it did.

I didn't go to lunch, but when the nurse came to get me, she insisted I follow her to the head psychiatrist's office. "He's expecting you," she said.

I entered a small, windowless room where the doctor was waiting. He was older, white-haired, and solid. He reminded me of Marcus Welby, M.D. After my encounter with the child doctor from the night before, I found his appearance comforting.

"Hello, Cadence," he said. "I'm Dr. Fisher. Please, have a seat."

I did as he asked, dropping into the hard, plastic chair on the opposite side of his desk. I wrapped my arms tightly across my upper body, rubbing my hands up and down the outside of my biceps.

"I understand you had a rough night."

I shrugged. I was still numb. I still felt like I didn't have the right to breathe. I stared at the floor.

"We're here to help you, Cadence. We have you on medications that will keep your alcohol withdrawal to a minimum. It can be very dangerous. Much of the reason you felt compelled to drink was physical. The craving was like an ache, wasn't it? A deep, burning ache?"

I dropped my arms to hang loose at my sides and slowly raised my eyes to look at him. "Yes. In the last six months or so, especially. When I tried to stop, my heart felt like it would explode right out of my chest. It was like my body would break wide open or turn inside out if I didn't give it what it wanted."

He nodded. "It was good that you did, then, to some extent. At least last night. People go into cardiac arrest from withdrawal every day. We'll help you get through the physical part of things safely. Then we can figure out the right treatment recommendations for you outside of the hospital."

"What kind of treatment?"

"For alcoholism."

It was the first time someone used that word in reference to me. I didn't feel up to arguing with him. I didn't feel up to anything. I felt as though the real me was floating near the ceiling, watching this strange conversation unfold. Like all of this was happening to another person.

"I can't just get what I need here?" I inquired.

He smiled and pushed his glasses back up the bridge of his nose. "You won't be here more than a couple of weeks for detox. We just get you stabilized. Treatment requires more time than that."

"How much time?" My voice was flat. I had no strength to fight him.

"In-patient programs are typically twenty-eight days. I'm going to recommend that for you." He glanced at a file lying in front of him on his desk. "I'm also going to put you on an antidepressant regimen."

"Why?"

"Because depression and alcoholism go hand in hand. People drink too much as a way to medicate their emotional pain. Some people overspend, some people smoke or eat or work seventy hours a week. You drank. Different behaviors, the same compulsion." He gave me a kind smile. "People who drink just have a harder time hiding the results."

His answer struck me mute. It was as though I was no longer human, but instead a mass of diagnostic labels: suicidal, depressive, *alcoholic.* I'd only ever been labeled as driven, goal-oriented, or successful. The discordance between these two descriptions was far too broad to comprehend them as both being part of who I was. It made me feel crazier than I suspected I already was.

"In the meantime," he went on, "you'll follow the daily routine here. You'll rest, and let your body start to heal."

What about my heart? I wanted to ask. *Can you heal that, too?*

"You also should call CPS," he said.

"CPS?" I repeated dumbly.

"Child Protective Services."

"I know what it is, I just don't know why you think I need to call them." My stomach threatened to heave its bitter liquid contents.

He paused to flip through what I assumed was my file, running the tip of his index finger up and down the pages until he found what he was looking for. "Ah, here it is. You told the intake physician that you left Charlie alone in the house one night to go purchase more alcohol?"

I'd said that out loud? I didn't remember the words leaving my mouth. I nodded once, tightly pressing my lips together to keep from crying.

"That's something we're required to report. But I think you should do it."

I shook my head in a brisk motion. "I can't."

He leaned forward and set the file down, resting his forearms on his desk. "You can. And you should. It's better if you self-report."

"Better how?" I couldn't fathom making this call. I couldn't fathom that any of this was happening at all.

"In case anything legal comes up, your calling is taking responsibility for the action."

"What do you mean, legal?" I asked, my blood pressure rising.

"Let's not worry about that now." He reached for the phone on his desk and punched in a number before handing me the receiver. "Here, I'll sit with you while you do it, okay?"

I put the phone to my ear and waited for someone to answer. When the operator directed me to the right department, I held the receiver back toward the doctor. "I can't do this."

He nodded and gently pushed the phone back at me. "Yes, you can."

I took a deep breath and spoke to the voice saying "Hello? Can I help you?" on the other end of the line.

"My name is Cadence Sutter," I began shakily, "and I need to . . . I want to let you know . . ." I looked at the doctor and he nodded encouragingly.

"You want to let me know what?" the man on the other end of the phone asked.

"I left my son alone in our house in the middle of the night so I could go buy wine." The words came out in a rush, tripping over one another.

"And how old is your son?"

I squeezed my eyes shut and a few tears made their way down my cheeks. "He's five." A sob tore at my chest. "Oh God, he's only five."

The caseworker took down the details of the night I left Charlie and I cried while he told me the incident would become a part of my permanent record.

I stumbled my way numbly through the next week. I talked to as few people as possible, choosing instead to sit alone at the table in what I learned was called the community room. I colored through my days. I spoke when spoken to, answered Dr. Fisher's questions in low, monosyllabic phrases. I took the pills the nurses gave me. The pills made me sleepy, so I slept. A lot. It was the easiest way to pass the days. Every time I woke, I slowly rose into the consciousness of where I was and what I'd done. It instantly felt like a huge boulder was sitting on my chest.

Wine, pills, hospital.

Charlie.

Gone.

When I thought about my son, my breathing became shallow and sharp. My insides hemorrhaged despair—it oozed through my body like hot, black tar. I found escape from this thought only through coloring, the focus on the pencil to the page. It was the only thing I could do.

"Your son will love these," a nurse said one afternoon as she looked over my shoulder at the picture I was working on.

My throat suddenly closed and my eyes blurred. I shook my head. I wasn't coloring these for him. I could barely allow myself to even *think* about him. I couldn't. It hurt too much. I knew he was okay; he was with his father. Still, anxiety swarmed through my flesh like a regiment of fire ants. I would have done anything to exterminate how I felt.

Another patient chose that moment to snap the television on in the other corner of the room. *Clifford the Big Red Dog* flashed onto the screen. The sight of the cartoon Charlie loved was too much for me. The sobs took over again.

This is how my time in the hospital was spent. Coloring and crying. Crying and coloring. Besides sleeping, it was all I could do. I lost track of what day it was. I didn't care. I hurt my son. I lost him. Nothing mattered but getting out of here and making everything right.

During my second week in the hospital, I finally brought myself to turn on my cell phone and check for messages. There were two from Jess, the first seeing how I was and the second to let me know that she had spoken to Charlie and he was doing fine with Martin. He missed me, but understood I was "sick" and in the hospital so the doctors could help me get well. The third was from a number I didn't recognize. As soon as I heard the voice, though, I knew who it was: Martin's divorce lawyer.

"Cadence? It's Steven O'Reilly. Martin tells me he has some serious concerns about your ability to take care of Charlie. He told me you've been drinking and things got bad enough that he had to come remove Charlie from your home."

My pulse began to ricochet through my veins. *Oh God. Oh God oh God oh God.*

"Martin has spoken to Child Protective Services and they've informed him you're on record putting Charlie's life in danger. He's filing for full custody and I've submitted the necessary paperwork to grant Martin temporary guardianship while you're incarcerated in the hospital. I certainly hope what Martin told me about what you've been doing is wrong, but if it's not, you're going to want to contact a lawyer at your earliest convenience."

"No!" I howled. I threw the phone across the room and it smashed against the wall. I grabbed the sides of my face with my fingers. My nails raked my skin as I dropped to my knees on the cold linoleum. The pain I felt was bigger than my body, bigger than the entire room. It pressed down on me and threatened to smother my every breath. A nurse rushed into my room.

"What is it, Cadence?" she asked, trying to wrap her arm around my shoulder.

I jerked away from her touch and fell to the floor, shrieking, "No!" over and over again. *He can't take Charlie. I won't let him. I'll die first.* My body longed to shed its skin and move on to being another person altogether. A person who didn't get drunk in front of her son.

The nurse pressed the red button by the side of my bed and a moment later, there was a rush of bodies around me and I felt myself lifted by strong arms into my bed. Next came the sharp sting of a needle in my arm. It took less than a minute for the drug to take effect, and I drifted off into restless sleep, only to wake a few hours later to cry again. *What have I done? What have I done?* This phrase played over and over in my mind. *Martin took Charlie. I've lost my child and I'm not going to get him back.*

I sunk down into that hospital bed and stayed there for two days, pinned down by agony. I wept. I didn't want to be here. I didn't deserve to have Charlie as my son. Not with what I'd done. Nurses checked on me every few hours and gave me the pills they said I needed to keep taking. I swallowed them, knowing they would let me sleep, the only kind of escape I had left. The nurses tried to lull me out of bed with promises of relief to be found in group therapy, yoga, and meditative walks. I shook my head and refused to budge. Finally, Dr. Fisher sat on the edge of my bed and set a warm hand on my shoulder.

"Cadence. You need to get up."

"No."

"If you don't get up for you, get up for Charlie."

I started to sob again at the sound of my son's name. Picturing his face brought on a tangible sensation of razor blades sliding across my skin. "I can't believe what I've done," I cried. "How did I let things get this bad?"

He moved his hand up and down my arm in a soothing motion. "I know it's hard. But if you don't get out of bed, what are you going to teach your son?"

"My ex-husband took him," I said, sobbing. "He's not even mine anymore."

"Of course he's yours."

I shook my head into the pillow. *He didn't know. How could he know? Had someone taken his son away?* "I don't want to be here. I don't want to do this anymore. I can't. I just can't. It hurts too much."

"I know it hurts. But if you give up, if you decide to kill yourself, Charlie won't have a mother at all. Not even a part-time one."

I paused, my tears finally slowing. Dr. Fisher squatted down next to me, his next words whispered right into my ear.

"Do you know what else might happen to him?"

I shook my head, rubbing my wet face into the pillow, knowing I did not want to hear what he might have to say.

"It's possible he'll kill himself, too. Studies have shown us that a child whose parent commits suicide is twice as likely to commit suicide themselves. Do you want that, Cadence? Do you want Charlie to someday swallow pills or shoot himself in the head because you couldn't find a way to step up and face your problems? Is this what you want to teach him to do when he can't handle his?"

For the first time in two days, I made eye contact with another person. Dr. Fisher had a sweet, round face; his eyes were gentle. I must have looked like a train wreck.

"Is that true?" I asked.

He nodded.

I got out of bed.

Ten

In the middle of February, when I first arrived at Promises Treatment Center—fresh from the psych ward and detox—I was surprised to find a three-story, nondescript steel gray Colonial-style house in an area of Bellevue where many homes have been converted into businesses. Promises' aged cedar siding was cracked in a few spots and the landscaping consisted of a yellow-lined parking lot and several groupings of slightly bent rhododendron bushes. The building wasn't broken down, but its weathered appearance did little to foster a sense of confidence in the establishment's healing capabilities. I voiced as much to Jess, who drove me there.

"It looks fine," she said. "And it's the only one your insurance completely covers." Her voice was uncharacteristically thin. It practically wavered. She was tired. Exhausted of me, I supposed, of the situation. She was the one who called all the available treatment facilities while I was on suicide watch on the psych ward. She was the one who agreed with Dr. Fisher that I should spend twenty-eight days as an in-patient at Promises. She further committed me to another six months of continuing care, during which time I would attend a weekly group session, as well as an individual meeting with a counselor twice a month. Jess picked up my mail and fielded furious calls from Martin. She relayed the details of what was going on with me to my mother. I still hoped I might wake up any moment from this nightmare. That none of this was real. Maybe I was playing a part—the alcohol-numbed woman stumbling her way into treatment. I could be a goddamn Lifetime movie of the week.

"Where's the Zen garden?" I asked. "I imagined sitting in a Zen garden while I pondered the recesses of my fucked-up soul." Sarcasm became a tic for me when I got nervous—worse than an eye twitch and just as impossible to control.

Jess sighed. "You can ponder your fucked-up soul among the rhododendrons."

"I don't know," I mused. "I was hoping for a little pizzazz. A welcome wagon of a massage therapist and personal dietician, at least."

"Let's go," Jess said. I went, unable to put off the inevitable.

I soon learned that Promises' understated front was for discretion's sake; rare is the woman who wants to be walking into an establishment which boldly proclaimed FORMERLY DRUNK WOMEN ENTER HERE! in neon lights. It was designed so she could be going in to see a dentist or get a massage. No one would be the wiser.

But now, two months later on the Monday morning after I'd dropped off Charlie with Martin, I arrived for my continuing care group session with Andi and three other formerly drunk women already a little irritated, so the vision of Promises' decidedly dowdy exterior serves only to irk me further. It is a drizzly, cold day—Lake Washington a perfect gray reflection of the angry, cloud-laden sky. Traffic had been a bitch over the 520 bridge; wet roads render a large portion of Seattleites into inattentive idiots behind the wheel. You'd think the opposite would be true. You'd think they'd be used to it, seasoned veterans made into stronger, better drivers in the rain. You'd think this, yes. But you'd be wrong.

"Hey," I say to Promises' daytime receptionist, Lily, as I walk in through the front door.

Lily looks up from her flat-screen computer. Her station is a delicate, scrolled maple desk in the entryway to what I assume was originally a living room, but now serves as a waiting area. It's painted a peaceful sage green and filled with three overstuffed couches and muted lighting. Tinkling piano music plays softly in the background and a tabletop river stone fountain sits over in the corner of the room. I imagine the space saying, "Hello, welcome! Please, sit comfortably while you prepare to visit your drug- and/or alcohol-addled loved one. . . ."

Lily is a young slip of a girl, twenty-one if she is a day, with a mass of blond poodle curls and watery, pale blue eyes. "Hi, Cadence," she says, blinking rapidly. She is polite, well-trained.

"Anyone else here yet?"

She nods, her curls bouncing like a clown's wig. "Serena's here, and Madeline. A new gal, too. She's meeting with Andi before group starts."

"Thanks." I step down a long, narrow hallway, past the poster-covered walls. "Let Go and Let God" one proclaims; "One Day at a Time" says another. I grimace a bit, still, at these phrases. They seem trite, as though a mess as complicated as my life could possibly be rebuilt through tiny, ineffectual sentence structures. To my left is the large, sunny yellow kitchen and dining area; to my right, behind the waiting area, the four small offices shared by the staff. At the end of the hall is a stairway leading to the third floor, where the twenty or so in-patient residents stay, grouped together in five rooms sleeping four each, complete with knotty pine bunk beds and two large community bathrooms.

I head downstairs to the group rooms and enter quietly.

"One day at a time, my sweet brown ass!" I hear Serena exclaim as I step through the door. She snorts. "More like one breath!" She is a short, pretty black woman with an intricate configuration of dark, shoulder-length braids hanging in shiny, thin ropes about her face, swinging around like jungle vines. She appears slightly coltish beneath her cinnamon skin, all joints and smooth muscles, with a complexion marred by nothing but disappointment in how her life has worked out so far. She manages a small downtown cafe that provides the kind of insurance that covers her trips to treatment. This one will stick, she is convinced. It has to. She looks up, sees me, dark eyes bright, and gives me a huge, white-toothed smile. "Hey, girl!"

"Hey." I smile, move to sit in the chair over by the window, facing the door. I drop my purse to the floor, release a deep sigh. I glance at Madeline. "Hey."

"Hi." Madeline smiles at me, a small movement, barely an up-turned lip. She is a whisper of a person, the pretty, platinum blond, stay-at-home wife of a high-powered defense attorney. Her haircut probably cost more than my entire outfit. Her parents were both raging socialite booze hounds, so part of me wonders if by being here, she is simply keeping up a family tradition, her drunkenness an act born out of sheer boredom—rehab as recreation. She came to Promises about three weeks after I did, and joined the aftercare group just last week. Her fragility makes me feel awkward, like one wrong move, one swift step in the wrong direction, would crush her.

Serena screws up her lips, pushing them toward her nose. "What's wrong with you?"

I shrug. "Nothing. Traffic, I guess. Bunch of morons out there."

"No shit." She pauses. "Hey, now. Wait. *I'm* one of those morons!" She cackles at her own joke, then jumps up, stepping over to stand in front of me. She holds out her arms, bending the tips of her fingers back at herself, beckoning. "Get up."

I look at her warily.

She throws her head to her shoulder and lets loose an exagger-ated sigh. "Get *up*." As the resident recovery veteran, Serena has taken it upon herself to guide me through the appropriate behaviors. You come to a group session, you let people hug you. They do this at AA meetings, too. Being hugged by strangers is one of the things I have had to force myself to learn to tolerate, like a child forced to swallow broccoli. I stand and let Serena embrace me, knowing that, much like with my sister, it's useless to argue with her. She'd likely kick my ass if I don't acquiesce. She pats my back hard with open palms, squeezes me tight. "There. That better?"

I sit back down. "Yes." I smile again, realizing this is a little bit true. Her hug was fierce—there is no denying the loving intent behind it.

Serena moves to stand in front of Madeline, who looks up at her like a mouse trapped by a cat. "How about you, lady? You need another?"

Madeline blinks, gives her head a quick shake. "No, thank you. I'm still a little bruised from the first one."

Serena's head snaps back with her laughter. "Damn, girl. You'd never know you've got a mouth on you from the way you look." She plops back down in her seat.

Madeline leans forward a bit, adjusting her crisp, white linen blouse over her jeans. "How do I look, exactly?"

"Like if I shoved coal up your ass, you'd turn around and squeeze out diamonds." She laughs again at the look of horror on Madeline's face. "What? You need to relax, girl, I'm serious. You're gonna be back poppin' those happy pills and sucking down classy white wine spritzers like Kool-Aid before you know it if you don't start laughin' at your damn self."

"And you've done so well, this being your fourth time here," Madeline says beneath her breath, but loud enough for Serena to hear.

To her credit, Serena hoots at this statement. "There's that mouth, again. You are *definitely* one of us."

Andi chooses this moment to swish into the room. She is wearing one of her trademark broomstick skirts, this one a slightly metallic, coppery brown, paired with a chunky, black cowl-neck sweater. She is a heavy woman and her fleshy exterior somehow looks inviting, like something soft and wonderful you'd want to curl up with beneath a blanket. She smells of lavender and her dark hair is pulled into a simple ponytail at the base of her neck, showing off dangling dreamcatcher earrings against her warm brown skin. "Hello, ladies," she says, moving to the side in order to lead another woman in the room after her. "I'd like you to meet Kristin. She'll be joining our group."

Kristin gives a small wave. She is tall, five ten or so, and her body belongs on a runway, not in the basement of a treatment center. Her pale face is all angles, framed by wispy brown strands of hair falling from what I imagine was meant to be a French twist. She might be pretty, but it's difficult to tell; her eyes are puffy and red-rimmed, as though she recently cried her makeup away. She stands with one arm across her belly, clutching her opposite elbow with a bony hand.

We all greet her and watch as she scans for a place to sit. She settles in a chair farthest from me, closest to the door, as though she is contemplating making a run for it. Andi drops into her seat next to me.

"How is everyone?" she asks. "How was your weekend?"

"Where's Laura?" I ask, ignoring her question. "She's usually the first one here." I am anxious to see her after our conversation yesterday morning at my sister's house. I didn't call her later in the evening, as I intended. I simply forgot. *It's no wonder I don't have many friends,* I thought. *I'd have to be a friend to have one.*

"I'm not sure," Andi says. "I haven't heard anything."

"I'm not sure if I'm supposed to tell you this," I say, "but she wasn't sick last week. Her mom lied to you. She relapsed."

"Damn," Serena says, slowly shaking her head back and forth.

Andi sits forward in her seat, looks at me intently. "How do you know this?"

"She called me yesterday when I was at my sister's house," I say. "She was upset. She said she felt like using again. She told me she relapsed and that's really why she didn't show up to group."

Andi pauses, absorbing this information, then looks at me. "How was it for you, to hear she'd relapsed?"

I don't respond. Andi stares at me, waiting for me to speak.

"I thought I didn't have to share if I don't want to," I say. I'm not comfortable delving into emotional territory with others present. Andi's asking me to talk about my feelings with the group is tantamount to her requesting I share my masturbatory techniques—there are some things better left unsaid.

"You don't." Though she manages to quickly rearrange her expression, a brief, disappointed shadow falls across her face. "Every alcoholic is different," she goes on. "There doesn't have to be some catastrophic event to 'cause' your drinking to get out of control or make you relapse. It's rarely that simple. We want it to be, of course. We want something or someone to blame for making us pick up the drink that eventually takes us over the edge. There's no cut-and-dried way we get here, nothing we can point to and say, 'oh, *that's* going to turn that person into an alcoholic.'"

"But your husband *died*," Madeline says, whispering that last word like it was a secret Andi didn't already know.

"You're right. He did." Even now, six years after the fact, the grief tightens the muscles in her face. "And for a while, I used that as an excuse. I felt terribly sorry for myself—oh poor me, the widowed alcoholic. My husband died of cancer. He was only forty years old. I *deserve* to drink. It's my *right*."

"Well, it was your right," Serena says. "In a way."

Andi looks at her. "How so?"

"You had the right to drink. You just didn't know you were an alcoholic when you started doing it. You still have the right to drink, don't you? I mean, you're a grown woman. You could walk out of here right this minute and go on down to the Quickie Mart and pick yourself up a six-pack, couldn't you?"

Andi smiles. "*Vodka* was my drink of choice, remember? I slipped it into a water bottle during one of my lectures? And then I had the bright idea to show my breasts to my students."

We all laugh. This vision of a sloshed, boob-flashing Andi runs entirely contrary to the woman we know to hold a Ph.D. in psychology with research published in several well-respected journals. After she completed treatment at Promises, she decided to leave the tenure track at the University of Washington in favor of helping other women rebuild their messy, mangled lives.

Before Andi has the chance to continue, the door swings open and Laura saunters in. "Hey, ladies," she says. "Sorry I'm late."

I give her a quick wave, noting how pale she seems compared to just a couple of weeks ago when I last saw her. Her dark hair is stringy and thin around her face, chopped in a harsh, angled bob, coming to sharp points near her chin. Her low-hung jeans barely cling to the exaggerated knots of her hip bones. Heroin-not-so-chic.

"You guys talking about me?" she asks. Her voice is strained.

"Sort of." Andi smiles, beckoning with a wave of her hand. "Come on in."

Laura walks across the room and drops into a seat next to me, reaching over to poke the top of my leg with a bony finger. "You were worried about me, weren't you?" she says. "Go ahead, admit it."

I bob my head and flash a smile at her. "I'm glad you came."

She grins. "Me, too." She looks around the room. "I take it Cadence gave you all the news of my unfortunate relapse?"

"Yes," Andi says. "Are you okay?"

"Yeah, honey," Serena says. "You all right?"

"I'm fine," Laura says, throwing one meager leg over the other. "It was a fucking bad decision, though. I guess I needed to test the theory of whether or not I actually have a problem with addiction." She puts her gaze on Andi. "What do you think, Madame Therapist? Am I an addict?"

Andi's mouth curves up gently. "That's something you decide for yourself, Laura. Addiction is pretty much defined by continuing to indulge in any behavior when we don't want to. Even though it hurts us. Does that apply to you?"

"Oh, hell yeah," Laura says. "I'm sorry my mom told you I was sick." She pauses. "Well, I *was* sick, just not in the way she probably made it sound."

"It's okay," Andi says. "This time. But you know you can't come back to group if it happens again." She shifts toward the new woman, who has registered this entire exchange with watchful gray eyes. "What about you, Kristin? Would you like to tell the group a little about what brought you to us?"

Kristin sits up, her long limbs rearranging themselves before she speaks. "Well, I'm an alcoholic. And an addict. This is my second time in treatment."

"What brought you back?" Serena asks.

Kristin drops her chin to her chest, her fingers pull at a loose thread on her purse. "The court. I was caught driving drunk."

"Blue-light special, huh?" Serena leans forward, elbows on her knees. "How many DUIs you got?"

"This is my first," Kristin says quietly. "My lawyer is trying to plead it down to reckless driving. I went to treatment before, about five years ago, on my own."

Serena looks confused. "And you got ordered here, for one DUI? What else you do?"

"Serena . . ." Andi warns.

"Don't let her bug you, Kristin," Laura says. "She's only jealous because she's had four of them."

"One for each husband," Serena says, brown eyes sparkling.

"No, it's fine," Kristin says. She meets Serena's gaze, her chin trembling. "My kids were in the car. I ran into a stop sign in a black-out. I barely remember it. My neighbor reported me, Child Protective Services got involved, and now I'm court-ordered to attend treatment before they give them back to me." Her voice shakes, tears begin to roll. She pushes the heels of her hands into her eyes in a vain effort to stop them.

"Who are they with?" I ask, unable to mask the emotion in my own voice.

Kristin sniffs, looks up at me. "What?"

"Your kids. Who are they staying with? Your husband?"

She shakes her head. "He left a few years ago." After a heaving breath, she goes on. "They're with my mom."

"Do you get to see them?" I am clenching my hands together, I realize. My fingers have gone white. This is the first time I have heard another woman speak of drinking in front of her kids. None of the other women in my group have children. I am riveted; I want to know everything about her.

She nods. "Yes. But I'm just so ashamed. I can't believe I let this happen. I'm smarter than this. I can't believe I let myself get to this point." She is crying again, swiping at the tears with the back of her right hand. Her shoulders quake as she sobs in silence. We are not allowed to give her a tissue—at Promises, it is taught that interrupting a person's emotional processing in this way quashes its resolution. If she wants a tissue, she'll have to reach for one herself. I found this a little hokey at first, until I cried the first time in group, and someone new handed me one; my emotions shut down, whatever dam that had broken suddenly rebuilt—the release of tears immediately ceased.

"Did you lose your license?" Serena asks.

Kristin shakes her head. "No, because it's my first offense." More tears well up as she speaks, and she is forced to stop talking.

Andi lets Kristin weep in silence for a moment. "We're glad you're here, too," she says to our group's newest member, then swings her gaze to me. "How was your weekend with Charlie?"

My eyes are still on Kristin, watching her feel her pain so easily, so out in the open for all to see. I am amazed by this, in awe of her ability to admit the gravity of what she has done to perfect strangers. It took me three weeks at Promises before I could say the words "I got drunk in front of my son" to anyone; they still feel like bits of sandpaper stuck in my throat whenever I'm forced to speak them.

I have to tear my eyes away to look at Andi, who I suspect is bringing my son up for Kristin's sake. "We ended up at my sister's place for the night," I say. "I took him to get a haircut, alone, though.

It went well, actually." I don't mention the episode in my sister's living room, my angry reaction to my child's behavior. I'll save that for when I meet with Andi alone.

Andi moves on to Serena and Madeline's weekend recounts. I listen, trying to stay focused on what the other women are saying, until it's finally time to walk out the door.

In the parking lot, I'm relieved to find that the drizzling rain has stopped and the sun is fighting to come out, backlighting the clouds with a fuzzy pale glow. I'm about to climb in my car when a voice stops me. "Cadence?" I turn to see Kristin approaching me, a black trench coat flapping around her long legs.

I stop. "Did I forget something?"

She approaches, shakes her head. "No, no. I was just wondering . . ." She pauses, bites her bottom lip, and then goes on. "Did you drink in front of your son?" Her voice is hesitant, clipped.

I give her a swift nod, not trusting my voice to speak. She gives me a look so vacant of judgment, so filled with compassion, it lends me some small measure of relief. I feel something inside my chest pulling me toward her, a whispery thin, silver line of connection.

"Can I call you sometime? Maybe we could go to a meeting?" she asks.

"Sure," I say. I swallow, grab one of my business cards, and hand it to her. I don't know what I'm doing—I'm in uncharted territory—but maybe, just maybe, I'll have an easier time of things if I choose not to handle it all alone.

Eleven

The morning startles me now, with its silence. On Tuesday, I open my eyes from a dreamless sleep and begin to lose Charlie all over again. I lose him in the absence of loud, clamoring early morning cartoons. I lose him when I realize there are no dresser drawers being banged shut as he tries on ten different outfits to see which best suits his mood. I lose him in the sad fact that the only person I have to cook breakfast for is me. Pancakes for one is a pitiful thing—I cannot bring myself to make them.

I try to escape. I pace. I walk around the house, into the kitchen, back out to the living room. I stand in front of the closed door to Charlie's room and can't bring myself to look inside. The sight of the bed he has not slept in is too much for me to bear. The tiny, lonely sock he left on the floor might as well be a dagger lodged in my chest. I'm not sure what to do with all I feel. I'm unwieldy. Unbalanced. I only want the ache to go away. I call Jess, but get her voicemail. I can hear what my mother would say without having to pick up the phone. She prescribes work for matters of uncertainty the way other mothers prescribe chicken soup for a cold.

I leave a message for Susanne, not really expecting to hear back. My not being able to drink with her has changed us. Andi warned me that it might.

"You getting sober shifts the dynamics in your friendship," she said. "Just like you would have a hard time being around her because she drinks, she might have a hard time being around you because you don't."

"So I lose her altogether?"

"You might," Andi said. "It's unfortunate, but sometimes, that's the way it goes."

I flash on the idea of turning this phenomenon into an article—when friendships fade. I sit down at the table and attempt to get a few words on the page, but I can't get anything done. What else can I write about? *When a Grown Woman Can't Take Care of Her Son? When Writer's Block Strikes? The Bitter Aftermath of Bad Choices? What to Do When You Don't Have Any Idea What the Hell to Do with the Rest of Your Life?*

Right. There's some high-quality journalism. My mind won't sit still. I feel like a ticking bomb.

I stand up and open the cupboards, cruising for something—anything—to eat. There's nothing—only a stale loaf of bread in my refrigerator and a single slice of moldy cheese. I've been living off coffee and takeout. I decide to go shopping and use up the hours and minutes that torture me with their lack of direction. I used to have a compass. I used to have Charlie.

It's the middle of the day, and the store's customers are mostly retirees and mothers with their children. *Damn.* I keep my head down and fill my cart with good intentions: lettuce, tomatoes, low-fat yogurt. I didn't make a list. I wander the aisles in a slow, haphazard pattern. I take time to read the nutritional content on a package of sharp cheddar cheese and am horrified at the amount of fat in one tiny little ounce. Still, I keep reading the packages before I put them in my cart. The longer I'm here, the less time alone I'll have to endure.

I turn the corner and there it is. The wine aisle. Oh God. A gripping, physical sense of longing fills me. An urge as primitive as hunger. My craving speaks to me in a hypnotic lover's voice. I feel like the woman who wants to return to the man who beats her. She convinces herself that this time he will be different; she'll just be more careful around him. Despite what I know, despite the fact that I'm in danger of losing my son, this voice entices me to believe that this time, the drink won't hurt. It makes the promise that this time, I won't end up black and blue.

I whip my cart around. I grab the makings for lasagna and stew, packages of precooked chicken and lunch meats. I think of the meals I made for the expectant mothers of Mommy and Me and start planning out menus in my head. Maybe I can fill my days with cooking, fill my freezer with food for my son. Chicken soup, taco meat, shepherd's pie. His favorites.

I take a deep breath and push my cart around the corner. I hear the bright, chirping chatter of a little girl speaking to her mother. "Can we get this cereal, Mama?" she pleads. "Can we, can we *pleeeeease?*"

I look up to see the mother's tired, haggard face as she responds. Her shoulders are hunched; she is carrying another child in a baby sling—a newborn. "No, honey," she says. "That's a sugar cereal. It's not good for us."

"But *please*, Mama!" the little girl begs, stomping her feet and shaking the brightly colored box a couple of times for emphasis. "I will clean my room. I will even throw away Trevor's poopy diapers."

The mother sighs quietly. "I said no, Emma. We have cereal at home." Baby Trevor starts to cry and so does Emma. Her face screws up and fat tears roll down her chubby pink cheeks. She plops down on the floor and sits cross-legged, her plump fingers gripped into angry fists on top of her knees. *"I want it!"* she screams. *"I want it!"*

Watching this scene unfold, my heart aches not only for the mother—who looks as though she'd love nothing more than to curl up for a good, long nap—but for myself. My heart aches for Charlie. I think of the countless times my son threw a fit exactly like this one in the middle of a store. How in those moments part of me wanted to plop him down on a shelf, paste a bright yellow price tag on his head, and leave him there for some other woman to take home.

You don't know what you have, I long to tell her. *I know it's hard. I know you feel like you might just collapse right here in the grocery aisle. But you don't know. You have no idea how horrified you'd be if you did something to lose this. If someone tried to take them away. You have no idea how much you'd hate yourself for thinking you don't want it.*

I move my cart down the aisle and look up only to see a box of Froot Loops. That's it. I lose it. I begin to weep. It's Charlie's favorite. A treat I rarely let him indulge in, but his favorite nonetheless. *Who really gives a fuck if he eats sugar cereal? There are so many worse things a mother could do wrong.* I grab a box and throw it into my cart. And then another. And one more. I want to be prepared.

I want to be ready for him when he comes home.

My attorney, Scott Watson, works out of a small space above a Thai restaurant on Capitol Hill. The tantalizing, spicy-sweet aroma of lemongrass and red chili paste serves as the dangling carrot for having to come see my lawyer; I do my best to plan my appointments with him around the lunch hour so I can grab an order of pad thai and swimming rama to take home.

On Wednesday, my stomach gurgles and growls as I walk up the stairs to Scott's office. I was referred to him by the team at Promises— he was the only lawyer who had the availability to take my case, and whose rates I could actually afford.

When I met him back in March, his open, flamboyant nature put me at ease right off the bat—during our first appointment he told me entertaining stories about his weekend dinner parties and his own dysfunctional family dynamics, giving me a glimpse of him as a human being, not simply an attorney who, while paid to be on my side, I feared might be quietly passing judgment. There is no sense of this about him; instead, he exudes an acceptance and confidence that I am incapable of at the moment—the proper balance of determination and optimism to make me believe he may actually be able to get Charlie back.

"Cadence, darling!" he exclaims from his desk, looking up as I step into his office. His legal assistant, David, had announced my arrival. "How are you?"

I shrug. "I'm okay. How are you?" Always immaculately groomed, he wears a well-cut black pinstripe suit, shiny black loafers, and a white handkerchief in his breast pocket. Not more than a few years older than me, he is still slight enough to make you think for a moment he is a teenager dressing up in his father's workclothes.

"Good, good." He shuffles a messy stack of papers on his desk, then motions to the chair I am standing behind. "Have a seat."

I step around the chair, sit, cross both my arms and legs. "Any news?"

He shakes his head, lips pursed. "Nope. You're meeting Mr. Hines at his office, when?"

"May fifteenth," I say, wiggling my foot in the air.

Scott sits back in his wing-backed leather chair, casually assessing my jittery behavior. "You had your first visit with Charlie, didn't you? How'd it go?"

"Good, for the most part." Again, as I had in group, I relate the conversation Alice and I had shared, but also how wonderful it was to be with Charlie.

He taps a pen against his phone. "You didn't bring him home?"

"No. Was I supposed to?" The muscles in my chest seize; I tighten my fingers around each of my biceps. The empty ache in my stomach suddenly vanishes and is replaced by nausea. Since Martin filed for custody, I'm basically at the mercy of the legal system. The process of trying to get my son back is out of my control—have I screwed up the one thing I could have influenced?

"You didn't have to, it just might have looked a little better if you had. Like you were confident in being alone with him."

"He wanted to see his cousins and his aunt," I say, immediately set on the defensive. "What's wrong with that?" *I'm not confident!* I want to scream. *I'm a pitiful, writhing mass of insecurity! Can't you see that? Do I really have to say it out loud?*

Scott sits back, places his hands over his rib cage, and pats them rhythmically, like he is playing the piano on his suit buttons. He is contemplating. "Nothing is wrong with it, it just doesn't paint the picture I was hoping your time alone with him would." He flips a hand in the air, dismissing the subject. "No worries, we'll handle it. The next weekend, though, you should bring him home, okay? Have him spend the night there."

"Okay." I am fighting the feelings as they rise in me: panic, fear, anger. I see Scott register this, and again, a concerned look passes over his face.

"Cadence, look," he says, tucking his hands flat beneath opposite biceps. "I'm going to tell you something, okay? I've thought about telling you this since our first meeting, but the timing just never seemed right. I trust you'll hold what I say in confidence?"

I nod, swallow twice, blinking back the tears.

He takes a deep breath. "I'm an alcoholic. Four years sober. I see the old me written all over your face, hear myself in almost every word you say. You're scared, defensive, smart as hell, but baffled as to how you got to this horrifying place. So believe me, I get this. I get how crazy you feel right now. I don't have kids to lose custody of, but I lost a lot in the process of getting sober."

"Like what?" My ears are perked now, my panic momentarily quelled by his revelation.

He laughs, a short, barking sound. "My boyfriend, for one. Steve. I was a very messy drunk and he got tired of cleaning up after me."

"I'm so sorry," I say. "How long were you together?"

"Eight years," he says. Wry regret cloaks his words. "He finally left after the night he came home to find me making boy soup."

"Boy soup?" I laugh, and must look as confused as I feel, because he goes on to explain.

"I brought home three other men from the bar. We were in the hot tub when Steve came in. Hot water, naked bodies . . . boy soup."

I suck a breath in through my teeth. "Ahh." And then, after a brief pause. "Wow. *Three* men?"

"What can I say?" He smiles, shrugging his shoulders almost imperceptibly. "I'm ambitious." He untucks his hands, presses them flat on the tops of his thighs. "That wasn't who I was, you know? I loved Steve. Drinking just totally changed my personality. It took away my dignity and my ability to make rational choices. My partner track with a well-known law firm went away, too." He motions around the small room. "I didn't set out to be a one-man practice, taking clients at rates less than a third an hour than what I was making. But it took what it took. I hit rock bottom and didn't get disbarred. I should have been. I was shit-faced in court on more than one occasion."

"How did you know when you hit bottom?" I ask, genuinely interested in his response, though simultaneously shocked and touched that he would share such frank, intimate details of his life. I find this at AA meetings, too, people just opening up, confessing the most appalling of sins with a comfort and ease I've never known. I can't decide if this impresses or horrifies me.

"When I stopped digging," he says, and something about this image makes sense to me; it clicks inside my head, a key fitting into a lock. I see myself at the base of a deep, dark hole, shovel in hand, face blackened, exhausted. I'm prodding the soil, digging here and there, the ground literally falling out from under me, right along with my footing. But it's me, I'm the one digging. I stop my jabbing movements and see myself lifting the shovel out of the dirt. I hold on to it still, unsure how to let go, where to put it, no clue as to what else I might use as a tool to find my way out of this deep well I've put myself in.

"How do I stop digging?" My voice is quiet. "I don't know how to stop."

"Put down the shovel, honey," he says. "That's all. Just put it down and start looking up."

Twelve

That night, on Scott's recommendation, I pick Charlie up from Alice for our newly scheduled weekly dinner and bring him back to our house.

"What did you make me for dinner, Mommy?" he asks when we arrive.

I turn around in the driver's seat and smile at him. "Brussels sprouts and spinach salad, of course. Your favorites."

"Ew!" Charlie says, scrunching up his face. "No *way* am I eating that."

"No way, huh?" I pretend to sigh. "Okay, I guess we'll have to settle for homemade pizza. And green beans." As long as the beans were slathered in butter, I could get my son to eat them.

"All right!" he says, and we head inside the house. I'd made the dough in my bread machine after my appointment with Scott, so now I let Charlie help me roll it out into two small pizzas—one for each of us. He slops pizza sauce, a mountain of mozzarella cheese, and three pieces of turkey pepperoni onto his and calls it good. I spread pesto, crumbled goat cheese, and toasted pine nuts on mine and pop them both in the oven.

"What do you want to play?" I ask him, brushing flour off my hands. "Blocks? Cars?"

"Can I watch TV?" he asks, clasping his hands together in front of his chest and batting his eyelashes at me.

I laugh. "Nice try, Mr. Man. But not right now. I don't get to see you enough. I want to do something together."

"But we can watch TV together," he says, his voice lifting up at the end of the phrase.

"Later. How about Connect Four?"

"Okay," he says. "I get to be red."

"You always get to be red," I tease him.

"It's my favorite color."

"I thought orange was your favorite color."

"Not anymore." He dashes into the living room and grabs the game from the shelf by the fireplace.

His favorite color had changed. I wondered if this happened when I was drinking, or only since he has been staying with Martin. Not knowing this feels wrong, like I'm deficient as a mother in yet another new and debilitating way. I take a deep breath as we sit down at the table, determined to not let this feeling ruin my time with my son.

After we play and eat, I let Charlie choose one cartoon for us to watch as we snuggle on the couch. "It's time to go, kiddo," I say when *SpongeBob SquarePants* is over. "I have to have you back to your daddy by eight o'clock."

Charlie throws his arms around my waist and clings to me. "No. I don't want to leave."

"I know, baby," I say, a lump already forming in my throat. "I don't want you to leave, either. But I don't have a choice."

"Why not?" he whines. "I want to stay here in my room."

"You have a wonderful room at Daddy's, don't you?"

He nods his head against my chest and I kiss the slightly musty mess of his hair. "Well, then, you get to stay there. And then, not this weekend, but the next one, you get to stay here. Okay?"

"Okay," he says, drawing out the word. He tilts his head back to look at me. "But you won't let any other little boys in my room, right, Mommy?"

"No way," I tell him, trying to swallow back my tears. "That room was made just for you."

The next morning, I am back at Promises for my individual session with Andi. She sits in her chair, notepad on her lap. Her outfit today is head-to-toe royal purple—a healing color, she says. After she tells me this, I feel somehow lacking in my jeans and emerald sweater set, as though I, too, should consider the influence the colors of my outfit might have on the people around me. We're discussing the bout of irritation I had with my son at Jess's house. This is normal, she assures me, for a newly recovering alcoholic or any other tired, stressed-out mother.

"All mothers get irritated," she says. "Kids are irritating creatures. You acknowledged you screwed up, apologized, and he forgave you. That's a good thing."

"How is it a good thing?" I ask, bewildered.

"It's good because Charlie gets to see that grown-ups make mistakes, too," Andi explains. She is ever-patient with my questioning. "He also gets to see his mom admit she did something wrong and apologize for it. That's called modeling positive behavior."

I sigh. "The way you say it makes it sound so logical."

"Forgiving yourself takes time," she says, the barest hint of exasperation lacing through her words. "Being a good mother does not mean being perfect every moment. We screw up. We get mad, we drink too much, eat too much, yell too much. A good mother learns from her mistakes and does what she can to not let them happen over and over."

"Well, I've failed that one," I say, taking a quick sip of my coffee. "Look how often I got drunk around him." Still, the words are like jagged pebbles caught in my throat. All the good things I've done as a mother—the books I've read, the countless hours I've spent snuggling my son, kissing his scrapes, dancing with him in the living room to the Wiggles—none of this matters. My drinking looms above it all, casting a thick, black shadow over anything I may have done right.

"And now you're here, doing everything you can to not let that happen again." She sighs, looks at me. "You don't have to go through any of this alone."

"I understand that, in theory. But allowing myself to rely on other people isn't as easy as it sounds. Kind of like the whole 'eat less, move more' mantra is supposed to work for weight loss. If it were that simple, everyone who struggles with their weight would just do it."

"I know. I've been through it, remember? Understanding how you ended up where you are isn't a one-shot deal. It's a process. My job is to help point you in the right direction so you don't land here again."

"Can I ask you something?" I say.

"Of course."

"I was wondering what you think Martin's reasons are for trying to take Charlie from me."

She looks pensive. "It's probably a combination of things. The most significant being that you were too drunk to take care of your son. At the point you were at in your drinking, it was right for him to take Charlie away."

Her words sting. My cheeks flush and the tears come again.

"I know that's hard to hear."

I can't even nod. I can't move. My eyes burn.

"Martin also sounds like the kind of guy who does the 'right' thing," Andi says, lifting her fingers to make invisible quotation marks around the word. "He's very logical, right? A left-brained thinker?"

This time, I manage to respond. "Very much so."

"So his brain takes the facts—as he sees them, at least—and lines them up, arranging them in a logical order so he can draw a conclusion." She sits forward, hands clasped, elbows resting on her knees. "We all wish life were logical. And admitting we screwed up and aren't capable of fixing something that has gone wrong is a devastating thing. We're used to applying our dizzying intellect to a problem and making it go away."

I raise one eyebrow at her. "I wouldn't call my intellect 'dizzying,' exactly. If it were, I wouldn't be in this god-awful nightmare of a mess, now would I?"

She smiles. "Don't be too sure. This is not a matter of intellect. It has to do with biology and emotion. Some of the smartest, most successful people I know are alcoholics. But for whatever reason, they never learned how to manage their feelings. So they drank to numb them out. But the underlying issue is not having the right emotional skills to manage the feelings in the first place. *That's* what you have to learn to do."

"And how do I do that?"

She sits back into her chair and smiles. "You feel them."

Later that day, I am sitting at the computer in my kitchen, browsing through the freelance writing job postings on Craigslist, thinking I might be able to make more money auctioning off a kidney on eBay, when the phone rings. It's Peter, calling from his office at the *Herald*. I picture him sitting behind his desk—a huge African American man—six foot four and well over three hundred pounds. His burly voice definitely matches his build; it used to shake the glass walls of his office when I worked in the newsroom.

"Have you sent a query over to Tara Isaacs over at *O* yet?" he bellows.

"Not yet," I say. "I'm still trying to come up with a good pitch." I don't tell him that what I'm really trying to do is figure out whether I want to be a writer at all. I'm not sure I still have it in me.

"Screw the pitch. Just make contact with her. Have you forgotten everything I taught you? Sell, sell, sell yourself. You'll never make it in the freelance world if you can't."

I sigh. "Then maybe I'm not meant to make it." Even as I say this, I realize how much this makes me sound like a victim, and I shudder.

"Bullshit. You're a talented writer. Get over yourself and send the woman an e-mail. Just a follow-up, 'hey, how ya doin', pleased to meet you, my friend Peter the sex god told me we might get along.'"

I laugh. "I might have to leave that last part out, but all right, I'll send the e-mail."

"Good girl. Let me know how it goes."

We hang up and I rest my fingers on the keyboard. This used to come so easily to me. I'd find the first sentence and the rest would spill out on its own. I decide to keep it simple. The e-mail Peter sent a couple of weeks ago has Tara's e-mail address as a direct link, so all I have to do is click on it and it opens up a fresh, blank e-mail screen.

Dear Ms. Isaacs,

Peter Baskin, the editor-in-chief at the Seattle Herald, gave me your contact information after meeting you at an event in Chicago about a month ago. My name is Cadence Sutter, and I've been a journalist and freelance writer for over seven years.

I've taken some time off lately to spend more time with my young son, but am very interested in the possibility of working for such a prestigious, well-reputed magazine as O. If you have a specific subject you believe your readers would like to see explored, please let me know. Otherwise, I'll be in touch soon with some of my own ideas.

I attach a list of the publications my work has been featured in, as well as a few of my best articles for her review, then cross my fingers before hitting send. I don't expect to hear back from her for a few days at least, but an hour later, as I'm scrubbing the outsides of my kitchen cupboards, the new e-mail alert sounds on my laptop. I rush over to check, and it is, indeed, from Tara. It reads:

> *Dear Cadence,*
>
> *It was certainly a pleasure to discuss your work with Peter—he did nothing but sing your praises when we spoke. I look forward to hearing back from you regarding what you think your writing could bring to our publication. I don't like to assign ideas to the freelancers I work with, as I find that they, most always, come up with something better than I could have ever dreamed.*
>
> *Take care, and I hope to hear from you soon.*
>
> > *All best,*
> > *Tara Isaacs*

Oh, holy crap. Now I have to come up with something. She didn't give me a deadline, but still, I'm not sure I can do it.

I may have just bitten off a hell of a lot more than I can chew.

I am alone over the weekend and Saturday night I go to bed early and lie in that all too familiar twilight space of not really asleep, not really awake. It's the space I used to escape by downing another glass of wine. A tangible remedy to an intangible ill.

Feel the feelings, Andi said. I don't understand why the thought of this terrifies me. Maybe because part of me believes if I don't acknowledge how I feel, then I don't have to acknowledge what I did. I'm terrified to face it. Around and around my mind goes while my body pretends to be asleep.

The phone rings, interrupting my thoughts. I end up fumbling for it, not looking at the caller ID. I bark an unfriendly greeting. The possibility flashes through my mind that perhaps it is Kristin calling me for the first time, in some kind of crisis, or maybe even Laura. But the demand behind my ex-husband's words is unmistakable.

"Why did you call our son a freak?" he says without so much as identifying himself. I exhale a heavy breath into the receiver, attempting to release the immediate tension that seizes my body the instant I know who it is on the other end of the line.

"What?" My brain is fuzzy but my heart is wide awake, already thumping an anxious pattern in my chest. The blood pushes quickly through my veins. "I didn't."

And even though I know what he's saying isn't true—I didn't call our son a freak—I do know he's referring to a week ago when I lost my temper with Charlie at Jess's house. The accusation hurts. I think of how easily I became irritated with my son, the grip of my hand on his fragile arm. How much more damage did I cause him?

"He said you did."

I rub my eyes and look at the clock: 9:00 p.m. I'd only been in bed for half an hour. "Why are you calling me about this now?"

"He didn't tell me about it until I was putting him to bed tonight," he says, his voice short. "And I'm meeting with Mr. Hines on Monday, so I want to be prepared." I grit my teeth at this classic Martin behavior. His mathematician's makeup prohibits him from allowing any unexpected scenarios in his life; he has to be ready for the most infinitesimal of possibilities. I can see him sitting at his desk, the light from the computer illuminating his face, a spreadsheet—color-coded, of course—created for the express purpose of documenting for his lawyer every moment I spend with our son. Any compassion I felt for him last week around his having to take care of Alice disappears.

I sigh, roll over in my bed, and throw my forearm against my forehead. It's amazing to me still the degree of animosity between us, how easily the daggers are thrown. He is not the tender man I married. I wonder sometimes how we ended up in this horrible place.

"I did not call him a name," I say, attempting to remain calm. "You know me better than that. He was jumping all over Jess's furniture and I said he was 'freaking out.' That's it, that's all. You can call Jess and she'll tell you the same thing." My stomach clenches, panicking, and I fall into a repair attempt. "Are we really going to stoop to this level?" I plead. "Can't we figure this out another way? I don't understand why you can't give me a chance to make this right." I paused, choosing my next words carefully. "There is nothing you can say about what has happened to make me feel any worse than I already do."

"Any worse about what you've *done*, you mean. Not 'what happened.' What you did."

"Yes. What I've done."

Martin is quiet a moment now. I allow myself to feel buoyed by a small flash of optimism.

"Treatment's helping," I say. "I'm starting to understand why it happened. I intend to make sure it never happens again." My voice is shaky. I'm not sure how convincing I sound. Part of me feels that after what I've done, I've lost the right to defend myself.

"Intentions aren't enough, Cadee. How do I know you won't drink again? How do I know Charlie will be safe?" He sighs, the old Martin I know coming through, if only for a moment, the ghost of the man who once loved me. I know part of him only wants to do the right thing by our son. But I don't understand how he could possibly think the best thing is for Charlie to be without me.

"It's probably better to leave it to the lawyers," he says. "I'm sorry I bothered you. Have a nice night."

Yeah, right, I think, as I hang up the phone. *No problem, I'm sure I'll drift right off to sleep now. Sweet dreams to you, too. Bastard.*

I flop over to lie on my side, punch my pillow, once, twice. I wriggle beneath the covers to find a comfortable position, unsuccessfully trying to blank my mind of any thought. I flip over one more time, wrestling around with the covers.

My relationship with Martin doesn't matter anymore. I can't fix it, I can't change it. What matters is my son. I miss him violently; there is a Charlie-shaped hole inside me. Is there one shaped like me inside of him?

Nighttime is the worst. The quiet makes me feel like I've lost him completely, like he might never be coming back. I watch moonlight graze the tips of its long golden fingers over my bedroom walls. Swayed by a gentle breeze, the laurel outside my bedroom window taps on the glass in a soft, staccato beat. Trying to find relief, I gather the nearest pillow I can find to my heart, hold it close, rock it. In the dark I pretend it is my son, soft and warm, quiet and sweet, my child peacefully sleeping.

Thirteen

I am about halfway through my second cup of coffee on Monday morning when I decide to start wading through my old clippings. I'm contemplating whether it would be feasible to reslant any of the stories into new, unbelievably brilliant article ideas. The first few years I did freelance work, I'd written several pieces about what it was like having a colicky infant—all the different methodologies I tried to help Charlie sleep through the night. Going for drives, feeding him homeopathic antigas tablets, and finally, eliminating all dairy and wheat from my own diet in case Charlie might have been allergic and I was making him miserable with my breast milk. I wrote about how none of those methods worked—I simply had a child who was only happy when I was holding him. Tears begin to well in my throat as I think about what I would give to be holding him right now. Obviously, in my current state, I can't write about parenting.

Sighing, I abandon my clippings, flip open my laptop, and start reading the headlines on a local news webpage, another technique I've used in the past for finding a seed to a story. A local man was arrested for flashing a group of teenage girls at a Tacoma high school. A profile piece, maybe? *The Man Behind the Trench Coat.* I roll my eyes to the ceiling at the absurdity of this thought. Scrolling down the page, I see a video clip about an organic produce delivery service. Five minutes later, I know more about cow manure compost and how it relates to a successful heirloom tomato crop than I ever thought possible. Where's the story idea in that? *The Road to Going Green Is Paved with Crap?* I sigh again. Honestly, this is pointless. How did I ever come up with good ideas before?

The phone rings, saving me. It's my mother, inviting me to come visit her at her office. I haven't spoken with her since the pancake breakfast at Jess's house, but it's as good an excuse as any to escape trying to write. Thirty minutes later, Keiko, my mother's reception-ist, lifts her eyes from her computer and comes out from behind her desk to let me in. She is a young, gorgeous Japanese girl, petite enough to make me feel like a lumberjack.

"Cadence!" she greets me, ushering me inside. She locks the door behind us, tucks her long, sleek black sheet of hair behind one ear. "Haven't seen you in a while."

"I know. How've you been?"

"Pretty good. How about you?" Her face immediately morphs into a look that tells me my mother has already informed her exactly how I've been. *Lovely—just what I need, a twenty-year-old receptionist for a judge.*

"Fine," I say brightly. The easiest answer often turns out to be the biggest lie. I smile. "Is my mom around? She's expecting me."

"She's in her office." She steps back behind her desk, reaches for the phone. "Want me to let her know you're here?"

"That's okay. I'm pretty sure I can still find it." I step down the hall past the wandering labyrinth of cubicles; Mom once told me she had the place designed so skittish patients would have a hard time making a last-minute run for it. I find her sitting at her desk and plop down in one of the buttery-smooth red leather chairs.

We sit in silence for a moment, my mother's eyes on me, my eyes on the floor.

"How's that grandson of mine?" she asks, her voice attempting joviality.

I look up. "I'm sure he's fine." I pause, the sudden wedge in my throat making it impossible to speak. The truth is, I don't know exactly how he is. I can't wait to see him for dinner on Wednesday. "And Mark? How is he?"

"You mean Mike?" She looks a little shy, then smiles, and it strikes me how similar it is to my own.

"Right, Mike. Sorry." Handlebar Mustache Mike, Jess had dubbed him. The new boyfriend. "How are things going with him?"

"Good. He's very sweet. He's teaching me how to dance."

"That's nice of him. Are you guys getting serious?" I ask this despite already knowing the answer is no.

"It's too soon to tell. I like him, though. He makes me laugh." She pauses, looks at the wall, then back at me. "So, honey. I have to ask you something."

"Okay . . ." I cross my arms over my chest, wondering if all women automatically go on the defensive around the person who brought them into this world. But I realize this can't be because it doesn't happen to Jess. I attempt to rearrange my face to keep this from showing too much.

Her expression is hesitant, but she leans forward, folding her hands together on top of the paperwork on her desk. "I've been thinking a lot. About your . . . problem. With alcohol."

"Join the club," I say, my own reach for levity. This conversation is dangerous; I should have suited up with protective gear.

She gives me a faltering closed-mouth smile. "I can imagine." She takes a deep breath in through her nose. "I've been wondering what I'm going to say when Mr. Hines asks me if I think you're ready to take Charlie back."

"Oh." My insides begin to shake; I grip the arms of my chair to steady myself. "Did you come to any conclusion?"

"That's what I wanted to talk to you about. Do *you* think you're ready to have him?" Her body is rigid as she speaks, welded into position, bracing herself for my response.

I cross my legs now, too, and proceed to uncontrollably wiggle my airborne foot. "Of course I am. I'm his mother. He's never been anywhere but with me." As I say this, I hate the hesitance in my voice. I want Charlie back. I ache for him so deeply I can barely breathe. But that isn't the question she asked. She wants to know if I am ready for it. I have not thought to ask myself that question. Scott hasn't even asked me that. My mother asking it of me now raises a wild, panicky feeling inside me. I don't know what to do with it. "He needs me."

My mother's features soften. "I have no doubt he needs you. That little boy loves you beyond belief, and I know you adore him. But I just . . ." she trails off.

"I'm not drinking anymore," I say. "Treatment is helping." I use the same phrase I used with Martin the night he called. This is not a case of me repeating something again and again, trying to make it true. It *is* true. I am better than I was two months ago. I'm a smart woman. I'll handle it. Children should be with their mothers; that's all there is to it.

"I'm sure treatment *is* helping." She unlatches her fingers, drumming them on the papers beneath.

I give a short, sharp nod, acknowledging she is right. The bright beep of the intercom on her desk makes me blink. My mother pushes a button.

"Yes?"

"Your ten o'clock appointment is here, Sharon."

"Thanks, Keiko. I'll be right up." She stands, gives me another dazzling smile. "Sorry. Can we talk later?"

I stand, as well. "I'll have to call you. I'm not sure what my schedule is going to look like." She stares at me, blinking, both of us knowing full well that my "schedule" consists of a fat lot of nothing.

"Sure. Just let me know."

We both move to walk out of her office, me a couple of paces ahead of her. I love her, but I don't know how to reach out to her. But then I don't have to, because it is she who sends out a hand and grabs me by the arm, pulling me to a stop.

"What?" I say.

"If you need me—" she starts, but I cut her off.

"Okay. Thank you." I cannot help but think, *Too little, too late.* I don't believe her. She knows how to say the right thing, just not how to do it. My bitterness tastes like a mouthful of pennies.

"I just—" she begins helplessly, but doesn't finish the thought.

"Mom. I know." I hate the way I sound. I want to thank her, I want to be the kind of daughter who can crumple into the safety of her mother's arms and fall apart. But I'm not. I'm the daughter she raised; the kind of daughter who pulls her arm away from her mother's touch and plans to keep on walking until no one can touch her at all.

Fourteen

Over the next couple of weeks, I rack my brain trying to come up with a good idea to pitch to Tara. Editors are always looking for the hook—there are very few truly original ideas, so my best shot is to find a new and interesting angle to bring to the table. *O* readers look for inspiring, self-help-oriented content, but I'm the last person on the planet to be giving out any kind of self-improvement advice. If *O* published something I wrote and a reader found out my current life circumstances, they might sue for misrepresentation. False advertising, at the very least. I was crazy to contact her in the first place; crazy to think I was ready to take on something so big.

Instead, I take on something small. On the Friday of the last weekend in April, I decide that not having Charlie with me is as good as any other time to do a deep clean of my house, so I head out to Target to pick up supplies.

I've never been an immaculate housekeeper, but when my drinking began taking up more of my day than being sober, my surroundings pretty much mimicked my inner struggle with chaos. I am loath to admit it, even to myself, but there actually came a point when I ran out of clean underwear and instead of doing laundry, I simply decided to stop wearing them altogether. With my alcohol-soaked brain, this seemed a perfectly reasonable act at the time; now, it seems desperate and sad . . . defective, really. I mean, what kind of person *does* that?

While I was in-patient at Promises, Jess hired the cleaning service she and Derek use for the houses they put on the market to come and scour the surfaces of my home. They ended up needing three days to complete the job, and I will never be able to repay my sister for her kind gesture. I don't even want to think about the mess they found, the wine stains they had to scrub out of my carpet, the thickness of scum built up in my bathtub. The gunk under the toilet rim was there long enough for me to consider giving it a nickname. Since coming home, cleaning brings me relief. Instead of finding solace in a bottle of wine, I attempt to find it in Comet cleanser.

After wolfing down a giant corndog and a diet soda from the concession stand for lunch, I wander the aisles, considering the numerous selections of countertop cleaning solutions. When my cell phone rings, I fumble for it, thinking it might be Jess, and pull my cart to the side of the aisle so I don't block other shoppers from trying to get around me. "Hello?"

"Hi, Cadence. It's Kristin. From group?"

"Oh, hi." My response is guarded.

"I'm sorry it has taken me so long to call you," she says. "I kept meaning to . . ."

"No worries," I say. I'd seen her at group a couple of times and thought about how she hadn't called, but it didn't bother me. Not really. Isn't that what most people do, say things like, "We should do lunch," or "I'll call you next week," and then you never hear from them again? I've rarely taken this kind of thing personally before and I don't see a reason to start now. I regard a picture of a genie on a bottle, promising me surface shine like no other, and wonder briefly if it's really true what they say about bald men being more virile than those sporting a full head of hair, and how one thing could have anything to do with the other.

"How are you?" I ask.

"I'm okay." She pauses. "Well, not really." Another pause. This phone call is going to take forever if she continues to do this. "Why do we do that?"

"Do what?" I say, thinking she might be talking about her pausing habit.

"Say we're okay when we're not."

I shrug, as though she can see me. "We're conditioned that way, I guess." The bottle with the genie convinces me to throw it in my cart. I start to move down the aisle, phone tucked between my shoulder and my ear. "Can you imagine what would happen if we started answering that question honestly? Like 'How are you?' 'Well . . . *actually,* I'm a mess. I started drinking heavily, and now I'm fighting for custody of my son.' People would run screaming down the streets."

She laughs, and I'm relieved. Most people would not consider the reference to drinking heavily very humorous. I'm not even sure I do, but there it is again, that sarcastic reflex. "Yeah, I guess you're right." She takes a breath. "So, I was wondering, do you want to go to a meeting this afternoon?"

"Hmm . . ." I murmur, turning my cart down the next aisle, my eyes searching for the packages of multicolor scouring sponges. "I was kind of planning on cleaning my house."

"Oh." Her voice is small. "Do you want some help? I'm completely fastidious. It's sort of a compulsion of mine." She gives a short laugh. "One among the many, I guess."

I hesitate—she hears this.

"I'm just . . ." she starts, then fades off. "I'm having a hard day. My house is so empty. My mom took the kids to Ocean Shores for the weekend and being totally on my own without being able to even visit them . . . the quiet is killing me." There is only the slightest quiver in her voice, but I hear it. I know what she's feeling. Silence is brutal for those accustomed to the constant noise of children. I also know what it must have taken for her to work up the courage to pick up the phone. Other than calling Jess, I have not had that kind of courage myself.

"Why didn't you go with them?"

"I couldn't get it approved by Child Protective Services. It's mortifying, having to get approval to spend time with my own children."

"I know. I'm sorry."

"Nothing to be sorry about. It's my own fault." She takes a deep breath. "So . . . you want some help?"

"You're not at work?" I ask, grabbing the largest pack of sponges I see. Leaning over to reach them, I almost swerve my cart directly into an older lady walking next to me. I mouth an apology to her angry expression. She purses her thin lips in disapproval, and I have to grip the handle of my cart to keep myself from flipping her off. Defensive *and* angry—I can't imagine why some man has not swept a catch like me right off my feet.

"I work from home a couple days a week," Kristin says.

"Doing what?" This perks my interest. For some reason, I imagined Kristin a kept ex-wife, fully supported by child support and alimony. Taking child support from Martin, no matter how much I did need it to help pay the bills, has been difficult enough for my pride to contend with. I keep a separate account for Charlie's expenses. I buy his clothes, many of his books and games, and cover the copay on his trips to the doctor with the money Martin pays me each month. If there's anything left over, I apply it to the other household bills.

"Graphic design," Kristin says. "I work for a firm over in Bellevue, but I really only go into the office for the social aspect of it, or to meet with clients. The actual work I can do from home."

"Huh, that's pretty nice." I review the contents of my cart. I'm ready to head home. "Are you really sure you want to help me clean?"

"Definitely. I need to get out of my head." Again, a statement I can relate to.

"All right then," I say. I give her my address to punch into Map-

Quest, and we agree she'll be there in less than an hour. I try to remember the last time I invited another woman to my house, outside of Susanne and Jess, and come up empty. *The only thing I have to change is everything.*

Andi will be proud.

I park in front of my house and the first thing that strikes me is the deteriorating state of the yard. This prompts me, on the way to my front door, to drop to my knees. I yank out the groups of dandelions and horsetails that have begun to overtake the bark-covered beds. I pull with vigor and intent, carelessly throwing the weeds behind me, not bothering to set them in any kind of a pile. My knees become damp—stained, I'm sure—but I continue to work, finding relief in eradicating imperfection with such immediate results. It's unfortunate that I can't apply the same process to my own failings.

I am working with such intent, I don't notice when a car pulls up in front of the house, a door slamming, or steps moving toward me.

"Cadence?" Kristin's voice pops through my concentration—a pin puncturing a balloon. I fall back onto my butt, my hand pressed over my heart, which is suddenly pumping like a jackrabbit on speed.

"Jesus! You scared me!" I look up at her. *Damn, she's tall.*

She pulls the corners of her mouth down, gritting her teeth, breathes in sharply. "God, I'm sorry. Didn't you hear my car?"

I look over to the curb and see a huge, tan Chevy Suburban. "I guess not." I flap my hand in her general direction. "It's okay, not a big deal. You just caught me by surprise." I take a slow, deep breath in an attempt to slow my pulse. "Did you have any trouble finding it?"

She shakes her head. "You're not too far from me. I'm just over in Magnolia." I notice she looks softer with her hair down; the angles of her face don't look quite so severe. She smiles prettily, and I notice one of her front teeth crosses slightly over the other. My mom would love to slap a set of braces across them.

"Ah." I stand up, brush off my jeans, and return her smile. "Well, welcome."

"Thanks." She eyes the yard warily, the weeds tossed haphazardly along the walkway, all over the grass. "Are we doing yard work, too? I sort of have a black thumb . . ."

I laugh, wiping my dirty hands on the seat of my jeans. "Oh, no. I just got a wild hair. Impulse control issues, according to the great and powerful Andi. No ability to pause between thought and taking action."

She smiles. "She doesn't miss much, does she?"

I shake my head. "Nope. It's highly irritating." I motion toward the front door of the house. We step inside, and I watch her take in the front room. She sets down her purse on the entry table.

"What a great little house! How long have you lived here?"

"About six years. We moved in when I found out I was pregnant with Charlie."

She glances at me sidelong, careful. Her eyes are the shade and shape of a newly minted quarter. "My son's name is Riley. He's six. Eliza is eight." Her eyes fill, her bottom lip trembles. "Sorry. I can't seem to stop crying."

"Don't be sorry. I know how you feel."

She gives me a grateful look.

I show Kristin the rest of the house, and then we start cleaning, me in the bathrooms, she in the kitchen. I turn the stereo up loud, selecting an eighties greatest hits compilation, figuring we are about the same age, so she and I weathered junior high and high school humming along to the same new wave tunes. We work for a couple of hours, talking only when she needs direction as to where to stash my pots and pans, or where I hide the vacuum cleaner. When we both end up in the living room—each dusting the shelves on either side of the fireplace—I tell her how since getting out of treatment, I've cleaned like never before.

"I so totally get that," she says, lifting up one of Charlie's many

Spider-Man action figures to dust beneath it. "Managing external circumstances to calm internal chaos. Like if my environment is orderly, maybe my thinking patterns will follow suit." She sets the toy back down, looks at me, and sighs. "If only it were that simple, right?"

She continues working, focused and motivated, seemingly oblivious to just having so accurately summarized my own crazy thought processes. She appears happy to have something other than her own life to think about. There is something incredibly comforting about having another person in my home, no pressure to pretend or entertain. She is here because she wants to be. And maybe, just maybe, she's here because she needs this as much as I do.

I am touching up the gross area on the floor around the toilet in the master bathroom when Kristin calls my name. She steps into my bedroom, grinning. "Hey, I think we've done it. This place looks totally awesome."

"Like, totally, dude," I joke. Thankfully, she laughs.

"Were you a Valley girl?" she asks. "I so totally was. I had a handbook and everything. I campaigned for *months* to get my mother to let me change my name to Tiffani. With an 'i.'"

We laugh about this, too, and I can't believe how normal I feel, how at ease I am with this woman I barely know. I don't do this kind of thing. I'm unsure how, exactly, it's managing to happen.

"Do you still want to go to a meeting?" I ask her, stepping into the bedroom. "I have a couple that I normally go to, but I'd be willing to check out something different, if you know of any."

Kristin looks in the mirror at her messy hair, her now dirty clothes. "I don't think I'm presentable enough to go to a meeting. I'm kind of a wreck."

"I'd offer you a change of clothes, but I highly doubt I have anything that would fit you. We have slightly different builds." It's automatic for me to resent her a little for her thin frame, though I really wouldn't want to be as skeletal as she is. Her clavicle looks like it could be used as a deadly weapon.

"I know." She sighs, regarding us both in the mirror. "I'd kill for your curves."

"Are you kidding me?" I give her a look like she is out of her gourd. We are the approximate physical imitation of Laurel and Hardy. "Everybody wants to be tall and thin."

"No, everybody wants boobs like yours. I look like a boy."

"You can *buy* boobs," I say, cupping my hands beneath my breasts and pushing them upward, where they belong. "I can't buy a faster metabolism."

She giggles. "Yeah, but what about men?" She holds out her arms, encircling an invisible partner, twisting her face into a moony, exaggerated romantic expression. "Oh, baby, oh, my love . . . let me gather you to my bosom. . . . Whoops, you just broke your nose on my breastplate!"

We are both laughing now, and a sense of release fills me. Tension lifts from my body with each breath.

"Should we just hit a meeting another time?" she says after we manage to get ahold of ourselves. "I actually feel a lot better. More centered, I guess. I can spend the rest of the weekend getting a couple of work projects done."

I nod. "Sure. I should probably try to get somewhere on my next article, too." First, though, I have to come up with an idea.

"You're a writer?"

"Well, sort of." I make a face. "A freelancer. For now."

"That makes you a writer." She winks. "Fucked-up, alcoholic creative type, like me."

I smile. There's something marvelous about four-letter words pouring out of the mouth on such a beautiful face. It strikes me how normal she seems. If I hadn't seen her in the group room at Promises, I never would have guessed she was an alcoholic. She is too polished, too pretty. It just doesn't fit.

"Haven't you ever noticed how many actors and writers have problems with substance abuse?" Kristin goes on. "Look at Hemingway. Or Britney Spears."

I laugh. "I'm sure Hemingway would *love* being lumped into the same category as Britney."

She smiles. "You know what I mean, though, right?"

"Sure. Robert Downey Jr. is brilliant, but a serious alcoholic and addict."

"Oh, I love him. I'm so happy he got sober."

"Me, too." I walk her toward the door. She stops short in the hallway, runs the tip of her index finger over a silver-framed picture hanging on the wall. In it, I'm behind my two-year-old son, chin propped on his right shoulder, my arms wrapped tight around his waist. It is an icy winter day; we are both bundled up in ski jackets and gloves. Our cheeks are red, our eyes bright. We have just finished building his first snowman. Our grins are ear to ear.

"Charlie?" she asks.

I nod, tight-lipped, two wide, tight bands of sorrow building up in the muscles of my neck. I made him hot cocoa that morning, and scones, which he mispronounced as "stones." Since that day, that is what they've been; when he'd ask for them, it was, "Mama, will you make me blueberry stones?" I never had the heart to correct him.

"Look how happy he is," she says. "He's got your smile."

"I miss him," I say softly. And then, barely audibly, "I'm so sorry for what I've done."

"I know." Her expression melts into compassion and she leans in and hugs me. It is a solid, strong embrace. I hug her in return, grateful.

"Thanks for letting me come over," she says, pulling away to move toward the living room. "I feel better."

"Anytime," I say, somewhat surprised to realize I mean it. "Thank you so much for your help." I'm pretty sure I'm not just talking about the cleaning. I don't know where to put all I feel. This woman fed something in me today that has lived a lifetime of starvation.

After she leaves, I throw in a load of laundry, and for the first time in months decide to fix myself something healthy to eat. Since there's nothing in the house, I swallow my angst about the local market and zip over the few blocks to buy some romaine, cooked chicken breast, cranberries, and pecans for a salad. I find a small loaf of par-baked French bread and imagine its fresh, yeasty scent wafting through the house.

On the drive home, I realize that this has been one of the more pleasant afternoons I've spent in a very long time. I can't remember laughing so much since Martin took Charlie away—long before that, really. I didn't get anything written for Tara like I'd hoped, but I also didn't obsess about what Mr. Hines's decision will be. I didn't cry. I didn't sit and roll around in mental misery over all the mistakes I've made. I got my house clean. And I think—in spite of every wall I threw up in defense—I might have even made a friend.

Fifteen

The first half of May goes quickly, jam-packed with fun fests anytime Charlie and I are together: on the weekends, we go out for a cheap breakfast at IHOP, where I allow him to indulge in strawberries and whipped cream on his waffles.

"Do you mean it?" he asks, his eyes widening when I say yes.

"Yep," I say. "Go for it."

"Hey, waitress lady!" he hollers, frantically waving his chubby hand in the air.

"Charlie, shush," I say, laughing. He is anxious, I'm sure, to get in his order before I come to my motherly senses. "They're not going to run out."

We don't spend much time in the house. Using the discount Charlie gets as the child of a Microsoft employee, we hit the aquarium, the zoo, and the Pacific Science Center. We eat messy homemade burgers and lots of ice cream. I let him stay up late and don't make him clean his room. He rarely misbehaves because I give him pretty much everything he wants.

"You're turning into one of those parents you hate," Jess said one Sunday afternoon we spent at her house. "Aren't you worried you're overcompensating a bit?"

I shrugged. "A little, maybe. But I don't care. I have a lot to make up for." I cradle a selfish and quiet hope that Charlie is going home and telling Martin how much fun I am compared to him or Alice. How much he wants to come back and live with me. *His mother*. I don't know how to explain to my sister how compelled I feel to be in constant motion when I'm with Charlie. Standing still puts me in too much danger of my drinking catching up to me. I'm terrified it might suck me back in.

Jess won't let it go. "What're you going to get him for his birthday this summer, a Corvette? A yacht?"

I stuck my tongue out at her. I did need to talk to Martin again about Charlie's birthday party. The last time we had dinner together, my son told me he wants his August party held at Bouncy Land—a popular, inflatable playground venue for six-year-old boys. When I'd dropped him off at Alice's house that night, Martin was already there, waiting to take him home. We stood on the porch while Alice helped Charlie gather his things.

"Okay," I said. "He told me he wants to have his party at Bouncy Land. I was thinking a Spider-Man theme."

"My mom said he wants to have it at her house. Just a few friends." The muscle above Martin's left eyebrow twitched, a tic that only appeared when he was annoyed. "I'd like to keep it simple."

What you'd like to do is not extend any effort and leave it all up to your mother. I took a deep breath before responding. "We can keep it simple at Bouncy Land. I'm happy to plan it. And it's what he said he wants."

Martin shook his head. "Not according to my mom. She's been spending a lot of time with him, so I'm apt to believe her."

And by extension, not believe me, Charlie's mother, who is barely allowed to spend any time with him at all. Martin didn't have to speak for me to know exactly what he was thinking. My blood began to simmer beneath my skin.

"Well, we have until August," I said. I didn't have the energy for this argument. "We can figure it out later. I'll send you an e-mail with my ideas." I already knew what cake I would make and the Spider-

Man-themed decorations I would buy. I had in mind the kind of party the likes of which little boys dream.

When Charlie's not with me, I try to write, to come up with something—*anything*—I might be able to sell, but it feels as though there is a logjam of words stuck in my brain. I go back to the very basics, utilizing techniques I learned in college for encouraging creativity. First, I type out two columns of random words on a page and print it out. Then, I draw lines linking two words together and see if an article idea emerges. The first two words I link are "tires" and "chocolate." That's a no-go. The next set is "firemen" and "salami." The thought flashes through my brain that I might be able to scrounge up an X-rated essay out of that last combination, but erotica isn't exactly what I want to add to my résumé. After a few more tries, I give up. I can't get anything on the page. I wonder if my drinking did some kind of permanent brain damage—if I forever ruined my own professional abilities. Another failure I'll have to endure.

I try to distract myself with AA meetings. When Andi first told me how many meetings I had to attend, I was incensed. "Are you kidding?" I said. "I have to do group, individual, *and* three meetings a week? Do you know how many hours that is?"

"Yes," she answered, nonplussed. "How many hours a week did you spend drinking?"

She had a point. I'm grateful now to have something to do. A reason to escape my house. The meetings I choose to attend are large ones, fifty people or so, where I can sit a few rows from the back and have less of a chance of being called on to share. I used to sit in the very last row until I heard someone refer to it as "relapse row." I try to blend in—not too much a part of things but not too separate. A couple of times I consider avoiding the meetings and signing my own slip with another person's name just to avoid the humiliation, but I'm too afraid I'll get caught. I'm unwilling to risk losing Charlie forever.

I do listen during meetings, but I'm not sure how much I actually comprehend. For the most part, the voices sound like the grown-up characters in Peanuts cartoons: *wah-wah-wah-wah*. Occasionally, though, a certain story or phrase will pop through my consciousness, like the man who spoke of driving his car into a tree in his neighbor's front yard. He came to lying in the grass a few minutes later, not remembering anything past leaving work that afternoon.

"I'd been in a total blackout," he said. "So when I saw the cop car's flashing lights approaching, the first thing I thought was, *damn, they're going to smell the booze on me.* In my stoned state, I thought about parsley . . . how it's supposed to clean your breath? I figured grass was the next best thing. So I took a mouthful and started chewing."

The room erupted in laughter as he told this story and I thought, *What the hell is so amusing? It's not funny. It's ridiculous and sad. The man was eating a* lawn.

But he was laughing, too. He held up his hands in mock surrender, then dropped them to his lap. "I know, I know. But that's where my drinking took me. Lying on the lawn, gnawing on grass like a cow, my neighbors watching in horror." The laughing ceased, replaced by a sudden, somber silence. The man gave his head a quick shake before he continued. "I heard a phrase when I first got here, something about the 'incomprehensible demoralization' alcoholics feel. And that's exactly what it was. I was demoralized beyond my previous understanding. I thought no one could possibly get how full of shame and pain and self-disgust I was. I lived in this dark, terrifying vortex. I thought I was unique."

"Incomprehensible demoralization." This phrase reverberated throughout my bones. It captured exactly how I felt about my drinking. About drinking in front of my child.

"I also didn't know how to talk about how I felt," the man went on. "I couldn't imagine telling anyone how deep my pain went or talking about the horrible things I'd done." He paused, and then seemed to look directly at me. "But then I heard something else. I heard that we're only as sick as our secrets. And I knew that I didn't want to be sick anymore. I knew that I was willing to do whatever I had to in order to get well, including telling the truth about all I had done. And it scared the hell out of me. But what scared me more was starting to drink again."

"We're only as sick as our secrets." Another phrase that managed to soak into my mind and wreak a little havoc. What were my secrets? The drinking, of course. That was the worst. How bad it got. I didn't want to talk about that. Certainly not the details—I could barely admit those to myself. Nor could I acknowledge how incompetent I sometimes felt as a mother. And a writer. And a wife. And a daughter.

Afraid that someone might encourage me to say any of this out loud, at the end of the meetings, I would zip out the door before anyone could lure me into too deep a conversation. The people I have spoken with are generally normal and nice, not the religious zealots I first imagined they would be, but still, I haven't let any conversations get much past hello.

This technique works well for me until the morning I attempt to make a beeline for the door at the end of a meeting in the basement of a church in Fremont, a neighborhood not too far from my house. There is a swarm of happily chatting people blocking the exit, and I stand there impatiently craning my neck, looking for a method of escape.

"In a hurry?" a low, gravelly voice says. I look to my left toward the source of the voice and realize it is the man who told the story about eating a lawn. Now that he is next to me, I see that he is attractive, dark-haired, and in possession of mischievous green eyes. He is dressed in a black suit with a shirt and tie—definitely appealing in a clean-cut, businessman kind of a way. My thoughts flicker briefly on what his arms might look like out of that suit.

"Kind of," I say, giving him a quick smile before glancing back to the doors. They're still blocked.

He grins. "You make the fastest exit in the West at every meeting I see you."

I stare at him, self-consciously smoothing down my curls. "You watch me?"

"It's kind of hard to miss someone moving at the speed of light." He winks and then laughs, a deep, vibrating sound. "I'm Vince."

"Cadence." I smile and relax a bit when I realize he's only teasing. I reach my hand out to shake his and he takes it. His grip is quick, but firm.

"How long have you been sober?" he asks, tucking his hands into the front pockets of his slacks.

"A few months," I say. *One hundred and three days, if I make it through tonight.*

"Did you get your ninety-day chip?" He rocks back on his heels, then forward to stand flat.

I shake my head, pressing my lips together. At every meeting, the chairperson asks people to announce if they're celebrating a sober "birthday," but I have yet to open my mouth.

"Why not?"

I shrug and give him a half smile. "I'm not sure, exactly."

"Intimidating, isn't it? Telling this room full of people you're an alcoholic." He smiles and the skin around his eyes crinkles. "Makes it all too real."

"I guess that would be true," I say. I don't feel like going into a detailed explanation with a stranger about my doubts of whether or not I actually *am* an alcoholic, so I take the easy route and agree with him. I glance toward the doors, but there's still no escape.

"It's the middle of the day," I say, wanting to change the subject. "Don't these people have somewhere to be?"

Vince laughs again. "They have to be here. It's sort of part of the deal for staying sober. I'm on my lunch hour."

"What do you do?"

"I'm an electrical engineer."

I cock my head and scrunch up my face a little. "An engineer in a suit?"

He chuckles. "I own the firm. Have to look sharp and fool everybody into thinking I've got my shit together." He digs into his pocket, rooting around with his fingers. I hear the jingle of change. A moment later, he pulls out a handful and starts flipping through it. "Aha!" he finally says, pinching a bronze-plated coin between his index finger and thumb. He pushes it toward me.

"What's this?" I ask, taking the coin from him.

"My ninety-day chip."

"Oh, I couldn't take that." I hold it out toward him, trying to give it back, but he flaps his hand back and forth, refusing to take it.

"I've got five years," he says. "And I like to pass it on. That coin's full of good juju."

"Juju?" I'm almost afraid to ask what this means.

"Mojo, energy," he explains. "'May the force be with you' kind of thing."

"Ah, I see." I look at him and raise a single eyebrow. "Are you sure you want to give it to me?"

He bobs his head. "Absolutely. Three months was when I found my solution."

"And what was that?"

"Coming here." He winks at me again.

"Why haven't you given it to someone else?"

He shrugs. "I'm not sure. I kind of carry it like a good luck charm. But I try to live in the moment, and it feels like the right thing to do to give it to you."

"Well, then . . . thank you," I say, unsure exactly how he could determine something like that. But it is a nice gesture, and he seems like a decent enough guy. "It was good to meet you."

"You, too. I'll see you around." He waves, walks off, and finally, I'm able to find a big enough gap in the crowd to make it out the door.

Sixteen

The day before my meeting with Mr. Hines, I sit down with my coffee to look over my bills and determine whether or not it's time to put my house on the market.

I can't keep fooling myself. Money keeps going out and nothing comes back in. I'm not writing, and there's no guarantee I will. If I sell, I can use part of the equity to buy a small, no-maintenance condo and the rest to pay off my credit card debt. That will at least buy me some time to figure out if freelancing is what I really want to do with my life.

Just as I put my hand on my cell, intending to call and talk with Jess about what I need to do to get ready to sell, the phone rings. I see Martin's number on the display and immediately don't want to answer. Curiosity gets the better of me, of course, and I pick up the phone. "Hello?"

"Mama?" Charlie's voice is small, so unlike his usual brashness, it sounds borrowed from a much younger child.

Immediately, my body softens. "Hi, baby," I say. "Are you okay? It's so early." There is a sniffing sound in my ear and I realize he is crying. "Oh, honey, what's wrong?"

"I had a bad dream." He sniffs in hard, blows a long breath into the phone. "I *want* you." Nothing else matters—not Mr. Hines, Martin, nothing. Only Charlie. My son, wanting me. And I can't be there.

Dammit. This isn't fair. There is nothing about this situation that is fair. Not to me, not to Martin, and especially not to our son.

"I want you, too, baby. I miss you so, so much." I drop into a kitchen chair, my breath quivering as I speak. "What was your dream? Can you tell me about it?"

"Well, first there was a car. And then there wasn't. And you were there. And Daddy. And a fire." He snuffles again. "And I was scared."

I sigh. "I'm sorry, sweetie. It's no fun being scared. I wish I was there right this minute to give you a huge hug. A huge *squishy* hug."

He giggles. "Cuz you're a squishy mommy?"

"Yep. You told me I was. Remember?" A smile plays at my lips, relieved that he laughed, and thinking of how he felt pressed against me the night we spent at Jess's house.

"Yeah . . ."

"I love you, Mr. Man. I don't get to see you this weekend, but I will next week, okay? And you can call me anytime and I will call you, too. Did you get my cards this week?"

"Uh-huh."

"Well, good. You'll put them in your special book for me?"

" 'Kay, Mama."

"Love you, Charlie bear."

There is a rummaging noise, muffled voices. I wait, steeling myself against another confrontation with Martin. I want to know how his meeting with Mr. Hines went. What did he say about me? About our marriage? Was he convincing enough for Mr. Hines to choose him over me? Does being Charlie's mother matter at all, or does my drinking erase any meaning behind the word?

Martin comes on the line. "He had a bad dream," he says.

"Sounds like it." I pause, waiting for him to continue. "Thanks for letting him call."

"He wouldn't take no for an answer." My first thought is: *Excuse me, you told him* no*?* But then Martin goes on. "I told him it was too early, and that he might wake you up, but he would not be deterred. He's slightly stubborn."

Again, I smile. "I wonder where he gets that."

"Yeah . . ." Martin lets out a hard breath, a cross between a cough and a laugh. "The kid doesn't stand a chance."

"Nope."

Again, I hear a muffled voice, Charlie's this time, then Martin's voice in my ear. "He told me to tell you he loves you."

God. Has there ever been anything as difficult as this? "Thanks," I say, pushing my fingernails into my palm to keep from crying. My chest feels hollow. A giant claw just reached through the phone and scooped out what is left of my heart.

When Kristin calls later that afternoon and asks me to go to a seven o'clock meeting with her, I find myself agreeing, thinking that after my call with Charlie, it isn't a good idea to be alone. She picks me up at 6:30.

We pull into the parking lot of a church and head inside. I scan the room, but don't see Vince, and find myself strangely disappointed. We sit in a circle of about twenty-five men and women, in various states of being here by choice, others by court order. There are old people and young, professional and those with clothes stained greasy from an honest day's labor. There's coffee and talk about God, only one of which I am comfortable with. The meeting has opened up for people wanting to share their experiences, instead of being called on by the chairperson. I can finally relax, no longer in danger of being asked to speak to the group about my experiences.

"Hi, I'm Kristin, and I'm an alcoholic/addict," Kristin says when the chairperson opens the meeting. Her voice is fairly quiet, but it still manages to surprise me. She hadn't told me she was planning to speak.

The room is still. I am amazed at how intently people pay attention to another person's sharing in these rooms. In a bar, lots of people are talking, and nobody's listening. In here, one person speaks, and every word is heard.

"Hi, Kristin," the group responds, and I flinch. The response still feels clichéd to me, mimicked, perhaps, too many times in the media for it to appear substantive or genuine. No one else seems to mind it.

"Hi, everyone," Kristin says. Her fingers are linked tightly together in her lap and she keeps her eyes on them. "It's good to be back to this meeting." She pauses, a nervous habit of hers, it seems, when she is unsure how to proceed. She looks up, smiles weakly at the faces around the room. "I came for about six months, and really liked it, you know? I stayed sober. But here I sit, five years later, with barely sixty days."

The room erupts in applause at her pronouncement. The people here applaud at every announcement of sobriety—thirty days, one day, twenty-one years. Twenty-one *years*? I silently questioned the first time I heard such a long sobriety date. If they have to keep coming for so long, this program must not work as well as they say it does. I mean, really, isn't there a point you finally get it, and don't have to come back?

Kristin smiles again, then continues. "I know now that I'm in the right place. I'm going to do it the right way this time. I'm going to get a sponsor, I'm going to do everything she tells me. Even when she's wrong. So, anyway, thank you. Thank you for still being here."

"Thanks, Kristin," the group responds. We listen to a couple other people share, and then the meeting closes with the group standing in a circle holding hands, reciting the Lord's Prayer in unison. I keep my eyes open and mouth shut; the words wriggle like tiny metal shavings under my skin. I'm not religious, and while I'm told I don't have to accept an organized religion version of a higher power—apparently, I can choose to use a doorknob if I want to—when the word "God" is thrown around these rooms like confetti, it's difficult to imagine any other concept. I have a hard time feeling like I fit in with all of this. It's a little cultish, really, the way they talk about turning their will and their lives over to some invisible spirit. It goes against everything I grew up believing about the self-sufficient woman I should be.

Kristin accepts several hugs from the women in the room, and though I am standing off away from her, I get pulled into a few embraces myself. One woman with flame orange tresses and a sequined, denim button-down shirt hugs me hard, then holds me out at arm's length. "Trying to be invisible doesn't work so well here, does it?" she says, smiling. Her candy apple red lips are not a good match to her hair color. She wears rimless glasses and dangling intricate silver earrings.

"Uh, um . . ." I say. I am not used to being called out on my crap, so this is my brilliant response.

She laughs. "Don't worry, I won't tell. I did the same thing at meetings when I first got here. I was scared to death that someone might talk to me."

I make a few halfhearted protestations, and she just smiles more. "Do you need a sponsor, honey?"

"I don't think so," I say, finally finding a way to get the words in my brain to travel out of my mouth. "I'm in treatment."

"Really? Well, treatment can't last forever." Leaning over a nearby table, she scribbles something on a piece of paper and hands it to me. "Just in case. I'm Nadine."

Minding my manners, I take the paper, slip it into my purse. "Okay, well, thanks. I'm Cadence."

"Isn't that an interesting name?" she exclaims. "Creative mother, I guess."

"Father, actually," I admit, finding it very odd to be sharing this bit of extremely personal trivia with a strangely exuberant, orange-haired alcoholic.

Kristin rescues me at this point. "Are you ready to go?" she inquires, smiling at Nadine. "Hi, I'm Kristin."

"Nadine." She reaches over to hug Kristin. "Thank you for sharing, honey. I really appreciate hearing from the newcomers. I hope you find something here that keeps you coming back."

Kristin returns her embrace. "Oh, thank you." After she pulls away, she smiles again. "How many years do you have, Nadine?"

"Thirty-seven."

"Wow," Kristin says.

"If I can do it, anyone can," Nadine says, winking. "You two take care, okay? We'll see you next week."

We wave on the way out the door, and I exhale as we climb into Kristin's car. She looks at me as she turns the ignition. "What?"

I give her a look. "Nadine."

She tilts her head, curious. "What about her?"

I push another breath out of pursed lips, snap my seat belt in place. "Nothing, really. She's just a character."

"Yeah, but she's got a huge heart." Kristin backs up the vehicle, looking over her shoulder, careful not to run over any of her fellow alcoholics. "I remember her from the last time I was here. I almost asked her to be my sponsor."

"Why didn't you?"

She throws the car into drive, starts to pull into traffic. "I don't know. I don't know why I didn't do a lot of things. I guess I wasn't ready." It's quiet for a moment, and then she continues. "Nadine said something once that really stuck with me. It's the reason I knew I could come back. I mean, I was so full of shame, you know?"

I nod. Yes, I did know. Of course I knew. "What did she say?"

"She said, 'We don't shoot our own wounded.'" She glances at me. "I can't think of anywhere else in the world you get that kind of reception after fucking up. It made it a hell of a lot easier to get help."

I consider this. "What choice did you have, really? I mean, with CPS being involved and the DUI. Didn't you have to get help?"

She is quiet, contemplating, then shakes her head. "No. I didn't.

I could have killed myself. Those were my options." Her voice trembles. "I went with the one where my kids don't have to grow up without a mother."

"That's a hell of a choice to make."

"I know."

We are silent for another moment. And then the words come. They are out of my mouth before I realize, in barely a whisper. "I had to make that choice, too."

She reaches over, grabs my hand for the second time that night, squeezes hard, then turns the corner so she's driving us the right way home.

Seventeen

I leave my house the next morning dressed simply in a lavender cardigan and dark jeans. I'm jittery with renewed determination to present my case to Mr. Hines. I weave my way south down Interstate 5, drive beneath the ill-advised, traffic-inducing monstrosity of the Convention Center down the freeway about a mile. Qwest and Safeco Fields are off to my right. I take the exit next to the Tully's Coffee roasting plant, a building that twenty years ago used to produce Rainier Beer. As children, when my mother drove past it, Jess and I debated the more accurate characterization of the scent in the air—urine or cornflakes? I much prefer the current, easily distinguished nutty bouquet of roasting coffee.

Driving up and over the West Seattle Bridge, I listen to the calm, computerized tones of my GPS directing me to follow Fauntleroy Way, cross over California Avenue, and down the hill toward Lincoln Park. I find Mr. Hines's office a few blocks away from the Fauntleroy Ferry terminal. It's disguised as a two-story, sky blue Victorian-style house, complete with sharp gables and white gingerbread trim. I had imagined I'd arrive at a nondescript office building, but the address is right. It's not until I find a tiny black sign tacked to the left side of the front door, emblazoned with scrolled brass letters—RONALD HINES, MSW, GAL—that I'm certain I'm in the right place.

My cell phone rings just as I'm lifting my index finger to press the doorbell. I reach inside my purse and flip the phone open.

"Hello?" The word comes out as a whisper, though I'm not sure why.

"Hey, I just wanted to wish you good luck," Jess says. "I love you. I know you'll do great."

The tension woven through the muscles of my chest relaxes a bit. "Thanks, Jess. I appreciate it." I take a deep breath. "I need to talk with you about selling my house, too, okay?"

"Yeah, sure, of course," she says. "I'll run a CMA to see what we can list it for."

"What's a CMA?"

"Comparative market analysis. It tells us what houses are going for in your neighborhood."

"Oh, okay. That sounds great. Thank you." I pause to take another deep breath. "I'm standing on the front porch of his office right now. I should probably go."

"Okay. Call me later."

"I will. 'Bye." I press the bell and hear the thud of a man's footsteps moving toward the door. It swings open and Mr. Hines stands in front of me. I'm not sure what I was expecting him to look like, but it wasn't this. His blond hair is unkempt. He's stocky, not particularly handsome; at least, not in the traditional sense of the word. The pale pink, striped dress shirt and khakis he's wearing are rumpled and creased.

"Ms. Sutter?" he inquires. His voice resonates in a low, deep timbre.

I nod, my lips pressed together, too afraid to speak. I'm afraid I might let loose a wild string of babbling hysteria, begging this man to give me my son back. I'm pretty sure that wouldn't go over well. My breath is shallow; my lungs feel like overinflated balloons behind my rib cage.

"Come in." He gestures for me to step inside a long, narrow hallway. He closes the door, slips past me with his back against the wall. I follow him into a small, square room with three long, rectangular windows. It's sparsely decorated with a couple of chairs, a round end table, and a bookshelf. He sits in one of the padded, forest green armchairs and looks at me expectantly. "Please, sit down."

I lower myself into the other seat. Our knees are barely a foot apart. This arrangement feels oddly intimate to me, so I angle my knees off to one side to create a slightly larger space between us. "I'm really nervous," I blurt. "I don't know what to expect."

He shifts his mouth in a small motion. It's not quite what I would call a smile. "I wouldn't expect you to," he says. "And I'm sorry you're nervous. We'll take this slowly." He reaches for a yellow legal pad and a pen, crossing his left leg over his right knee. "Why don't you start by telling me about your marriage to Martin?" He drops his eyes to the notepad and waits, pen poised just above the page.

"Okay." I take a deep breath, unlacing my fingers and setting my hands flat on the tops of my thighs. I give him the short version, how Martin and I met, dated, and then decided to get married when I found out I was pregnant with Charlie.

He looks up when I say this. "Charlie wasn't planned, then, I take it?"

"No," I say. "But it only took me about two seconds to know I would keep him, once I knew I was pregnant."

"How did you feel about becoming a mother?" His eyes are intent on mine and I have to force myself to not look away.

"A little scared," I say, wanting to be honest with him, knowing this is what Martin most likely said about how I felt, too. "But aren't all mothers scared, the first time? I know my sister was. It kind of goes with the territory."

"So, how was being a mother once Charlie arrived? Were you still scared?"

I consider this, drumming my fingers across my thighs. "Well, in a different way, I suppose. I loved him immensely. I had never felt anything like it, to tell you the truth. I was scared I wouldn't be a good enough mother to him." As soon as the words are out of my mouth, I want to reel them back in, to somehow make it so they hadn't been spoken.

"Really." He looks thoughtful. "Why was that?"

I struggle to find the right words, panicking that he has just now, within the first thirty minutes of our conversation, decided I shouldn't have Charlie with me. "I think it was because my own mother was absent a lot when I was growing up. She was a single mom, and there was this part of me that was afraid that since I hadn't seen how to be a present, loving, involved mother, I wouldn't know how to do it myself. But I learned." I tick off the list of all the activities Charlie and I took on during the first couple of years of his life. I talk about teaching him some basic sign language, the classes we took, the play dates at the park.

"What did you find hard about being a mother?"

"Well . . . hmm." I fiddle with the hem of my shirt. "Mostly it just took time for me to adjust to how much Charlie needed me. For everything. It felt like a lot of pressure to get it all right."

"All of what right?"

"Everything. I wanted to give him the kind of childhood I didn't have. I wanted to be with him every minute of every day. I wanted him to feel treasured. I wanted to play pat-a-cake and peekaboo and hold him every minute he'd let me." I make a quivering, throaty noise I hope he interprets as laughter. "That was easier to do when he was a baby. Now he only lets me hold him when he's tired. The rest of the time he whirls around. He's a very energetic kid."

"Are you?"

"Energetic?"

"Yes. Do you feel like your energy level matches your son's?"

"Does *any* adult have the same energy level as a child?" I'm answering his questions with another question, an old habit from my reporting days. Deflect a subject's questioning of you with another question. He starts tapping his pen against his jawline. I try again. "I'm not an athletic person, if that's what you mean. My idea of exercise tends toward pacing back and forth in front of my computer when I can't think of a story idea."

"I see." Mr. Hines looks down to his notepad, scribbles a bit, then raises his eyes back up to me. "And your marriage? Why do you think it ended?"

I push a breath out between my lips before speaking. "There's a complicated question."

"I realize that. Can you at least try to answer it for me?"

So I do, first giving him the background on Martin's changing careers, then how our relationship shifted when Charlie arrived. "Martin was an only child," I explained. "It was just him and his mother from the time he was two years old. I think in some ways he got used to having a woman focus all her attentions on him. And only him. I sort of took over that role when we were dating, and our relationship worked. But then Charlie came along and I couldn't do that anymore. Martin had a difficult time adjusting."

"So you're saying you got divorced because he was jealous of Charlie?" Mr. Hines's silver irises peek up at me underneath twin blond caterpillar eyebrows. He appears doubtful.

"No, no, of course not," I backtrack, shaking my head. "Martin loves Charlie. But he wasn't around very much. For either of us. I tried talking with him, I even tried to get him to see a counselor with me. He refused."

"Ah," Mr. Hines says, scribbling another note on the page in front of him. "I see."

"There was so much distance between us," I say. "He was working an insane amount of hours, Charlie and I barely saw him, and when we did, he and I argued over parenting issues. Or his mother. Basically, whatever the subject was, we argued. He retreated, and I didn't want to rock the boat and make things worse, so nothing was ever resolved." My gaze lifts out the window before I bring it back to Mr. Hines. "It just wouldn't have worked. At least not for me. I felt like if he couldn't even acknowledge we had issues we needed to address, there wasn't enough of a foundation for us to try to build the relationship back up again. He abandoned us emotionally long before I filed for divorce."

"And when did your drinking begin?" He asks this as if he is inquiring when dinner might be served.

I swallow once, hard. "About two months after he left." I told him of my inability to sleep, the anxious thoughts that would spin like a top in my head. About having a glass of wine at night to relax. How it progressed slowly, over a period of months. How one day, a year later, I woke up and alcohol had taken over. "It didn't feel like a choice anymore," I say. "My body *demanded* that I drink. If I didn't, I got so ill I couldn't function. It wasn't like I just up and decided one day, oh, I think I'll start drinking on a regular basis so I don't have to think about my problems anymore," I explain, basically repeating what I'd told the doctor who admitted me to the psychiatric ward. "I didn't realize it was happening. I didn't know what was wrong with me."

"Did you tell your doctor how much you were drinking?"

Does anyone? I wonder. *Oh, yes, Doctor, I'm downing a good eight glasses of merlot a night.* "No, I didn't."

"Why not?"

"Well, I think at that point I didn't realize how much I was drinking. Or maybe I just couldn't admit it to myself. It felt pretty much next to impossible to admit it to her. It wasn't until I got to the psych ward and the doctor on duty that night asked me how much I drank that I got honest about it."

"I see." He makes another note. I resist the urge to snatch the pad from his lap and read what he is writing about me. "Why didn't you ask for help?"

"I just kept thinking I would find a way to manage it. I felt like there was something incredibly wrong with me that I couldn't just handle everything on my own."

"No one is completely self-sufficient," Mr. Hines says.

I raise an eyebrow at him. "You haven't met my mother yet. She worked two jobs, went to college, and raised two little girls entirely on her own. Martin's mother is like that, too. She raised Martin and ran a successful business. I had all these strong, successful women around me. I wanted to be one of them."

"So you pretended that you were and drank to alleviate the knowledge that you weren't?"

I look down at my fingernails. "That's simplifying it a bit, but yes. I suppose you could say that."

"What about your sister? You couldn't talk to her?"

"By the time I started to suspect I might have a problem, she was busy with infant twins and trying to sell houses. I didn't want to be a burden." I take a deep breath and look back up at him, wanting to direct the conversation back to a more positive note. "The good news is, I'm learning a lot about choices in treatment. That I can learn different tools to manage my unhappiness. Alcohol just happened to be there. I had no idea it would take me over the way it did. I understand that part of it is physical, but for me, it was more emotional and mental. I feel like knowledge is power, you know? I know better now, so it won't happen again."

He nods, listening. "So knowing you're an alcoholic enables you to stop being one?"

"Well," I say, drawing out the word, "to tell you the truth, I'm not exactly sure I'm an alcoholic."

He cocks his head to the side. "Can you elaborate on that?"

I pause, carefully considering my words. "Well . . . I think most alcoholics have trouble with drinking their whole lives. I haven't. I listen to people in meetings talk about the first drink they took when they were twelve years old. And it didn't happen like that for me. I drank socially for years without any problems, so I guess it feels more like a bad episode for me. A rough patch. Like I said, I'm used to being independent, not asking for help." I shrug. "I understand that I need to, especially now that I'm on my own. When Martin left, I was in unfamiliar territory, and I drank to relieve the discomfort."

He looks at me, his gaze sharp. "Alcoholics, by definition, have a life that has become unmanageable. Would you say that your life was unmanageable while you were drinking?"

"Yes," I start, not wanting to argue with him, but also wanting to be as honest as possible about my thoughts. "But it's not anymore. I'm managing it. I'm getting treatment. I'm learning the right way to handle my stress." I lean forward, my fingers linked, elbows resting on my knees. "I swear, I am going to do everything in my power to make sure I never pick up another drink. I'll do whatever my treatment counselor tells me. I'll go to meetings, get a sponsor, whatever it is I need to do." The tears come now, despite my valiant efforts to keep them at bay. "Charlie is everything to me," I say, my voice cracking on the words. "He's my life. I need to have him back with me. I want him back more than I've ever wanted anything." I sit back, wiping away the tears with the edge of my hand. "He needs me. I'm the first face he's seen every morning since he was born. I've given him every bath and kissed every scratch he's ever had. I taught him his alphabet. I tickle his back every night. He says he can't sleep unless I do this for him . . . I'm scared he's not sleeping . . ." I lose it at this point. The tears take over.

After a minute or two of me weeping, Mr. Hines quietly leans over and pulls a few tissues from the box on a table next to him, then hands them to me.

"Thank you," I sniff. "Sorry about that."

He waves his hand, dismissing my words. "No need to apologize. I'd be more worried if you didn't cry, to tell you the truth." He sighs. "I think that's enough for today, Ms. Sutter. If I have any more specific questions, we can save them for when I come visit the house."

"Okay," I say, hesitating. "Are you sure? I'm happy to stay."

"No, no. I've got enough of the basics here. Thank you for your honesty. I know this is hard to discuss."

"Yes." I reach for my purse, then look at him with what I hope is the clearest expression of gratitude I can muster. "Thank you for your time."

I want to say more. I want to beg him to just give my child back to me. *Anything,* I want to tell him. *I'll do anything you tell me to. Jump off a bridge, stand on my head, take night courses on healthy parenting for the next ten years. Whatever you decide, I will do. Just give me my child. I'll get down on my knees, right here. Please. I want my child back.*

My cell phone rings the next afternoon. I fumble for it, hoping by some miracle it might be Scott calling to tell me Charlie would be on his way home by the end of the week. I'd spent the day after my meeting with Mr. Hines in front of the television, waiting. Instead, Jess's name pops up on the caller ID.

"Hey, there," I say, flopping back into my well-worn groove on the couch. I click the mute button on the television remote.

"Hey," she says. "You never called me back."

"Sorry," I say. "I kind of vegged out watching the Food Network when I got home."

"Your personal porn channel, you mean?"

I laugh. "Pretty much." I don't tell her that I also ate six pieces of fried chicken I brought home from the grocery store, topped off with a full pint of Ben & Jerry's Crème Brûlée ice cream. Nor do I tell her I roamed the cupboards after eating all of that, looking for more, even though it felt as though my stomach might burst. Different behavior, same compulsion, Andi would say.

"Okay. Well, I was worried." I hear her take a deep breath. "So, how did it go?"

"Fine, I guess. I lost it, totally cried my eyes out in front of him talking about losing Charlie. It sucked." My throat thickens again just thinking about it.

"Well, he'd probably be more concerned if you didn't lose it."

"That's what he said." I don't want to talk about this anymore. I don't even want to be living through it. "Anyway. How are you? How are the boys?"

"I'm good, they're a couple of terrors. When do you get Charlie again?"

"Not until the weekend. I've been relegated to the status of 'every other mother.'"

"It'll be okay, Cadee." She knows me too well to ignore the sadness in my voice, however well I try to mask it.

I clear my throat. I can't cry again. I just can't. "I should go. I'll talk to you about the house stuff later?"

"Okay. I love you."

"Love you, too."

I hang up, grateful for Jess's heartfelt assurance that all will be well. I want desperately to believe her, but we are sisters, after all. Her desire to soothe me might compel her to lie the same way drinking taught me to lie to myself.

Eighteen

Four days after my appointment with Mr. Hines, I'm pacing the house. I want to call and talk to Charlie, but it's early afternoon and he's with Alice. She always lets my calls go to voicemail so there's no point in trying. He was with me over the weekend, but it wasn't enough. The muscles in my arms literally throb from wanting to hold him. I sit down at the kitchen table, edgy and uncomfortable. I try to work.

I revisit the idea of writing an essay about how adult friendships fade. There has to be a market for something like that—maybe I could query my old contact at *Woman's Day* and see if she'd be interested. I think about my friendship with Susanne and why it doesn't seem to be working anymore, but realize I'd have to write about my drinking problem in order for the essay to make any sense. Plus, if I was going to do a really thorough job, I would have to talk with Susanne to get her side of the experience in order to present a well-rounded picture of the situation. *Scratch that idea.* I run a couple of Google searches on random thoughts—switching careers in your thirties, how to lose ten pounds eating ice cream—but I can't concentrate. All I can think about is Charlie. Shutting down my Internet window, I open Outlook and send Martin an e-mail, giving him the rundown on the pricing at Bouncy Land for Charlie's party.

It's not that expensive, and it includes pizza and juice for the kids. So all we'd have to do is bring the cake, which you know I will make. And some goody bags for the kids, which I'll do, as well. Let me know what you think.

He sits at his computer all day for work so his answer only takes a few minutes to come back to me.

I think it's better if we do it at my mom's house. She wants to make the cake, too. If you want to do the goody bags or balloons or something, that would be fine. We'll take care of the rest.

This is wrong. It just feels so incredibly wrong. I have always planned Charlie's birthday parties. Not Martin. Me. He shows up, gives the other children airplane rides or fills up water balloons for them. Who the hell does he think he is? I screwed up, yes. But does that completely erase my worthiness as Charlie's mother? Does that mean I don't ever get a say in anything about his life ever again?

"God*dammit*," I say out loud to an empty room. I make a strange growling noise and pound my fists on my desk.

I can't *stand* this. I can't do it. I feel wild. Unstable. I need to get away from myself. I decide to head over to my favorite neighborhood coffee shop, convinced that outside of going to a meeting, a white chocolate mocha is another perfectly legitimate motivation to leave the house.

The door at Wholly Grounds jingles as I step inside and a barista gives me a welcoming smile. I glance over to the corner opposite the fireplace where the owners have set up a twenty-foot-square, gated-off area filled with kids' tables and toys. A large sectional couch sits right outside this enclosed play area so mothers can chat and sip coffee while keeping an eye on their children. There are four women sitting on the couch today and a handful of kids in the play area. My eyes flicker across them quickly, doing my best not to let my emotions get the better of me at seeing mothers with their children. I can't keep melting down. There'll be nothing of me left.

"Cadence!" a voice calls out. I stop in my tracks and look back to the sectional, only to realize that the women sitting there are Brittany, Renee, Susanne, and another woman I don't recognize.

I give them a hesitant smile and a quick wave. I'm not in the mood to talk. I want to get my coffee and run back to my house. But Brittany beckons me over, so I take a deep breath and go to say hello. "Hey, everyone." I smile at the woman I don't know, feeling oddly unnerved. "I'm sorry. I don't think we've met."

"I'm Julia." She motions over to the children, who all appear to be about Charlie's age. "And that's Cody over there, in the brown T-shirt. With the whipped cream on his face."

I smile, but my chest feels tight. It's hard to breathe. I feel like the specimen smeared on a glass slide under a microscope.

Brittany sits forward and sets her cup on the table in front of them. "I haven't seen you in ages. How have you been?"

"I'm good. Busy with the writing, as always. How are things going for you?"

"I'm wonderful." She beams, running her palm over her abdomen. "Pregnant again."

"Really? That's great." It must be early in her first trimester; her stomach is completely flat. I swallow hard. I just want to get my coffee and go home. I look over to Susanne, who hasn't said a word. "How's Anya?" I ask.

"She's fine." She flashes a swift smile, then looks immediately away. *What's the deal with that?* I know we haven't been talking much, but I didn't expect it to be this awkward between us.

"Where's Charlie?" Renee asks, peering over the top of the couch, searching for my invisible child.

My arm reflexively reaches out behind me as though Charlie were standing right there. As though I could hold his hand. I read once about a man who lost a leg at the knee after an accident. He talked about reaching for his right foot to put on a shoe every day for years, even after the leg was gone. I imagine how I feel in this moment is a little bit like how he felt when he had to pull back from reaching to his foot.

My cheeks explode with heat as the other women watch me drop my arm back to my side with quizzical expressions on their faces. I scramble for the right explanation. "He's spending some time with Martin today," I say, finally settling for an abbreviated version of the truth. *We're only as sick as our secrets.* "Father-son bonding time."

I catch Susanne throwing a quick sidelong glance at Brittany, whose eyebrows lift almost imperceptibly. A sense of trepidation begins to coil in my belly.

"That's important for them to do," Renee says. "Rick spends every Tuesday night with Juan. They go to the park and then out to dinner so I can get some alone time."

"Huh," Julia says. "Alone time? What's *that*? I couldn't get Steve to spend an evening with his son if his life depended on it."

"You don't have to pick up Charlie any time soon, do you?" Brittany says. "You should join us. Get your coffee and come have a seat."

"Oh. Okay. Great. Thanks." *What else could I say?* I shuffle back from foot to foot, looking at Susanne for some kind of support, but she still doesn't meet my gaze. I guess what Andi said was true—our friendship has shifted for good. Or maybe it wasn't a friendship at all. At least not the kind that is good for me.

"Great." Brittany smiles again. Susanne stares at her coffee cup, Renee looks over to the play area, checking on her son. My eyes follow hers, automatically searching the group of children for my son's face. Though it shouldn't, not seeing him there startles me. My heart jumps a beat in my chest before I remember he's not here.

As I step away from them, the whispers start. It's Renee, just barely loud enough for me to hear. "Does she think we don't know?"

And then Brittany: "Martin told me she's an absolute mess. He had to step in."

"Of *course* he did," Renee agrees, keeping her voice low. "I mean, really. Wouldn't you?"

"What?" Julia asks. "Does she think we don't know what?"

Susanne doesn't say a word.

My throat seizes up. My stomach clamps down on itself and I freeze where I stand. They all know. It had to be Susanne. She told them. How could she *do* that? I can't drink with her anymore, so she starts gossiping about me? What the *hell*? And I'm sure once Brittany got the scoop about my going to treatment, she must have talked to Martin at Charlie's preschool and pumped him for all the details.

I want to run away. I want to pick up my feet and force them right out the door. But I don't. Instead, I spin around to face them, my eyes bright. I swallow, trying to keep the tears at bay. I don't want to give them the satisfaction. They stop talking and look up at me. They're caught.

"You know what?" I say, staring straight at Susanne. "I actually need to work today. I don't have time for coffee."

Susanne drops her eyes to the floor again and Renee simply stares back at me. Julia looks confused.

"Oh," Brittany says, the only one who doesn't look away. "That's too bad."

Yeah, too bad. I want to defend myself. I want to ask each one of them if they've ever done anything shameful in their own lives. If they've ever hurt anyone they love; if they've behaved in a way they'd do anything in the world to erase. My blood feels like fire beneath my skin as I consider what they must think of me. I might as well be standing naked in front of these women.

I might as well still be drunk.

Nineteen

Since Charlie is with me over Memorial Day weekend, I invite Jess and Derek and the boys over to my house for a barbecue. Jess and I have talked a bit about what amount I could list the house for, but Derek wants to do a once-over on maintenance issues and ways I might fix the place up for a quicker, more profitable sale. Jess and I get the chicken and vegetable skewers ready for the grill while Derek completes his inspection.

"Well," he says as we sit down to eat at the picnic table in the backyard, "it might need some electrical work to come up to code. And a few of the rooms need fresh paint. But otherwise, it's pretty solid. I think if we spruce up the yard and price it just under what others have listed for in your neighborhood, it'll go quick."

"That's great," I say. "Will I lose anything?"

Derek shakes his head. "You shouldn't. You bought the place before prices really started to go up around here. You'll come out ahead, for sure."

"I don't *want* you to sell our house, Mommy," Charlie says. "I like it."

I smile at my son. "I know, baby. I wish I didn't have to, but we'll find another place just as nice."

"Like Daddy's house? We could live there, since Shelley doesn't stay there anymore." He looks hopeful.

Jess gives me a bemused smile and I chuckle. "I don't think

that would work for us very well, either, Charlie bear. Don't worry, though. Uncle Derek will help us find something." I swing my gaze to my brother-in-law and he nods.

"Absolutely. There are some great deals to be found. I'll keep my eye out for a repo or short sale on a condo. In Edmonds, maybe. Near the water."

"We could live near the beach, Charlie," I say. "What do you think about that?"

"Yeah!" Charlie says, and I am relieved he is so easily appeased.

When the kids are out of earshot and Derek is in the house grabbing another soda from the fridge, Jess turns to me. "Have you talked to Mom since you went to her office?"

I shake my head. "Has she said anything to you?"

"Not really. She's acting weird. Maybe you should try again."

"Maybe," I say. "We don't have the best track record when it comes to communicating."

"Emotional crap makes her uncomfortable. Where do you think *you* got it?"

I laugh. "Yeah, how did you luck out?"

She shrugs. "I dunno. I'm just wired differently." I wonder if this is true. She and I basically had the same childhood, yet I'm the one with all the issues.

She sighs and looks over to the kids. "So, you're really going to sell this place?"

"I have to. I can't afford it anymore."

"What about work? Have you sold anything lately?"

"Don't ask. I'm totally procrastinating."

"Well, you know what procrastination and masturbation have in common, don't you?" She waits a beat, then answers her own question. "When it comes right down to it, you only end up screwing yourself."

* * *

The following Wednesday, for my weekly dinner with Charlie, I decide to invite my mother to come along. I've been regretting my petulant behavior from the last time we talked, and after my own meeting with Mr. Hines, I am even more anxious to know what she plans to say to him. I call her first thing in the morning on Wednesday and Keiko offers to convey the message to her since she is already busy with a patient.

"She told me she'd love to," Keiko says when she comes back on the line. "I'll make reservations for you at the Spaghetti Factory, if you like. Sharon said it's Charlie's favorite place."

I smile, touched my mother managed to remember this detail about her grandchild. "That would be great. Thanks."

I pick Charlie up from Alice and we meet her at the restaurant near her office around seven o'clock. Even after a long day with patients, my mother's brown hair is sleek and her casual khakis and white cotton sweater are still smooth and spotless.

Charlie runs to greet her. "Nana! I'm having 'sketti for dinner. Do you want it, too?"

My mother hugs him and laughs. "I think Nana might have to settle for a salad, but I might have to steal a bite or two of yours, if that's okay."

"Sure!" Charlie speeds back to his seat and clambers up into the chair next to me. "You sit there, okay, Nana?" He points to the chair across from him with his chubby index finger.

"Okay," my mother says, and she slides into her seat. "Hello, darling." She gives me a big smile. "How are you?"

"I'm doing okay," I say, which is about as honest an answer as I can muster up. "How are you?"

"I'm well. Busy as always."

We place our orders and before our food comes, my mother helps Charlie color on his placemat. "Look, Mommy," he says. "Look at me color with the blue crayon."

"Yes, sweetie. You're doing a wonderful job."

"Try to stay inside the lines, sweetie," my mother says.

"He doesn't need to, Mom," I say. "It's creative, like thinking outside the box."

She sits back in her chair and sets the crayon she'd been holding back on the table. "Okay." Her expression is blank; we've clashed on issues like this before. I want Charlie to know it's okay for him not to do everything perfectly; she spent much of my childhood expecting me to do nothing less.

The server delivers our food and outside of both of us talking to Charlie, my mother and I don't say much to each other for the rest of our meal. I'm anxious to ask her if she's come to any kind of decision about her meeting with Mr. Hines, but it's not appropriate to talk about it with Charlie here. She gets up to leave before I've paid the bill.

"I'm exhausted," she says. "Thank you so much for inviting me, though." She waggles her fingers at Charlie. "Nana loves you, honey."

"I love you, too!" Charlie says. He slurps a single noodle up into his mouth and specks of marinara sauce spatter all over his cheeks.

"'Bye, Mom," I say, grabbing a napkin to wipe my son's face. "You're a monkey, you know that?"

"Ooo-ooo-ooo!" Charlie says, mimicking a chimpanzee's call.

I laugh. "You silly kid. I love you so much."

"Love you, Mommy! All the way to the stars and back."

Alice is waiting by the front door when I drop Charlie back off half an hour later.

I hug my son and try not to cry as I drive away. I grab my cell and punch in my mother's number. She has to be home by now.

"Hi, honey." Her voice is tense. My pulse speeds up.

Why is this so hard for her? Why can't she just say, yes, of course you should have Charlie? Isn't that what any good mother would say? I decide to dispense with any niceties and ask her the hard question. "Are you worried I'll start drinking again, Mom? Is that why you haven't decided what you're going to say to Mr. Hines?"

She is silent for a moment. "Yes," she finally says.

I have to swallow a couple of times to keep from crying. "I guess I understand that," I say. "There are no guarantees I won't."

"No, there aren't," she says. Her voice is barely a whisper.

"I'm doing everything I can."

"I know. It's just—"

"Just what?" *Tell me. Please, just tell me why you think I'll fail.* "Do you think I'm like your mother? That I'm crazy?"

Her sigh is ragged. "I don't think you're crazy, Cadence."

"You've told me my whole life I'm like her."

"I said you *looked* like her."

"You said I was her carbon copy! You said she was crazy, then you told me I was just like her. I was a kid. Did it even cross your mind what conclusions I'd come to about that?" *I will not cry,* I chant internally. *I will not cry, I will not cry, I will not cry.*

"My mother wasn't crazy."

"What?" I ask.

"She wasn't crazy!" There is the hitch of tears behind her words. "That's just what they called alcoholics when I was growing up. That's what my dad called her. It's what I was used to calling it. I didn't know how to talk to you girls about it, so I just called her what I'd always called her. It wasn't until my father left that I really saw what was wrong with her. That it was the drinking that brought on her crazy behavior. She climbed into bed and drank for days and days. She wouldn't shower. She screamed at me. I'd try to cook for her. I'd try to make her the kinds of things she liked to eat so she would stop drinking, and she would throw the plate of food at me as I walked out the door. Later, she said she was sorry. She made me climb under her covers with her and then she cried. She cried and she told me how much she hated me. She said she wished I was never born." Her breath heaves.

Trying to process what this all means, my thoughts spin to the point of feeling dizzy. "God, Mom. Why didn't you *tell* us any of this?"

"You were too young. It's not exactly the kind of knowledge little girls need. When you got old enough, there wasn't a reason to tell you."

"Until now, maybe? You didn't think when all of this happened with me that that might have been a perfect opportunity to say something? Maybe at the family session at Promises? That would have been a perfect place to bring it up."

"Of course I did. I just . . ." She trails off and I have to prompt her.

"Just what?"

She sighs. "I've never talked about it to anyone. I certainly wasn't going to say anything in front of all those strangers in that group. I didn't even know how to say it to *you.*"

"Are you afraid I'll end up like her?"

"If you keep drinking, you *will* end up like her. And when I meet with him in July, if I tell Mr. Hines you should have Charlie, and you start drinking again . . . well, then it would be my fault." Her voice is tired, wrung dry.

"What would be your fault?" I whispered.

"It would be my fault if Charlie grew up the same way I did. Scared of his own mother. Terrified to do or say just one tiny wrong thing for fear of it setting you off. I wouldn't be able to live with myself if you hurt him the way she hurt me."

"But I'm not her," I say quietly. "Mom. I don't ask you for much. I never have. You taught me that. I'm so capable. Why would I ever need help? But I need your help here." The words feel heavy and foreign, falling at strange angles throughout my mouth as I deliver them.

"I'm sorry," she says. "I don't know what else to say."

"Sorry for what? Are you going to tell Mr. Hines I shouldn't have Charlie?" My lungs feel like they're about to collapse from the pressure surrounding them.

"I don't know what I'm going to tell him," she says. "Not yet. I just wanted you to know why."

*   *   *

I call Jess the next morning, wanting to tell her about our grand-mother but knowing it's something I probably shouldn't do over the phone. I half expect her to already know anyway, since Jess is usually our mother's first confidante. Though I am the oldest I can count on one hand the number of times I've known something that significantly affects our lives before she does.

"Marley, get away from your brother with that crayon!" she says instead of hello. I hear the boys screeching in the background. "God, I'm sorry," she breathes into the phone. "The little shits."

"Uh-oh, bad day?" I smile as I say this, even though I know full well it's not nice to feel happy that my sister has bad mommy moments, too. I can't help it, though, I do. It makes me feel less defective.

"Not bad, really. Just busy. I'm trying to get three offers put together and faxed to the appropriate agents and Marley decided to get artistic on the septic addendum. Now he's trying to color his brother's brain periwinkle blue. Through his nasal passage."

I laugh. "Tell him Aunt Cadee said to go with burnt sienna."

"Uh . . . no," she says. "So what's up?"

"Can you come over for dinner tonight?" I ask her.

"That depends," she says. "What are you going to make me?"

I smile, knowing exactly how to lure her. "Green chili enchiladas with gobs of jack cheese and sour cream?"

"Sold! I'll get Derek to hang out with the boys and be there at seven."

I fill my day by going to the grocery store for all the ingredients I need to make my sister's favorite meal, deciding at the last minute to grill some corn on the cob for a roasted corn salad with red bell peppers and cilantro-lime dressing. I love how easy it is to get lost in my thoughts while I work in the kitchen. Following the steps in a recipe and ending up with exactly what I expect is a huge comfort. Right now, I'll take predictability wherever I can find it.

Jess shows up at about 7:15 wearing black leggings and a long, red T-shirt. She inhales deeply. "Oh my God, I could smell this all the way down the street." She walks in the front door, pulls her shirt up, and uses a hooked thumb to extend the elastic waist of her pants. "I dressed appropriately."

I laugh, taking the fancy bottle of citrus sparkling water she brought to go with our dinner. We sit down and after serving her a spoonful of each dish, she moans appreciatively as she eats. "Oh, man," she groans. "You are the best cook."

I smile, and my whole body fills with pleasure at her compliment. "Thank you."

We eat in silence for a few minutes, until I set down my fork and rest my hands in my lap. "So," I begin, "I have something I want to talk to you about."

Jess sets her fork down, too, and gives me an apprehensive look. "Uh-oh. This isn't just a sisterly bonding meal? There's an agenda?"

I release a short laugh. "Not exactly. But I do need to tell you about a talk I had with Mom." I repeat what our mother told me about our grandmother being an alcoholic.

"Wow." Jess breathes the word out heavily, dropping back against her chair as she keeps her eyes on me. "Well, it makes sense, doesn't it? She *hated* talking about her mom with us. All those stories about taking her to the psych ward and how horrible it was checking her in—" She stops suddenly and drops her gaze to her plate. "I'm sorry. That was rude. I didn't mean—"

I wave off her apology. "Don't worry about it. I *was* in the psych ward. And I belonged there." I give her a wry smile. "For a little while, at least." I roll over a few phrases in my mind, unsure of the proper etiquette for thanking my sister for delivering me to the loony bin. I'm pretty sure Hallmark doesn't have a card for this occasion.

Jess looks relieved. "Yeah, can you imagine what it was like for our grandmother back then? Having a drinking problem and instead of getting to go to treatment like you did, everyone telling her she was a nut job?"

I pause for a moment, considering what my sister has said, and she starts to look worried again. I reach over and squeeze her forearm. "I've just never thought of it that way. That treatment is something I 'get' to do as opposed to 'having' to."

She nods, looking pensive. "Man, our poor grandmother." She pauses. "Our poor *mother*. It has to bring up a lot of crap for her. She probably has no idea how to deal with your situation."

"That's something we have in common then."

She reaches her arm around my shoulders and pulls me to her for a hug. I let her hold me for a minute, resting my head on her chest. "So, you haven't asked how *my* conversation with Mr. Hines went," she says.

I jackknife upright. "What? You talked with him? When? You didn't tell me you had a meeting with him. Scott didn't tell me he was planning on talking with you."

She holds up her hands in a gesture of surrender. "Whoa there, Nelly. I didn't know. Your lawyer didn't know. The man just called me this afternoon, out of the blue."

"What did you say to him, Jessica?"

She drops her hands back to her lap. "What do you think I told him? I said you are the most amazing person I've ever known. I told him you are creative and smart. I said you are loving and generous. I told him I would not be the person I am today without you as my sister."

My throat begins to close and my eyes mist. I open my mouth to speak, but no words come out, so I close it again.

"You're welcome." Jess touches my cheek with her warm hand. "I meant it. I love you so much."

"I love you, too." A couple of tears slip out and she wipes them away with the edge of her thumb.

"But that's not what you really want to know, right? You want to know what I told him about whether you should have Charlie back."

I nod, unable to speak again.

"Well, I've thought about it a lot. How could I not, right? I saw how ugly it was that night I came to get you." She looks at me with glassy eyes. "I barely recognized you. There was this . . . I don't know, *vacancy* in you. Like you had already stepped away from your body. It scared the hell out of me."

"I'm sorry," I whisper.

"I know," she says, using the bend of her wrist to wipe away her own tears. "It just seemed like you were fine one minute and the next time I looked, you were way over the edge."

"That's how it felt, too. *Exactly* how it felt."

She takes a deep breath. "The good news is, I see all these changes in you already. You seem to be calmer than you were even a week ago. I'm not sure what it is exactly. But I told Mr. Hines you've always been a role model for me and you're a role model for me now."

"Really?"

"I know, frightening, isn't it?" She winks at me.

I give her a halfhearted smack. "Jess."

"I also told him you're the parent Charlie should live with."

A sob grips my chest and I curl back up against my sister. "Thank you," I whisper. "Thank you so much. And not just for saying that to Mr. Hines. Thank you for everything. For being there for me that night. For helping me."

"Eh. What else are little sisters for?" She kisses the top of my head.

I look up at her. "I'm the big sister. I should be *your* hero."

"Be your own," she says, and the thought flits through my mind that it might be possible for me to do just that.

Twenty

Nadine sits across from me at a meeting the morning after my dinner with Jess. Her flame orange tresses are spiked in a wild, porcupine mess and her vermillion lips stand out as a striking but friendly gash carved against her pale, powdered face. Her skin has the softly wrinkled quality of a slightly overripe apricot. Sparkling green eyes regard me from behind her glasses as she talks about the peace she finds in AA.

"I've got ANTs," she says with a grin. "Assorted negative thoughts. They crawl through my brain causing trouble, but what I hear in these rooms manages to squash them, so I don't have to reach for a drink to drown them out. Little bastards keep coming back, though, so here I am. You all are my exterminators. That's all I've got. Thanks."

As she picks up the knitting project she had set in her lap while she was speaking, the other people in the room give a collective chuckle, including me. This is such an accurate image of how my own head feels most the time: my brain as an ANT farm.

I came because I knew Nadine would be here. I need to get a sponsor. Someone to help guide me through how to do the work. I have heard about it constantly during the meetings, these "steps" I need to take. I have no clue how to begin. I have a bizarre suspicion this mouthy, brilliant-haired, ANT-ridden recovering alcoholic might just be the person to walk me through.

After the meeting ends and I'm waiting to talk with Nadine, Vince approaches me. A petite woman who appears to be about my age, with dirty blond hair and shaking hands, walks next to him. She wears baggy blue jeans and a heavily pilled, oversize green sweater.

"Cadence," Vince says, "I'd like you to meet Trina. This is her first meeting."

"Hi," I say, keeping an eye on Nadine to make sure she doesn't slip out before I get a chance to talk with her. Asking her to become my sponsor is not the kind of conversation I want to have over the phone.

"Nice to meet you," Trina says in a tiny voice. She doesn't lift her gaze from the floor.

"How've you been?" Vince asks me.

"Okay," I said. "I guess. Hanging in there."

"Just taking the next indicated step, huh?"

I nod, though I'm not exactly sure what he means. Another reason I need to get a sponsor. There are moments I feel like I need a translator for some of what gets said at meetings.

"I thought you might be able to give Trina your number," Vince says. "Being that she's new and all."

"Oh," I say, pulling my chin back into my chest a little. "Okay. Sure." I rummage through my purse and manage to find an old grocery receipt. I check it to make sure it's not one with a wine purchase listed, then scribble my name on the back with my phone number and e-mail address.

"Thank you," Trina practically whispers as she shoves the paper in the front pocket of her jeans. "I have to get going." She gives us a short wave and speeds out the doors.

Vince laughs. "See? You two have something in common already."

I smile at him. "Cute."

"Who, me?" he says. "Why, thank you." He gives me a quick, unexpected hug, and my nose is suddenly pressed into his neck. Along with a natural, slightly wood-smoke male muskiness, his skin has a clean soap-and-water scent. My stomach lurches a bit as I realize just how long it's been since I've felt a man's touch.

I pull back and look at him, unnerved by the glint in his green eyes.

"Are you bothering this poor girl, Vincent?" Nadine says as she approaches us.

"Now, why would you say that, Miss Nadine?" he says with a smile. "Excuse me, ladies, I have to get to the office. I'll talk with you later, Cadence."

"'Bye," I say. "Take care." I turn toward Nadine. "It's nice to see you again."

"You're becoming a regular." She leans in to hug me, a quick, voracious movement. There is such power, such an emphatic under-standing in her touch. I want to know how to have this, how to give it to others.

"Do you have time to grab a cup of coffee with me?" I ask. I'm not sure where this courage is coming from. Something is compelling me to push past the usual fears that would normally hold me back.

"I do." She smiles. "There's a shop just around the corner, Wholly Grounds? Do you know it?"

"Yes," I say, trying not to think about what had happened there with Susanne and the other mothers. "I'm a regular. See you there in a few minutes?"

Once we both arrive and order our drinks, we settle into the plush, dark brown velvet chairs by a flickering faux fireplace.

"Mmm." Nadine leans back, holding the large mug with both hands, palms wrapped around it to warm them. "I love my coffee, don't you?"

"Definitely. Another addiction of mine, I suppose." I sip my own drink, unsure of exactly how to do this. Nadine must sense this, be-cause she takes a swallow of her coffee, then speaks.

"So, tell me, Cadence. Why am I here?" She is nothing if not direct.

I laugh a bit nervously. "Well, I'm in a treatment program at Promises?"

She nods. "I have several sponsees who've gone there."

"Oh." I pause. "So I need to get a sponsor. I know you offered to before and I'm not sure exactly how this works and what it really means. But I think I need one. I've got so much going on and I'm going to eventually lose Andi—she's my counselor at Promises—and I think she's really the only person I've trusted in a long time, you know?" I take a deep breath after rambling all this out on a single exhalation.

Nadine smiles, sets her coffee on the flat stone surface next to the fireplace. "Slow down, honey, you'll hyperventilate."

I grimace self-consciously. "Sorry." I take another slow breath in. "I know I haven't shared much in meetings. I've been too scared when I get called on, so I've passed. But I'm in the middle of a custody dispute for my son." I reach into my purse, pull out a picture of Charlie, and show it to her.

"He's gorgeous," she says. "Look at that grin. How old?"

"He'll be six in August," I say, and for some reason, a lump begins to form in my throat. I set the mug down on the squat wooden table between us. "So, is there an application process or something for this sponsor thing? Is this like a job interview? Do you have to get back to me?"

She chuckles, eyes sparkling in amusement. "No application necessary. It's not that formal a process, really." She smiles warmly, but the expression behind her eyes is clearly serious. "I would be happy to be your sponsor, Cadence. We can talk more about what that means as we go along. But the first thing is I need to know if you are willing to do what I suggest."

"What, exactly, are you suggesting?" I ask warily.

"That you be willing to do what I suggest." She gives me a closed-lipped smile, and I have to rein in the bit of frustration I feel for fear she'll see it on my face. None of this makes sense to me. "For example," she goes on, as though sensing I need further explanation, "how would you feel if I asked you to go to ninety meetings in ninety days. Would you be willing to do that?"

I consider this. My immediate reaction is *hell no.* "Ninety? In a row?"

"Without missing one. If you do, you start over." She cocks her head to the side, giving me a bemused smile. "How would that feel to you?"

"Irritating," I say, and she laughs again.

"Well, honesty is good. I'd rather that than have you try to blow sunshine up my butt." She clasps her creased, slightly leathery hands together as though in prayer. "You've been in treatment, so I won't ask you to do the ninety-in-ninety thing. I *will* ask that you call me every day. And we should get together at least a couple times a month outside of meetings. How does that sound?"

I nod, a little stilted. "I think I can do that. What are we supposed to talk about when I call?"

"Anything you need to. Whatever's on your mind. How you're feeling, whether you slept poorly, if your ex-husband is pissing you off . . ." She gives me a meaningful look. "They have a nasty tendency to do that, you know."

"Oh, I know." I ask, reaching for my coffee again to finish it off, "Are you divorced?"

"Yep. Four-time loser."

"Four?" It's impossible to keep the astonishment out of my tone, or off my face.

"Yeah, I'm a slow learner." She grins. "I'm dating someone right now, though. But I'm only using him for sex."

It's my turn to laugh loud enough to turn the other patrons' heads. I'm starting to really like this woman.

"What?" Nadine bats her eyelashes in an unsuccessful attempt to look innocent. "I'm not dead yet."

"Definitely not." I swallow the last of my coffee, savoring all the gooey sweetness at the bottom of the cup.

"What do you do for work?" she asks me, setting her empty cup on the table next to her.

I sigh, fingering the edge of my mug. "I'm sort of in limbo right now. I was a reporter for the *Herald,* and then a freelance writer, but all of that pretty much went by the wayside when I started drinking. I've had a hard time getting back into it. I think it might be time for a career change." What *kind* of career change, I still don't know.

Nadine gives me a concerned look. "What do you do all day, then?"

I shrug. "I go to treatment and meetings. And cook a little, for my son. Things I can put in the freezer for when he comes home." My voice shakes as I say this last sentence. "I probably watch too much TV."

"You need more structure than that," Nadine says sternly. "You need to get out in the world. Isolation is bad news."

"I have no idea what else I could do."

"What you do is not as important as the fact that you get off your duff and do it." She glances over to the counter. "Maybe they're hiring here."

"Um, I don't think I want to be a barista."

"Why not? Serving others is a great lesson in humility."

"I think I've humiliated myself enough."

"Humiliation is about shame. Becoming *humble* is about being of use to others. It helps you get off the self-pity pot and stop wallowing around in your own crap." She grins. "Think about it, at least."

"Is that a suggestion?" I tease her.

"You bet your sweet bippy it is." We stand and begin to gather our things, getting ready to leave. "Oh, and just so you know," she says, "one of my other 'suggestions' is no dating for at least the first year of sobriety."

"That shouldn't be a problem. It's pretty much the last thing on my mind."

"Uh-huh." She gives me a pointed look. "I've seen Vince talking with you. He's a charmer. A good man, but a charmer nonetheless."

"Nadine, he was just introducing me to a woman who was at a meeting for the first time. That's it. I promise."

"*And* he gave you his ninety-day coin a couple of weeks ago."

"How did you know that?" I ask with a single raised eyebrow.

"He told me." She pats my forearm. "Now, I'm not accusing you of anything, honey. I just want you to be careful with your heart. Let's say we help you get to know it better before you just give it away."

Twenty-one

I sit in my living room on a Tuesday morning after a busy weekend spent with Charlie. I took him swimming at the YMCA on Saturday morning, then to a free, bring-your-own-popcorn outdoor movie at Discovery Park that night. Sunday morning we went around Green Lake two times—Charlie rode his bike and I walked, carrying a bag of stale bread crumbs to feed the ducks.

"Look, Mommy!" Charlie said, pointing his finger at the water. "That one has babies!"

I turned my gaze to where he was pointing. "You're right, sweetie, it does."

Charlie jumped up and down once and clapped his hands. "She's a good mommy," he said. His tone was matter-of-fact. "Like you."

"How can you tell?" I asked him, my heart glowing a bit from his words.

He shrugged his small shoulders. "I dunno. I just can," he said, and something that had been broken inside me began to stitch together and heal.

Now, I set my laptop on my legs as I stare out the front window at my glistening willow tree. A misty but persistent shower has blurred the outside world since Saturday. It's the kind of rain true Seattleites are used to; the kind that transplants from sunnier lands swear will gradually drive them insane. I check my e-mail and see a brief note from an address I don't recognize. I click on it, and realize it's from Trina, the woman who Vince introduced me to at the meeting.

Hi Cadence, it says. *I've heard at meetings I'm supposed to try and reach out to people. So, I guess this is me, reaching out. I'm not sure what else to say, but I thought I'd drop you a note to at least say hello.*

She's farther along than me, I think. Besides asking Nadine to be my sponsor and chatting with Vince, I haven't had the courage to talk to many other people at the meetings. Why did she choose me? Was I the only person she'd met, the only contact information she had? If so, I'd better respond. I shoot Trina back a quick message, ending it with my phone number and a suggestion that we try to have lunch together sometime soon.

The phone rings. It's Scott, so I take a deep breath before answering. "Hi, what's up?" I try to sound less tense than I feel in anticipation of what he might have to tell me. I lean over, set the journal on the coffee table, then lounge back with my now-lukewarm mug of coffee in hand.

"Mr. Hines sent over his notes from his interview with you. They were here when I got to the office this morning."

I am about to take a sip of coffee when my arm freezes in midlift. "What did he say?" Adrenaline begins to speed through my veins.

I hear papers rustling in the background on Scott's end of the line. "Which do you want first—good news or bad news?"

"Good." *Please,* I think. *Please, please, please.* Let him say he thinks I should have Charlie back.

"Okay. So, he says that he believes you have a deep bond with Charlie. He says that your love for him is clear."

I nod, as though he can see me. "That's good, right? Really good?"

"Yes, it is. Are you ready for the bad?"

"Jesus, Scott, will you just tell me?" My blood is pumping so fast, my heart pushes against my rib cage. I barely have time to take a breath.

He sighs. "He thinks you're just going through the motions of treatment so you can get Charlie back."

His words slam me back against the couch. I can't speak. There are a million things racing through my brain and not one of them will come out of my mouth.

"Cadence? Are you okay?" Scott asks.

"I don't know. No." That's it. That's all that will come out. My mind is whirling.

"Cadence, listen to me. This isn't the end of the world. He goes on to say that you are most likely still in the denial stage, moving toward acceptance. He says that most alcoholics go through it." Scott laughs. "Hell, I could have told him that." He pauses a moment. "He does say in his notes that you don't think you're an alcoholic. Did you say that?"

"I said I was struggling with it. At least, that's what I meant to say." The tears are right there again, threatening to take over. "Oh God, did I screw it up? Did I just completely screw up my chances? I was trying to be honest, Scott. Everyone was telling me to be honest, so I was."

"It will be okay, Cadence," Scott says. His tone is low and soothing. "He still has to talk to your mother, plus whatever he thinks about Martin and his mother is going to make a huge difference in any kind of final recommendation."

"Okay," I say, trying to believe him. I can't believe anything else.

"There's one more thing. He wants to meet with you and Martin together, too."

"Oh. Is that normal?"

"It depends on the situation."

"Okay. So is it a good sign or a bad sign?"

He sighs. "It just means he wants to see how you two interact. The dynamics of your relationship, how you communicate with each other. I suppose you should see that as good. Hopefully, it means he hasn't made up his mind after meeting with each of you alone. He needs more information. It'll be fine. "

"Okay." I hang up the phone. I remain on the couch for a while, continuing to stare out the window, numbly replaying the memory of my meeting with Mr. Hines. I can't go back, I realize. I can't change what I said or what he thought. I just need to figure out how to move forward. I need to find a way to fix this.

I write a note to my son. I tell him how much I love and miss him, and that I can't wait to hug and snuggle him in a few days. I include the joke: "Why is eight afraid of seven? Because seven ate nine." After getting a stamp on it, I put it in my purse, deciding I'll drop it in the mailbox on my way to the *Herald* to see Peter.

In addition to putting the house on the market, I've decided to ask for my job back. Nadine is right. Not only do I need to make money, I need a set routine to keep my mind on task so that I don't venture into dark, dangerous territory. For now, at least, wide open stretches of time are just too much freedom. It's the equivalent of a dog tearing loose across an open prairie when it is much better suited to the safety of a securely fenced backyard.

Walking back into the newsroom is a little like returning to my childhood home. I'm immediately struck by the familiar sight of reporters hunched at their desks behind stacks of paper, furiously typing away at their computers; the pungent scent of fresh ink pressed into paper. The buzz of voices and phones ringing soothes me—I used to be able to write with anything going on around me. It wasn't until Charlie was born that I lost my ability to focus. A panic button set off inside me at the sound of his cry; as a result, I suddenly became hyperaware of every little sound, unable to block extraneous noise.

I walk over to Peter's office, nodding hello to the few people I recognize.

"Knock, knock," I say, stepping through the doorway. Peter looks up from his computer and his furrowed brow falls smooth. A smile erupts across his wide, round face.

"Hey, Cadence!" he booms. "To what do we owe the honor?" He

hoists himself up from behind his desk and lumbers over to hug me. Beneath a heavy dose of his spicy cologne, he smells of ink and sweat.

I take a deep breath and release it before answering. "I want to talk with you about getting my job back."

He pulls back and looks at me with large, brown eyes. He has shaved his beard since last I saw him, and his jowls appear bigger without it; there's no delineation between his jaw and neck. "Have a seat," he says, and gestures to the chair on the opposite side of his desk. He walks around and sits down, too.

I comply and smile nervously, linking my fingers in my lap. "I know things have to be tight around here, staff-wise. I thought my experience might come in handy. I can do anything you need me to."

He sighs. "You know I'd love to hire you back."

"Great! When do I start?" I laugh nervously, feigning a confidence I don't feel.

He gives me a wan smile. "It's just not in the budget right now, Cadee. I can't do it." He pauses. "The freelance market is tough, I know."

"Even if it weren't, I'd still be having a hard time coming up with anything to write about," I say quietly. "I thought maybe if I got back on the paper, working the old standard stuff I'm used to, I'd get my groove back."

"Writer's block is a myth, and you know it. You just sit down and put words on the page. Something will show up. If I taught you anything, I taught you that."

"I've tried," I say. My voice shakes. "Nothing comes." I look at him, tears in my eyes. "I really need a job, Pete. I need the money. So I can take care of Charlie."

His expression falls from a smile to one of compassion. "I understand, Cadee. I wish I could help. But my hands are tied. The economy sucks. And people aren't buying papers the way they used to. It's all online. I'm not even sure how much longer *I'll* have a job."

I stand up and give him a fake smile. "I understand. I figured it couldn't hurt to try."

"It was good to see you," he says. "Keep in touch. And keep writing."

I nod and head back out of the building. The rain has stopped, so I decide to take a walk instead of going home. *There's nothing for me there.* I turn down Second Avenue, thinking I might head toward the Pike Place Market and get lost among the sights and sounds of the vendors. I try to figure out my next step. I've only walked a couple of blocks when a familiar voice pulls me out of my thoughts.

"Cadence! Hey, girl!"

I stop and look over to the entrance of a small cafe and see Serena standing there in black pants and a white, button-down blouse. Her cinnamon skin glows, and her dark braids are pulled back into a ponytail at the base of her neck. She is smiling.

"Hey, there," I say, walking over to her. "How are you?"

"I'm good." She hugs me. "You look like you've seen better days, though."

I give her a half smile. "Yeah, I guess I have."

"Come on, I'll buy you lunch." She takes my hand and leads me inside. "Welcome to Le Chat Noir. The Black Cat." There are black leather booths along the wall and we end up sitting in one closest to the kitchen. I look around, taking in the aged, red-brick walls and brilliantly hued, Picasso-esque paintings hanging on almost every available inch of space. The tables are a warm-hued pine, accented by royal purple napkins with centerpieces of yellow gerberas.

"This is nice," I say. "How long have you managed it?"

"Oh, let's see. Since about two relapses ago?" She chuckles. "That would be ten years, give or take. What are you doing in this neck of the woods?"

I tell her about my visit with Peter. "I'm just feeling really discouraged, you know? Nadine, the woman I just asked to be my sponsor, says I need a reason to get out of bed in the morning. Something to structure my day. Not to mention the fact that I'm practically broke."

She nods, then sighs and leans back against the booth's cushioned backrest. "What else can you do besides write?"

"Not much," I say. "I like to cook, but I don't have any kind of training or experience where I could do it professionally."

A sudden grin spreads across Serena's face. "I need a server. Think you could do that?"

My chin jerks in toward my chest. "I don't know," I begin. "I'm not really sure . . ." I don't want to disappoint her, but it has never crossed my mind to be a waitress. It's right up there with my barista aspirations.

"You don't have to be sure. It's only four shifts, but it's busy as hell around here. You'd make pretty decent tips." She laughs. "Nothing you could retire on, of course, but it'd at least keep you occupied. It comes with insurance, too, if you work at least twenty hours a week."

"Hmm," I say. Besides my mortgage, my health insurance is one of the highest bills I pay.

"No 'hmm' about it. I'm sure your sponsor told you to get out and be of service. Mine always does. Well, ain't *nothin'* more of service than being a server!" She laughs, and the sound is so infectious, I can't help but laugh, too.

"Are you sure?" I ask, a strange mix of trepidation and excitement brewing in my gut. "I might be terrible. You might regret it."

"I don't regret nothing. And I'm not taking no for an answer." She smacks the table with open palms. "Now, let's feed you and get you an apron."

I spend the rest of the afternoon in training. Serena shows me how to punch an order into the computer at the servers' station and where it pops up on a screen back in the kitchen for the cooks to get started. I feel awkward at first, but focus on what she tries to teach me.

"Smiling's the most important skill of this job," she says. "Even if you don't mean it, even if you're having a shitty day, you put that smile on your face and look like you've never been happier to see anyone than the people sitting at your tables."

"I should fake it, you mean." *Oh, the irony. Wait until I tell Andi.*

"Yep. Happiness only, though. Not orgasms." She grins and I laugh.

"I don't think I'm in any danger of that," I say, though my mind flips briefly to Vince's handsome face. It's been so long—I'm not sure my body would remember what to do.

Serena has me take an order from a sweet old man who walks in about three o'clock. He uses a cane and wears a plaid fedora. "This here is Samuel," she says. "He's one of our regulars. Sam, this is Cadence. She'll be taking care of you today."

I give her a panicked look, but she just gives me a little push toward the table.

"Hi," I say. "What can I get for you?"

Sam pulls off his hat to reveal a pale, shiny scalp, smiles at me, and says, "I'll have my usual."

"Um," I murmur, throwing my gaze over to Serena, who has walked back to the kitchen.

Sam laughs, a broken, coughing sound. "Just kidding you, honey. I'll take the curried roast turkey wrap with fruit instead of fries."

I gulp as I scratch down his order on the notepad Serena gave me earlier. "Anything to drink with that?"

"Coffee, sweet and creamy." He winks at me. "You're a pretty lady. You're gonna do well."

I smile at him, feeling a bit more relaxed. "Thank you. I appreciate that."

Under Serena's supervision, I take on six more tables over the next couple of hours, surprised by how quickly I pick up timing serving a table's order and when to deliver the bill. By the time I'm through, I've made fifty dollars and for the first time in a while, I feel like I've actually accomplished something. It isn't rocket science, but it distracts my brain from the custody dispute and how much I miss my son.

"You're a waitress?" Jess squeals when I stop by her house on my way home to tell her about my new job. "Do you get to wear roller skates?"

"Shut up," I say, blushing a little. "It's a nice place. And it'll get me out of the house."

She smiles and squeezes my hand. "I'm just teasing you, Flo. I can call you 'Flo,' right?"

"I'm going to smack you if you're not careful."

"Okay, okay. I'm sorry. It sounds like a good plan for you right now." She pauses. "Have you talked with Mom again?"

I shook my head. "I don't really know what to say to her right now."

"I think she's struggling, Cadee."

"That makes two of us."

She sighs and gives me an exasperated look.

I shrug. "I just feel like until she knows what she's going to tell Mr. Hines, I'm not really sure what else we have to talk about."

Jess snorts. "Oh, please. Only twenty years of unresolved conflicts."

I think about my sister's words on the drive home. I don't know how to tell my mother how much I need her now any more than I did when I was a child. My mouth wouldn't even know how to form the words. Still, I make myself pick up the phone when I get home.

"Can I ask you a question, Mom?" I say.

"Sure," she says, though her tone is guarded. She is waiting for me to grill her about what she's planning to say to Mr. Hines. But I won't. I'm going to leave it up to her to tell me when she's ready. If I push her on something she doesn't want to talk about, she'll clam up completely. That's a trait I know we share.

"I've been wondering, since you told me about your mother, how you dealt with how she was. With her drinking . . . and everything."

"I've dealt with it just fine, I think," she says. "I haven't let it control my life."

"Okay, but *how* did you deal with it?"

"I don't know, Cadence. I just lived. I worked."

"My counselor at Promises says work can be an addiction, too. A way to escape your feelings."

"I'm not addicted to work," my mother snaps. "I'm passionate about what I do. Please don't psychoanalyze me."

"I'm sorry," I say, backing down. "I didn't mean to." I had no idea how to have these kinds of conversations with my mother. We've always kept so much to the surface; trying to connect with her on a deeper level feels like fumbling around for a light switch in a pitch-black room. I decide to take a different tack. "Can you at least tell me what was it *like* for you, growing up with your mom?"

"I thought I already did."

"You told me what she did, not how it *felt* to be around her. I need to know . . . I want to understand what Charlie might be going through . . . so I can help him." Tears break up the words in my throat and they come out disjointed.

"Oh, honey." Her voice softens. "I'm certain you didn't get as bad as my mother. She really wasn't in her right mind. She'd been drinking so many years, the doctors called it 'wet brain.' She used to swish her mouth out with perfume to keep me from smelling the alcohol on her breath."

"Oh my God," I say. "Is *that* why you didn't let us wear any?"

"Yes."

"That's awful."

"The worst part was more the unpredictability, really. Never knowing what to expect." I hear her take in a shuddering breath. "I tried to be a better mother than that to you girls."

"You were." I realize this is true. She may not have been the most available parent, but we never doubted she was working so hard because she loved us and wanted to give us the best that she could. She did the best she could with the tools she'd been given.

We are both quiet for a moment, unused to this kind of emotionally charged exchange. She is the first to speak. "I still don't know what I'm going to tell him," she says softly, referring, I know, to Mr. Hines.

"It's okay, Mom," I say, blessed with a sudden understanding that it isn't the mature, capable woman talking with me who doesn't know what she is going to say. It's the little girl trapped inside her who still can't stand the scent of perfume.

Twenty-two

The following Thursday, after we rehash everything that happened with my mother over the past couple of weeks, my new job and my new sponsor, Andi and I talk about the friendship I've started to forge with Kristin.

"Did you really think you were that unique?" she asks. "Plenty of mothers use alcohol to manage their stress. You just happened to get caught. That makes you one of the lucky ones."

"How do you figure that?" I say, now fiddling with the edge of my cardigan. I can't seem to keep my hands still. My body feels like lit sparklers are lodged beneath my skin.

"Well, let's look at the facts. How many times did you go to jail?"

"Never." *Uh-oh*, I think. *Here she goes, questioning bullets, my name etched on each one of them, no one else to cushion her barrage.* I sink down a bit in my chair, wishing there was a place where I could take immediate cover.

"Okay. How many times did you deserve to?"

"I don't know what you mean," I say, locking my hands together, drumming my fingers on the backs of my hands.

"Sure you do." She is unflappable, leaning forward in her seat. "How many times did you drive with Charlie in the car when you were wasted?"

I squirm. "Okay. I get it. I know what you're saying."

"Do you? Charlie's not dead. You're not dead. Ergo, you are *lucky*." She keeps her eyes on me, reading my reactions like a hawk. "Did you ever kill anyone else?"

"No," I say quietly, now holding my body completely immobile. I don't want to give her any further ammunition. I want to run away—it's more difficult to hit a moving target.

"Again, lucky. Women go to jail every day because of their addiction issues, Cadee. They kill people. This disease isn't picky about who has it."

"But I didn't kill anyone."

"Yet." She holds my gaze steady with her own. "You haven't killed anyone *yet*."

"I hate how that feels."

"How what feels?"

"That I have a 'disease.'" I hook my fingers into invisible quotation marks in the air around the word "disease." "It sounds so pitiful."

She cocks her head toward her right shoulder. "Is it pitiful if someone has cancer?"

I sigh. "That's not the same thing."

"Really? Why not?"

"Because," I say, throwing my hands up in the air, then letting them drop back down. I try to withhold another sigh. "Cancer is tangible. People feel compassion for you if you get cancer. Not so much if you're an alcoholic. And a mother who drinks? Forget it. Straight to hell. Big, fat scarlet letter 'A' branded on our foreheads for life. Me and Hester Prynne? Like this." I hold up both my arms in front of me, crossing my fingers to emphasize just how intimate the heroine from *The Scarlet Letter* and I could be. "Same letter, different sins."

"You want people to feel sorry for you, then?" Andi tilts her head to her other shoulder, squinting.

"No!" I say. "I didn't say that." How can I like this woman as much as I do when she so thoroughly manages to piss me off?

She ignores this, straightening her head, and looks at me head-on. "Oh. I see. You feel sorry for *yourself.*"

I cross my arms over my chest and press the tip of my tongue into one of my lower molars, but don't respond. I'm too irritated to be in control of what might come out of my mouth. She does not seem to be bothered by my silence, which serves only to annoy me further.

"It also sounds like you're still stuck on wanting alcoholism to be a matter of morality or willpower," she goes on. "It's not a character flaw, Cadence. It's a disease. It's diagnosed by a set of observable and consistent clinical symptoms."

"Okay, so how exactly do I accept the diagnosis?" I ask, taking a deep breath in and releasing it, attempting to let go of the tension clinging to my body. I know I need to stop arguing with her. But defiance seems to be littered throughout my psyche. I keep stumbling on it unexpectedly, and then find myself shocked when I continue falling down: *Well. How did* that *happen again?*

"Most of it you've already done."

"I have?" I'm sure I look confused.

"Sure." She smiles, references my file on her lap. "You admit you couldn't control your drinking, even when you tried. You tried to stop, over and over again, and you couldn't. Right?"

"Yes." Something inside me is crumpling, like a pop can under pressure. I feel myself giving in, capitulating beneath the weight of the facts laid plain before me.

"You admit your life became unmanageable, right? Things got completely out of your control—your work, your ability to parent Charlie?"

I give her a curt nod. Her words feel like they are skinning away a warm blanket from my body on a cold winter's night. I hate this. I hate that I cannot rationalize my way out of what she is saying. I feel trapped, yet oddly hopeful at the same time. A pinprick of optimism that says if I can accept this about myself, I might be able to find a way to manage it. Maybe I can put down the shovel, gather some different tools.

"That's step one in accepting. If you weren't an alcoholic, things wouldn't have progressed to that point. You could stop drinking when you tried. 'Normal' people decide to stop and they stop. End of story."

I think about how I see myself in the women I've met and the people I've listened to in meetings. I'm like Kristin and Serena and Laura; I'm like Scott. I'm even like Vince, who took a mouthful of lawn. They all understand what it is to feel that sense of incomprehensible demoralization. *The compulsion, the shame, the secrets, the lies*—I can relate to it all. Alcoholism isn't a physical diagnosis. It frustrates me to no end that there's no blood test I can take that will tell me definitively, yes, you're an alcoholic, the way I'd know I had diabetes or cancer. Instead, it's looking at the circumstantial evidence that led me to this place. When I do, it's impossible to ignore that whether I like it or not, odds are that I am an alcoholic.

Great. That's just great. I had hoped that admitting this to myself for the first time I might find relief, as Andi had. What I feel instead is a sense of folding in on myself—dull, reluctant surrender.

"So, I need to tell you that Laura won't be returning to our group," Andi says, interrupting my thoughts.

"Oh, no," I say. "Did she relapse again?"

Andi nods, her lips pressed together into a grim line.

"Shit." I sigh. "Can I still call her, though? Just to see how she is?"

"Of course you can. She's going to need all the support she can get."

I don't have Charlie the second weekend in June, so I ask Serena to schedule me for double shifts at Le Chat Noir to fill up my days. Nadine is right—having structure definitely helps me get out of my head. When I'm at the restaurant, I'm much too busy to think about anything other than not dropping the enormous tray I'm carrying, or whether the woman with the red-rimmed glasses wanted home fries or fruit with her egg-white omelet. I'm not wallowing in fear—I'm taking care of an immediate task.

Another unexpected benefit of the job is the constant interaction with customers. It forces me to be friendly in a way I've never really been, and I quickly learn that my openness encourages theirs; a big smile and a sincere inquiry about their well-being goes a long way in making them feel like there's nothing else I'd rather be doing than taking care of their needs. Letting down my guard is uncomfortable at first, but the more I do it, the more natural it feels. It's also great to go home with cash in my pocket, and while I don't think waiting tables is something I'll do forever, it's enough for me while I figure out what exactly it is I really want to do with my life.

Around ten o'clock on Saturday morning, I am slammed with two parties of six people and a handful of other tables thrown in just to make things interesting. Sweat trickles down the back of my neck as I fly between the kitchen and the dining room, mindful to keep a smile on my face while I pour fresh-squeezed orange juice and ask the line cook to, pretty please, add a side of thick-cut, peppered bacon to one of my orders.

"Looks like you're kicking ass and taking names," Serena says, watching me carefully balance an enormous round tray filled with plates.

"I'm surviving," I say with a grin. "For a little while, at least."

"A single just sat down in your section," Serena points out. "Want me to get Barb to take it?" Barb is the other daytime server at Le Chat Noir, a tough-talking, big-hearted veteran in the food service business who has worked for Serena for five years. She has taken me under her wing, relieved to finally have a coworker who isn't young enough to be her grandchild.

"Nah, I've got it," I say. "Just have to get this food out and I'm good." I deliver the tray to my awaiting table of eight, happy that Barb taught me the trick of making a seating chart on the back of my notepad to keep track of who gets which order. I learned quickly that customers get annoyed when I accidentally put the wrong meal in front of them. When all the food is sitting in front of the proper person, I flip around and walk over to the small table in the back corner of the restaurant, reviewing my tickets as I move across the dining room floor.

"Well, now, look who it is," Vince says as I approach.

My gaze lifts from my notepad and there he is, sitting at my table, alone. "Vince," I say, stopping short. "What're you doing here?" He wears gym shorts and a white T-shirt; his dark hair is slicked back like he's just stepped out of the shower. I can't help but notice how the short sleeves cling to the muscular cut of his arms. *Damn. Look at those triceps.* I feel a sudden, familiar pull in my pelvis. *Oh, right. That's lust.*

He grins. "Well, I was hoping to eat."

My stomach flutters nervously. "Do you live near here or something?"

"My office is just around the corner, so I belong to the gym in the building. I didn't know you worked here."

"I just started a couple of weeks ago." I glance over toward the kitchen and see Serena is leaning over the beverage bar, watching me with great curiosity. Smiling, I turn back to Vince, pen poised above my notepad. "What can I get you?"

"How about the chorizo breakfast burrito and a cup of coffee with my waitress?" His green eyes twinkle as he smiles at me again.

"Very funny. I'm working. But I appreciate the offer." I notice an appealing dimple in his left cheek and spark briefly on the vision of sticking my tongue into it. *Man, he is cute.*

"Are you free later?"

I lower my voice and lean down toward him. "My sponsor told me I'm not allowed to date yet."

"Date?" he says with a playful edge to the word. "I was just going to see if you'll be going to the Fremont meeting tonight."

My face flushes pink and I pull back, unable to meet his gaze. "Oh. Sorry," I stutter. "I didn't mean to presume."

He laughs. "Cadence, you're not reading this wrong. I'm attracted to you. But I know how early recovery goes and I'm not looking to screw that up. I'd just like to get to know you."

"As friends?"

He nods. "Yes. I think the great Nadine might allow that."

I smile. "I think so, too." I go back to the kitchen and put his order in the system.

"Who is *that*?" Serena asks. "He is one fine-lookin' man."

"Just a friend," I say, and force myself to believe I'm telling the truth.

Twenty-three

On Tuesday afternoon the following week, I go to the home store to find paint for the master bathroom Derek thinks I need to spruce up before putting the house on the market. I find a gallon of pale butter yellow on the mistake rack while I talk to Nadine about seeing Vince at the restaurant.

"Ha, I knew it," Nadine says. "I could see it in his eyes."

"I need to wait, right? I shouldn't sleep with him."

"You can sleep with whomever you choose," she responds. "But I wouldn't recommend it. Not yet. If he's truly interested, he'll wait."

"I think I can live with that," I say, and I hang up, smiling.

Later that night, I'm standing in the kitchen sipping my coffee, staring out at yet another drizzly June evening. Just as I work up the motivation to get started painting the bathroom, I get a call from Scott.

"Mr. Hines wants to meet with both you and Martin at his office next Monday," he says.

"What should I be prepared for?" I ask, marking the day on the calendar. June 20.

"He just wants to see how you two interact. Be yourself. Be as kind as possible."

"What if I can't be kind?"

"Then at least be polite."

After working my four shifts at the cafe, I spend the weekend with Charlie, who asks, after I suggest a city bus trip to the Children's Museum downtown as a way to escape the rain, if we can just stay home. He is tired of the continuous activity I've put him through the last few weekends we've spent together.

"What do you want to do, Mr. Man?" I ask once he has his things settled in his room.

"Hmm . . ." he says, tapping his index finger against his cheek. "I know! Let's build Spider-Man's fort! You can be Mary Jane!"

"Oh . . . great!" I attempt to manufacture enthusiasm as we spend the afternoon building a cavelike structure in the living room out of blankets and the kitchen chairs. Part of me feels edgy and impatient as we do this—in the past, it's the kind of activity I have needed a couple glasses of wine to get through. I manage to quell that feeling and throw myself into creating a superhero's luxurious secret lair, complete with a gigantic spiderweb made out of some black string I found in the garage. Charlie dons his slightly-too-tight Spider-Man Halloween costume and decorates the space with all of his Spider-Man stuffed toys. In the spirit of things, I pull an old pair of bright red tights over the top of my head and sashay around the living room.

Charlie scrunches up his face at me. "What're you doing?"

"I'm being Mary Jane!" I say, swishing the skinny red legs of the tights around my neck. "Don't you love my red hair?"

He giggles and finally the unrest in me begins to settle down.

"Help me, Spider-Man, help me!" I prance around the dining room table and look back over my shoulder. "I'm being chased by the Green Goblet!"

He laughs out loud, snorting a bit as he tries to talk. "It's the Green *Goblin*, Mommy. Not *goblet*."

"Ohhhh," I say. His laughter soothes me further.

"Can we sleep out here?" he asks as we stand back to admire our handiwork.

"Sure. I'll get the blow-up mattress for you and I'll sleep on the couch."

"What about movies? Can we watch movies in our fort?"

"Sounds good. With pizza. And ice-cream sundaes for dessert."

"Woohoo!" My son lunges at me with a full-force embrace. I soak up his affection like it was the sun.

For the most part, it is a good, calm weekend and so on Monday, I use it. When I am on my way to Mr. Hines's office and my heart begins to rattle behind my ribs like a wild monkey in a cage, I think about how my son smells. I focus on how he felt curled up with me on the floor Saturday night while we watched *The Lion King* for the hundredth time. I picture his wide smile when he saw the amount of hot fudge and whipped cream I put on his sundae and how the pride in my heart swelled to an almost unbearable level when he generously offered me his maraschino cherry.

After I arrive at his office and Mr. Hines steps down the hall in front of me, I can't help but feel that I'm being led to a guillotine. Again, I think about Charlie. I tell myself I am strong enough to survive this meeting. I have to be. I need to do this for my son.

Martin is already in the room we enter, which is different from the one I sat in during my first meeting here. It's a little larger with a grouping of comfortable, coffeehouse-style chairs and the same ugly, paisley-patterned carpet. I imagine this would have been the living room if it were still someone's home. The shades are drawn and a single table lamp lights the room.

Martin gives me a perfunctory smile as I sit down in the chair directly next to him. If someone were to draw lines between our three chairs it would form a perfect equilateral triangle with Mr. Hines sitting at its peak.

"So, thank you for coming," he begins. "I've gathered some important information from both of you, but I think there are a few things each of you might need to hear from each other. From the horse's mouth, so to speak."

I nod enthusiastically, my eyes wide. I want to be sure to appear engaged in this process, despite the dread I feel bouncing along through my blood.

"Like what kinds of things?" Martin asks.

"Well, Martin, I'd like you to talk a little bit about when you first started to suspect your ex-wife had a real problem with alcohol."

My face immediately flushed. I expected we'd talk about Charlie, what we each thought was best for him. Not this. And he's always called me "Ms. Sutter," but he calls Martin by his first name. What's up with that? I am instantly plagued by the fear that Mr. Hines's decision has already been made.

"Aren't we here to talk about our son?" I ask.

"We are," Mr. Hines says. "And your drinking relates to him. Would you disagree?"

I shake my head, chastised.

Mr. Hines bobs his head. "Martin?"

Martin clears his throat and throws me a quick glance before moving his eyes back to Mr. Hines. "Well, I think the first time I noticed her drinking was back in September of last year when I came to pick Charlie up for the weekend. Her face was red and I could smell the wine. I thought maybe her friend Susanne had been there and they'd had a couple of drinks. But then that kind of thing happened maybe two times before Christmas, and that's when I really started to think something might be wrong."

"And why did you think that?" Mr. Hines says.

"I brought Charlie back to Cadee's house the day after the holiday. It was about seven o'clock, I guess, and she came to the door with a glass of wine in her hand. I could tell I woke her up—her hair was messy and there were creases on her cheek, like from a pillow. But her eyes were glassy. And she was slurring her words a little. And it wasn't like she didn't know we were coming. I thought it was strange. Especially that she'd obviously just woken up and decided to grab a glass of wine before she even answered the door." Martin speaks as though he's giving an oral book report in front of a class; his voice lacks any noticeable inflection.

I shift in my seat and attempt to keep my back straight. I remember that night. I barely made it through Christmas Day at Jess's house without Charlie. I was halfway through my third bottle of wine in twenty-four hours by the time Martin showed up. I remember thinking I looked fine. I felt fine. I remember thinking there was no way Martin would suspect I was drunk.

"Do you remember this night, Ms. Sutter?" Mr. Hines asks.

I nod curtly. There is nothing left for me except honesty.

"Would you say Martin's assessment of you was accurate? Were you drunk?"

Again, I nod. "That was a very rough holiday for me. Charlie being with Martin and Alice. I'd never been without him for Christmas morning."

"So that makes it okay?" Martin asks.

"No, that doesn't make it okay," I snap. "I'm just saying how I felt. That's all." So much for being polite.

Mr. Hines scratches down something on the notepad he holds on his lap. "Any other times you were concerned?" he asks Martin.

My ex-husband stares straight ahead, his eyes on Mr. Hines. "There were a few times on the phone. She would call me, wanting to talk."

"What?" I say, incredulous. "I did not."

Martin swings his gaze to me, his lips pressed into a hard line before he speaks. "Yes, you did."

I don't say anything, but cross one leg over the other and shake my foot wildly. I feel a sinking sensation in my abdomen. He might be telling the truth. I hate that my mind is so foggy. Heavy cotton gauze is wrapped too thickly around certain images for me to see them clearly. I have a vague recollection of calling him, but I can't for the life of me remember what was said. I feel ill thinking what he's about to reveal.

Martin takes a deep breath. "The calls were always late at night. She would cry and tell me she was scared, but she wouldn't tell me what she was scared of. And it was odd, because she isn't someone who cries a lot. Her words were slurred and she'd repeat herself over and over. I'd usually have to hang up on her."

"Are you sure you don't remember any of those calls?" Mr. Hines asks me.

"No. Maybe. I don't know." I look at Martin. "I guess I more re-member the *feeling* of them."

Martin's head whips around at the same words he used to de-scribe his memory of his father on our first date. His eyes flash, but he doesn't say a word.

I drop my gaze to the floor. Quiet, fractured memories drift through my mind. Memories of things I'd said to Martin with my phone in one hand and a glass of wine in the other. Memories of tears. But the specific conversations were just out of reach.

"Is it possible you blacked out during them?"

My stomach twists and I stop shaking my foot. "Yes. I suppose it's possible." *Probable, actually.*

"Did you ever ask Charlie about his mother's drinking?" Mr. Hines asks Martin.

Out of the corner of my eye, I see Martin nod. "After Christmas, I asked him if he had seen his mommy drinking out of a wineglass. He told me yes. I asked him if it was a lot, and he sort of shrugged and wouldn't look at me. I told him it was okay that he tell me and he said 'yeah.'"

"Yeah, what?" Mr. Hines pushes.

Martin sighs. I recognize the sound; he's not exasperated, only tired. He's not enjoying talking about these things any more than I am. "Yeah, she was drinking a lot. He told me she was sleepy a lot, too. And had headaches."

Tears burn in the back of my throat. I swallow twice, hard, try-ing to keep them down. The muscles in my chest feel like they're trapped in a vise. I take a couple of deep breaths and then turn to look at Martin. "If you were so concerned," I ask, "why didn't you say anything? Why didn't you sit me down and talk to me about it?"

"I don't know," Martin says. "I guess I trusted you on some level. That you'd keep a handle on it. You've always held everything together."

"Did you think you might be imagining it was happening?" Mr. Hines asked Martin.

My ex-husband shook his head. "No, not imagining. More thinking that it wasn't every night. She wasn't a heavy drinker when we were together. Or before that, as far as I knew. I thought maybe it was something she'd do a couple of times and then stop. Like maybe it was some kind of weird phase she was going through."

"But she didn't stop."

"No."

I am quiet, trying to breathe. My face is on fire.

"Are you all right?" Mr. Hines asks me. "Is hearing these kinds of things difficult?"

"Of course it is," I say, my voice low. *What a stupid question.*

"A little frightening, too, I imagine, not remembering things that you've done."

I nod. I hate this. Incomprehensible demoralization.

"When did you decide you had to act, Martin?" Mr. Hines asks. "When did you begin to worry Charlie might be in danger?"

"When his preschool teacher made a couple of comments to me about Charlie being late a lot and then being out sick a few days in January."

I feel him look over to me, but I can't meet his gaze. The tightness in my chest rises, pushing up through my throat until the tears trickle down my cheeks. I can't stop them. I keep my eyes on the floor, still listening.

Martin sighs. "Cadence hadn't said anything to me about it, which I thought was strange. She usually let me know if he had a cold or something like that if I was going to have him for the weekend. The teacher also said something about Cadence looking like she'd been fighting something off for quite a while. Like she had the flu. I knew she looked more tired than I remembered seeing her before, but it made me more aware, I guess, when the teacher pointed it out, too. Like I should be looking out for something." He took a deep breath. "And then the teacher called me one morning and said Charlie wasn't in school again. And that Cadence had called before and didn't 'sound right.' So I got in my car, went to her house, and took him away." His eyes leave me and direct their attention back to Mr. Hines.

I'm afraid I might throw up. *Oh God. Who is this woman they are talking about? It can't be me. It can't.* And yet I know it is. I rip open the gauze and I see the truth. I'd never been so drunk—I knew I couldn't drive. I thought it was better to keep Charlie home with me. I remember my son letting his father in the door. I remember being so drunk I couldn't protest when Martin took him away.

I remember a few hours later, wishing I were dead.

"What happened then, Martin?" Mr. Hines asks.

"She called and left me a message on my phone. She said she'd taken some kind of medication and had a bad reaction to it. She was completely drunk."

I remember doing this. I remember the desperation I felt—the sheer unadulterated desperation. It was close to the sickening shame I feel now.

"And then?" Mr. Hines asks.

Martin rolls his shoulders back like he's trying to alleviate tension in his neck. "Her sister called me the next day and told me Cadence had admitted herself to the psychiatric ward and would be going into treatment for the drinking. I told her I would keep Charlie, of course. And then I called my mother and asked her to watch him while I figured out what to do. She suggested I call Child Protective Services and get their advice."

I'll bet she did. I attempt to wipe the tears from my face. *I'll bet she offered to make the call herself.*

"You've been quiet, Ms. Sutter," Mr. Hines says. "Are you okay?"

I give a quick nod. *Sure, I've been sitting here weeping, reliving the most horrific night of my life. But I'm fine. Just great.*

"Do you have anything you'd like to ask Martin?"

I take a deep breath, not wanting my voice to splinter when I speak. It does anyway. "Why did you have to call CPS? Why didn't you just wait for me to get into treatment and then *talk* to me? We could have found a different way through this. Charlie could have stayed with you while I was in treatment and then come back home. Or we could have worked out some other kind of schedule, so you'd feel more comfortable that I was better before he came back. You don't need to take him *away* from me."

Martin attempts to look impassive, but I can see the emotion wrestling around behind that mask. "I wanted to talk to a professional. They recommended I file for custody. I did what I thought was best for Charlie. I want to protect my son."

CPS and his lawyer have told him that the correct response to an ex-wife's drinking problem is to file for custody. Nothing I say will change his mind.

"What if we were still married and I developed this problem?" I ask, still ridiculously optimistic I can frame it to him in a different way. "Would you have immediately picked up and left me and taken Charlie away? Or would you have helped me get through treatment and find a way to manage it with our family still intact?"

"Our family's not intact," Martin says. His tone is guarded.

He might as well have slapped me. I suppose whatever mistakes he has made are now irrelevant. In his mind, my drinking trumps them all.

Still, we hold each other's gaze for a moment. I see two distinct moments from our life together: his wide smile the first night we met, then the light in his eyes when I told him he was going to be a father. My heart aches.

"I would understand it better if I had done this more than once,"

I finally say. "If I was going through treatment for a second or third or fourth time. Or if I wouldn't go at all. But I'm not. I screwed up. I take total responsibility for what I've done. I'm also starting to understand that my problem with drinking isn't only about alcohol."

"Really," Martin says, doubtful. "What's it about then?"

"I guess it's more about how I think. How I've learned to push down any kind of negative feelings. Some people get addicted to food or shopping or work or sex. I got addicted to alcohol."

"I'm sorry, but I think that's kind of a copout," Martin says. "Like you're not responsible. I think it's easy to say, 'Oh, I have a *disease* that made me do this.'"

"You think this is *easy*? You think *anything* about what I'm going through right now is easy? You're trying to take my *son* away from me. *None* of this is easy." My voice escalates; I pause for a moment before continuing. "I'm not making excuses, Martin. How many times do I have to tell you I've owned up to what I did wrong? And now I'm doing everything I know how to to get help and never let it happen again. Trying to take custody away from me is just making things worse. For everyone. Charlie included."

Mr. Hines clears his throat. "What do you mean?"

"I mean my son isn't used to being away from me. I mean he has to be struggling with why everything has changed."

"Do you talk to him about it?" Mr. Hines asks.

"In a way," I say. "I tell him his daddy just wants some extra time with him right now. I think he's too young to understand a complicated concept like custody. I don't want him to feel like he has to choose between us."

Mr. Hines nods, and I hope this means he approves of how I'm handling the issue with Charlie.

"What about you, Martin?" he says.

"I've told him I want things to stay like this, his living with me, but there's a very smart man who's going to help us decide if it's the right thing to do."

Oh, please. Brownnose, much? It takes all my strength not to roll my eyes to the ceiling.

"Is there anything else you'd like to say to Martin?" Mr. Hines asks me.

"Like what?" I don't take my eyes off Martin, who won't look at me. The tips of his ears are red—proof positive I've ticked him off. I didn't set out to make him angry, but part of me can't help but be a little bit happy I did.

"I don't know. That's why I asked."

I look back to Mr. Hines. "No. I don't think there's anything else I need to say."

I can't defend myself after what I've done. There's nothing I can say to change my past behavior or how Martin reacted to it. He only hears what he wants to hear. He only hears what allows him to continue to be right.

"How is Charlie doing with all of this?" Mr. Hines asks Martin.

Martin breaks out his jocular grin. "He's great. I've kept his routine as close to what he's used to as possible." He goes on to recount Charlie's summer day camp activities and play dates at the park.

I close my eyes. I can't do this anymore. There's nothing left to say. I *gave* Charlie that routine. I am his *mother*. It was my job, and I lost it.

Twenty-four

Though he told me not to expect to hear from him unless something significant came up, when there's no immediate word from Scott about my joint meeting with Martin and Mr. Hines, I become even more twitchy and unsettled. Working at the restaurant and getting the house cleaned up and ready to sell does help, but there are still too many hours in the day where my mind wanders into dangerous places. I worry that my mother's silence means I'm not going to like what she has to say. I worry that treatment won't make a difference, that Mr. Hines has already made up his mind and is simply going through the motions to make his decision look impartial.

"You don't know that," Nadine tells me when I call her and tell her my fears. "And you can't control what he's thinking or what decision he's going to make. The sooner you come to peace with that fact, the better. When I get as wound up as you are right now, the only thing that works for me is getting out of myself and doing something to help another alcoholic."

"Help them how? Like clean their house? Or make them soup?"

"Sure, if you want. Or, you can just pick up the phone. Listening to what someone else is going through is a great way to quit moping around."

I'm not moping, I think, but then realize she is right, which irritates the hell out of me. It dawns on me that I've spent a lot of my time over the past couple of years feeling sorry for myself for one reason or another—sorry that my career didn't turn out the way I wanted it to; sorry that my marriage ended and that I couldn't stop drinking. Poor pitiful me.

I decide to send Martin another e-mail about Charlie's birthday party. E-mail feels safer than talking with him on the phone; something about the sound of his voice makes it difficult for me to keep my emotions under control. Charlie's birthday is only six weeks away and if I'm going to convince Martin to hold our son's party at Bouncy Land, I'm going to have to do it soon.

> *Dear Martin,*
>
> *I understand that you and Alice want to have a low-key birthday party for Charlie this year. I just feel like we should maybe respect what Charlie wants, too, and he told me he wants to have his party at Bouncy Land. I'd also really like to make his cake—he wants the same chocolate mud cake I've made him every year. The one with all the gummy worms on it? It's kind of a tradition.*
>
> *I'm not trying to start an argument with you. But with all that is going on, I just want to give Charlie the birthday party he deserves.*

As usual, I get Martin's prompt response.

> *Cadence,*
>
> *I talked with Charlie after our last e-mail about this. He told me he wants a backyard pool party at his omi's house. So that's what we're going to do. Again, if you want to bring the goody bags for the other kids to take home, that would be great. But my mother is going to make the cake. I really don't feel like we need to discuss this anymore, okay? See you later.*

This is nuts. Why is he being such an ass? I suppose, like everything else right now, I have to find a way to let it go. Now if someone could just tell me how the hell to make that happen, I'd be fine.

Discontent and frustration weight me to my chair. Though I know I should, I don't want to go to a meeting. Andi's voice plays in my head: *When I don't want to go to a meeting is when I probably need to be there most.*

I decide to do what Nadine suggested and call Laura instead, see if I can help her in some small way. I don't understand why I'm sober and she's not. We went to the same treatment classes, we did the same assignments. We wrote about our "losses" and "yets"— things we lost due to drugs and alcohol and things that we have yet to lose, but will if we drank or used again. Was her list of losses not significant enough? All I wrote for my list of losses was a single word: "Charlie." The fear of that loss becoming permanent has been sufficient to keep me from drinking. Maybe Laura didn't feel like she had anything left to lose.

She squeals happily when I ask if I can take her to dinner, telling me she'll be waiting at the curb. Punching the address she gives me into my GPS, I follow the lulling, computerized instructions to a neighborhood not too far from Northgate Mall. The beginning of dusk drapes a misty purple curtain around me as I drive along; the feathery arms of towering evergreens fall black against the quickly fading sky.

I see Laura standing on the parking strip in front of a pale yellow, two-story Craftsman, as she promised she would be. She climbs into my car, leans over to hook a skeletal arm around my neck, hugging me to her. I catch a whiff of alcohol on her breath. Or maybe I didn't. Maybe I just imagined it.

"Hey, lady," she says. "It's *so* good to see you." Her voice is thin, tired, a mere shadow of the robust girl I first met at Promises. I am only a little over a decade older than Laura; still, I always feel rather maternal around her—something about the hard-ass but false shell she presents to the world, I think. Some part of me feels compelled to warn her against the long-term hazards of maintaining that kind of bravado.

I smile. "You, too." I glance at her out of the corner of my eye as we drive away from the curb, attempting to surreptitiously assess her emaciated appearance. She wears a fitted, short-sleeved lavender T-shirt, exposing enough skin for me to see a collection of angry, abusive bruises splattered across her forearms. They stand out like piles of ripe berries smashed against a snow white blanket. The left side of her face, right beneath her eye, is swollen and stitched in a two-inch, crisscrossed, black-bloody line. I make a low, whistling noise. "What happened? It looks painful."

She shrugs, fiddling with the controls of my stereo. Her fingernails are chewed to the quick; bloody, ragged skin frames each one. "I don't remember, really," she says. "The docs in the ER say someone beat the hell out of me." She laughs, an empty, joyless sound. "Obviously. It looks worse than it feels."

"I'm so sorry," I say quietly.

"Don't be," she says. "You didn't have anything to do with it." She attempts a cheery grin. "Where do you want to eat?"

"You choose," I say. "You look like you could use a steak." *And a couple gallons of ice cream,* I silently muse. *Daily, for a couple of weeks, at least.* If she's been drinking, maybe the food will help sober her up.

"I could use ten steaks," she agrees. Her tone is flat, a pummeled thing.

It doesn't take long to find a steakhouse back near the mall. As we walk inside, the low, soothing moans of Miles Davis's *Kind of Blue* album pour out of artfully hidden speakers, rich and smooth, subtly muting the conversations of the other diners. Heavy velvet scarlet curtains line the walls, dim-lit candelabras and flickering hurricane candles only serve to add to an atmosphere of quiet intimacy.

I'm glad for this atmosphere, conducive to private conversation, even though I'm not entirely sure what to say to her. And yet, I want to ask her what happened. *How did you get here?* I'll say. *Tell me what I should do to keep from ending up in the same place.*

"So," I begin, haltingly. "How are you?"

She drops her chin to her chest, looks up at me from under dark, lifted brows. "You want the honest answer or the I'm-hooked-on-recovery, can't-wait-to-get-well-again answer?"

"Honest." I watch as she fiddles with a packet of Sweet'N Low, tearing it open and pouring it into a tiny white mountain on the table between us, then destroys it with a single swoop of her hand. She glances up at me.

"I'm all sorts of fuckered-up." Her dark, almond-shaped eyes are ripe with a pain too big for her tiny frame to carry. Her words are slightly slurred. I tell myself she's tired, that it can't be anything else.

"Do you want to talk about what happened?"

"Why not?" She shrugs, then proceeds to take a couple of swallows of the giant Coke the waitress has set in front of her. She looks at me, takes a deep breath in, releasing it in a fast, hard push. "Well, William—that's my ex, right?"

I nod.

"Okay. Well, he took me out, you know? I know, I know . . . Andi told me to stay away from him, but I really wanted to give him a chance." She smiles wistfully, the innocence of her youth shining through an otherwise haggard appearance.

"He took me to this real nice place downtown, too," she goes on, "all filled with candlelight and tablecloths and all that fancy shit, and I'm thinking, *wow, look at this classy place, he's trying to support me, I might really be able to kick it this time.*" She gives another dry laugh. "Then he goes and orders a bottle of champagne. He was all, 'C'mon, baby, you can have some, you're addicted to the needle, right? One drink won't hurt you.'" She swallows, shaking her head as though not believing the words that were coming out of her own mouth. "I said no at first, you know? I was strong. But then he poured the glass, set it in front of me, and the smell, it got to me. I took a sip, and it was like liquid relief pushing through my veins." She looks at me, tilting her head in question. "You know that feeling?"

I nod. "Yes. Of course." I would take a swallow of wine, feel it hit my bloodstream like a gush of warm water. If I close my eyes and imagine it, I can almost feel it again.

She nods, too. "So, the moment I got that feeling from the booze, I wanted to shoot up." She gives me a heartbreaking smile. "William took me to that hotel we used to like to go to and we scored. We shot up for a few days. When we ran out, he called some friends of his over and let them have sex with me. He took their money, left to go score, and that's when I got beat up, I guess. I vaguely remember saying no to the fifth one. That didn't go over so well with him." She gestures to the evidence of this under her eye, her tone flat, completely matter-of-fact. "After he was done, I called nine-one-one."

"Oh, Laura," I say, my throat constricting with tears. Horrible images are filling my mind: her sprawled out helpless on a hotel bed, scabby, disgusting men circling her like vultures. "Did you file a police report?"

"Nah," she says, giving me a quizzical look. "Why would I?"

"Because they *raped* you?" I say, trying to keep the incredulity out of my tone.

"Oh. Yeah, well, it'd get thrown out, I'm pretty sure, even if they could ID the guys. There's no physical evidence, since they didn't rape kit me. They probably figured I'm just a junkie, turning tricks to score. Which, technically, I was. Not like I haven't been arrested for that before."

Aghast from this astonishingly unemotional dissection of her attack, I can't think of a lucid response. Our server approaches, sets the dip in front of us, admirably avoiding too prolonged a look at Laura's battered arms and stitched-up face. Laura digs into the dip, slathering a crostini half an inch thick before putting it in her mouth. My appetite is momentarily quelled by her story, so I only sip at my soda, trying to dislodge the heavy lump lodged in my throat. It only takes her a few minutes to demolish most of the appetizer on her own, washing it all down with the remainder of her drink.

"Yum," she says, smiling. "That was tasty." She looks at me askance. "What's wrong?"

I don't know how she can talk about being gang raped, beaten, and then eat, as though we were having a conversation about shopping for shoes. I shake my head, pressing my lips together, unable to verbalize the thoughts that are racing through my mind.

She sighs, reaches over to squeeze my hands with both of hers. Her fingers are bony, but her grip is strong, reassuring. "It's okay, Cadee. I barely remember any of it."

"Not remembering it doesn't make it okay that it happened," I say, gritting my teeth.

Our server places our dinner salads in front of us. "Can I get you two anything else right now?" she asks.

"Yeah," Laura says. "I'd like a martini, please. A double, with three olives."

"Of course," the server says, then departs.

"Laura," I say. "Do you really think that's a good idea?"

She laughs, pulling her hands off mine, then leans back against the leather booth. "Why not? I already fucked up. What's the point?"

I don't know what to say. A strange panic swells in my belly.

Laura spears at her salad, lifting her fork, hesitating right before putting the bite into her mouth. "So anyway, I spent the night at Harborview, and then they kicked me out." She laughs, takes her bite, chewing as she speaks. "And since I can't afford Promises, I'm screwed. My mom won't take me back in 'cause I used again, so I'm staying with a few chicks I knew from my last stint in detox. It's supposed to be a sober house, but you know, whatever." She rolls her eyes. The server brings the martini and Laura slithers her hand around it. She puts the rim to her mouth and takes two long swallows, draining half the cocktail glass.

"You can call me anytime, you know that, right?" I say, grasping at the only thing I can think to offer. "We can take a walk around Green Lake, or go to a meeting. I'll come get you."

She forces a smile, blinking back the tears, pats my hand. "Sure. That'd be great." Fear is peppered across her face, though she fights hard to disguise it, lifting her jawline almost imperceptibly. She lifts the drink to her mouth again and finishes it.

Our server returns with our dinners and Laura waggles her empty glass. "Can I have another, please?"

There is an agonizing, sinking feeling in my stomach. I ache to offer her something, anything, but there is nothing more I can think of to stop her. I feel grossly ill-equipped.

"My mom's such a *bitch* for not letting me move back home," she says suddenly. Her words are coated with venom. "How am I supposed to kick this shit without her support? You know, because *she* didn't have anything to do with my turning into an addict. Same thing like your husband." She repeatedly pierces the same piece of lettuce over and over again, attempting more to maim it than eat it.

I pause, considering how best to respond. I don't blame Martin for my drinking. I never did. Laura drew that conclusion on her own. No one *made* either of us do anything. No one stuck the needle in her arm. No one poured the wine down my throat.

The server delivers Laura's drink along with our dinners. She gulps it down, like a parched man after crossing the desert, emptying it without setting down the glass. That's it. I can't stand it anymore.

"You need to stop," I say. I want to pull the words back as soon as they leave my mouth. They're only going to piss her off.

Her skinny shoulders twitch, as though she was trying to shake off something uncomfortable against her skin. "What?"

I lean in, try to grasp her hand in mine, but she yanks away. "I can't be around you when you're drinking, Laura. I didn't know you were already drunk or I wouldn't have picked you up."

"I'm not drunk!" Her eyes are wild, indignant.

"Yes, you are." My eyes fill. "I'm sorry, but I can't be a part of this. It's too hard."

"Whatever. I need to go to the bathroom."

She tries to stand up, pulling the tablecloth with her. I have to grab her untouched dinner plate to keep it from landing on the floor. As she stumbles toward the ladies' room, I take a few deep breaths. I feel sick. Was that how I looked when I drank? How I spoke, smelled, acted? Is that what Charlie saw every night, his mother loose and out of control?

I pull my cell phone out and call Nadine. "I don't know what to do," I say when she answers and tell her what's going on with Laura. "I don't want to be around her when she's drunk. It's completely freaking me out."

"Then don't be around it," Nadine says. "Put her in a cab."

"I can't leave her alone like that."

"Why not?" Nadine is matter-of-fact. "She didn't think about how her being drunk would affect you. She'll be fine. You need to keep yourself safe right now, Cadence. Trust how you feel."

A few minutes later our server approaches the table. "Your friend is getting sick in the bathroom," she says quietly.

"Oh God," I say. "I'm so sorry. Can you please call her a cab?" I hate myself for it, but I cannot take Laura home. It's too much. I can't have her in my car. I can't handle it. This is horrible. This is not the night I had planned.

"There's already one outside. They sort of count on this kind of thing happening on Friday nights."

"Thank you," I say, handing her a stack of bills from my wallet. "I'll go take care of her." I head toward the bathroom, only to find Laura spread out on the small couch in the waiting area. The hostess is looking at her like she is a disease. I squat down next to my friend, push her hair out of her face. She smells strongly of vomit and booze. I have to swallow back the gorge that rises in my throat.

"Laura?" I say. "Come on. They have a cab waiting for you."

She grunts but doesn't move. I stand up and sigh, reaching to pull her into a sitting position.

"Hey," she slurs, lifting an arm in sloppy dismissal. "Leaf me 'lone."

"I can't. You have to get up."

"Sleep," she groans.

I look up just in time to see our server stepping over to help me. "Thank you," I say, relieved.

"No problem," she says. Together, we manage to get Laura to her feet and shuffle her out the door into the waiting cab. I give the driver her address, a stack of cash, and ask him to take good care of her.

After she is gone, sadness presses through my body as a physical ache. I bend at the waist, bowed by the kind of grief that will not allow me to stand. The server places her hand flat against my back. "She'll be okay," she says, I'm sure assuming my posture is due to worry over my friend. "Someone will get her well."

I don't have the heart to answer, to tell this woman how wrong she is. No one can do this for Laura. Or for me, for that matter. If she wants it, she'll have to do it herself.

Twenty-five

The next day, I call Martin's cell phone and it rings four times before he picks up. One more and it would have gone straight to voicemail; he must have been deliberating whether or not he was going to talk to me.

"Hello?" he says. The word is short and hard in my ear.

"Hi," I say. "I was wondering . . . I know it's not my weekend, but I'd really like to see Charlie. Just for a little bit. An hour or so." I am missing my son; there is something in me too hollow to be filled by anything other than having my child in my arms.

Martin pauses before he answers. "Why?"

I have to take my own deep breath to keep from snapping at him. "I just miss him." *Please,* I think. *Can you please just do this for me? He's my son, for God's sake. He came out of* my *body.* Heated humiliation floods my cheeks. I shouldn't have to beg to spend time with my child. Only another few weeks, I remind myself, and the decision will be made and he'll be back with me. I won't have to go through this anymore.

"I'm sorry to hear that." There is a sturdy wall built around his words. His pause is expectant—awaiting further explanation. I can picture that handsome face, elevated eyebrows raising impatient waves across his forehead.

"Martin," I say after taking a few calming breaths. "Please." I can hear the contemplation ticking through his mind.

"He's at my mom's," he finally says. "I'll call her and let her know you're coming."

I let go a sigh of relief, despite having to endure another encounter with Alice. "Thank you. I appreciate it." I know, despite the custody dispute, at his core, Martin is a good man. The part of him that loved me once understands how much I need this.

He pauses. "Are you okay?"

"No," I say. For some reason, his question brings on an onslaught of tears. "But I will be." I hope he realizes I'm not just talking about today.

"Okay." He hangs up without saying good-bye. I redirect my car toward Alice's house. All I can think of is pulling Charlie into my lap, feeling his solid little body pressed against mine. I need to be reminded that there is good left in the world. Charlie is the best evidence of this I've ever known.

I park and take a couple more deep breaths to calm me before going inside. Dusk has already fallen, the pale afternoon haze melted into fuzzy gray shadow. She is waiting at the front door, opening it just as I am raising my fist to knock.

"It's nice to see you, Alice," I say, stepping inside. I look around, noting how little her house has changed in the years I've known her. Flat white walls, salmon velour couches, and teal plush carpeting grace the living room. Every windowsill and flat surface holds hundreds of porcelain trinkets collected over the years at garage sales. This is probably the only thing about Alice that clearly frustrated Martin, a minimalist. Dusting was a daily ritual with her, a habit she tried—and failed—to get me to adopt.

"Mama!" Charlie rushes in from the kitchen, throws his arms around me. Tears flood the muscles in my throat in response to his touch. I squat down, pull him close, breathe him in.

"I love you so much, Charlie bear." There is more ache in my heart than it can hold. I feel it spilling throughout my body, weighing me down. "I missed you." I can't help it; the tears start to fall.

Charlie pulls back, looks at me, worried. "What's wrong?"

I shake my head, try to wipe back the evidence from my cheek. "I'm okay, honey. I just had a hard couple of days."

"Oh," Charlie says.

I look up at Alice, who stands back, regarding the scene. There is an odd look on her face. I might venture to call it compassion.

"It's cool out," Alice says.

"It is," I say, nodding, wondering if we'll ever be able to talk about more than the weather.

"We were just about to have some cocoa and cookies. Why don't you come join us?"

I know the invitation is born out of manners but I accept anyway, wanting Charlie to witness us getting along. I settle myself down in one of the breakfast nook chairs with Charlie on my lap. He chatters away about his day while Alice sets a plate of shortbread before us and begins to warm milk on the ancient avocado-colored stove.

"And then Omi took me to the park and I climbed to the top of the monkey bars and she told me to get down from there so I didn't break my neck."

"Ah," I say with a smile. "That was probably a good thing. I've seen you on monkey bars. You fell once, remember?"

"I fell?" he asks. "Did I bleed?"

I nod, reaching up to touch the small scar over his right eyebrow. "You needed two stitches. Right there. I was very, very scared."

"See, Charles?" Alice says. "Even your mother agrees with me."

"Wow," I say, hoping the intended levity in my voice comes through, "we might want to mark this as an historic day, huh, Alice?"

To my surprise, she laughs, though her smile doesn't quite reach her eyes. She stirs powdered cocoa mix into three mugs, setting Charlie's in front of him, then turns to open the cabinet above the stove where I know she keeps her liquor. She pulls out a bottle of Bailey's Irish Cream, unscrews the lid. "I hope this doesn't bother you," she says. "I just like to have a drop in my cocoa."

I watch her pour substantially more than a drop in one of the mugs. I lean over and wrap my fingers around the handle of the mug she left alone, pulling it toward me. "Doesn't bother me a bit," I say with a smile. I'll be damned if she's going to get the response she's looking for: me eyeing her drink longingly, or rushing home because I can't stand to be around the booze.

I snuggle Charlie in closer. "Want to go read a book after we're done with our snack, honey?"

"Okay!" he says, kicking his legs out and letting them fall back again. His heels smack against my shins.

"Sh— Ouch!" I'm thrilled that is the only word that pops out of my mouth. It could have been—and almost was—much worse. "Watch it, there, Mr. Man. Your mom bruises easily."

He twists his head around and lands a wet, cocoa-scented smack on my lips, then looks up at me with adoring eyes. He knows I'm a sucker for his kisses. "Sorry, Mama. I didn't mean to."

I set my forehead against his. "I know you didn't. It's okay."

"Martin was that way, too," Alice says, sipping from her mug.

I lift my gaze to her. "Really? What way was that exactly?" I'm not sure how successful I am at masking the automatic defiance I feel. *Don't you dare criticize my child,* I think. *Don't you* dare.

She lowers her drink, curls up the corners of her mouth. "A little careless with his movements." She shrugs. "Not intentionally, of course. Just a little wild."

"Huh." "Wild" is not a word I'd associate with my ex-husband. Ordered? Definitely. Charismatic? When he wanted to be. Moody? Too often. But wild? Not that I'd ever seen.

"Charles reminds me so much of his dad." Alice winks at Charlie, which makes me think she must have something in her eye. Charlie happily munches away on his second cookie. "Don't you?"

"Yep!" Charlie exclaims, spraying crumbs onto the table in front of him and into my cocoa. I set my drink down.

"Charles, be careful!" Alice says, though not as sternly as I've heard her be with him before.

"Sorry, Omi." He bats his big blue eyes at her and I see her body immediately soften. That's something new. A few months ago, she was barking at him for staining his jeans. Apparently, he's learned how to charm her.

"It's okay." Alice looks at me and lifts her jaw, blinking a couple of times. "He's a good boy, Cadence. I want you to know that."

I hesitate, unsure what to say. Maybe the Bailey's is stronger than I previously thought. Or maybe she started drinking it before I got here. I can't think of any reason outside of inebriation that she would be this nice to me.

"Mommy knows that, Omi," Charlie jumps in, saving me. "She helped *make* me, remember?"

Alice watches my face and I don't let my eyes drop. "You're right," she finally says. "She did." She stands up, steps over to the counter. She grabs a dish rag from the sink behind her and vigorously wipes the stove of invisible spills. "Stay as long as you like," she says.

"Thank you," I say. I take her words for what they're worth. It's as close to a truce as we're likely ever to come.

After leaving Charlie at Alice's house, I try not to think about what Mr. Hines might have gathered from the meeting with Martin or what further conclusions he is coming to about me, my ability to parent, my drinking. The fact that I ever put my child in danger causes my heart to constrict. It threatens to stop beating altogether when I allow myself to consider the possibility that I won't get him back at all. The thought strikes me that Martin might really succeed here—he might take my son away from me.

There's still my mother, I think as I pull into my driveway. *But who knows what she's going to say.* I've left her alone since our last conversation, not wanting her to feel pressured to give me an answer, considering all the painful memories my drinking brought up for her. And yet. She is my mother. Part of me wishes she could just let down her guard and show up for me once in my life.

Then I remember how her own mother abandoned her. First emotionally, with her drinking, then physically, when she died. Tenderness wells up in me as I close my eyes and put my mother in Charlie's place—a little girl, unable to protect herself from her mother's unstable, drunken rage. How she must have hidden herself—first in her room beneath the covers, then in the deepest recesses of her own soul. The walls she built were high and strong; I knew, because as her child many years later, I couldn't break through them. She learned that cutting off emotion was the only way to keep herself safe, the only way to survive, then she passed that lesson on to me. If I hadn't stopped drinking, I wonder if Charlie would have eventually learned that same thing from me.

We do what we're taught, I suppose, unless life comes along and gives us a chance to change direction. Getting sober is my chance. And now I need to consider what kind of example I'll be for Charlie. I could give in to this disease I have and teach him what my own mother learned—that a bottle of wine is more important than his life—or I can step up to the plate and learn a new way to live. A way that teaches my son that while his mother is fallible, she is also strong and capable of turning her life around. I'll never know how my mother's life could have been different, if my grandmother had found a way to get sober. But I do know I'm determined to undo any damage I've done to my child. I'm determined to teach him his worth.

Twenty-six

Over the next few weeks, a natural rhythm evolves to my days. On the days I work at the cafe, I rise at around five o'clock so I can make it to my shift at 6:00. I slip on a swishy, black skirt and white, button-down blouse, flip my hair into a quick updo, and head out the door. The morning shift is decidedly unglamorous, but I love it.

"Let me set up your caffeine IV," I joke with the surly, sleep-deprived customers as I pour coffee into thick, white restaurant mugs. This comment almost always earns me a smile and at least a twenty percent tip. Le Chat Noir is popular among the nearby business set; on a good day, working both breakfast and lunch, I go home with a couple hundred dollars in my pocket.

"You're a natural," Serena says. "Like you've been doing this all your life."

"I'm just acting out the part of sassy waitress," I tell her. In that sense, I suppose I *have* been doing it all my life. Acting out my part. The good daughter, the good student, the good wife. Whatever the situation demanded of me, that's what I became. The situation I'm in demands I find a way to pay my bills, and writing wasn't cutting it.

"I feel really strange about it," I say to Vince one night after a meeting. "It's everything I've ever worked for. But I just don't think journalism is really what I want to do."

"It's okay for you not to know what you want to do with your life," he tells me with a grin. "Just as long as you're not sitting on your ass drinking."

As soon as I get the yard cleaned up and all the painting done, Derek gets my house listed for sale and we begin looking for an appropriate townhouse or condo for me to buy. I spend my Wednesday nights with Charlie, and the weekends he is with me we work on sorting through all our things in preparation for an eventual move.

"I want to keep *all* of my toys, Mommy," he says.

"We won't have room for all of them, sweet boy," I say, reaching over to touch his soft cheek. "You can fill these two boxes with everything you really, really want and the rest we are going to give away to other little kids who don't have *any* toys to play with."

"And that will be a very nice thing for me to do," he says, repeating what I've already told him.

"Yes, it will." I give him a big hug. "I'm very proud of you, Charlie. You are a *very* nice little boy."

"Yep!" he says with a confident smile, and he puts another toy in the box.

When I get home from my shift at the cafe on the Thursday in the second week in July, I call Scott to ask if Mr. Hines has sent over his report. "I haven't seen anything from him yet," Scott says. "I promise to call you the minute it lands on my desk. You have Charlie this weekend?"

"Yep," I say, my cell phone tucked between my shoulder and ear as I rinse out my coffee cup, glancing out the kitchen window at the newly flowering forsythia in the corner of my yard. A true Northwest summer has finally tiptoed in—slightly overcast mornings balanced by bright and sunny afternoons, verdant foliage, and sweet, clean-smelling air. I've heard it said that if you don't like the weather in Seattle, just wait a minute and it will change. A little bit like my moods. "Charlie's coming here," I tell Scott.

I hear the shuffling of papers in the background. "Have you heard anything from your own mother? I haven't gotten any notes from Mr. Hines about their meeting, either. It was yesterday, right?" There is an edge of panic in his voice.

"It's tomorrow, actually. And she's coming over for brunch with Charlie and me on Sunday. I'll talk with her then, okay?" I set my mug upside down next to the sink to let it air dry. My mother sent me an e-mail earlier in the week, asking if she could bring Charlie and me breakfast "so we could talk." I am trying not to take it as a foreboding sign that she didn't just call me and tell me what she was going to say to Mr. Hines.

"You can think of it however you want to," Nadine said when I called to talk with her about it. "You can imagine the worst or the best. It's your choice."

"Everything's always a choice," I said, a little annoyed she didn't offer me the comfort I'd been looking for.

"Ah," Nadine said. "*Now* you're starting to get how this whole program works." I hung up slightly irritated, but with a smile, which was becoming par for the course at the end of my conversations with my sponsor.

"Sounds good," Scott says now. I hear more paper being shuffled, someone whispering to him in the background.

"I'll let you go," I say.

"Sorry if I'm distracted," he says. "I'm due in court in an hour. You're doing great. I'll talk to you soon."

I hang up, then immediately call Alice's house. I want to tell my son I can't wait to see him. I drop into my chair, listening to the phone ring and ring. No one answers. I set my phone down on the desk, maybe a little more forcefully than I should, resentful that I'm not part of his daily schedule. I don't know where he is or what he's doing. There is something inordinately wrong with a mother not knowing exactly where her child is at any given moment. I say all of this to Andi later in the afternoon during my individual session.

"Holding on to resentments is like drinking poison and hoping the other person will die," she says after I've had my little tirade. "That kind of anger is a luxury an alcoholic can't afford to have. It's toxic."

I throw my hands up in the air, then drop them into my lap. "Great. I'm not only an alcoholic, I'm a *toxic* alcoholic."

Andi shrugs, tucks the sheet of her long black hair behind one ear, showing off sparkling silver hoops. She doesn't appear impressed by my first time admitting to her that I am an alcoholic. I hoped for a little more hoopla, considering how long it took me to say the words out loud. I imagined the swell of violins in the background, a dramatic, emotional crescendo reached as I finally find the courage to admit the truth about who I am to my treatment counselor. No such luck. "Well," she says instead, matter-of-factly, "you know what happens when you take the alcohol out of the alcoholic, don't you?"

I shake my head almost imperceptibly, gritting my teeth. "No, but I'm sure you're going to tell me."

"You're left with the 'ick,'" she says, then tells me my time is up.

Twenty-seven

With my mother due to arrive any minute the following morning, Charlie and I cuddle on the couch, him sitting between my legs, leaning up against me, using me like a lounge chair. I sip my coffee over the top of his head while he giggles at the easy, educational silliness of *Go, Diego, Go!*

"Mom?" Charlie says.

"Hmmm?" I lean down and kiss the top of his head, still slightly matted and warm from sleep. God, he smells so good. I wish I could bottle it and keep it with me always.

"What's an alcoholic?" He asks this the same way he has asked me to define a thousand other things: an accordion bus or an avocado. My child, simply seeking explanation.

Still, my head lifts. Where was this coming from? Martin, I assume. It has to be Martin. Or Alice. The two of them, talking about me in front of my son. How do I answer this? Truthfully, I decide. Always the safest route to take. "Well, honey," I begin a little shakily, "it's kind of like having an allergy."

"Like Anya's 'lergic to peanuts?'"

"Kind of. Only an alcoholic is allergic to alcohol. They have one drink of something like beer or wine and they can't stop. That's *their* allergic reaction."

He twists his head so he can look up to me. "Like you drink wine?"

I tap the tip of his nose with my finger. "How I *used* to drink wine, yes. I'm not doing that anymore, remember?" *Oh God, please tell me he doesn't talk to Alice and Martin like I'm still drinking.*

"Oh yeah!" he says, reaching up to touch my cheek. "That's good. I didn't like it when you did. Remember that time you spilled that bottle all over the floor?" He turns back to the muted television. "You swore. A *lot*. The F word, even."

"You're right, I did." I pause, remembering that day, not too far from the night Martin came and took Charlie. I was in the kitchen and had just opened what would have been my second bottle of the night when I turned and knocked it with my elbow off the counter and onto the floor. It didn't break, but it did make a horrible mess. And Charlie is right—I dropped enough F bombs to destroy a small nation. "I'm sorry for doing that. Mommy shouldn't swear."

He shrugs his pointy shoulders against me. "It's okay. Daddy does it, too. It makes Omi mad."

I smirk at this, probably taking more pleasure than is healthy for me imagining Alice dressing down Martin regarding the evils of profanity. I take a final swig of coffee, then reach over to set my empty mug down on the table next to us. Just as it touches the surface, there is a sharp rap on the door. I carefully disengage myself from my son, who wraps his arms around my leg and mockingly threatens to not let go. Another rap at the door.

"Just a sec," I call out, lightly bopping Charlie on the top of his head. "Lemme go, buddy. I need to get the door." I swing open the door and there stands my mother, smile as bright and wide as ever. She should have it patented. She wears jeans, a red knit sweater, and black boots.

I tuck the errant curls popping loose from my ponytail back behind my ears. "Hi, Mom."

"Nana!" Charlie exclaims as he leaps off the couch and into my mother's arms. My mother hugs him close, covers his face with kisses.

"Hello, baby boy," she says, stepping into the house. Charlie clings to her leg now. Her movements are awkward, weighed down by a five-year-old boy. She gently detaches from him and closes the door behind her. She sets down a bright red Macy's shopping bag. "I brought breakfast," she continues, surveying the living room as though she was seeing it for the first time. I can't remember when she was last here.

"What did you bring us?" I ask, trying to keep my voice light.

She reaches down into the Macy's bag, pulls out a brown paper sack, and hands it to me. "Bagels and cream cheese. Nothing fancy, I know, but they're still warm. I picked them up at the PCC."

I open the bag and the warm, yeasty scent wafts up into my face. I breathe in deep. "Mmmm," I murmur. "They smell great." Closing the bag, I hold them out to Charlie. "Can you be a big boy and take these into the kitchen for Mommy? We'll be right there."

He snatches them from me. "Can I have one? Can I make it myself?"

I smile. "Sure, honey. Just be sure to use one of your safe plastic knives and not one of mine, okay?" I've always encouraged Charlie to be as independent of me as possible, to learn to do things for himself. He already ties his own shoes and picks out his own clothes. He races off and I am left standing in front of my mother, who is squinting at me like she doesn't quite recognize me. "What?" I ask.

She presses her lips into a thin line, shakes her head. "You just look good. Healthier, I guess. Like you've lost weight."

"I wish. But thank you." I'm less puffy, I suppose, now that the alcohol aftereffects are working their way completely out of my system, but I haven't dropped an ounce of fat. Even with all the running around I do at the restaurant, my flesh grips on to each calorie I feed it with the same vigor that I hold on to Charlie. It professes no plans to let any of them go.

My mother and I are quiet a moment, listening to the noise of Charlie in the kitchen, opening and closing drawers, the squeal of his pulling out a chair from the table. The air is heavy with unspoken words, weighting down the moment more than I am comfortable enduring. I can't make small talk. I can't pretend there isn't an elephantine issue smack in the middle of the room. I decide to make the first offering, step directly into the fire. I have to unclench my teeth in order to speak.

"What did you tell him?" I ask.

She twists around, sending her arm out as though she was reaching to do calisthenics, setting her purse down on the table by the front door, then back to face me. A muscle above her right eyebrow twitches rapidly as she speaks.

"Honey, I'm sorry I didn't tell you what I was planning to say to Mr. Hines. I honestly didn't know myself, so I thought that saying nothing was the better way to go. You seemed so . . . angry. I didn't want to upset you any more than I already had."

"I understand why you're having such a hard time with this," I say, pulling my arms back to cross them over my chest. "I get it. And I feel for you. But waiting . . . I'm not going to lie, Mom. It's been hard."

She sighs, leaning her head toward her shoulder while crossing her arms over her chest, too, rubbing her biceps up and down, a soothing self-hug. "I wish I could have figured it out and told you right away. But I didn't want to tell you one day I thought Charlie should stay with you, and the next day say something different."

Charlie screeches another kitchen chair around in the kitchen—likely moving it back from the counter where he stood to prepare his bagel. I experience the vague sensation that this might not be the best time for me to be having this conversation with my mother—I should be spending time, every moment I have, alone with my son—but I have to see this through. I have to tell her how I really feel—it's taking up too much space in my head. My mind can barely hold another thought.

"Like I said, Mom," I begin, "I know that my drinking must have brought up a bunch of ugly memories for you. Things you haven't thought about in a long time."

She nods, a tiny movement.

"My heart aches knowing you had a mother who treated you like that. Who treated *herself* like that. But I've been thinking about it a lot. And I have to wonder, if she had had a family who supported her, if her mother was in her life and had offered her the kind of love and acceptance that she needed, maybe she could have gotten well." My voice breaks and I have to wait a moment before I can go on speaking. "I can't change who she was to you. I can't change what she did. But maybe you can give to me what her mother couldn't."

"What do you need?" my mother asks, her voice barely above a whisper.

"I need you to believe in me, Mom. That I'll find a way to manage this."

She unwraps her arms, lifts up her hands slightly—a gesture of surrender.

"So, what did you tell Mr. Hines?" I set up internal emotional scaffolding, bracing myself for the worst possible outcome.

"I told him I think you should have Charlie," she says. "I told him you are the most tenacious person I know, and when you set your mind to accomplishing something, you don't rest until you've given it everything you've got. I told him I can't imagine you doing anything less than that when it comes to recovering from all of this." I see the truest sense of pride in her eyes. Something deep inside me finally relaxes, a tight grip letting go.

Closing the gap between us, I slip my arms up around her shoulders, resting my chin on her shoulder. "Thank you," I whisper in her ear, the feeling of tears thick in my throat once more. I'm beginning to suspect there is no end in sight to this new weepy tendency of mine. "Thank you so much."

My mother hesitates a moment before hugging me back. She's surprised, I think, to have me display such affection. She reaches up, presses her hand against the back of my head. "I'm not very good at showing it, I know, but I do love you, Cadence. You're my daughter.

I'll do whatever I can." She pulls back and looks at me. "In fact, I already have."

I tilt my head and squint at her. "Uh-oh. Should I be nervous?"

She smiles. "Not at all. Derek told me you listed the house for sale."

I nod. "I can't afford it."

"Well, I can. I signed the offer yesterday. I'm hoping you'll let me buy it, and you can rent it from me at an extremely reasonable family rate until you're back on your feet. Then, you can either buy it back or find somewhere else you and Charlie want to live."

My jaw drops. "You want to be my landlady?"

"If you'll let me." She grabs my hand and squeezes. "You and Charlie have been through enough in the past couple of years. The stress of moving is the last thing either of you need."

"I don't know what to say, Mom. Are you sure?" I run a few quick calculations in my head. If she buys the house for what I'm asking, I can use the profit to pay off all my credit card bills. Living off my wage from the cafe won't be easy, but if she's serious about charging an extremely low rent, I might actually be able to bounce back from financial catastrophe.

"I'm positive," she says. "What good is all my hard-earned money if I can't help my child when she needs it?"

"I don't know what to say. Thank you." My eyes fill, and Charlie chooses this moment to come bounding back from the kitchen, interrupting us. The wooden door that sections off the two rooms swings wildly back and forth. His face is messy with smears of cream cheese, his eyes are bright. "I need help, Mom!" he says. Amazing. At least my child has no issue with asking for assistance when he needs it; I've done that much well with raising him. "I want some milk but the holder thing is really full and I don't want to pour it and make a mess even though I know spilled milk isn't anything to cry over, I still don't want it to spill."

My mother and I both laugh, wiping our eyes, but it is she who steps forward first. "I'll help you, sweetie. Can you get the glass down you want to use?"

He doesn't answer her. Instead, he regards us with a quizzical look. "Why are you crying? What's wrong?"

"Nothing, sweetie. Nana and I are fine."

"Grown-up stuff again?" he asks, sighing with an edge of informed exasperation far beyond his years.

"Yeah, but it's the good kind of grown-up stuff," I say. "Guess what, monkey? We don't have to move!"

"Really?" he exclaims. "I get to keep my room?"

"Yep."

"What about my toys?"

"Those, too." I reach for my mother's hand, pull her along with me toward the kitchen. "C'mon, I hear that sesame bagel calling my name."

Charlie turns and races in front of us, beating us to the kitchen. "Bagels don't talk, Mom," he says.

"Are you sure?" I say, winking at my mother, who is smiling, still holding my hand. "I just heard the plain one ask for peanut butter and strawberry jam instead of cream cheese."

"Mo-om," he groans. "Stop it."

"What?" I say, my eyes wide, innocent. "Maybe it's allergic to dairy, like your cousin."

He laughs, his head thrown back, mouth open wide, a bright and beautiful sound that reaches inside me and makes me happy, too.

My mom leaves around two o'clock, promising to call me during the week. "I mean it," she says, hugging me at the front door. "And make sure you get those papers signed with Derek, so we can get the ball rolling on the house."

Charlie and I occupy the rest of our afternoon together baking his favorite chocolate chip cookies. I let him drop the butter, sugar, and eggs into the mixer; I handle the messy job of adding the dry ingredients. He sneaks a couple of handfuls of chocolate chips when he thinks I'm not watching. I let him get away with it.

"Can I take some of these to Omi and Daddy?" he asks after the last cookie sheet comes out of the oven. "I can telled them I baked them."

"You can 'tell' them, honey, not 'telled.' And of course you can take them. That's very thoughtful of you." I help him fill a plastic container to the brim.

"But Mommy," he says when he sees the container, "then *you* don't have any cookies to eat."

"Oh, Mommy doesn't need to eat any more cookies. Trust me."

When I get back home from dropping him off, I sit down at the kitchen table and turn on my computer, breathing a little sigh of relief. I lean back in my seat, stretching my arms far above my head. The muscles in my back are tight and tense, but as I stretch it hits me that I was never this relaxed when Charlie lived with me. My house was never this clean, my work was never quite done. I always felt like I wasn't good enough at anything I tried to do. When I was working I felt like I should have been with Charlie. When I was with Charlie I should have been working. I was never in the moment—I was always looking in the direction I thought I should have gone.

Something within me drops down—an elevator plunging too fast, weighted by leaden guilt for having this sort of thought. I'm not supposed to find any kind of pleasure in my child not being with me. Isn't it a requirement for mothers to constantly pine over their children when they are away from them? Maybe I just don't have it in me to be a parent. I shake my head, as though to remove it of these heretical thoughts.

I push away from the table, just reaching to log off and power down my laptop, when my phone rings. It's Vince.

"I missed you at the meeting today," he says. On the weekends I don't have Charlie, I've been going to a smaller meeting in Vince's neighborhood, telling myself it isn't to see him, but to meet more people in recovery.

"I had Charlie," I tell him, "so I couldn't make it. How was it?"

"Good, actually. That gal, Trina? The one I introduced you to at the Fremont meeting? She shared a little about drinking around her kids. It was pretty powerful."

"I didn't know she was a mom." My nerves suddenly jangle around inside my body. After the e-mail I sent to her, I never heard back and hadn't seen her at any meetings. Again, it becomes apparent I need to work on my friendship maintenance skills.

"Yep," Vince says. "Her husband doesn't know she's going to meetings. She said she's still drinking, too. Trying to figure this whole thing out."

"Why are you telling me this? I thought we were supposed to be anonymous."

"Not always. At least not among ourselves." He sighs. "Anyway, I really just wanted you to know I missed seeing your smiling face."

We hang up, and I drop back into my chair, feeling guilty for not making more of an effort to get in touch with Trina. If what Vince said is true about her drinking in front of her kids, I know her pain. I can feel it as alive in me as my own. Just like Kristin felt mine. It's then that I realize what is saving me. It's what Andi talked about—having a group of women who get me—who don't judge, who understand my thoughts and know why I do and say the things I do. It's not being on my own to face all of this. It's having someone to talk to, to call. I think about how the people in AA talk about moments in their lives when their idea of a higher power gives them a flash of clarity and they're given an opportunity to pass on what they have learned. If I have a higher power, maybe it's giving me a chance to offer Trina what I didn't have the courage to ask for myself.

I don't give myself the option to think too much about what I should do; I'd only succeed in talking myself out of it. Steeling myself with a couple deep breaths, I sit forward again, poise my fingers above the keyboard, and begin to type an e-mail.

Dear Trina,

I hope you don't mind, but when Vince mentioned you shared at a meeting today about being a mother who drinks, I felt compelled to write you.

You are not alone. I am a mother who drank in front of her son. I was drunk almost every night for a year, and toward the end I was drinking pretty much around the clock. I went through an ugly divorce, and I sat in front of my laptop with an enormous goblet set next to me, sipping away at a bottle of wine until I passed out. I was a terrible mother. I have shame that runs deeper than I know what to do with.

I have been where you are, not so long ago. Killing myself seemed a viable option compared to the misery I was living in. I sat in my kitchen staring down a bottle of pills, ready to end it. I have been in a treatment program for almost five months, and have finally managed to admit that I have a disease called alcoholism, medically diagnosed, and treatable on a day-to-day basis. I realized I am not alone, that I am not the only mother who has gotten drunk in front of her children—I just happened to get caught. I didn't agree with my counselor when she told me this makes me lucky, but I'm starting to now. I have just begun this process myself, learning how to stay sober, to avoid the emotional traps that might lead me to drink again. I have a long way to go, and so much to learn.

My ex-husband is trying to take custody of my son away from me. I have more turmoil in my life than I know what to do with most days. I'm riddled with levels of shame and guilt that I'm not sure I'll be able to endure.

The help I can offer you is the knowledge that you don't have to do any of this on your own. There are treatment programs available, and the meetings, as you, of course, know. But I'm here, if you want to write or call. You can say anything you need to. I want you to talk to me like I know exactly how you feel, because I do. You are not alone. You're just like me.

With love,
Cadence

Puffing up my cheeks, I push out a long, tired breath, reading what I've written twice over. It's the most words I've put on a page in months. I throw out a quick, cosmic request to whatever powers that be for Trina to send me a return e-mail in the morning.

Powering down my laptop for the night, my insides are battling with an equal measure of exhaustion and elation. Thankfully, exhaustion wins out, so I make the rounds in the house, turning off the lights, going about the business of saying good night. I tumble into bed. Sleep slips in fast and easy. I want to believe it's not exhaustion but instead the immediate side effect of deciding to do the right thing.

Since I don't have to be at the cafe, the alarm jolts me from a deep slumber at 7:00 the next morning. I wake with my face smashed into my pillow, a tiny stream of drool leaking out of the corner of my mouth. *Lovely,* I think, wiping my cheek with the edge of the sheet. *What man wouldn't want to wake up to this? Would Vince?* I smack the clock to get it to stop screeching at me and remind myself with a heavy sigh that I'm not allowed to date. I need to stop thinking about him that way, at least for another six and a half months, when I celebrate my first year of sobriety. Not that I am counting.

Check e-mail is the next thought in my head. In less than two minutes, I throw back the covers, pull on the nearest set of sweats, and am in the kitchen firing up my laptop. While my computer boots up, I get my coffee started.

It's done about the same time as my computer is warmed up. I open the new mail option and it's instantly as though I've stepped off the edge of a skyscraper. My insides plummet, terror lands with a thud somewhere down near my pelvis. I scroll down, panic twisting in frantic, zigzagging patterns throughout my veins. There's an e-mail from Tara at *O*, and the subject is *Drunk Mother*. Oh shit.

> *Dear Cadence,*
>
> *I was a little confused by the e-mail you sent, and believe you sent it my way accidentally, but I have to say, the editor in me thinks it's a compelling subject. I hope you'll consider what I have to propose.*
>
> *I'm so moved by the compassion you showed "Trina"— sharing your story with her makes me think that you'd do an amazing job sharing it with O's readers. I'd love to talk with you more about putting your story into an essay, and how we could make it fit into a themed issue around women and addiction.*
>
> *I want you to know I'll keep you in my thoughts. My aunt is in recovery from an addiction to prescription painkillers, and while she doesn't have children, she has worked hard to maintain her sobriety. She is one of my biggest inspirations.*
>
> *I look forward to speaking with you soon.*
>
> *All best,*
> *Tara*

"Oh my God," I say to the empty kitchen. "Holy shit." I pop open the e-mail I sent the night before, and there it is, addressed to "Tara" instead of "Trina." Outlook must have autofilled the address when I typed in the letter "T." I was obviously too tired to notice.

"Oh no," I groan. "Oh no, oh no! Please, God, tell me I didn't do this!" But there it is, in pretty black script. Maybe if I blink hard enough, it will disappear. I blink. It doesn't work. I blink again. *Dammit.* No luck.

I grab my cell phone off the table, call Jess, and tell her what I've done.

"That's fantastic!" she says. "I'm so proud of you!"

"Wh-what?" I stutter. "Proud?" *I can't believe this is happening.*

"She loves the idea, right?" Jess chatters on. "You've been struggling to come up with something and here it is!" I can hear Derek mumbling something in the background and she shushes him.

"I didn't *mean* to do it!" I wail, throwing my free hand up into the air, then slapping the top of my thigh. I take a quick intake of breath. "Holy shit, Jess, I have to write her and tell her it was a fictional e-mail or something. Something I was writing for a story." I move to click on the screen, prepared to take the appropriate measures to write that e-mail.

"What?" Jess exclaims. "Are you kidding me? Lying to her would totally screw with your professional credibility."

"Oh, and my confirming that I'm an alcoholic in danger of losing her child in a custody dispute won't?" I hesitate, though my hand is hovering over the mouse and my eyes are still glued to the screen.

She sighs. "People feel better if they know you've got some personal experience you can relate to theirs with. She obviously connected to you because of her aunt. This is a good thing, Cadence."

"I don't know," I say, completely rattled. My heart is still pounding in my chest.

"You don't know what?"

"Should I really leave it alone?"

"Absolutely. But make sure you send the e-mail to the woman you meant to send it to in the first place, too."

"Good point. Thanks." We hang up and I carefully copy and paste the e-mail Tara received, making sure Trina's e-mail address is in the correct place before sending it.

Next, I decide to Google "mothers and alcoholism." A spark of my old journalistic tendencies ignites as I read; I smell a good story.

Getting sober for women is different than it is for men, I find on a website dedicated to recovery.

> **Social stigma, labeling, and guilt are enormous barriers for females to receiving treatment. Women are often subject to the madonna/whore continuum theory, which states that all women fall on one end of the spectrum or the other—either you're a whore or a saint. If you're an alcoholic, society tends to label you as the whore, even if it's only metaphorically speaking. If a woman is a mother, the expectation is for her to be a saint, so if you're both, an alcoholic and a mother—even a sober alcoholic—that preset prejudice comes into play. Generally speaking, society assumes you're not a good mother.**

I am utterly engrossed in my reading until the phone rings and I see Kristin's cell on the display screen. "I'm on my way," she says too quickly for me even to say hello to her. "Do you want a mocha from Wholly Grounds or have you already hit your caffeine limit for the morning?"

"What?" I say, puzzled.

Kristin sighs in my ear. There is the subdued roar of her car engine, indicating that yes, indeed, she is on her way to my house. "We're carpooling to group, remember? We talked about it on Saturday?"

"Oh, oh, that's right." I press a palm to my forehead, sitting back in my chair. "Sorry." I glance at the clock: 9:00 a.m.

"So, do you want a coffee?" Kristin presses.

My eyes fall onto the untouched, forgotten, and cold remainder of the cup I'd poured when I first got up, something that suddenly seems a lifetime ago. "Yeah, that'd be great, thanks." I take a deep breath. "Can you make it a double?"

Twenty-eight

Calling Tara at O magazine is one of the most intimidating things I've ever done. Even with Nadine and Andi urging me on, it takes me a little over a week to muster up the courage to pick up the phone. I wait until I get home from my Friday shift at the cafe, take a shower, a deep breath, and then punch in the number she listed in her e-mail.

"Tara Isaacs speaking," she says when she answers.

"Hi, Tara," I say. My mouth is dry, so I swallow once to avoid sounding like I have cotton wrapped around my tongue. "It's Cadence Sutter."

"Oh, *Cadence.* I'm so happy to hear from you. When you didn't respond to my e-mail, I was afraid I might have scared you away."

I laugh nervously. "Well, I'm definitely a little scared to be talking with you. Embarrassed, really, to tell you the truth."

"Why? Because you accidentally sent me the e-mail? Don't be. It happens to the best of us." She chuckles. "My husband's name is Owen, so I can't tell you the number of times Oprah has been sent a note asking her to pick up milk on the way home from work."

I laugh again, this time a little more comfortably. "Thank you for that. It's scary to be talking about this at all. I haven't really advertised what happened with me."

"I'd imagine not," she says. "But that's all part of the story, right?

How hard it is for women to tell the truth about what they're struggling with and get help?"

"I think it's more that it's hard to *ask* for help. Especially mothers who might have a problem. If we tell someone, 'Gee, I think I might be drinking too much,' what if our kids get taken away?" My throat catches on that last sentence, so I cough to clear it.

"See? It's a great angle. I want all those kinds of details. How you started drinking, how it progressed. Do you think you could get me five thousand words to start?"

My pulse quickens. "Um, I don't know. I haven't written anything in a while. And the custody decision hasn't been made yet. I'd feel a little strange writing it without knowing the outcome." I can't imagine writing about what I've done, detailing the days I chose alcohol over my son, committing my sins to the page.

"There's no rush," she says. "Why don't you just take your time, and send me whatever you come up with when you're ready? Or not, if you decide you aren't comfortable doing it. We'll be going ahead with a women and addiction issue, but haven't picked the month yet. It's at least a year out."

"I'll definitely think about it. I just wanted to say thank you for the opportunity. And your kindness."

"You're very welcome," Tara says. "I'm rooting for you."

"Thanks," I say. "I can use all the cheerleaders I can get."

Later that night my in-box blinks with the e-mail that has finally arrived from Trina. Tiny, panicky bubbles begin to bounce along in my veins as I click on it, and with a deep, unsteady breath, I whisper a quick thank-you to the empty room. It reads:

Dear Cadence,

   Thank you so much for your honesty. For letting me know
I'm not the only mother in the world who has done this in

front of her children. I can't tell you how much it means to know that I don't have to do this alone.

After I read your e-mail, I took a deep breath and went to the HR department in my company to ask about my treat-ment benefits. It turns out they are extensive. I wept as I told my husband I need help with the girls while I do whatever it takes to stop drinking like this. He cried and told me he would support me through this. You are right—I am not alone. My girls would not be better off without me, they would be better off without me drinking. I will keep in touch and let you know how I'm doing. And hopefully, see you at a meeting soon.

All best,
Trina

Relief flows through me. It worked. What I offered was actually of help to her. Maybe there's hope for me yet.

Twenty-nine

Charlie's birthday falls on what is forecasted to be the hottest day of the year. After Martin's last e-mail on the subject, I managed to grit my teeth and give up the fight to have the party at Bouncy Land, settling instead for putting together ten goody bags filled with a variety of tacky, easily breakable loot his little preschool friends will adore. Rubber balls, plastic sunglasses, toy cars. And candy. Lots and lots of candy.

"Just do what you can do," Nadine told me. "Being there for your son is the most important thing. Not where the party is held or who makes the cake."

"Oh, I'm still making a cake," I said.

"Didn't you tell me Martin insisted Alice was making it?"

"Yep."

"And you're making another one?"

"Yep."

"Without telling him?"

"Yep."

Nadine shook her head, but smiled. "Kind of ornery, aren't you?"

I smiled, too. "Maybe just a little." Charlie told me what kind of cake he wanted and he was going to get it. I make it for him every year. Case closed.

I invite Kristin and her kids to come along to the party, along with my mom, Jess, Derek, and my nephews. I feel like I'll need protection of some sort, being among the Mommy and Me Mafia again, though after what happened in the coffee shop, I didn't invite Susanne. My stomach twists at the thought of what the other women say about me, the judgments that are made, but Andi encourages me to try and let those thoughts go.

"What other people think of you is none of your business," she says. "You can't change it, you can't control it. The only thing you can control is your reaction to it. Focus on Charlie. Take lots of deep breaths. Have a place where you can go take a break from the party if you need to—your car or something. Keep your friends close and you'll be fine."

I follow her advice and spend the drive over to Alice's house taking huge yoga breaths. In through my nose . . . and out through my mouth. I imagine the tension I feel releasing and traveling outside my body through every breath. I sit in my car, continuing to breathe until I see Jess and Derek pull up with the boys. I step out onto the parking strip and she comes over to hug me.

"You ready?"

I pull back from her embrace and give her a big smile. "As I'll ever be. Can Derek carry the box with the goody bags? I need to get the cake."

"Sure." She calls him over and he takes the large box out of my trunk. Together we walk up and around the side of the house to the backyard, where the party is being held. Marley and Jake immediately race off to find their cousin, who I see already splashing around in a sizeable wading pool. He sees me and waves. He is wearing Spider-Man swim trunks and Spider-Man goggles. Of course.

"Hi, Mommy! It's my birthday!" He flaps his hands in the water, emphasizing the excitement he feels.

"I know, sweetie! I'll be over in a minute."

"Okay! I'll be right here!"

The sun is a brilliant, roasting ball in the sky. The heat lies over my bare shoulders like an electric blanket. Marley and Jake, wisely dressed only in swim trunks, jump into the pool with Charlie. Martin and Alice are nowhere to be seen.

"Come with me into the house?" I ask Jess. I still can't help but feel apprehensive about being alone with Alice for very long. I want a witness in case she decides to dangle a glass of merlot in front of my face.

"Of course. Hey, honey," she says to Derek. "Why don't you set those goody bags on each of the plates on the picnic table."

"Yes, ma'am," Derek says.

Jess and I go up the back steps into the kitchen, where I see Alice at the table, putting finishing touches on a large white sheet cake decorated with bright yellow sunflowers.

"That's very pretty," I say. *A ten-year-old girl would love it.*

"Thank you," she says, looking over with a smile. The smile disappears when her eyes register the dark chocolate Bundt cake I carry. It's covered in fudgy frosting and crumbled-up Oreos. The middle is filled with gobs of gummy worms, which spill up and over the top of the cake in a slightly gross, squirmy fashion. A Spider-Man action figure is posed on the top of the cake, wrestling with two gummy worms in a battle for his life.

"What's that?" she asks. Her voice is flat.

"A cake," Jess says with a smile. She loved that I decided to bring it despite Martin telling me not to. "Can we put it in the fridge so it doesn't melt?"

Alice's face is like stone. "I'm not sure if there's room."

"We'll make room," Jess says cheerfully. I don't think I've ever loved my sister more than in this moment. Talk about ornery. She steps over to the refrigerator and shuffles a few things around before reaching for the cake and sliding it onto a shelf. "There! Perfect."

"Where's Martin?" I ask.

"He's finishing wrapping presents in my bedroom," Alice says. "He'll be down in a minute."

Jess and I go back outside, where Derek is now spraying down squealing children with water from the garden hose. Brittany and Renee have arrived along with Julia, the woman I'd met at Wholly Grounds back in May. Their children are already in the pool, too. I plaster a grin across my face and decide to force myself to go say hello. Just as I'm about to move toward them, Kristin steps through the gate with Riley.

"Hey, glad you found it okay," I say. "Where's Liza?"

"Home with Grandma. Apparently, attending a little boy's birthday party wasn't high on her list of priorities."

"Ah." I smile at Riley. "I'm glad you came, sweetie."

"Thanks for inviting me," Riley says, standing shyly next to his mother, still holding her hand.

"Why don't you go play in the pool?" Kristin says, giving him a little nudge.

I crouch down next to Riley and point out my son. "See the boy in the Spider-Man getup? That's the birthday boy." I call out his name. "Charlie? This is Riley, my friend Kristin's son."

At the sound of my voice, Charlie stops playing and waves vigorously. "Hi, Riley! Do you like water fights?"

A bright expression falls across Riley's face. "Yeah!" Any hesitance he felt seemingly forgotten, he races over to join the other children in the pool.

"Hi," my sister says to Kristin. "I'm Jessica, Cadence's sister." She extends an arm to shake hands.

"Hi," Kristin says. "It's nice to finally meet you."

"Sorry," I say. "I should have introduced you."

"Yeah, especially since I'm so shy," Jess teases me. She shakes her head a little as she watches her husband gleefully wield the hose. "I'd better go over and make sure he doesn't get them too worked up. It's all fun and games until somebody gets excited enough to pee in the pool."

Kristin laughs, and then reaches over to run her hand down my arm. "You okay?"

I put my hand over hers and give it a quick squeeze. "So far, so good. Just don't leave me alone."

"You got it."

"Let me introduce you to the Mommy Mafia," I say under my breath. I have told her about my run-in with them at Wholly Grounds and she vowed not to allow that kind of crap to happen again. We step over to the other group of women, who all give us big smiles. Only Julia's appears genuine. I introduce Kristin to her first, then to Brittany and Renee.

"Where's Martin?" Brittany asks me. She wears a sleeveless maternity top, which only partially conceals the basketball-size bump of her pregnancy.

"Inside, finishing a couple of things, I think. You look great, by the way. How far along are you now?" *Kill her with kindness.*

"Six and a half months. The heat is killing me."

"How are you doing?" Julia asks me. "We didn't get a chance to chat that day at the coffee shop. It was so sweet of you to invite Cody to come, too."

"I think Martin organized the party, didn't he, Cadence?" Brittany points out.

Kristin shoots her the stink eye. Brittany doesn't miss it.

I take a deep breath. "He did the invites, yes. I'm responsible for the five-pound goody bags, though."

Julia laughs. "So *you're* the one to blame for the sugar high Cody's going to suffer from later."

"Especially after you see the chocolate mud cake I made. With gummy worms."

"Oh, boy," Julia says, "he's going to love that. He begged for one on his last birthday, but I'm more of a store-bought-cake kind of mom."

"It's pretty simple," I say. "I'd be happy to get you the recipe."

"I'm not sure if having a recipe will help my baking-gene deficiency, but I appreciate it. Thanks."

Alice and Martin descend from the back of the house carrying a tray of hot dogs for the kids and Polish sausages for the adults. Derek relinquishes his hold on the hose to help Martin get the grill started for lunch. The kids race back and forth between the picnic tables for handfuls of chips and pretzels and hunks of watermelon, screeching and hollering when they jump back into the pool. Jess polices the crazy scene while Kristin and I chat with Julia. Brittany and Renee wander off to sit in the shade of a large pear tree in the corner of the yard. Another couple of Charlie's friends show up and join the fun in the pool. For a moment, I almost manage to feel normal. I'm just a mother at a birthday party, not an alcoholic stuck in a custody dispute for her son.

My mother finally arrives just as the kids are sitting down to eat. Despite the heat, she is still in her workclothes—a pair of linen slacks and a short-sleeved, white button-down shirt.

"Sorry I'm late," she says, coming over to kiss my cheek. "An appointment ran over. Stubborn wisdom tooth."

"Is there any other kind?" I say. "I'm glad you're here."

"Nana!" Charlie cries out. "Where's my present?"

"Charles Sutter!" I reprimand him. "Are those good manners?"

My son hangs his head for a moment. "No."

"What do you say?"

"Thank you for coming to my party, Nana."

"Of course, sweetie. And your present is in the driveway."

"Awesome!" Charlie exclaims, and races off toward the fence. Forgetting their lunches, all the other children follow, squealing like a bunch of baby pigs.

"Good God," Brittany says. "Too bad I'm pregnant. I need a drink."

"Me, too," Renee agrees. "I'll have an extra one for you."

"There are beers in the cooler," Martin says. "Derek, you want a beer?"

My brother-in-law shakes his head. "No, thanks. I'll pass. Need to keep on my toes around this many monsters. Can't let them get the upper hand." He winks at me and I give him a grateful look.

Kristin squeezes my hand. I wonder if this is uncomfortable for her, too, watching other people drink. I know where alcohol will take me, and truly, I don't *want* to drink; in fact, my stomach gets queasy just thinking about it. But I can't help but be a little jealous that other people *can* drink and I can't. It's a sizzling-hot summer day. My mind tells me a Corona with a squeeze of lime would sure taste good.

"Nana got me a car!" Charlie screams from the fence. "A car, a car, a *car*!"

I swing around to face my mother. "You got him a *what*?"

She gives me a closed-lipped smile before speaking. "A Spider-Man jeep. Child-size and battery-powered. He can zip around the playground."

"Geez, Mom."

"Oh, stop. He'll love it. And so will you."

"He should keep it at my house, don't you think, Sharon?" Martin asks. "Since he's there more?"

"No, Martin. I think he should keep it at his mother's."

"It sounds dangerous," Alice chimes in from her seat at the picnic table. "What if he falls over?"

"Then he'll learn to get back up," I say.

"Not a bad skill to teach a child," Jess says. "You don't want him relying on his mama to rescue him for the rest of his life."

I have to turn away quickly so Alice won't see me smirk at my sister's not-so-subtle dig. Derek's shoulders shake in an effort to conceal his amusement. I don't look at Martin, but I'm pretty sure he's fuming.

"I think I'll go check this new ride out," I say, stepping away from the group. I'm halfway to the front yard when I realize Julia has followed me.

"Cadence?" she calls out, and I stop. The kids come tromping back toward us, running to the table to finish their lunch.

"It's so cool, Mommy!" Charlie says as he races past.

Julia and I both laugh. "He's not amped up or anything," I say.

"Typical, right?" she says. "I thought Cody was going to turn inside out, he was so excited on his last birthday." She pauses and looks like she's trying to figure out how to say something more. After a moment, she finally does. "So, I hope this isn't totally out of line, but I wanted to talk to you about that day in the coffee shop when we first met."

I bob my head once, suddenly apprehensive. "Okay . . ."

"Brittany and Renee told me what's going on with the custody dispute."

My heart seizes in my chest. I didn't think anyone would bring the custody issue up at the party. Not really. I thought I could skate by on sheer determination. Or maybe it was denial.

"Oh," I start, but then don't know what else to say.

She gives me a soft smile. "I just want to tell you my sister-in-law has been in recovery for eight years now, and she's the best mother I know. She wasn't always, but she is now. My brother stuck with her through some pretty tough times."

"Oh," I say again, and something inside me relaxes.

"And again, I hope you don't mind, but I told her I met you and she said to give you her number, in case you ever want to talk. She's in the program." She hands me a piece of paper.

"Thank you," I say, taking it from her, then glance over toward the rest of the party. "I'm sorry to cut this short, but we should probably get back. It's about time for cake."

Back at the table, we sing a hearty rendition of "Happy Birthday" to Charlie and the kids finish off the messy mud cake in about two minutes flat, leaving most of Alice's cake on the table. I thought I would enjoy this, but I don't. I feel oddly bad about bringing mine, even though Charlie was thrilled to see it and asked to have his candles nestled among the gummy worms instead of the sunflowers. I have a big piece of Alice's cake, as do the rest of the adults.

"It's really good," I tell her and everyone murmurs in agreement. It's a fantastically light almond cake with thick, homemade raspberry filling. The kind of authentic European, melt-in-your-mouth confection she spent years creating at her bakery.

"Not a little boy's favorite, it would seem," she says, shrugging.

"Yeah, but they'd devour a box of sugar cubes if I left it on the table," I say. "What do they know?"

Martin hugs his mother. "Cadence is right, Mom. It's the best cake I've ever eaten."

Alice smiles, leaning her head against his chest. "Not the best."

"The best," Martin insists. He mouths the words "thank you" to me over the top of his mother's head.

I give him a quick smile in return and experience another brief flutter of hope. Maybe we can do this. Maybe after everything is said and done, we can find a way to be friends.

Thirty

What's going on?" I ask Scott toward the end of August. My desperation to get Mr. Hines's report is evident. "Why is it taking him so long? It's a pretty simple decision, isn't it? Me or Martin. One or the other. The end."

"He has to review all the documentation," Scott explains patiently. "Your medical files, the reports from Andi at Promises, the declarations from both your and Martin's references, plus take into account what he has learned from his interviews. It's a lot of material to go over. Then he has to put it into a succinct report for the judge."

"And we can fight it, right, if he recommends Charlie stays with Martin?"

Scott sighs softly. "Yes, but Cadence, more often than not the court will go with the GAL's initial recommendation. If things go Martin's way, you can spend thousands of dollars going to court and end up with the same result, or you can accept the decision and find a way to cope with it."

"It won't go Martin's way," I insist. "It can't." I can't allow myself to believe for a moment I won't get Charlie back. Not even a millisecond. I won't have to accept it, because it won't happen. I say as much to Nadine, who I am calling each day as she asked.

"I'd like to think I'm that powerful, too," she says. "I'd love it if just because I want something to turn out in my favor, it will."

"I think you get what you put out," I say, mildly irritated that she's not being more supportive. "If I believe I'll get him back, I will."

"I know it's hard to come to terms with," she says, "but you're not in control of this decision. You've done what you can and you have to leave the rest."

"Easy for you to say."

"No, honey, it's not," she says, her tone laden with grief. "I spent years trying to will my son into not drinking himself to death. I thought that if I got him into treatment program after treatment program, if I supported him and believed in him, if I took him to meetings with me and all that good motherly stuff, he would get well. He didn't. It wasn't up to me."

"That sucks," I say sourly.

"Yes, it does," she agrees. "But that's life."

Our conversations are brief and all seem to go like this. I tell her what's going on with me and she points out the holes in my thinking about a situation, or how she handled something similar. I know on some level she's right. This isn't my decision and it royally pisses me off. I can do all the right things, and still, I could lose custody of my son. How does that make sense? Do the right things, and the right things should happen. I want to live in a world where this simple concept bears true.

I go through the motions of my days during the week, sticking to the usual schedule as much as I can, despite the thoughts racing through my mind. I'm distracted and edgy, attempting to remain focused only on the task in front of me—brushing my teeth, taking a shower, drinking coffee. I work at the cafe four days a week. Serena moves me to dinner shifts, where the real money can be made. I have lunch with Jess and my mother, go to a meeting with Kristin or Serena, have mildly flirtatious conversations with Vince. I'm only half listening when people speak. Too many thoughts pound through my brain to hear their words. *Please,* I think. *Please let me have him.* I'm itchy inside—allergic to uncertainty—with no easy way of relief.

I keep myself busy. My mother and I work out the terms of our arrangement with the house. I pay my bills, do the laundry, and plant hopeful bunches of bright-eyed yellow and purple pansies in my flowerbeds. It helps some, but still, it is not enough.

I spend the weekends with my son. We have dinner with my mom, Jess, and her family. After I drop him back with Alice the Sunday of Labor Day weekend, I decide I need a project. My night is too empty, the house too quiet. All it takes is a quick trip to Home Depot and four hours later the pale, powder blue walls in my son's room are replaced with an earthy, armed forces green. The next day I pick up new camouflage sheets and top them with a thick, dark brown comforter—grown-up colors for my grown-up boy. *A welcome home gift,* I think, as I smooth the bedding and fluff up his pillow. For when he moves back in.

Later that night, I am standing in Charlie's newly painted room, looking out his window. The sky looms heavy with ponderous black clouds, the air is thick and cold with the threat of an incoming late-summer storm. I think of Charlie, how he races into my bed at the earliest rumble in the sky, at first sight of a threatening steel wool sky. He is terrified of the loud, wall-shaking booms and the brilliant flashes of lightning. During a rainstorm when he was three, a fir tree fell directly next to his bedroom window, freaking the living daylights out of him. For months to come, *any* loud noise—a door slamming, a toy clattering to the hardwood floor—would send him directly into my arms. *Who is holding him now,* I wonder. *Alice? Or Martin?* It should be me. There are some things mothers are specifically made for—holding their children during a storm is one of them.

I'm finishing hanging the curtains edged with embroidered green tanks when my cell phone trills on Charlie's bed, where I tossed my purse. A quick glance at the clock tells me it's most likely Kristin calling to see what time she can pick me up for the meeting tonight.

As part of her plea agreement, her lawyer worked out a deal for her to get Liza and Riley back at the end of next week, so she's trying to get in at least a meeting a day before having to rely on babysitters.

"I'm ready when you are," I say into the mouthpiece of the phone. "Just finishing up with Charlie's room. You should see it."

"Cadence?" a man's voice says. "It's Scott."

Everything inside me freezes solid. All my organs, my breath, every cell in my body become immovable. "What did he say?" I ask. Terror pulls down on the muscles of my face until it feels as though it has hit the floor.

"I'm sorry," Scott says. His voice sounds broken apart, as though recently pushed through a wood chipper. "I just got the e-mail. He made the recommendation for Martin."

"No" is the only word I can get out. My eyes close and there is a sudden rushing river in my ears. My body sways and I gasp for breath, my hand splays flat across my chest, trying to force the air to move in and out of my lungs. This can't be happening. I'm not here. I am not this person, this is not happening to me. It's not. The same words I said in Jess's car the night she drove me to the hospital. The night I wanted to die.

"His report says that your thoughts about suicide are too recent," Scott goes on, "and it's too early in your recovery to say for sure that you won't relapse. If it's going to happen, it's usually in the first two years, so that's where that's coming from." He is quiet, waiting a moment, and when I don't respond, he prompts me. "Cadence? Are you okay?"

What a stupid fucking question. While I think this, I manage to restrain myself from saying it. Instead, I take a deep breath and answer him. "I don't know."

"As you know, your mother and Jess both said you should get him back," Scott says. "Andi's reports all said that you're making remarkable progress and your prognosis for continued recovery is good."

"But it didn't matter," I say, my voice devoid of emotion. None of this has mattered. I did everything I needed to and I lost him anyway. There was no point in even trying. The decision was made the minute Mr. Hines knew I was an alcoholic. I was instantly tried and convicted.

"It matters for you, Cadence," he says. "And for Charlie." He sighs, a deep, laborious noise. "I'm so sorry."

I push my forehead into the palm of my right hand, trying to press the thoughts racing through my brain into submission. "It's not your fault. You did everything you could. It's me." The words are rote, robotic.

"It's not you," he says, "it just is. I'll call you tomorrow, okay? So we can talk about our next move?"

"I thought there wasn't one. I thought this ends it." Every word is an effort. I force myself to speak.

"Only in terms of the decision, but we need to figure out the specifics of the parenting plan with his lawyer, so it's likely we'll all have to meet."

"Okay."

"Don't be alone tonight, okay? Will you promise me that?"

"Sure," I say. "I'm going to a meeting with a friend." I say this at the same time I'm devising the excuse I'll use to tell Kristin why I'm not going. I can't. What's the point now?

"Call your sponsor, too. She sounds like a great lady."

"I will. She is." I am reduced to smaller and smaller syllabic structures. Again, I don't intend to call Nadine.

"You'll get through this," Scott says. "Just hang in there."

"Okay. Thanks." I hang up, sink to the floor. I put my face in my hands, curl my back against the wall, elbows against my thighs.

Oh, Charlie. My baby. He's going to think I don't want him. When he wakes in the night from a bad dream, I won't be there to hold him tight. Every day, in a thousand ways, he'll need me and I can't be there for him.

The pain is like shards of glass in my blood.

A black, shuddering sound creeps up from my belly into my throat and at first I think it might melt into tears but instead, a raging, gravelly scream blasts out of my mouth like a bomb. After my breath is spent, another scream crawls up through me and goes off, and then another and another. The sharp edges of the noise tear at my flesh, slashing and burning the muscles in my neck until I wonder if it's possible to choke to death on your own rage. I've never felt anything like it, this forcible, ravaging fury. Adrenaline pumps every cell in my body to twice its normal size—it feels as though I might very well be about to explode.

I scream. I scream until my throat is raw, until the ache there matches the one already throbbing in my chest. I don't want this. I don't want this pain. It's an emotion laden with stones, pulling me down into a dark hole from which I'm not sure I know how to escape. I look for the logical action to take.

There is no logic here.

The phone rings. Kristin. I take a few deep breaths, answer. My voice is hoarse. Good. My lie will only be more convincing. "Hello?" I creak.

"Cadence? What's wrong?"

"I'm sick," I say, not having to fake the pitiful, weak edge to my words. "I've been throwing up all afternoon." When in doubt, tell people you've been vomiting. They'll steer clear.

"Oh, ugh." She pauses. "You seemed fine this morning. Is it something you ate?"

"I don't think so. It came on pretty suddenly. Chills, fever, all the fun stuff." *Hang up. Hang up now. I don't want to talk to you. I don't want to talk to anybody.* "I'm going to stay home."

"Obviously. Want me to bring you anything?"

My son.

"No, I don't want you to catch this. Especially with the kids coming back next week." I practically choke on this last sentence, but I know it's the one that will convince her to stay away.

"Okay," she says. "You're probably right. I'll call you tomorrow to see how you're doing."

I hang up. Pulling myself into a standing position, I drag my feet down the hall, careful not to look at any of Charlie's pictures. I step into the laundry room and gather up the sheets I just took off my child's bed, then take them with me back to his room. I drop face-down onto his bed, smothering my face in the earthy scent of him. I cry in earnest: the kind of body-racking, stomach-rending sobs that I know will leave me feeling as though I've been stoned by an angry crowd, beaten black and blue. Only the bruises I've earned are all on the inside, tucked away from anyone's view but my own. Self-inflicted abuse that I'm sure only scratches the surface of what I deserve.

A flood of emotion rides through my body and I endure each wave, hopeful the next one will be the last. The storm that had hinted at its arrival earlier now begins to rage. Rain hits the gutters like raw grains of rice machine-gunned into a metal pan. A north wind leans its powerful shoulder against the window strongly enough to make me think it might just push its way through the glass. Night deepens in the room; black air surrounds me like a cold, wet blanket. Darkness answers me only with more tears and so I decide to welcome them, to give myself over to the one thing that might eventually grant my heart reprieve.

An hour passes, then three. Gradually, mercifully, the weeping tapers. I roll out of bed and step over to the dresser. I'm hesitant to register my reflection in the mirror, unsure if I want to see whether my current physical state matches the horror of the emotional. When I finally look, I see the veins in my forehead pounding in violent blue rivers beneath my skin; my hair is stringy, mashed and wild, my eyes flash the inky black of a thundercloud. *Oh God. Who is that? How am I going to survive this?*

I groan. I want to do anything to alleviate this pain. My stomach bends in on itself from the weight of it; my heart seizes up in my chest with every breath that holds the thought of my son. I wonder if this is what it feels like to be drowning.

I have grabbed my keys and I am out the door before I know it. My body's mission for oblivion has overtaken my mind's ability to give its opinion. The rain is a torrent against me, wet little nails hammering against my body. My car already knows the path: two blocks down, four more on the right, and I am there. It's late—there aren't many cars in the lot. A few soccer moms getting their shopping done after the kids have gone to bed and their husbands are home watching the news; the bachelor buying his week's worth of frozen dinners and cold cereal. And then there's me.

The wine aisle is right where I left it. Staggering rows of glossy green and black glass soldiers—the army of my past destruction. *What difference does it make now?*

I contemplate which poison I should choose. I'm not picky about it, really. I drank red wine because I thought it was the classy choice. Tonight, I don't care. The only thing that matters is escape. I run the tip of my finger over a liter-size bottle of merlot. Shiny silver labels attract my eye. I load six bottles into my cart and head up to the cashier. Usually, I'd buy some fancy cover items: boxes of crackers, wedges of expensive cheese. Not now. Not tonight.

"Did you find everything you need?" An exorbitantly cheery young redhead greets me at the register as I'm setting the bottles up on the conveyor belt. She says this without looking up, and when she does, there is no mistaking her double-take at my appearance. Swollen eyes, straggling hair, six liters of wine. I doubt she has trouble doing the math. Nor does anyone else in the surrounding lines. They look at me as though I might be infectious.

"Yes." I stare at her with heavy, dead eyes. The real answer is no. What I need is my son back. What I need is to not feel any pain like this ever again.

She looks away, carefully running each bottle over the reader. "Having a party?" she asks, trying to keep her voice light.

"No." I reach in my purse, pull out my debit card, and pay for my purchases.

"Would you like help?" she says, her smile bright and false as she hands me my bags. She looks right over my shoulder; her expression is pleasant, but her eyes cloud.

I laugh at her choice of words. *Help? What's the point?*

"I've got it," I say, and head out the door. A chill of remorse tickles up my spine—a spider scaling a wall. I shouldn't be doing this. I need to stop. But I can't.

Another staredown with a bottle. No pills this time, but wine bottles lined up like a firing squad on the table in front of me. A single glass is poured. The rich, acidic scent wafts upward, my fingers toy with the rim of the water glass I've filled to the brim. I thought that banishing my wineglasses from the house would somehow keep me from drinking. At the moment, this doesn't look likely.

The wine talks to me. "Go ahead," it says. "Here I am. You might as well."

"No," I tell it. Or maybe it's not the wine speaking. Maybe I'm hearing the voice in my head, the one Andi has always called my addict.

"It will trick you," she said. "It lured me into thinking it was worth it. It wasn't."

I slump in my seat, pulling my fingers away from the glass. Charlie will stay with Martin. I don't know how to reconcile this thought in my head. I never believed it would happen. Not really. I believed that children belong with their mothers. I didn't beat him. I didn't lock him in a dark closet and leave him to starve. Those are the kinds of women who should have their children taken away. Not me. Yes, I drank too much—I can admit I am an alcoholic. But if it's a disease, why am I being punished like this for having it? Would they do this to a woman with any other disease? If she was getting treatment, if she was doing what she needed to do to get well, would they still take her child away?

The phone rings. It's late, past 11:00. I see Jess's name on the caller ID, wonder why she would be calling so late. I don't answer. Let her think I'm already asleep.

Hours tick by. I stare at the bottles. They stare back at me.

I don't sleep. The wine beckons.

Such easy, immediate relief. It calls to my pain, offers to cradle it gently, then obliterate its very existence. The tears rise again in my eyes, flooding my vision. Do I really want Charlie to grow up without his mother? Do I want to do to him what my grandmother did to my mother? If my child isn't with me all the time, am I still technically his mother?

I don't know the answers. I don't know anything at all.

The pain is astonishing. I don't know what to do. I don't want to drink. I know what happens down that road; I know I don't want to end up there. What I don't know is where this new road I've been placed on might lead. I don't know where to turn, how to feel, how to act and move and breathe in the world where someone else decides how often I see my child.

A low groan escapes me, a natural companion to my tears. *He won't be here every morning. I'll have to find a reason to get out of bed each day without him with me. How am I supposed to do this?*

I know other women have been here. I know they have managed to get through it without taking a drink. People in AA talk about acceptance, about finding serenity in the realization that the only thing you have control over in this world is your reaction to what life throws your way. How? I want to know. How do I find these things? I understand that on days where the sun is shining, when my car starts and I have a good job and enough money and my husband loves me, it's easier to do. How—in moments like this, moments where I can't see anything but darkness in front of me—*how* do I find the sliver of hope that leads me back into the light?

My heartbeat quickens. I can barely see for the swell of tears in my hot, puffy eyes. I know what I have to do. Now I just have to work up the courage to do it. Eventually, I manage to stand and slowly carry each of those six treacherous bottles of wine to the counter. I pour them down the sink, shuddering out harsh, rough sobs of relief.

When the wine is gone and my tears are finally spent, I look through the kitchen window into my backyard. The sky is the royal hazy blue of impending day. The storm clouds have passed, leaving a faint netting of stars to adorn the sky. I swallow to calm the nerves that jiggle in my throat. I will find a way to get on with things. I'll gather up my black, fluttering scraps of guilt and resentment and pain and somehow knit them together into a way to survive. And though I'm afraid, though shame claws at the gates of my mind, I walk over to the table and I reach for the phone.

I'm doing the right thing. I don't worry if it might be too early to call.

Epilogue

About a month after the custody decision came down in Martin's favor, Andi told me she was leaving Promises. It was my final appointment with her there. Everyone else had already graduated; Andi said I could keep coming to see her—every day, if I had to. Which I often did. I was fragile and tearful, my edges held together with gossamer threads. Threads placed there by other women. They held them tight for me, gave me as many as I needed, until I worked up enough strength to fabricate my own.

"I want to start my own practice," Andi said that last morning in September. She wore chunky squares of turquoise jewelry paired with a fabulous Stevie Nicks–style white summer dress, complete with the raggedy, uneven hem. She made it look good. "Working in groups is great, but I find the most satisfaction in the one-on-one counseling."

"Can I be your first client?" I asked. There was so much I had to work through, layers and layers of emotions to peel back. Andi was one of the few people I trusted to expose those tender places without the fear that she might drive something sharp and wide directly into them.

"Absolutely." She smiled, and it lit up her eyes like someone had plugged her in.

A year later, I still work with Serena, waiting tables five nights a week at Le Chat Noir. It's not a glamorous job, but it pays my bills and it is work I'm proud to do. I've even spent some time in the kitchen there, learning basic knife skills and how to build a perfect white sauce. Cooking still calms my mind, lulling me into a lovely, predictable world, so much so that I've recently enrolled in culinary school. At thirty-five, I'm older than most of the other students there, but Serena is convinced that as soon as I graduate, I'll become Seattle's next celebrated chef. I'll be happy if someone is just willing to hire me.

It took me a while to get used to the idea of not being a writer anymore, but over time, I've come to peace with the knowledge that at least for now, that chapter of my life is through. I did buy a copy of *O*'s issue on women and addiction when it came out. Other writers did an amazing job describing the struggle other women—other mothers—have faced in trying to get sober. I read their stories and related to each and every one of them, but I only tell mine in meetings, even though speaking in groups still isn't something that comes naturally to me.

What does come naturally is being Charlie's mother. I soon discovered that not having him waking up in my house every morning did not make me any less a parent to him, any more than it made Martin less of his father when Charlie was living with me. Every Wednesday and three weekends a month he is at my house. Martin and I split the holidays. The mediator also recommended I keep Charlie with me full-time two months during summer, which, surprisingly, Martin agreed to. It's a standard parenting plan, it's just that I'm the Disneyland Mom, instead of the Disneyland Dad, as the saying goes. Martin had enough class to not ask that I pay him child support, though by law, he is entitled to it. He signed that right away as part of our agreement.

"I make over five times your salary," he said during our mediation settlement. "To ask you for any of yours would be stupid." His lawyer protested and tried to change his mind, but to no avail. I respected Martin in that moment—brief amnesty from the count-less hours of fury I had already endured at the thought of him. My relationship with him is one of the thicker layers I need to work through.

I find solace in the little things, like the fact that my child is awake with me more hours on the weekend than he is with Martin during the week. I'm sure of this. I counted. Kristin recently pointed out that if a father spent as much time with his child as I do with Charlie, if that same father worked and went to school, and still somehow managed to see his child that often, the world would can-onize him. They'd probably throw him a parade. "How does he do it?" they would ask in wonder. "What an amazing man!"

This is not the experience I have had as a mother who does not have primary custody of her child. Expressions aren't that hard to read. I see the very core of my character being questioned. A few people have the gall to ask why I don't have custody of my son. I've heard the whispers, questioning what I must have done to lose him. These are not people I invite to share my life; these are people I have to restrain myself from ripping a new orifice. There are those, too, like Julia and Tara, who understand and respect the work I do each day to stay sober, the commitment I've made to strive toward the best version of myself I can be. Still, the shame hovers just beneath the surface, though I'm doing what I can to let it go. It's progress, not perfection, Nadine reminds me. She says I cannot regret the past, nor can I shut the door on it. I can't regret it because it brought me where I am today; it taught me the lessons I needed to learn. I can't shut the door on it and pretend it never happened, because that hinders my ability to apply all that I've learned. I believe her. Some days. Others, I want to play like a potato bug—curl up and make believe the rest of the world doesn't exist.

I have friends now, though, who won't let me do this. My phone rings incessantly; I always have someone to spend time with if I need it. Kristin is still sober, and so is Serena. I wonder sometimes, too, if Laura is still drinking, but since I never heard from her after that night in the restaurant, Andi reminds me time and again that the only person's sobriety I can be concerned with is my own.

To this end, I hit three, sometimes five meetings a week, if I need it. They keep me focused on a solution to my problems rather than the problems themselves; they teach me I must accept my current circumstances as being exactly the way they are meant to be. For me, acceptance is an action, something I have to practice day by day, sometimes moment by moment. It's not a one-time event—it's a process I have to learn to apply to the events of my life. I used to view acceptance as capitulation, me throwing up my hands and admitting that I am weak. I see now that it is much the opposite. It's realizing the strength it takes to gently embrace what is, going with the flow of my life instead of against it. It's understanding what I can change and what I can't. It's believing I have the tools to become the person I am meant to be. I cannot change society's concept of me as a mother without custody of her son, but I can change my reaction to it. I have to, or eventually I will drink again. And that, I know, is a path I'm unwilling to walk down again.

My mom has turned out to be an excellent landlady, and while I have argued with her over the minuscule rent she allows me to pay, I am grateful for this new and more open relationship with her. Over time, she has told me more about my grandmother, and has even started attending Al-Anon, a support group for the loved ones of alcoholics. She, like me, is learning a new way to handle what happens in her life instead of trying to barricade against it. Neither of us is perfect in our approach to how we interact, but we are trying, and that's more than we've done before.

With Nadine's blessing, Vince and I went out on our first official date the night I celebrated one year of sobriety. He brought me coral roses, because after nine months of talking almost daily, he already knew they were my favorite. He took me to dinner at the Space Needle in a private room for two, where the view displayed the lights of Seattle looking like diamonds scattered across a swath of black velvet.

At the end of the evening, he stood at my front door, took me in his arms, and kissed me like I'd always imagined he would. Soft, yet insistent; passionate, yet sweet. Six months and countless kisses later, we're still going strong. Wherever we go, he opens the door for me, puts his hand at the small of my back, and tells me he loves my Wild Woman of Zanzibar curls. He knows more about me than any man has before—he has seen me overcome by emotion, dissolved into tears over missing my son. He does not run away, nor does he try to fix me. He holds me, supports me, and lets me find my own way.

When Charlie isn't with me, Vince and I talk into the wee hours of the morning, after our bodies have tired and we lay snuggled together in one of our beds. We talk about our pasts and what we hope our future might be, though for now, we are moving slowly, content with how things already are.

I waited several months to introduce them, but once they met, Charlie and Vince became excellent friends, often locking themselves away in Charlie's room to build elaborate Lego cities or act out scenes from *Star Wars* while I throw together our evening meal.

"I like Vince," Charlie tells me. "He's funny. You can marry him if you want."

"Oh, sweetie," I say. "I'm so happy you like him. But Mommy's not quite ready to get married again. Not yet." My son's stamp of approval almost means more to me than my own.

Tonight I will not see Vince. Instead, I am on my way to Alice's house. She still watches Charlie for Martin after my son gets done with school. So I pick him up there. It is a cool, late September evening; the sky is lit up with brilliant brushstrokes of scarlet, sunflower, and amber. I pull up in front of Alice's house. Charlie stands on the porch, waiting for me. He jumps up and down when he sees me, races down the stairs. Alice watches as she steps out the front door. My son throws himself into my arms when I get out of the car and I wave to Alice. She nods and gives me the barest of smiles. It's still not easy between us, but at least I don't find myself searching out ways to purposely make it unbearable. That's progress, I suppose. More than I ever expected to achieve.

It's Friday, and Charlie and I are heading over to Kristin's place for pizza and Dance Dance Revolution excitement. Jess and the twins will meet us there. The children will play, Kristin, Jess, and I will talk. Charlie and I are in charge of bringing the ice cream; we'll stop at the store on the way and I'll let him pick out the flavor. I will breathe deeply to retain my patience as he examines each and every carton in the case—he'll review his options only twice, if I'm lucky. I will remember to be grateful for each moment I have with my son. If I fail and snap at him to hurry up, to just pick a flavor, I will tell him I am sorry. I'll kiss him and hug him, and start the night all over again. My son has the kind of heart that will let me do this. He is resilient. He is beautiful. He is mine.

Acknowledgments

This book would not exist without the support and encouragement of a few fundamental people. My amazing agent, Victoria Sanders, whose loyalty is only surpassed by her publishing savvy. Benee Knauer, who patiently held my hand through more versions of this manuscript than either of us would probably care to count. Thank you both for trusting that the story I held inside me would eventually find its way out.

It has been such a gift to work with my editor, Greer Hendricks. She is impossibly kind and insightful, and I am beyond grateful for her wisdom and gentle guidance. Thank you for believing in this story, and for laughing and crying in all the right places.

Also, thanks to Sarah Cantin, Greer's assistant, who provided a wickedly organized timeline and the perfect resolution to a troublesome plot point—you are a gem!

To my dearest friend, Tina Skilton, who read portions of this manuscript in its various iterations upward of a hundred times and never failed to provide constructive feedback along the way. Thank you for laughing with me, crying with me, and always, always knowing the right thing to say.

To my mother, Claudia Weisz, for perspective and unwavering support. To my children, Scarlett and Miles, who are, without a doubt, the reason I'm here.

Some of the best and most brilliant people I've ever met walk with me along the path of recovery, and I cannot say enough about their unconditional love and support. My deepest gratitude goes out to Sally C., Lisa X., Sherrie S., Loretta M., Carmen B., Carol F., Kurt J., Liz W., Cheryl P., Tim T., Cheri S., Jon T., and too many others to name. I am privileged to know you all.

And finally, my love and appreciation to my husband, Stephan Hatvany, who had the courage to stand by me in my darkest hours and continues to be the kind of man I used to believe could only be conjured on the page. You are my happy ending.

Resources

www.aa.org

www.anonpress.org

(Help lines, phone numbers listed by state)

www.aalivechat.com

(24-7 online AA meetings/support)

Best Kept Secret

Amy Hatvany

A Readers Club Guide

Questions and Topics for Discussion

1. Do you think the pressures that moms feel today are different from those that previous generations of mothers have faced? How do the challenges of balancing work and family fit in? Discuss to what extent this was illustrated in the novel.

2. Cadence's doctor and Andi both use the phrase "different behaviors, same compulsion" when discussing addiction and recovery. What do they mean when they say this? Can you think of other addictive behaviors that women adopt in an effort to "escape"?

3. Cadence says that her mother, Sharon, never discussed the end of her relationships with the men she dated. Do you think this had an effect on Cadence? What was your opinion of how Sharon reacted when Cadence called her father?

4. Did you agree with Martin's decision to file for custody? In your opinion, what were his motivations for doing this?

5. Alice is one of the novel's most enigmatic characters. Did your opinion of her change from the novel's beginning to its end?

6. Forgiveness is an important theme in this novel. Discuss instances within the narrative where it is offered freely, and those instances where it is withheld. Is forgiveness something that should always be available to people who are repentant?

7. Cadence's grandmother is arguably one of the most important characters in the novel, and yet we never see her or know her, beyond secondhand descriptions. How did your opinions of both Sharon and Cadence shift once you knew more about her?

8. Did this novel change the way you think about (or talk about) your own drinking habits, or those of your friends? Did it change any of your preconceptions about addiction and addicts?

9. *Best Kept Secret* is about one woman's mistake that she can't undo. Is there a decision or choice that you have made in your life that you regret? Were you able to rectify it?

10. The truth of Cadence's grandmother's alcoholism is a long and closely guarded family secret. Are there any family secrets that you only learned about as an adult?
11. Did the ending surprise you? Who do you think should have received custody of Charlie?

Enhance Your Book Club

1. Many memoirs have been written about addiction (*Lit* by Mary Karr, *Wishful Drinking* by Carrie Fisher, *Drinking: A Love Story* by Caroline Knapp, *Smashed* by Koren Zailckas). Consider selecting one to read as a group, or having members bring in one that they have read that they found particularly moving. How is reading a memoir about addiction different from reading a novel about the same topic?
2. Mothers who drink have been in the news in recent years. Do some research online and revisit the stories that made headlines. Do you have a different perspective on these women after reading *Best Kept Secret*?
3. Think about the portrayal of alcoholism and addiction in films, and consider watching one as a group. Some examples include: *Barfly*, *28 Days*, *Requiem for a Dream*, *Rachel Getting Married*, *Blow*, and *Postcards from the Edge*. Do you see a distinction in how male and female addicts are depicted?

A Conversation with Amy Hatvany

What inspired you to write *Best Kept Secret*?

I began writing the story as a direct result of my own emotional experiences around being a mother and a recovering alcoholic. While the characters and plot are fiction, Cadence's emotional turmoil during her descent into addiction and her journey back to sobriety are largely based on what I went through. As I worked on the emotional side of getting sober, it became clear to me that there is a special, intense kind of shame that accompanies being a woman who has been drunk in front of her children. It's that shame which forces so many of us to keep our addiction secret, for fear of what might happen if we tell someone the truth. We're terrified of the stigma and possible consequences, but keeping this secret can have devastating—even deadly—results.

I wanted to write a story that would hopefully illuminate how this can happen to anyone. How quickly a seemingly innocent behavior can destroy an otherwise successful, strong woman while she attempts to keep the balls in her life in the air so no one will suspect what's really going on. I wanted to emphasize how many women, whether or not they end up becoming alcoholic, face incredible amounts of pressure to do everything in their lives perfectly. And when we fail, we experience such profound levels of shame and self-loathing, even as we smile brightly and tell ourselves that we can't expect to *always* be perfect. But deep down, perhaps subconsciously, I think we still believe that we "should" be. So we reach for behaviors that drown our shame out, at least temporarily. And then we become ashamed of the behavior, and a vicious cycle emerges.

When do you find the time to write? Do you have a special workspace, or any writing rituals?

Since I still have a day job, I pretty much fit in writing time wherever I can. Early in the morning, late at night, or on the weekends when the kids are still sleeping. My ritual is to get my butt in the chair and keep it there until I hopefully get at least two thousand words on the page! I wear my most comfy pajamas so I can sit cross-legged while I try to ignore my two adorable dogs, who constantly pester me for attention. Like Cadence, I need total and complete silence in order to write, but I'm easily distracted—"Oh, look! Shiny things!"—so my husband's Bose noise-canceling headphones are one of my favorite accessories.

You're the author of two other novels (published under the name Amy Yurk). How was writing this novel different than your previous two?

It was different for me in many ways. Because of various circumstances, I hadn't written anything substantial in more than five years, so I felt pretty rusty and stilted when I started out. Obviously, the emotions behind this story were incredibly personal, more so than with my first two, because in revealing Cadence's secret I was revealing my own. There were dark memories I had to revisit, and it took some time to build up the courage to get the emotional side of those experiences fully onto the page. I worried about being judged for my alcoholism, but the idea that if I told the truth it might help even one woman who is still suffering alone in silence made it worth the risk of what others might choose to think of me personally.

Since this is admittedly such a personal story for you, why did you choose to write a novel instead of a memoir?

I chose to write a novel primarily because that's the genre I feel most comfortable working within, but at a deeper level, I also wanted to address broader themes around the pressures women face every day in all our roles: as mothers, as professionals in our chosen careers, and as wives, daughters, and friends. Unfortunately, feelings of not being good enough, self-loathing, shame, and guilt are common to most women in our culture, and it was important to me to speak to all women—not just alcoholics and addicts—about the dangers of letting those emotions get the better of us. Fiction allows me a much wider canvas to explore the complicated issues at play.

Part of Cadence's struggle is that she feels like she can't measure up to other mothers—that her peers in her Mommy and

Me group have it "together" in a way that she does not. Is this a sentiment you've observed in women you know?

Absolutely. Society places an increasing amount of pressure on mothers to maintain ridiculous levels of expertise. We're supposed to be mindful of every possible effect our actions might have on our children and edit ourselves accordingly. We're expected to be psychologists, nutritionists, teachers, doctors, and organic farmers (or, at the very least, shop only at local, sustainable farmers' markets!). If a mother is thinner or better-dressed, or has taught her three-year-old how to ask for juice in Mandarin Chinese, it's a common reaction for many women to feel somehow "less than" in that woman's presence.

I think what's dangerous about this feeling of inadequacy is that it's entirely based on our *perception* of what a woman appears to be on the surface. But the truth is we rarely know what's really going on behind closed doors. Maybe that thin woman has a terrible eating disorder, or the better-dressed woman has a hidden online-shopping addiction that is about to bankrupt her or end her marriage. And so on. When I find myself feeling unworthy next to a mother who manages to work full-time, runs the PTA, and bakes delectable gluten-free goodies for her children, I remind myself that every one of us is fighting some kind of battle. Everyone suffers.

Cadence finds some peace and satisfaction in cooking. Do you have a similar activity that relaxes you and gives you a sense of fulfillment?

Oh, I'm a total foodie, too! I adore cooking—the creative side, of course, that comes out of whipping up something glorious to put in my mouth, but also the calming, Zen-like effect the process has on me. If you do the right thing in a recipe, you get an expected result. There are very few things in life that predictable, so I find a lot of peace in the kitchen. (And on my couch, watching the Food Network! Ina Garten—the *Barefoot Contessa*—is my personal culinary hero.) I post some of my favorite recipes on my website and on Facebook, and I always love it when readers send me their favorites, too!

At the end of the novel, Cadence notes that "if a father spent as much time with his child as I do with Charlie, if that same father worked and went to school, and still somehow managed to see his child that often, the world would canonize him." Do you agree that this double standard exists? Do you think we tend to expect different things from mothers and fathers?

I do see a double standard. As the traditional nurturers, mothers are expected to put their children first, and as the typical primary breadwinners, fathers are expected to put their careers first. If a family's situation differs from these standards, our sense of normality is disrupted, and we're not quite sure how to respond to the people involved.

This is especially notable in the standard perception that after divorce, children should remain with their mother and the father should have visitation rights. How many men are judged or looked down upon for spending their allotted two weekends a month with their children? People don't make moral suppositions about his character. They don't automatically wonder what horrible thing he did to not have primary custody. He's just doing what fathers should do. If he manages to do more than that, he is lauded as going above and beyond.

Now, put a mother in that same scenario, working hard at her career, paying child support, and spending two weekends a month or more with her children. What is your core emotional reaction? What does it bring up in you? Are you immediately horrified, assuming she must be a druggie or a prostitute not to have been granted custody, or at the very least a selfish or immoral creature? The underlying belief is that in order to be a good mother, at least as society defines it, a woman needs to have her children with her the majority of the time. Mothers without primary custody are typically ostracized.

Some might say these expectations are shifting, but I would argue that overall they have not. Our culture's belief systems around gender roles are deeply entrenched, and judgment comes much easier to most of us than acceptance.

When Cadence researches mothers and alcoholism, she comes upon the madonna/whore theory of societal expectations for feminine behavior. Can you tell us a bit more about why you chose to mention this in the novel? Do you think that women face more of a stigma with alcoholism than men do?

My decision to include this reference goes back to societal expectations around how women should behave, especially once they become mothers. The idea that a woman should aspire to a sort of self-sacrificing sainthood once she has children is one of the chief obstacles that keeps a woman struggling with addiction from getting the help she needs. Even if she isn't a mother, the cultural preset notion is that female alcoholics are sexually trashy. Male alcoholics are often seen as sexually indiscriminate, too, but sexual prowess in men is encouraged, if not worshipped, in our culture, whether the man is an alcoholic or not. The lens society uses to view women who suffer from alcoholism is a much different prescription than the one used for men.

Our culture is more comfortable with absolutes around sexuality—a woman is either the madonna or the whore. This categorization is so ingrained in people's minds that many aren't even aware of their own prejudice. And how many women do you know who would step up and admit their problem with alcohol or drugs knowing this label (drunk = whore) would be applied to them? The fear of this is a significant contributor to why so many women go without the help they need. They're diagnosed by their doctors as depressed or anxious, and the terror of that damaging stigma keeps them from talking about the real trouble they're in.

Both Laura and Susanne are friends of Cadence's who struggle with addiction, and both are unable to overcome their reliance on drugs and alcohol. How much do you think someone's ability to overcome an addiction depends upon the network of support they have, and how much of it is contingent upon the individual themselves?

That's a tough question, because I think it takes a balance of both. The first step toward overcoming an addiction is the realization that you can't "fix" the problem yourself. This was a serious challenge for me in getting sober, because I was someone who had actually accomplished quite a bit in my life before alcohol took me over. Whatever goal I set, I reached. But I couldn't make myself stop drinking, and it totally baffled me. It wasn't until I finally surrendered and said, "Okay, I need help," that I moved toward healing myself and my life. The trickiest part of alcoholism or drug addiction is that it is a disease that tells you you don't have a disease. Even after you're sober, the "addict" in your head will always be there, telling you things weren't really that bad, you aren't *really* an alcoholic.

That's where having a support system comes in. I need to be surrounded by other people in recovery, because our brains work the same way. They have addicts in their heads, too, spouting off some crazy stuff. (I think it's Anne Lamott who says, "My mind is a dangerous neighborhood not to be entered into alone.") They understand why I did the things I did. They felt the same compulsion and the same profound self-loathing I suffered from when I couldn't stop drinking. These people don't judge me. They taught me that no matter the things I'd done, or how much I'd beaten myself up for them, I am worthy of love. And now I try to help other newly sober people understand the same thing.

Unfortunately, there's no way to determine whether someone will overcome an addiction. There isn't a personality type or social group that has a better chance at sobriety. When you're emotionally fit, you're able to use more effective tools to manage your life; when you're not, you can easily fall back into unhealthy behavior, including using alcohol or drugs. Twelve-step programs are designed to help develop and then maintain that emotional fitness, and only the individual can decide if they are willing to do that kind of daily, continuous work on themselves.

Both Cadence and Martin were raised by single mothers, and both are determined to "do better" than what they were raised with—Cadence wants to be a more present mother, while Martin is determined to be a stable provider for his family. Do you think that the adults we grow into are inevitably reactions to (and perhaps against) our upbringing?

I think for the most part this is true. Though I certainly don't take the stance that we should blame our parents, or whoever it was that raised us, for all that goes wrong in our lives. I believe we all do the best we can with the tools we are given. As adults, it's up to us to take a look at what works for us and what doesn't. If a behavior isn't serving us anymore, or if it's damaging us or the people we love, it's our responsibility to reach out and gather new tools so we can grow as individuals. We need to ask ourselves if something we're doing is a result of programming or if it's something that contributes to the kind of person we want to be. And then we need to act accordingly.

What do you hope readers will take away from this novel?

Overall, I hope that women, especially, are able to see the similarities they share with Cadence, rather than the differences. I hope that the story widens the readers' understanding and compassion, and perhaps makes them reevaluate any preconceptions they might hold about women who suffer from alcoholism and mothers who don't have primary custody of their children.

I also hope that any woman in the throes of active addiction sees herself in Cadence's story and finds the courage it takes to reach out for help.

For me, that's the inherent beauty of books—each person will walk away with something different from a story. My hope as an author is that readers will find a need met, perhaps one they weren't aware they had to fill.

Do you have any plans for another novel?

I actually have another novel completed, though I'm sure I'll have more revision to do! It tells the story of a woman searching for her homeless and mentally ill father, from whom she has been estranged for twenty years. I used alternating viewpoints, flashing back and forth between father and daughter as well as between past and present. It was a different approach for me, and I felt stretched as a writer, which was a good thing!

I'm also about to start my fifth novel, which will explore what happens when a woman is suddenly and unexpectedly thrust into the role of full-time mother and is forced to confront the complicated reasons behind her previously hard-and-fast decision to remain childless.